In Time of Duty

Christopher B Legg

ISBN 13: 978-1-9997491-4-9

Published by Christopher Legg

www.christopher-legg.com

www.curious-writer.com

To Helen my sister who has always been a friend

CHAPTER ONE

15th August 1936

The wind howled along East Street and bit into her face. Nicole Kingson wanted change: but what? She would have liked her life to be blown on the south-westerly. The leaves in the maple trees joined the orchestra of town noises: milk churns banging, people chattering, car engines revving as horses whinnied and neighed, impatient to move on with deliveries. Nicole felt perspiration on her forehead, after the exertion of walking up from the station. She walked past Rax Dairy as horse-drawn milk floats returned. Milkmen hopped off and busied themselves, returning emptied churns. She continued past F.W.R. Woolworths with the gold lettering and red background. She looked behind her and waited for Connie, her stepmother. Nicole was late again and was sure she would get picked on by Edna Palmer, her old aunt. Family meant nothing to Edna; it was all work, work, work; and she took huge delight in giving Nicole all the worst jobs in the netting shed. Including mending the large trawling nets bound for Newfoundland. The town was built upon the rope industry, the fields in North Allington, Pymore and towards Ashcombe suited to flax and hemp. In every war Britain faced, Bridport had flourished, always with the best quality ropes: for rigging, then for the hay nets in the Great War. Nicole knew she was lucky to have the job; it was a quiet time for netting. Bridport boomed when the demand from the army and navy was high.

The maple leaves – slowly turning from green to brown, but not yet autumn gold – quivered as the wind gusted; they were not yet ready to fall. The sky was grey and overcast. Wasn't this supposed to be summer? It didn't feel like it. Autumn would soon rip the leaves from their homes.

Why was she always so short of time? It was because she didn't sleep at night. The only sleep she got was in the light of the morning, when the darkness was gone, when she was exhausted.

It was the nightmares. There had been a time when she had been free of them; but even that seemed in the distant past now. A time when she had been innocent and still a child. When Connie and Redver had married and brought the two families together; a time of bliss as she and Lily became friends. A time when they played, dressed up, ran in the fields, ordered Thomas around. Those summers as children when it never rained, the sky always wide perfect blue, and they ran free in the fields. Dad putting her and Lily atop of Topsy, the large shire horse, with Thomas plonked in the middle, still young, and Connie holding baby Hamilton in her arms, smiling up. Yes, they were happy times. It had all begun to change for Nicole when she became a woman; yes, that was it: that was what had started the nightmares.

'Come on, Mother, keep up.' She pulled her black beret-style hat down; waves of silky brunette hair cascaded free to her shoulders. The sound of their shoes on the pavement echoed from the stone facades of the Midland Bank. Cars, lorries and horses and carts jostled for position on the wide street.

They crossed over West Street. Nicole could smell stale beer from the doors of the Star as Aida Burwood mopped out. As she bent over, Aida's dark brown hair escaped from the side of the multi-coloured headscarf in which it was wrapped. Her pinny was clean and bright yellow. She gave a jovial greeting as they passed.

'You go on, Nicole love; don't let me keep you and make you late,' Mother called from behind. Nicole turned and waved. Why did she now feel like an outsider looking in? Why did she feel she didn't belong? Was that all she wanted? To feel that this was where she was meant to be? She felt that Connie loved Lily more than her, that she loved Hamilton more than her, and she was sure that she loved Thomas more than her. It wasn't true, but it's how she felt. Did Thomas have these feelings? She didn't think so; he was far too young when it had all happened in France. He didn't even know Connie wasn't his natural mother.

'I'll see you later.' Nicole pushed on, walking faster, her brunette hair flowing to her shoulders. Mother waved as she entered the *Bridport News* office on West Street, where she was editor. Nicole wished she was as tall as Lily; she wasn't short but her legs were not long and lithe like her half-sister's.

Could summer be over already? She breathed in as she came to Colman's, the bakers. The smell of freshly baked bread filled her nostrils. She stopped to savour it. The Bedford delivery lorry was parked neatly by the kerb, its engine running. Nicole stood and looked through the window; she couldn't see him. She inched forward, the smell of bread stronger, her nose close to the glass. A patch of mist formed. She looked to the back of the shop. Where was he?

'Hey, Miss Kingson, you looking for me?' she heard him call. She chuckled. She looked round and saw Romily Colman approaching, holding a large baking tray full of loaves. He was tall, his brown hair slicked with Brylcreem. He was clean-shaven even though he must have been up by three or four that morning. He looked athletic and his arms held the tray easily. He had a slim face which made his dark blue eyes stand out; they looked sharp and intelligent. He was dressed smart. Clean white shirt, brown trousers and black polished shoes.

'Course not, I was just going to see if your mother was around. Mother wanted me to ask her to put two cottage loaves behind.' She held her smile in.

'Sure we can, Nicole; for you and Mrs Kingson, anything.' He smiled, keeping his head down and avoiding her eyes.

'Ahh, shut up; you say that to all the girls! Don't forget I've a sixth sense.' She touched her ear with her finger.

Romily moved to the back of the lorry and put down the large tray of bread.

'Will you be coming to the water polo on Sunday? It's the last match of the year.' His eyes seemed to plead. He stood next to her, his chest pushed out and shoulders up. He stood to his full height of six feet yet he seemed more like a schoolboy than his twenty years.

'Might do, might not! Me and Lily thought we would go to Weymouth.' The air seemed to drain from him and his shoulders slumped.

'Oh, I thought you would be coming, as you've been to every other home game, ain't e.' His smile dropped from his face.

'To be honest, it's getting a bit boring, watching from the sidelines; with all that splashing around we can't see what's happening half the time.' She held her grin in.

'Oh, come on, you love seeing us all in our swimmers, don't e?' He looked up, his eyes flicking to hers.

'We can't see anything; you are all under water!' She giggled.

'Oh, come on, Nicole, I'll buy you a tub of cockles.' He raised himself up.

'If you put it like that, how could I refuse!' She felt her cheeks warm. She spun around and walked off. Romily had a way of lifting her spirits.

'See you Sunday, Nicole!' Romily shouted. She made sure not to turn around; she was grinning broadly. She walked past Bridport Motor Company, the strong smell of petrol replacing the aroma of fresh baked bread. Her feet felt light as she came in to St Michael's Lane. She passed the Hope and Anchor and crossed the street. She passed three more houses in the terrace, rounded the corner and faced the netting shed: W.M. Gale & Sons painted in white on the red brick. It was a shed with a low roof, long, more than four cricket pitches laid end to end. A throwback to when rope had been made. Her mood lifted. She was glad to have bumped into Romily.

'You're late again, Miss Kingson; don't think I didn't notice the other times this week,' Edna Palmer said, glowering at Nicole. 'Just because you happen to be some kind of niece of mine don't go thinking you're getting any special treatment,' she continued, standing there dressed in her black work dress. Nicole thought she looked Victorian; she was happy she didn't share her nose. Her father called her 'the big old conker' and would cross the street rather than talk to her.

'Yes, Mrs Palmer.' Nicole took off her hat and coat and hung both up with all the others and hurried to take up her station. 'Bloody old witch,' she said under her breath as she joined Alice Dunford and picked up her large wooden netting needle. The Ackerman machine clanked away busily at the end of the shed filling the room with noise, working on netting tirelessly, watched over by the foreman.

Alice was dressed in a white, black-patterned short-sleeved blouse tied at the neck in a large bow, and a long black skirt. Her dark brown, luscious hair was parted on the side and brushed back from her forehead like all the other girls. It was annoying if the hair fell in your eyes. Nicole knew Alice was only a second away from producing a wide cheeky grin on her pear-shaped face.

'You can work on after everyone leaves at lunch, Miss Kingson, and we ain't paying 'e for gossiping either!' Edna shouted, then turned and went to her office.

'Yes, Auntie Edna; hope you rot in hell.' Nicole nodded and forced a smile in Edna's direction. Then she sighed, brought back down to earth.

'Nicole, where have you been?' Alice said as she worked her needle through the tennis net. "Av you been chatting to Romily again?'

'Might have, might not! It was the train that made me late; then you know Mother doesn't walk as fast as she used to.'

'Oh, come on, pull the other one! I know you've been stood outside Colman's.'

'No, not at all! Well, I might have stopped; I had to ask for a couple of loaves, didn't I; Mother always wants a couple on a

Saturday.' Nicole threaded the twine without looking.

'What was he wearing today? Had his arms out, did he?'

'I might have happened to bump into him accidentally whilst I was waiting for his mother.' Nicole couldn't help but smile. She tried to suppress it; she didn't want Edna coming out and seeing her happy.

'You like him, don't ya?'

'He's all right, I suppose. He's always so smart, his shoes always sparkling. I suppose he's all right.'

'Why can't you admit it!'

'There's lots of other nice boys about; Billy Crabb, for one,' Nicole said.

'Yes, I suppose; but that's three mornings this week you've been late.'

'Oh, you know me, I'm always late; think I'd be late for my own funeral, wouldn't I!' The girls giggled.

After an hour, the net was finished. Nicole and Alice folded it over and put it on the pile and started a new one. They made sure to keep working. They turned their backs so Edna couldn't see them talking from her office window.

Robert Paul came to collect the nets, his ginger hair falling into his eyes. His baggy work trousers were covered in dirt and dust. He mumbled to the girls, picked up the pile of nets, loaded them onto his hand-pulled trolley and carried on down through the shed.

'He'd be nice-looking if he had his hair cut, don't you think?' Nicole said.

'Robert Paul? Nicole, no! You don't like him as well, do you?'

'A girl's got to keep her options open, and it keeps them on their toes if they think they have competition, don't it!'

Edna stomped out of her office, her face a picture of thunder.

'If I've told you girls a thousand times, you're not here to gossip,' she said, shaking her head.

Nicole looked down, not wanting to look at Edna.

'Nicole Kingson, you are the bane of my life! You can go out in the yard and make a start on them fishing nets.' Edna shook her head. 'And make sure you do 'em right; I'll be checking; don't doubt that I will.'

Nicole didn't like the rotten smell of fish and she didn't like being on her own; her thoughts had a way of returning to her nightmares, of her real mother Marie, of her grandfather and that fateful day. What if she was capable of doing what her grandfather had done? What if everyone she loved would be ripped from her life like what had happened to her mother? She wanted to feel at home, she wanted to feel she belonged.

I saw it, I saw the blood; I saw Maman; I saw it and then I ran and hid. I saw it all; I saw Grandfather do it.

CHAPTER TWO

16th August 1936

Nicole, Lily, Alice Dunford and Rosa Colman got off the steam train at West Bay Station. Rosa, the youngest and shortest of the girls, like her brother Romily had dark hair and blue eyes and was in a white blouse with a flower pattern and matching skirt. Nicole waited for Thomas and his friend Arthur Fooks to catch up. Thomas, eleven years old, was dressed in shorts, his blonde hair bleached lighter in the summer sun. Arthur had dark hair and was podgy-looking. They were excited and only allowed to watch the water polo because Mother had made Nicole and Lily promise to keep a close eye on them.

The station was busy with a small crowd; the weather was warm and sunny. Nicole could smell that day's catch wafting from the harbour: the mackerel to be taken to town. It reminded her of working on the nets and her stomach turned over. They stopped to let the long wagon trains of horses and carts full of shingle pass.

The three older girls wore dresses. Lily was in yellow, matching her blonde hair, and Nicole wore her favourite dark green and white striped dress. Nicole was glad to be free from work, getting a few hours of bright sunshine on her back. She looked over at the view of the harbour, trying to ignore the smell of fish. There was a high tide; the small fishing boats bobbed up and down and fishermen worked at cleaning down their decks.

The four girls found space on the wall overlooking where the river met the harbour wall opposite the small riverside café. The boys sat further down. Here, the river, held back by the sluice gates, formed a large pool which today had been roped off for the penultimate water polo game of the year. Rowboats for hire stood on one bank, ignored for the moment; the elderly bearded rowboat owner sat smoking his pipe, watching the proceedings.

Nicole wiped down the wall with her handkerchief before sitting with her legs dangling over the edge, the river feet below.

'I don't like heights; is it safe?' Rosa asked.

'Don't be so silly, you'll be fine,' Lily said, sitting down on her handkerchief so as not to dirty her dress on the dusty wall. Seagulls squawked above.

'I don't know why we're here so early,' Rosa said.

'I do,' Alice said.

Nicole looked over her shoulder but couldn't see any of the players for Bridport. A couple of cars passed. Then an old jalopy of a charabanc turned up, carrying the team from Lyme Regis. The players got off and went into the building on the quay. As they went in, the Bridport team ran out in their swimming trunks. Nicole saw Thomas clapping and cheering as he stood on the wall with Arthur. He'd better not fall in; Connie would kill her.

Nicole looked back over her shoulder. Billy Crabb and Romily Colman ran over to the women on the wall. Billy was only an inch shorter than Romily and had short cropped hair. His dark brown eyes were sharp and curious, his chest muscular and well-formed from all the farm work. He looked like a young version of her father's favourite boxer Tommy Farr, the "Tonypandy Terror".

'Hey up, girls; see you've the best seats in the house,' Billy said. 'Wanted a good view, did 'e?'

'No, Billy, these were the only seats left,' Lily said.

'Yes, we've only just got here,' Nicole said. Romily came and stood next to her. He smelled of baked bread.

'Robert Paul: he ain't showed up. Reckon you must have scared him in the shed or Edna Palmer has taken him prisoner,' Billy said.

'What we going to do? We're one player short,' Romily said.

'What about your brother?' Billy said.

'He's too young.' Nicole shook her head; there was no way he could play water polo at his age. 'Mother wouldn't want it.'

'He's old enough and he can swim, can't 'e?' Billy pushed out his chest. 'Come on; bet he would like to.'

'Billy, he can't. He's not that strong a swimmer,' Lily joined in.

'Go on, he will love it! He's got to start sometime. He must be the same age I was when I started,' Billy said.

'I don't know. Lily, we shouldn't let him, should we?' Nicole asked.

'Look, he could go in goal; he won't have to do much. I'll have the ball down the other end.'

'If you're worried, Nicole, I'll keep an eye on him for you,' Romily said.

'Come on, Nicole, the team needs him,' Billy said. 'I'll ask him now. I bet he wants to. Look how he's cheering.'

'Oh, all right then, I suppose. But Billy and Romily, you keep an eye on him, mind,' Nicole said. She didn't have a good feeling about this; but when Billy went over and asked Thomas, he jumped at the chance and his face looked so excited.

'Mother is going to kill you if this doesn't go well,' Lily said.

'I guess,' Nicole said. That would be nothing new. Romily stepped closer.

'Don't worry, I'll keep an eye on him. Ready for your cockles?' he whispered in her ear.

'Might be. If you lose I think we will go straight home; I don't want to miss the train,' Nicole said.

'I better make sure I score plenty today, then! Should be no problem; you'll set me up a few goals, won't 'e, Billy?' Romily said.

'Ay; these lot will be a bloody pushover.'

'Billy, don't swear; it's not gentlemanly,' Lily said.

'That's because I ain't no gentleman.' He winked at Lily.

'I've known you long enough to know that,' Lily said.

'You better get yourselves warmed up,' Alice said. 'Here comes Lyme.'

The Lyme team all sprinted out of the hut and dived one after another into the lagoon. Nicole thought the crowd that had gathered must be well over two thousand.

'They look pretty keen this year, don't they?' Rosa said.

'Bye, girls; see you after,' Billy said.

Romily waved his hand at Nicole and ran off to join his teammates before they all dived into the murky brown river. Thomas looked so small as he climbed down the ladder and got into the water. He swam slowly over to the Bridport goal that backed onto the sluice gates.

'Now do you see why we were here early?' Lily said.

'No; it was only me brother and his mate,' Rosa said.

'Come on, Rosa, you're telling me you don't like looking at Billy and his teammates?' Alice said.

'Look, they're starting!' Lily said.

Romily contested the tip-off as the umpire threw the ball up in the air. He patted it to Billy, who swam hard at the Lyme defence. Romily shouted for the ball and Billy threw it in his direction, only to be intercepted by the Lyme defender. Lyme counterattacked, the ball thrown down to their end. Thomas looked petrified in goal; his head looked so small. Nicole worried, but it was too late to do anything.

'Come on, Bridport!' Nicole shouted out.

'Shush, Nicole! What will people think?' Lily said, and giggled.

'I don't care... Come on, Bridport! Come on, Thomas!' she shouted, and stood up on the wall. Lily got up and the two young women shouted out together. Rosa and Alice looked at each other, shook their heads from side to side, and stood up with the sisters.

Romily swam hard using front crawl, pushing the ball out in front with his spare hand. He paddled face down, turning to come up for breath. He passed out to Billy, who swam past his Lyme opponent; he stopped, looked up and threw a looping pass over the last defender and into the hands of Romily. Romily gathered the ball and threw it at the Lyme goal. The goalkeeper moved too late and the ball found its way into the net for a goal.

'Yes, Romily!' Nicole shouted out. She cheered and both she and Lily jumped together on the wall.

'Watch it, you two; you're going to have me off and into that dirty mess, if you ain't careful,' Rosa said.

Nicole looked over at Romily, who put his hand up in her direction, waving. She waved back. She looked over at Thomas; it looked as if he was shivering.

At the tip-off Lyme raced down to the Bridport goal. They went to shoot. Thomas tried to position himself and rise out of the water but the goal was massive. As the Lyme player brought his arm back to shoot, a shriek went up in the crowd. Nicole took her eye from the action.

'Look, look! What's that?' Rosa said, pointing up river. Nicole turned her head to where Rosa pointed. The players, sensing the lack of interest from the supporters, stopped and trod water.

Nicole's gaze went upstream. The crowd was silenced. 'What's that, what is that, in the water?' There seemed to be a floating bundle.

'It's wool, it's a pile of wool... It must have fallen off someone's wagon,' Lily said.

'It's not, it can't be...' Nicole could hardly believe her eyes. 'It's not a bundle of wool, it's a bloody sheep!'

'What!' Lily said.

'You're right, it's a bloody sheep. Oh, Lily, they have to get it out! Look, it's still alive!' Nicole said.

The crowd started pointing as one, calling for the players to help. Billy, first to realise, swam over. Romily went to help him. As they swam to the sheep, a dog in the crowd got loose and launched itself into the river. The dog swam gamely, but realising its folly turned around and headed back to the bank. It was no sheepdog for sure, Nicole thought. Billy and Romily managed to get hold of the sheep and between them they pulled it onto the low bank near the café. The crowd gave them a huge ovation. They stood on the opposite bank and took a bow.

Nicole looked to wave at Thomas. He wasn't in the goal; where was he? And the water was flooding out of the river. The sluice gates were open, the torrent pouring into the harbour.

'It's Thomas, Lily! Look, he's –' Nicole tore off her shoes. Time seemed to slow down. She dived straight in. She held her breath, waiting to come to the surface. Her mouth closed tight, she opened her eyes. It took an eternity for her to surface. Her intuition told her that Thomas was in grave danger. Whoever had been so stupid as to open the gates like that? She got to the surface. She couldn't let Thomas suffer. As she swam, her dress billowed and slowed her. She sensed another body alongside, also in the water. It was Lily; Lily must have realised, too. Thank god for Lily by her side. Stupid thoughts tumbled through her mind at a million miles an hour. How stupid to think she could go for cockles with Romily; how Edna was such a bitch; how she wanted to go back to France. She felt the flow of the river rip at her ankles and legs, pulling on her; and she felt her head go under as the water rapidly emptied the basin and flowed under the road and into the harbour. The water was dirty and full of silt. She couldn't see a thing. Nicole felt her head come up. She took a deep breath and looked for Thomas. There was no sign. Was she to lose her brother, too?

She dived down. It was pointless, hopeless. The water raged, now in the harbour, flushed and spat out. Lily was there; they looked at each other. Their eyes communicated and they dived down. She couldn't see her hand in front of her face, let alone see Thomas. Then in the murky pit of the harbour, she saw his tiny leg float in front of her nose. She grabbed it for all she was worth and with her other hand she swam for the surface. She struggled, the river's force dissipated but still pulling at her, her strength deserting her. Then she felt Lily's hand on her own. They worked together; they pulled Thomas clear. The fisherman helped pull them in a boat. Nicole looked at Thomas. His face was ashen white, drained; he was traumatised, but breathing. She sighed with relief. All three hugged, wet through, bedraggled and alive.

CHAPTER THREE

16th August 1936

They bundled Thomas into blankets and towels and got on the train with him. Arthur Fooks sat next to his friend, quiet and shocked. Nicole looked at Lily, who shook her head.

'Mother is not going to be pleased,' Lily said.

Nicole craned her neck and tried to wring out her hair; it stank of the murky silt that had been in the river. Thomas looked so young, the colour not yet back in his cheeks. He didn't speak. His teeth chattered under the old towel.

'Can't we just say he fell in?' Nicole said.

'What? And lie? That will only make her ten times madder,' Lily said, her hair wet and straight.

Their dresses were ruined, covered in mud. The other passengers gave them queer looks.

'Well, let's make out it wasn't as bad as it was,' Nicole said.

'Bad, Nicole, bad? Thomas was nearly dead! God, he looks half dead now. He hasn't hardly said a word all the way home. What do you think? We can hide him in his room.'

'I just don't want to face Mother's wrath; I'm going to get the blame for this. I didn't know some idiot would open the sluice, did I.'

'I did say, didn't I, that we shouldn't let him play.'

'He's got to grow up; and he wanted to play.'

'I know, but we should have been firmer. I should have put my foot down. I'm going to be in trouble too.'

'I'll take the blame,' said Nicole. 'I said he could. There is no need for you to be in trouble too.'

After twenty minutes the train pulled in. They saw Arthur to his door and took the short walk to Home Farm. Nicole held her breath as she walked into the kitchen. Mother and Father were sitting in the armchairs. In front of the range her brother Hamilton lay on the floor on the old rug, curled up with Dusty, the female sheepdog, who was glad to be inside and was asleep, with her black silky coat of fur, a wet shiny nose and patches of white on her face. There was the kitchen dresser against the far wall, to the side of the larder door. It had yellow cupboard doors, yellow fronted drawers, a pull-down flap that made a shelf and two glass sliding doors on the upper section. One door pulled in front of the other, not able to be closed because Father had stuffed six years' worth of farm papers inside. To keep the dresser even on the bumpy floor Dad had made wooden wedges which he'd put under one side. There was only one rug in front of the range; the rest of the floor was bare flagstones, which mother would scrub every Saturday morning, her morning off from her work as editor at the *Bridport News*.

Mother, with her sharp, piercing green eyes, who seemed to be able to read all of their minds, who always knew which of her children had misbehaved. Her hair was blonde with streaks of white and grey. There were creases on her forehead. She had a slim figure; she loved to read, any book or newspaper, when the work was done and she could sit next to Father in the chairs in the kitchen or – on the odd occasion they wanted peace – they would go to the front room. What with looking out for the four children, keeping Father in line and working as editor at the *Bridport News*, Mother didn't seem to have a moment's peace. Mother was just as good around the farm; after all, she had been the shepherd's daughter. She could catch a ewe and flip it on its back just as fast as Father could; and she was neat with shears when she needed to be. What Mother said was law.

Father, seated in the opposite chair after a day on the farm and after the evening meal had been eaten, would doze as Mother read. He was slim and the tallest in the family. His hazel eyes often looked tired with the early mornings. There were deep furrows on his forehead. His brown hair was flecked with grey. When he didn't shave, his stubble was white. When in the fields he would always pull his flat cap down over his forehead. Nicole didn't even take notice of his wooden foot, so normal was it; he had lost his own in the Great War. He didn't talk about Marie, his first wife, the birth mother of Nicole and Thomas. Connie – or Mother, as she was to Nicole now – was the same: she didn't talk of her life before, when she had been married to Sampson Fox, the squire's son, the natural father of Lily. Lily was Nicole's step-sister, but more than that: they were best friends, and as close as they could be. Maybe they had different natural parents, but now they were a close family. The only child Mother and Father had had together was Hamilton. He had been born six years ago, about the time they moved into Home Farm. When Lily's grandfather, Admiral Fox, had given Mother and Father the tenancy, Nicole had been eleven at the time, the same age as Lily; Thomas had been five then. It seemed to Nicole that when they had moved in it had been such a happy time: choosing their bedrooms, sharing with Lily, Thomas into his own room; then not long afterwards, baby Hamilton appeared. Of course, she and Lily spoiled the baby. So much joy was in the farmhouse! Mother didn't take a long break; she was soon back to work, carrying Hamilton with her everywhere she went and keeping him in her office as she worked.

There was a wooden kitchen table and six chairs, the two old armchairs either side of the range. The high-backed armchairs had once had a vivid, colourful pattern of flowers., Nicole could remember in her childhood tracing the flowers with her finger and wondering why they didn't smell like real flowers. There were big roses, violets, buttercups, snowdrops and bluebells. The sink and draining board were under the window that looked out over the small farmyard of Home Farm. A dog-eared box of Persil washing powder sat on the windowsill, used for dishes and the washing of clothes. The bird cage in the corner housed Ol' Parrot, a cocky bright green and red bird who had been a gift from Dad's old mate Geordie Tucker.

'What on earth?' Mother said, getting up from her armchair.

'He's all right, he's all right,' Nicole said.

'He doesn't look all right. He's white as a sheet!'

'He's fine; it was nothing.'

'Whatever happened, you two were meant to be looking after him,' Mother said as she coddled Thomas, kneeling down, rubbing the towel over him.

Nicole looked at Lily. She wanted to lie, to say it was an accident, that he had fallen in. Lily returned a look and shook her head. Father put more coal in the range and opened the vent fully. Mother put the kettle on top and made more tea.

'Are you all right, Thomas?' Mother said.

'Yes, Mum. I would have been fine if the sluice didn't open.'

'The sluice? What?' Mother said.

'He was playing polo; the team was short; he wanted to,' Nicole said.

'I don't care: he doesn't play. And you can do the tea every night for a week; I'm going to be busy at the paper.'

'But Mum…' Nicole said.

'And you, Lily, you can help.'

'But I didn't want him to play,' Lily said.

'There is no buts; you can both do it. You're old enough to make decisions for yourselves, and you both let him,' Mother said.

'Put the kettle on. Put the kettle on. Put the kettle on,' Ol' Parrot squawked.

'You can shut up,' Nicole said, sitting down on the wooden chair at the table and picking up her mug. Mother poured, then opened the old biscuit tin and gave Thomas a biscuit. A small perk to have before tea.

'Don't go sitting down, my girl; you can start straight away.'

Father looked up and winked.

* * *

A week later, Nicole and Lily went and watched Bridport beat Seatown in the last match of the season. Billy had scored a hat trick. And now they were celebrating in the Bridport Arms. The low ceiling with large black timbers made the taller men crouch.

'Come on, Nicole, try some.'

Billy handed his pint glass to her. The beer froth ran over the lip and onto her hand. She hoped it wouldn't spill on her dress.

She looked at Lily, Rosa, Romily and Alice. They all nodded. She brought the glass to her lips and tipped the glass back. She gulped it down. She hated it, but Rosa and Alice had drunk some, and Rosa was younger than her. Only Lily was holding out. It was disgusting; she didn't like it. She handed the glass back to Billy. It was awful. She swallowed the foul-tasting liquid. She tried to look as if she enjoyed it but she couldn't hide her distaste. The others all laughed. She felt more embarrassed. She wanted to wipe her wet hand.

'How can you drink that stuff? It's awful!' Lily said.

'Come on, Lily; you as well,' Billy said.

'I'm not touching that horrible stuff.' Lily sighed and shook her head. 'And besides, Mother said we were not to.'

'Do you always do what your mother says?' Billy said, and laughed.

'Most of the time. And she's right.' Lily held her head straight and Nicole could see she was holding Billy's eye. Nicole wished she could stand up to him like her sister did and not give into the peer pressure. If she had done, then perhaps Thomas wouldn't have gone through what he did last week. And now she was having to work and make the meals every night.

'It's my nectar, like honey, 'tis,' Billy said, taking back the glass. He downed the remainder without hesitation.

'Hey, Billy boy, slow down and behave! We're in the company of ladies,' Romily said.

'I am going slow,' Billy laughed out as he put his glass down on the table.

Nicole looked into the harbour and saw fishing boats returning. The seagulls followed them in, ready, hopeful to pounce.

'Why don't you all come up with us to town? We will start at the Tiger, down to the Dolphin, then to the Nelson, the Packhorse, the Star, the Sun, eh? And then the Lily; you've got to come, Lily, to the Lily, ain't you?' Billy said.

'The Packhorse is so rough, Billy; it's full of drunks and down-at-heels. I don't want to be seen dead in there,' Nicole said.

'Me neither,' Rosa said.

'Look, why don't we have one more 'ere and then have a quiet drink in the Hope and Anchor?' Romily suggested. Nicole looked up and caught Romily looking at her; he held her gaze, then she glanced away.

'The Hope and Anchor? That's an old man's pub, Rom.' Billy moved over to Romily and put his arm around him. 'We've won the bloody league this year and I'm top scorer! It's time we celebrated, not get out our pipes and sit in the bloody corner playing dominoes.'

'Don't you even care how Thomas is after all that?' Nicole said. 'And Romily, you said you were going to keep an eye on him.' You couldn't trust them.

'I'm sorry, Nicole; it was that bloody sheep, wasn't it,' Romily said. She could see the pleading in his eyes.

'He's all right, ain't 'e; 'e's alive and well; was under the water for a minute – no worse than that dunking I gave them Seatown ladies, 'tis it,' Billy said.

'There's nothing wrong with dominoes; I quite like a game,' Rosa said.

'Oh Rosa, my dear sweet sister,' Romily smiled. 'Don't think I'm even ready for my pipe and dominoes yet. All right, maybe not the Hope and Anchor.'

'Come on, girls: say you'll come! Just come to the Tiger, have a bit of fun,' Billy said.

'We can't stay out too long. Mother said we had to be back by nine,' Lily said. 'And she hasn't forgiven us for last week.'

'I will have you back, don't you worries. Billy will get 'e back, of that I promise.'

'Is that another promise that will get broken, is it, Billy Crabb?' Nicole said. She should go home, be with her brother.

* * *

'I think we should be going, don't you, Nicole?' Lily said. Nicole knew they had stayed out too late but she wasn't sure where the time had gone and her head felt cloudy. They said goodnight to Rosa, Romily and Alice on the corner of Barrack Street. They stood either side of Billy and he put his arms around their shoulders.

'You sure you don't want me to help you with him? He's a right handful when his belly is full of beer,' Romily said.

'No, that's fine, Romily, we can manage and it's way out of your way; you walk Rosa home,' Nicole said.

'You're so good to me girls; so good of 'e,' Billy slurred. Nicole buckled as he leaned on her. He stank of beer; it was as if he'd taken a bath in it. He towered above them.

'You're my good girls; you two and your father; 'e've all been good to me. I wonder what me own father was like. They say he was as quick as a flash, my old man; he won so many prizes. Guess I takes after 'im.' He stumbled, and Lily and Nicole worked together to hold him up as they lurched past Stevenson's garage and Doctor Oliphant's surgery towards East Street Station. 'You two are two lovely girls, looking after me, and your old man he's looked out for me too; he was with my old man you know when.'

'He's never told us, has he, Nicole?' Lily said.

'No, he won't talk about it to us, ever,' Nicole said.

'He did tell me, a year or so ago, when we'd had a few parsnip wines,' said Billy. 'He told me 'bout his time in France. He told me all about it, said my dad was a hero saving others he was, saving others.' Nicole wondered what else her father had told him.

'I love you twos! Nicole, you're like a radiant marigold; and Lily,

21

you're tall, like pretty as a bluebell. You will break men's hearts.'
Nicole couldn't stop her face from turning beetroot.

'Shut up, will you, Billy; you don't know what you're saying,'
Nicole said.

'You're full of lather, you are, Billy, especially when you're full
of beer,' Lily said.

They struggled with him at the station, pulling open the carriage
door. They tried to make him look presentable, straightening his
cap and doing up the buttons on his shirt. He slumped in his seat
and dozed off.

'Do you dream about your father?' asked Nicole to Lily, once
they were on the train. 'Not Redver; I mean your real father.'

'Not so much. I mean, I don't feel like a Fox, not with the home
we've been brought up in. It's difficult being related to them and
all, but I don't feel part of that family. I know they try and all and
it's nice to see his photograph. I don't remember him that well.'

'Don't you ever think how different it could have been, thinking
you would have been a young lady of the manor?'

'I don't think I would be as happy as I am. I might never have
had a sister like you.' The girls smiled at each other.

'You know what? There is so much we don't know,' Nicole said.

'Don't know about what?' Lily looked Nicole in the eye as the
train rattled over the wooden sleepers.

'About our parents, all of them, about the war.' Nicole stared
out of the window. 'You know what, I can't even think of fighting,
of fighting for a cause. I can't imagine why Father went. Why, for
heaven's sake, would I want to do that?' *When I have my own mind to
fight.*

The train pulled through Wellbourne and along the cutting. It
passed through the fields with their hedged boundaries. There
were small pockets of green pasture where she saw the red
shorthorns grazing. In adjacent fields the white specks of Dorset
Horn sheep wandered, looking for lush grass. Nicole looked out
of the dusty window and at the manor house. She remembered

the long journey, holding Thomas in her arms, then seeing Connie and Lily for the first time. The thoughts of the nightmares wouldn't be far behind. Maybe the drink would help her sleep. How close she had been to losing Thomas! Did everyone close to her get taken? It didn't bear thinking about. Then it came up from the pit of her stomach and hit her. The guilt. She couldn't look after Thomas, she couldn't protect him. She should never have let him in the river. She was weak and she was guilty of not looking after him, of not being the person she should be. And she was guilty that her real mother was dead. It was her fault. Thomas had so nearly drowned; that was her fault, just as Marie's death was her fault; she was to blame. She was guilty.

They staggered out in the fading light at Moreton Station. Mr May came out from the waiting room in his stationmaster's uniform, bent over double. Seeing his grandson, he shook his head from side to side.

'Not again, Billy lad, not again. What's his mother ever going to say?'

He helped the girls get him inside. Violet was sitting in the lounge, knitting. Her hair was grey and she was plump. Still the same old Violet, Nicole thought. The needles clicked at speed as she didn't look up from her knitting.

'You can get on to bed; you don't deserve any tea, staying out getting in such a state. When will you ever learn? If your father could see you he would be so embarrassed.'

'Tha's the trouble though, ain't it: he don't see me. I don't see him, only in my nightmares. I ain't never seen 'im, hav' I.' Billy lurched from his support and headed out and made his way to the stairs. Nicole could hear him stumble and bang his way up the wooden steps, colliding with the wall and the banister, his hobnailed boots banging loudly on the stairs up to the landing. He slammed his bedroom door shut; the noise echoed through the small railway cottage and Nicole could feel the floor vibrate.

'I'm sorry, girls; he's getting worse and worse and there ain't nothing I can do; he won't listen to me, his grandfather, his great uncle or even Redver.' She put down her knitting and looked at the girls. 'He doesn't seem to care about nothing. He was such a sweet young boy when he was growing up. Well, I don't need to tell you two; but these last few years he don't listen at all, he don't; spends all his money going out and all. It's lucky if he don't end up in a fight. It seems like only yesterday that all you young 'en's were playing together.'

'It must be hard for you, Violet,' Lily said.

Nicole, caught up in her own thoughts, was glad Lily was with her; she always knew the right things to say to make conversation. They'd been to the same village school and both been taught by Miss Appleworth; but Lily had a way with words that she didn't.

'It is,' replied Violet. 'It would have been better for him if I'd married again, got him a father; but there was no way I could. I was so in love with his dad. I still am; I think of my Jimmy every day. I can still remember him, still picture him, I can. There wasn't anyone that ever came close to him. I shouldn't have thought like that; I shouldn't have.'

'Violet, you can't blame yourself. You did your best,' Lily said.

'It wasn't good enough, was it? It wasn't fair on the young lad.'

'He'll grow out of it, won't he,' Lily said. Nicole felt uncomfortable, standing talking to Violet, being so close and not being able to soothe her, and feeling she had the same demons as Billy.

'I hope so, dear; I really do, for his sake as much as mine. But he gets so angry, so angry with me. I thought it was a phase he was going through, that he would be different when he was older, that he would mature; but he don't seem to. Anyway, you two don't want to be listening to an old maid like me. You better get on home before your mother wonders where you are.'

CHAPTER FOUR

23rd August 1936

'Why have I got to go, Nicole?' Lily asked.

Lily was seated in front of the mirror brushing her light blonde hair, dressed in her full length blue Sunday best dress. Lily liked the thin blue and white stripes; the blue contrasted with her green eyes. She seemed to have more freckles on her face. She was glad she shared the room with Nicole and had her close to confide in. If only they were the same dress size, then they could have swapped them. Of course, Nicole was shorter, petite and so pretty with her long dark brown hair and dimples on either cheek.

Lily, slim-waisted and with long thin legs, stood back from the mirror and pushed down her dress, which ended above her ankles. She pulled her hair back from her neck and looked side on. The dress fitted well.

'They are your grandparents, after all.' Nicole picked her dress from the hanger and stepped into it, pulling it up and over her shoulders and over her undergarment.

'Can't you come in with me and keep me company?' Lily was born a Fox: the daughter of her mother, Connie, and Sampson Fox, the youngest of Admiral's two sons. Her life could have been so different.

'They're not my family; they don't want me in the big house, do they? I'll walk up the drive with you but there isn't no way I'm going in,' Nicole said.

'Why do I have to go on my own all the time? Can't Mother come with me, just once?' Lily tried to brush a stubborn tangle from her hair. She saw her own face grimace back at her from the mirror.

'You know she will never set foot in there! Crikey, if she ever sees anyone from that family you know she'll duck and hide or look the other way if she can. Go on, how bad can it be? Least you've got grandparents; it's more than I have,' Nicole said.

'I don't want to go! They're different to you and me, they don't have any fun. It's all so stuffy, it all smells so fusty, and they're always being morbid or melancholy. The place is all so dark,' Lily said as she brushed her hair and looked at Nicole in the mirror. 'It doesn't feel homely, it doesn't feel safe. I feel on edge up there.'

'What do you remember of your father? I mean not Dad, but you know,' Nicole asked.

'I think he was kind. I can remember sitting on his lap and he read to me in the library. He was ill a lot and always seemed to be taking to his bed. He didn't really have time, what with being out managing the estate. I was too young. I remember hearing arguments. It was him and his brother or Mother and Nanny or all of them. Nanny was no fun, I remember that.' Lily put the brush down and got up. She looked out of the window into the garden and saw Thomas, who was kicking the football against the wall. Hamilton ran towards the ball; her father came from the path, picked Hamilton up under one arm and passed the ball to Thomas. Hamilton shrieked with laughter as Father held him upside down.

'Father doesn't talk about much, does he, from before, I mean,' Lily said, smiling down as she watched her father and brothers pass the ball to each other.

'Only to say some silly stories about himself, Geordie Tucker and Billy's dad.'

Lily handed Nicole the brush. Nicole sat on the stool and took it from her.

'I like to think I'm like my real mother; I'd like to have talked to her, like we are doing now.' Nicole brushed her long brunette hair. 'Connie's so nice; and the fun we've all had growing up; I should cherish what we have. It's just the damn nightmares that don't stop.'

'I know, I know. It's like my natural father; just to have known him… We are so lucky, so lucky we've all got each other. I'm so glad you're my sister, Nicole.'

'Me too, Lily.'

'Come on, let's go show the boys how to play football,' Lily said.

* * *

The tall pine trees stood like soldiers to attention lining the drive. Lily felt the wind blow through her hair and the sun shone down, hot. How much better it would be if she could stay with everyone else and go for a long walk and picnic by the river. She could play with Hamilton and Thomas, and talk with Nicole. Why was it she was forced to do what she was told and had to go and see her stuffy old grandparents? After all, what had they ever done for her? Then there would be her Uncle Theodore and his wife Elizabeth and their son Montague. Her uncle acted like he was the squire already, and he was intimidating. They all intimidated her. All their airs and graces, their way of doing things. Then having the butler serve them! Spencer was nice, but it wasn't the same as home.

The walk from Home Farm to Kingcombe Manor was less than a mile, up the lane and then left down the drive. The distance might as well have been a thousand miles, given the difference between the two worlds. They might be cramped, Lily thought; they might have little, but there was love and there was fun and there was joy. The Manor, for all the trappings of wealth, didn't fill her with the security she had at home. Yes, she was related to them; but she didn't belong in that world. Sampson – the father she could only faintly remember – had been her link; even his memory was a shadow that was fading. There were pictures of him in the Manor. Lily didn't know if her memory of him was of the real him or the picture hanging in the hall.

'Don't have too much fun without me, will you,' Lily said, trying to sound upbeat and happy.

'I'm sure we will. You don't have to stay all afternoon, do you?' Nicole replied.

'Mother said I have to stay and have dinner with them; they don't eat till late so who knows when I will be able to escape.' Lily walked, dragging her feet. 'Oh, Nicole, I don't want to go in. Go on, come in with me! Come at least to the door.'

'I don't think I should; they don't like me, do they.'

"Course they would like you if they knew you.' Lily ran her finger through her hair and down her cheek. She felt her stomach turn over. Why did she always feel like this? They were family. 'Let's go to the back door; we can sit and talk to Auntie Dot and Mary for a bit. Come on, please.'

They rounded the corner and followed the path round the back of the Manor House. Aunt Dot was coming across the yard. Good old Aunt Dot. She ran the kitchen; she was married to George Kingson, the brother of her father Redver. Lily liked Uncle George and Auntie Dot. It was common for them to be around Home Farm, even though they both worked for Admiral. Uncle George as shepherd she had always known, and Auntie Dot in the kitchen at the Manor. Mary, too, her cousin, following on in the tradition working under her mother. Auntie Dot was a fulsome woman. Once, mother said, she had had the best figure in the village; but the long hours had taken their toll. Now she hustled and bustled, her figure filling out the blue flowered pinafore. They were down to earth; no airs and graces. Aunt Dot: her face wrinkle-free with busy hazel eyes, her dark blonde hair tied up in a bun. She was sharp and too intelligent to be a cook. Auntie Dot's only flaw was a birthmark on her cheek. Mary was taller than her mother, her face rounder, less defined.

'Hey, you two young beauties, come 'err!' Auntie Dot said as she put the pan down and hugged them both. Mary greeted her cousins, then carried on in through the door.

'Hello, Auntie Dot,' Lily said.

'What you doing 'err?

'I've to visit Grandmama and Grandfather; Mother has insisted, said it was my duty,' Lily said.

'I'm keeping her company 'cos she's too scared,' Nicole said.

'I'm not. I just don't want to come,' Lily said.

'Well, you two can 'av a cup of tea with me and Mary first, can't 'e.'

Aunt Dot motioned for them to join her in the kitchen. It was massive, four times as large as the kitchen at Home Farm. There was a vast fireplace with a huge range, there were large coppers, and the walk-in larder was as large as their front room. The walls were pristine whitewash, the place kept immaculate by Aunt Dot and Mary. The kettle was boiled and Aunt Dot handed out mugs of tea.

'You know you've nothing to worry about. Admiral has a heart of gold; it's only bluster and talk. He puts on a show most of the time.'

'I don't know; I can't talk to him. He scares me.'

CHAPTER FIVE

23rd August 1936

Lily left the warmth of the kitchen behind and walked up the steps into the tiled hallway. She looked at the oak staircase and it seemed smaller every time she visited. She walked down the hallway and into the library. In her blue and white dress, her prettiest, she felt awkward and ugly compared to the beauty of the Manor House.

As she entered the library she looked out of the tall windows; on the southern edge on the large lawn she saw her Uncle Theodore, who was playing croquet with his son Montague. She slowed down. Montague, his only child. He had been a long time coming, her cousin. The village gossip-mongers, no doubt fuelled by Auntie Dot, had gone into overdrive when news of Elizabeth Fox's pregnancy had got out; the men even worse, saying that Uncle Theodore didn't have it in him. That something must have happened to him in the Great War; that he would never have children; but then, after all the years… Then, there he was, a cousin on this side of the family, related but hardly ever talked to. Montague was a year or so younger than Thomas. He was a ginger-haired boy, like his mother. He seemed happy out playing with his father.

Theodore walked over, ruffled his boy's hair and congratulated him on a good shot. He was tall and upright, over six feet tall, shoulders back, blonde hair. She knew he had been a captain in the war. And Father hated him with a passion; there had been bad blood forever. He was dressed in tan slacks and blue blazer. When not holding the mallet, he would walk with his cane.

Lily walked further, into the library. She saw her grandmother at the far end, sitting with a book in her lap. Ignoring the book, she was staring out of the window. She looked up. Lily thought she looked much older: so thin, her hair grey and white. As Lily neared she could see her grandmother's slender frame. Her pale skin seemed to hang from her. Lily had very few memories of her when she was younger. She didn't remember her grandmother having much to say. It was the sound of the men arguing and talking, or Nanny ordering her what to do, that she remembered. Now, her grandmother looked frail and she looked old.

'Grandmama.' Her grandmother didn't move to get up; she put her hand out for Lily. Her hand was limp and cold and bony.

'Lily, it is so nice of you to come.' Her voice was weak and quiet and Lily strained to hear it. 'Sit, sit down here; I'm so glad you have come. I did so hope you would have come last week or the week before. I've missed you since your last visit; how long ago was that?'

'I think it's only a month or a bit longer; it's not been long.'

'Oh, it seems like so long ago. I'm glad, anyway, to see you here now. You are looking so pretty and you're getting tall like your mother. That dress really brings out the colour of your eyes; you should wear blue more often. You're taking after your mother, except you have Sampson's eyes. At least, when he was young, not like when he got older.' Josephine coughed and cleared her throat. 'You know, I still miss him every single day. It's not right for a mother to outlive her children, is it? And of course when he was young I didn't get much time with him, and your grandfather insisted that Nanny knew best. 'Course, Nanny spent more time with him than I ever did.' She shook her head and looked over at Lily from behind her glasses.

'You know, your mother stood up to Samuel, Theodore and Sampson; took them all on. She's a brave woman all right. And of course she led the village, didn't she, saved them all, dug with her bare hands, she did.' Grandmother paused, taking in a long rasping breath. She picked at her nails, her hands moving constantly. 'I wanted to do more, to make her feel more welcome. I wish I had;

but it's hard standing up to the men in this household. They always get their way in the end.'

What was that? What had her mother done? Dug with her bare hands?

'You don't know about the train, the landslide?' Gran seemed to read her thoughts. 'The way your mother and Violet toiled out there all night was inspiring. We thought we'd lost them all; we thought Sampson was dead, but your mother, she led the way. If it wasn't for her… I'd thought I'd lost him. It was so cruel; he died later. He never recovered from the trauma.'

Lily caught her breath; she was taken aback. 'What was Sampson like when he was a boy?'

'Oh, he was full of life! Of course, he was younger than Theodore, and of course older siblings always want things their way. He was a happy child most of the time, I think; and when he was older he loved his motorcar.'

'He had his own car?'

'Oh yes! Drove everywhere; and it was forever breaking down, as far as I can remember.' Lily chuckled to herself. 'He doted on you.'

'I remember. I remember being in here with him. I was on his lap.'

'Do you, dear? Do you?'

Lily watched as Grandmother seemed to force her lips to smile, which she didn't quite manage.

'Oh yes.'

'He would be so proud of you, of how beautiful you are.' Josephine reached over and touched Lily on the arm. 'I want you to know that we might not show it but we do care about you, Lily; you are still part of this family, even though… well, even though… well, you know.'

'Thank you, Grandmother.' Lily didn't know what else to say. It was nice to hear; but she didn't get much sense that it meant anything, that the sentiment would be shared by the Admiral her grandfather or even by Theodore. She didn't think it meant anything; the words sounded hollow. And she didn't even want them to do anything for her. She wanted to achieve things on her own merits, not have them given to her on an inherited plate. She'd been brought up to work hard and to persevere, not sit back and take a helping hand.

The sound of footsteps approached and Lily looked up to see her Uncle Theodore stomping into the library, with his cane under his arm. Montague was nowhere in sight and must have been sent to his room. Probably to the governess. She held her breath, waiting for his intrusion. His blue blazer was crumpled and his tan slacks were creased. His normally immaculate blonde hair stood on end, like stooks of corn blown by the wind. It looked like he hadn't bothered to shave. His forehead was covered in lines, his eyes shadowed by deep purple bags. He stood tall and imposed himself.

'I see you're talking to my niece. How nice for you. Are you finding out what life's like down on the little farm with all the little piglets? Speaking of which, how many of you are there?' Theodore looked down at Lily. 'It must be awful, shoe-horned into that cramped cottage. God alone knows why your mother was so keen to get out of here. I suppose we've to put up with you at dinner.'

'It doesn't feel cramped at all; we have plenty of room,' Lily said.

'Don't, Theodore; we are having a pleasant conversation,' Grandmother said.

'Oh, pardon me! And I didn't realise we had royalty in the house.' Lily hated the smell of cigar smoke and her uncle reeked of it.

'It is not often I get to speak to Lily and I was so keen to hear what her plans were once she left school.'

'Don't let me stop you from talking; this would be good.' Theodore pulled up a chair. 'Go on; this I'd like to hear.'

'I don't know; I haven't thought about it much,' Lily said, not wanting to talk in front of her uncle.

'Don't let him put you off. You should do something; your mother has been doing such good work at the newspaper.'

'That common rag!'

'Theo, if you haven't got anything good to say, then don't say it at all. With your upbringing I would have thought you would behave better.'

'I'm just stating my opinion.'

'Lily and I were having a nice conversation; we don't want you interrupting.' Lily had never heard her grandmother raise her voice much above a whisper, but she did it now.

'I know when I'm not wanted.' Theodore got up and pushed the chair back against the wall. 'Oh, you can tell your father we are putting up all the rents for the tenants; they have been far too low for far too long. Tell him Mr Grey will be around in the morning.' Uncle Theodore stomped out.

'I'm sorry, dear. Go on, tell me: what do you think you might be interested in? It's so nice to have female company to talk to. Elizabeth doesn't think me worth her time; and you see what Theodore is like, and – well, Samuel is always down in the study thinking about the estate.' Josephine crossed her hands in her lap and continued to pick at her nails.

'I don't know, Grandmother; Mother says I could go with her to the newspaper, only as a junior to start with; or I might go into teaching, like mother once did; or I might go to college, something like that.'

'You have time to decide. You don't have to make your mind up right now anyway, do you?' Josephine looked over at Lily; her lips didn't quite open.

'If I can give some advice,' she continued, 'I never had the confidence or the mind to stand up for myself, not like your mother did. I've a lot of respect for that. You know, the way she stood up in this house, the way she has gone out to work. Lily, take it from me: stand up for what you believe in, stand up and be counted; and don't ever let a man put you down. You promise me that, will you, that you will do that? Don't let bullies like Theodore rule you. You go out in this world and you get on, you make something of yourself and don't let men ever dictate to you.'

Lily wondered where this was all coming from.

'Yes, Grandmother, I promise I will try.'

'Now go on and see your grandfather; he's got something he wants to talk to you about.'

CHAPTER SIX

23rd August 1936

Lily made her way back up from the Manor. She was exhausted. It was tiring, the digs from her uncle, having to be on her best behaviour, remembering every please and thank you. She could see the sun setting to the west over Snowdrop Hill. She picked at the early blackberries as she walked, putting them in her handbag. She went up to the top of the drive and paused at the junction. She saw Billy Crabb come down the lane from Kingcombe Farm. He was covered in dust from a long day in the field. His skin was tanned, dark as the earth. His arms were thick and his hair was tousled. He whistled as he walked up.

'Hey up, Lily, been down the Manor? Still part of the gentry, is 'e?'

'I wouldn't exactly say that. It wears me out, it does; my mother and grandmother insist I go.' She sighed, happy to be talking with someone younger and full of life.

'Was nice of your grandfather; he made sure to bring out cider for us all. Been so hot, it has; I felt I was going to die of thirst out under that sun. I'm glad I've seen you, Lily; sure does brighten my day seeing something so beautiful. Mind you, you're only the second most beautiful creature I've seen all day. The first was the most stunning goldfinches; perched on the tractor they were when I got there this morning. I do think they are the prettiest small bird, with their sleek feathers, and their flash of red, like red hats. Two of them; must have been husband and wife, that pair.' He smiled from ear to ear and looked her in the eye.

'You were lucky to see them; you don't often see them out like that. They're normally up in the apple trees in the orchard,' Lily said. 'That's where I like to see them.'

'I know it; it must be a sign. Come with me; let's go down the orchard, see if we can see them and watch the sunset.'

'I don't know. I should be getting back.'

'Oh, come on, Lily, you can spare your old friend half an hour, can't 'e?'

'All right, Billy Crabb, let's go.' She knew she shouldn't. Mother would be waiting and wouldn't approve.

Lily took off running with her hair blowing behind. She raced down the lane and into the orchard. She knew Billy was letting her get ahead. She looked round to see him chase her, his smile broad across his face.

They sat on an old tree stump. Lily could smell the full and deep apple. It was a pleasant release from the smell of old tobacco and cigars that seemed to follow Admiral and Uncle Theodore around the Manor.

'Listen: can 'e hear that?' She heard what sounded like a child's cry. She knew it was the goldfinch. She couldn't see it, the leaves too thick and green. They both listened as the bird cried out. She concentrated her hearing. She looked from branch to branch but couldn't see it.

'There, up there to the right.' Billy pointed up to the highest branch; and perched on the end was the small bird, calling.

'I see it, I see it!' Lily smiled. Billy brushed his arms against hers and she felt his warmth and his strength.

'Up there, look up there; you can hear it, too.' Billy pointed to the light blue sky. 'There's a skylark.'

'It is, Billy, it is.' Lily looked up and heard the skylark as it hovered high over the pasture to their left. 'It's perfect.' The sky was like the most comfortable smooth velvet curtain, rippled, with shades of dark orange, light pinks, soft blues, and thin veils of white cloud.

She felt him bring his arm around her shoulder. The first time a boy had ever done that. It felt warm and good; she felt safe and content.

'This is the best day of my life! I think it's so perfect. It must be my lucky omen, seeing them birds. I reckon it's my old man looking down on me.' Billy used his hand to stroke her shoulder.

'It could be. Sampson's there, too, somewhere.' They sat there, watching as a family of four rabbits came out and chewed on the short grass. What with the Dorset Horns and rabbits grazing there was no need for mowing in the orchard.

Billy pulled her closer. His touch was soft and delicate; his hand was rough, which only added to the sensation on her naked arm. She was curious.

'Have you been with many girls?' she asked.

'I might have been with a couple; nothing serious, you know.'

'You always seemed keen on Molly Hansford at school. That's what me and Nicole thought.'

'You've been talking about me, then?'

'We can't help but talk about you, Billy, what with everything you're always up to.'

'Me? I'm a virtuous boy, goes to church every Sunday and says my prayers.'

'Yes, but what about Saturday night? Where do you go and which altar do you go and kneel at? Is it the Royal Oak, the Dolphin, or the Tiger?'

'I might do, but after working all week a man has to have some pleasure. You can't deny him that, can you?'

'I don't think I'd want any boyfriend of mine going out drinking as much as that.'

'If I had a girlfriend as pretty and clever as 'e, girl, I wouldn't need to be going out having a drink.'

'I wouldn't want him getting drunk or looking at other girls. I'd be wanting to be taken to the pictures or a daytrip to Weymouth.'

'I would do all that and in style.'

'You haven't even a car, Billy.'

'That's no problem; I can't see that being any problem at all.' He turned to face Lily. He kissed her full on the mouth. She was surprised by his sudden action. Her first thought was to push him away; her hands went to his chest. She could feel his heart beat through his shirt. His chest was full and taut. His lips were soft. She should stop him, but she didn't.

* * *

Billy walked Lily to the door and came in with her. They were all gathered. Mother and Father sat in their armchairs, Thomas and Hamilton sprawled on the floor, Thomas reading his *Boy's Own* comic and Hamilton leafing through *The Beano*.

Everyone said hello to Billy. It wasn't unusual for him to stay for the evening meal. Nicole came into the kitchen.

'You look a picture, Nicole.' Billy winked at her.

'Shut up, Billy Crabb.' She passed him and went to the sink.

'Why don't you boys go out and play football?' Mother said.

'Go on, Dad, go on, come out with us. And you, Billy; can 'e show us?' Hamilton said.

'Ay, all right then, I show 'e I can still shoot it straight.' Father got up and patted young Hamilton on the head. Thomas ran on and Billy followed behind.

With all the men and boys outside, Mother began to talk.

'You two, listen to me. Billy is like family; and my god, he is like a son to us. Violet has always been good; she looked after all of you kids so I could go out and work.' She looked at them. Nicole and Lily sat down at the kitchen table.

Mother got up from the armchair and walked to the head of the table, pulled out the wooden chair and sat down. She looked determined. Lily felt her stomach sink. What if mother found out she had been in the orchard with Billy? Her life wouldn't be worth living! What if he said something? What if someone had seen? She felt guilty; she felt sure her mother had guessed. Lily felt so transparent; Mother could read her thoughts for sure. She hadn't meant for it to happen. She would never kiss a boy again! It had felt so good; how could something so nice and good be so bad?

Mother still looked young for her age, her blonde hair full and luscious, with not much grey and white. Lily knew she still caught the eye. She could count the number of times shopkeepers would joke: 'Here are the two young sisters.'

Mother continued speaking. 'Yes, he's like one of our own, and I won't hear a bad word said about him outside these four walls, so what I'm about to say makes it very hard. I've heard… no doubt you've heard the same gossip around the village about him and Molly Hansford; and we all know what she's like.'

The girls nodded and knew better than to speak when Mother was talking. Lily knew it; he must be seeing Molly. He must be. She hadn't believed it; she knew what the village was like. God, what if her name got bandied about like Molly's? She would die of embarrassment! She wouldn't be able to look people in the face. Then what would Gran have to say about that, and Admiral and Uncle Theodore? She wouldn't be able to hold her head up, she wouldn't be able to leave the house. And Mother wouldn't talk to her for a week; then there would be the punishment. Cleaning out the chickens, helping with the horses, god forbid feeding the pigs or having to clean them out too; that didn't bear thinking about. It was bad enough having to help cook the meals.

'My god, it's been hard for Billy without a father, and we've tried; your father's tried to take him under his wing and make sure he didn't miss out; but there's only so far he can go. We all know him, so this is hard for me to say. I know you're sensible girls. You're to watch out. Men his age, they are only after one thing, seems to me these days. Be careful; I don't want you gossiped about like Molly Hansford, is that clear? You two promise me now you will wait till you're married.'

'Yes, Mother, I promise,' Lily said.

'Yes, Mother,' Nicole repeated.

'And you are to go nowhere near Billy Crabb on your own, is that clear, you two?' Mother stressed, her tone harsh, the look in her green eyes icy and set. She looked Lily straight in the eye and

Lily felt her mother's eyes look down into her heart. She felt she knew where she had been and what she had done.

She knew Mother was right; she always was; and she said: 'Yes, Mother, I promise.' Mother nodded. Lily watched as Nicole did the same.

Lily felt her cheeks blossom as she walked up the stairs with Nicole. As they sat on the end of the bed Nicole looked at her with a quizzical glance and saw a flicker of recognition as the penny dropped. Oh god, how was she going to keep this from Mother, if Nicole could read her? She should stop herself right now from falling any deeper for Billy. There was no way on earth she could go against her mother.

* * *

'You like him! How much?' Nicole asked.

What should she tell her sister? Lily thought. They were lying in bed, the house in darkness.

'I don't know; I do; how can I, now Mother has spoken? I'm going to stop it.' Lily sighed.

'What have you done? You haven't…'

'It was only a small peck on the cheek, really.'

Nicole whistled through her teeth and said: 'You kissed him.'

'Shush! Mother will hear! You know she's got the hearing of an owl when she wants.' Lily turned over and faced her sister.

'What was it like?'

'It was so lovely! I can't explain how lovely it was; it was lovely!'

'Lovely, lovely? Come on, Lily, you can do better than *just lovely*! Tell me! I want to know. It wasn't like them sloppy kisses we got when we played kiss chase around the schoolyard, was it?'

'No, no, it was soft and gentle. I couldn't believe it was him. And it gave me goosebumps down my arms and on the back of my neck.'

'You like him, you do! What are you going to do about it?'

'Nothing! What can I do? Mother's given the last word on it and made me promise. I can only tell him it's to stop and I'm not

41

interested.' She was glad to have Nicole to talk to, to share it with. She'd had her first proper kiss and it had felt more than lovely; it had felt wonderful. He might be an oaf, but he knew how to kiss. His lips so soft and gentle; the feeling was like nothing she knew before. She wanted more; but she was sure she wasn't going against Mother.

CHAPTER SEVEN

6th September 1937

It was the first day of school. The day when Thomas would walk down Palmers Hill and up School Hill though the gates and sit down at the wooden benches. Except that today, Thomas Kingson wouldn't be going to school. He would be with his dad, of course; he'd worked plenty of days with him. He would work all the holidays, like he had again this year. He would work on the weekends when Father asked. But this was the first proper day, the first day he would be with his father for the rest of his life; he didn't have much doubt of that.

Thomas had dressed in his work clothes. Shirts and trousers handed down from his cousin Charlie Kingson, who was older and taller than him. Twelve years old and he should be taller, much taller. The brown cord trousers were baggy and he had to put extra holes in the belt to tighten them. They annoyed him as he had to hoick them up every five minutes.

He sat next to Father on the wagon, Topsy and Turvy pulling on in front. When they got to the field under the copse he jumped down and threw up the stooks of wheat. Father drove the horses through the avenue. Thomas loved the earthy smell of the land and the musky scent of the corn. The sun was out and he was glad he didn't have to go to school any more. There wasn't a cloud in the sky. He was glad to be finally working full-time with his dad; he would be much more help here. He was glad to be out from Miss Appleworth's class at last. His father seemed so much taller; he hoped he would grow up like him. Dad had his flap cap pulled down over his ears.

"Err, young 'en; you ain't at school now, there ain't time for

"

daydreaming,' Dad said.

'I know; give 'e a chance.' He smiled up at Father who had a broad grin across his face. They walked up the line. Topsy and Turvy, happy to be out too, neighed with satisfaction. Their tails swatted at flies. Thomas walked, increasing his pace to keep Father happy. He began to sweat as the slope of the hill rose to meet the edge of the copse. Father tied the horses to the fence and got down; he moved more slowly. Thomas knew his knees were giving him more pain. He saw his father wince.

The sound of blackbirds and sparrows chattered out of the wood. The men worked hard, loading the wagon together. When it got to ten-thirty on Father's pocket watch, they stopped for breakfast. They moved out of the strong autumn sun and sat together under the canopy of the large oak tree, using the trunk as support to their backs. Dusty the sheepdog came and lay down, so happy for the rest and hoping for a scrap of bread or cheese; she wouldn't want any of the raw onion.

Flies came to Thomas's face and he swatted them away. He got up and filled the horses' feed bags with oats and tied them off so they could eat breakfast too. He looked up in the sky and thought he heard a loud buzzing. On the horizon to the east he saw three aeroplanes heading their way. High up, descending, the loud thunder of their engines roaring. They looked massive; so much more exciting than the pictures in his comics. They seemed to be planning on attacking, practising their dives, following on the tail of the one in front. The lead plane then pulling up, and falling in behind.

'Them must be from Portland,' Dad said, pointing up to the sky.

'What are they?' Thomas asked.

'I reckon they be Hawker Hurricanes; they have massive Merlin engines, tha's what 'e can hear.'

The buzzing grew into a massive roar, flying low. Thomas looked up at the wide undercarriage with its camouflage paint and red and blue circles. He thought he could see the pilot.

'Mother reads the paper; they have some new Chancellor in Germany, making trouble just like they did before. Won't surprise me if it all kicks off; and I thought that would never be, not in my life.'

The three planes making noise like thunder in the sky raced across at less than a thousand feet. As they did, Topsy became spooked; she pulled at her loose tether, got free and bolted.

Father reacted fast. He leapt up, dropping his half-eaten piece of bread, and dashed after Topsy. Thomas, watching the plane, was slower to react. His father was running at full speed after the horse who, scared by the loud noise, was galloping at full throttle down the field. Thomas gave chase after his father, who was up alongside Topsy. She stood tall above Father. Thomas sprinted as fast as he could. Father was grasping for the reins as well as running across the uneven stubble. Thomas gained on them slowly, his short legs unused to the rough ground, his feet slipping in the heavy boots which were one size too large. He watched as Father grabbed hold of one loose leather rein. The horse was large and his father looked small up against the old mare. Thomas could see she was enjoying having the freedom to run free. He knew enough to know that if a horse was not caught it could outrun a man and be gone for hours; and – worse still – could injure itself.

With a hand on the rein, father got hold, and using his strength he dug his boots into the earth. It wasn't enough; he was pulled with ease by the large shire horse. At the headland, the horse turned and ran for the gateway. Father stopped pulling and ran with the horse. He got alongside its face and began to talk, stroking her mane and coaxing her. The horse, calmed, slowed, then stopped as Thomas caught up.

'I don't be needing that sort of exercise every day, now then, Topsy,' Father said and laughed, catching his breath. 'I think 'e will need to be practising ee's running, boy. It will be a job for 'e next time.'

Thomas looked at his father and smiled. He was surprised how fast his father could run on his wooden foot.

* * *

He was hot and tired but happy. The long working day was coming to an end; the sun was low in the red and orange sky. He was high up on the rick and was loving it. Father was showing him how to thatch it off so it wouldn't let the rain in. The thatched pitch would mean water would drain away and keep the wheat dry until threshing time.

It was the first time Father had ever let him up on top or showed him how to do it. Father had even said 'well done' and 'good job' which made him feel useful. He slid down the ladder and joined his father at the bottom.

'Tha's it for today, young 'en.' Father said. 'Let's go and see what's for tea.'

Thomas walked on behind his father, satisfied that he had been of help. They walked across the yard and through the back door of the farmhouse. Dusty ran in front, glad to be getting a lie-down. The smell of cottage pie filled the small kitchen.

'Coalman's 'err, coalman's 'err, coalman's 'err.'

'Shut up, will 'ee, you daft parrot!' Father said.

'Coalman's 'err, coalman's 'err, coalman's 'err,' Hamilton said, jumping up to hug his father.

'Don't 'e go encouraging 'im! He's daft enough.'

Dusty began to bark at the commotion, sitting up to see what all the fun was about.

'What is it with these animals round here?' Dad said.

Dusty barked and the red and green parrot kept squawking in between announcing that the coalman was 'err. Mother looked over from the sink and shook her head with a smile.

'Dinner won't be long,' she said above the commotion and the wireless playing in the background.

Nicole and Lily were laying up the table and Hamilton began dancing with Dusty who stood on his hind legs.

CHAPTER EIGHT

7th September 1937

Thomas crept down the stairs, the morning light flickering through the window. He wanted to grow up and be strong like his father. He had to grow taller. It was early, the dawn chorus just beginning with chattermags, blackbirds and sparrows singing outside. The kitchen was quiet, his sisters, brother, father and mother all asleep above. He positioned the chair, reached up with his hands. This was sure to stretch him taller. He held his breath and held onto the doorframe with his fingers. He held his breath and tried to pull himself up; he scrunched his face. He couldn't do it. He felt his fingers losing grip. Before he fell to the flagstone floor, two girt hands grabbed hold of his legs and held him up. It was Father, creeping up behind.

"E will have to do more than that to grow, young 'en; 'e will have to eat all Mother's cottage pie, won't 'e, boy?' Father laughed and plopped him on the floor. "E won't be like Tommy Lawton unless 'e does that.'

If only he could be like Tommy Lawton, the best striker in the football league! This season he was going to be playing for Everton. Thomas read every report in the papers. Tommy Lawton, who could head the ball as well as he kicked it.

'When will I grow, Dad?'

'Won't be long; 'e will be like me, 'e will shoot up in no time.'

'What if I don't and I end up short, like Nicole?'

'Well, boy, 'e can't decide; what will be will be. You will have to make the most of whatever 'e is.'

Thomas looked at Dad. He seemed so tall and strong. It was about time he grew; other boys his age were already taller than him.

''E shouldn't worry 'bout that; you will be fine, whatever 'e turns out like.' He smiled. 'And hanging off the door ain't goin' help 'e much! You should keep your energy for later; we've a long day ahead.'

'I've plenty of energy, Dad; I can keep going.'

'I know; you takes after me in that regard.'

'And Mother; I take after her too, don't I?'

'Ay, son, you do; and I's been meaning to talk to you about that.'

Thomas knew what he meant. He was a farmer's son, after all. He knew all about the birds and the bees; he knew where babies came from. After all, that's what all the children had been talking about in class in his last term. And he had seen plenty of calves born; he knew it was after the bull had been on top of the cows and it happened nine months later. He didn't want to kiss any girls. If he wasn't working he wanted to play football, or read about Preston North End and Arsenal in the paper.

Thomas carried out his chores and put leftovers down for Dusty. She ate quickly and quietly. Thomas then pulled the sheet from over Ol' Parrot's cage and fed him some nuts. Dad made the tea and they sat at the table.

'Look, 'e should know, Thomas.'

'I know, Dad; don't go on! I know where babies come from. Don't worry, I'm not after any girls; they're boring and don't like football.'

'That's beside the point! Look, you know my old friend, Geordie: he's coming here in the next couple of days. Well… look, this is hard for me to say.' Dad took a sip from his mug. 'I ain't never been good with words; it's your mother, it's Connie who is good with that sort of thing.' After a pause he continued: 'I've wanted to tell 'e for sometime, and it don't get no easier. Well, there was a time before I was with your mother; you know we woz in France, where I was with Geordie.'

'I remember; you were in the Great War, you and Geordie in the big metal tank, and Billy's dad before he died.'

'That's right, son, and… well…' His dad stopped, got up and went to the breadbin. He took out the loaf and the wooden board and large knife and put them down on the table.

What was his dad saying? He knew he'd been in the tank. He knew he'd been taken prisoner. 'Course, Dad hadn't told him. It was only Lily and Nicole who had told him a few things. Thomas thought he might like to be in the army. If he had the chance. He wouldn't go in the navy; he was sure of that. He'd been put off water for life.

'Son, I can't think of any other way of saying this… You have a right to know.'

Know what? Thomas was finding it hard to follow his father this morning. What on earth was he spouting on about?

Dad buttered the bread and dished out the slice to Thomas.

'I'm glad you're working with me, boy.' Dad took a large bite of bread and chewed. He spoke with his mouth full. 'When I was your age, I worked with my dad, your grandfather. He was a good man, hard-working, Hamilton, he was; a good worker. Mr Grey said there was none better.' He paused again. 'Son, Connie is always your mother; you know that, don't you?'

"Course I do, Dad; I'm not a noggerhead.'

'I know; I know 'e's no noggerhead.' Dad smiled at him.

'And you gave our Hamilton Grandad's name?'

'I did, young 'en; he has your grandfather's name.'

'And my name Thomas, why did you give me this name?' Thomas watched his dad with his brown hair going grey. Dad gulped, then slurped his tea. He was still tall and strong, like a good tree.

Dad cut another slice of bread. Thomas heard footsteps above; someone else was getting up and making a start on the day. 'I tell 'e later; it's time we started milking.'

* * *

Thomas fed Topsy and Turvy their breakfast of oats and chaff. He stroked their noses and then treated them to some carrot, holding it out on his hand to feed them. He never felt more contented than when he was with the animals. They neighed and he felt their whiskers and wet tongue on his palm. They smelled musty and warm.

Thomas picked up the brush from the stone windowsill. Spider webs hung from the corner in big large spirals. He watched as the spider reacted and fled to his hidey-hole in the corner. Dad returned with the harnesses. Thomas brushed Topsy's mane.

'Dad,' Thomas said.

'What, son?'

'What was it like in the tanks?'

'You don't want to hear about that.' Thomas put the brush back, then knelt down to buckle the harness under Topsy.

'I do, Dad; I was reading about it in the comic.'

'Well, it's nothing like what they make it out like. In the tank, first thing you notice is there is no fresh air. I tell 'e, your sisters might moan about cleaning out the horses and the smell of shit and all, but that ain't nothing.'

'What do you mean?'

'Well, you know what the fumes are like from the tractor? You imagine you are sat in that all day, right next up to the engine; it's hot, very hot; you put your hand out and you burn it. Well, we was right next to the engine. I was gearsman; see, there was eight of us to drive them first ones. I was on one side, Jimmy –Billy's dad – on the other. Then of course there's Geordie; he was on the guns. He'll tell you all about it when he gets 'err; you won't stop 'im.'

'And did you get shot at?' They moved over to Turvy. Thomas brushed his mane first. Dusty came in, her black and white coat covered in bits of straw, picked up from rolling around.

'All the time; and don't think that metal saved us. Them bullets cut through it like it was no thicker than paper, then. You know war isn't what they make out in them comics.'

'Is that how's Billy's dad got killed?'

'Something like that.'

'When did you meet Mother?'

'We lived next door. Her father used to be the shepherd, like Uncle George is now.'

'Is that where you got my name from?'

'No, his name was Stephen; a good, fine shepherd he was. Come on, boy, it's time we got out to the field.'

CHAPTER NINE

21st September 1937

Thomas looked out of the farmhouse window and up the lane. He felt excited. Hamilton, his seven-year-old younger brother, stood by him, wanting to look out too. Thomas reached down, grabbed hold and hoicked him up so he could see. They had been waiting all day for them to turn up. Father had said they would be here; the wait was dragging on and on. This week was massive. First, the Tuckers were all coming from France. Dad had said to Mum when he thought no one was around that they must be 'doin' bloody well in that old hotel if Geordie can bring his family with him on holiday'. Dad had said Geordie was bringing his wife, Eliza, and three of their unmarried daughters. Thomas had overheard Dad saying that Geordie was hoping he could 'get 'em all married off soon, as he'd only got rid of one so far, and the other three was eatin' 'em out of house and home. If 'e could marry 'em off to someone in England then even better, as 'e didn't want to be changing more nappies for grandchildren.'

So, there was going be Catherine, Edith and Emma as well as Geordie and Eliza. Thomas didn't much like girls around. What he was more excited about that Friday was the Melplash Show ploughing match, and this year it was being held on Admiral's land, and Dad had entered with Topsy. He could hardly breathe. Dad was in and Uncle George said he had a bloody good chance, given that Topsy could walk straight and all Dad had to do was hold on the reins.

There was a break in the cloud and the last sun of the day shone down in streaks. Birds were busy getting a last feed before they went to roost. The evenings were growing shorter as the last of the summer died away and autumn took hold. Thomas looked away, fed up with the wait. He would find something to read, or get his football.

The sound of the motor car honking its horn filled the lane. The birds scattered to their night-time perches.

Thomas spun around and saw the car pull to a stop in the lane. He saw a man with black hair streaked with white get out, wearing a huge beaming smile. The man must have been a couple of years older than his father. Thomas ran, tripping over Dusty who was lying behind them.

'Redver Kingson, where are you, boy?' the man shouted as he stretched himself out. Thomas ran through the front door, then stood stock still, Hamilton racing after him. He didn't know what to say; and there were a lot of them.

'It's Thomas! What, how you've grown!' the lady in the passenger seat shrieked. She got out, moved round to him, then gave him a suffocating hug. 'Last time I saw you, you was only a babe.' She kissed him on the cheek. 'You look just like your father, that's for sure.'

'And this must be Hamilton,' she said, moving to his younger brother. He felt his cheeks going red and wondered where the rest of the family was; it wasn't for him and Hamilton to be the greeting party.

The three young women got out of the car. The shortest, Emma, was about the height of Nicole and had short dark brown hair. She came and hugged him and squealed. He was too old for all these hugs and kisses. Why couldn't this man have had sons who could play football? It was all getting a bit boring.

Dusty came running out, barking and licking anyone she could, followed by Dad, then Nicole and Lily, and finally Mother, looking shy; she hung back. Nicole went straight to Emma and they embraced, like old friends.

Thomas felt overwhelmed. He got a hug from the one called Edith, who was taller and had dark hair like her father, then finally the eldest, Catherine, who had a pointy nose and seemed quieter than the rest.

'Redver Kingson, as I live and breathe, it's been too long.' The man was now shaking Dad's hand, yanking it up and down like a lever on a pump and slapping him on the back.

Thomas found his football by the boot scrape, started bouncing it and kicking it against the wall. He started passing it against the wall, fed up with all the noise and yelling.

Then to his surprise, Emma hitched up her skirt, ran over, controlled the ball with her foot better than any boy he'd seen at school, and took it away. Dribbling it round the car; then she passed to Geordie. Geordie blasted the ball over to him.

'Come on then, Redver; Tuckers versus Kingsons. After all, you've one more than us. I'll put a pint on that.'

Thomas smiled. He couldn't believe this; everyone joined in, even Mother, and she never played. Everyone was smiling and playing; and however hard he tried, he couldn't tackle Emma, she was too fast, too quick; and every time he went to tackle, she shielded the ball from him, passed it away or dribbled past him. She was much better than his sisters. He tried his best to score past Eliza at the other end. Dad managed a goal or two, and even Hamilton was passing well. Topsy and Turvy looked over the top of the stable door, neighing in support. Those Tucker sisters were just too good for them all.

They played for hours in the yard, longer than ever before. By the time they stopped it was dark and everyone was exhausted.

'Emma, you were brilliant,' he said, walking in with her.

'"Course I am, *magnifique*,' she said, throwing him the ball and laughing. She had a funny accent but apparently this was French. The girls could speak both languages and there had been a lot of swearing from Geordie in French and English; and even Dad was swearing. Thomas liked this girl. She was pretty and she could play football and she smelt nice. Now he was thinking he should be older.

They all crowded into the front room. The last time this number of people had been in here was at Christmas. They pulled in the armchairs and chairs from the kitchen; there weren't enough, so Thomas sat on Father's armrest and Hamilton shared with Mother. Eliza and Geordie squeezed with Catherine onto the sofa, its flower pattern still vivid as it was only used for special occasions. If Mother had her way she would never have removed the wrapping. Emma and Eliza sat on the kitchen chairs, along with Lily and Nicole.

Dad lit the fire and they all warmed up, crowded in. Thomas couldn't help looking at Emma, who smiled at him.

'You owe me that pint now, Redver lad,' Geordie said.

'I can do better than that,' Redver said. He got up and walked out. Thomas knew what was coming.

'I've to say, Connie,' said Geordie, 'that Redver: he never stopped talking 'bout you when we was prisoners, but he was right. What a woman you are! I didn't think he'd have it in 'im.'

'Oh, Geordie, don't! You'll embarrass her.' Eliza pulled on Geordie's arm. 'You're to forgive my husband; he thinks before he speaks.'

Dad came back in with the milk jug full of wine he'd been brewing.

'I think you will like this one; 'tis my own. Rhubarb, I think it is.' Dad poured out the wine for the adults. 'I'd put you up but I don't have the room.'

'Don't worry, boy, I've done a bit of a deal with the landlord at the Farmer's.'

Nicole, Lily, Catherine, Edith and Emma got up and went to the kitchen. Least it meant Thomas could sit on a chair. The talk went on, all about the old times; for hours they seemed to talk. Thomas tried to keep up, but his eyes were getting tired. Mother sent Hamilton to bed and said Thomas would have to go up next.

'And now we have it all happening again, don't we? I can tell you, that Germany, they're coming again. We've been too harsh on them; it's made them frightened and vengeful. They're coming, mark my words! I for one won't be surprised,' Geordie said.

'Do you think so, Geordie?' Mother said.

'I do, I'm afraid. I've no doubt this man Hitler, he wants power; he's no more than a school bully. And I'm afraid you don't get away by giving them what they want, do you? He will keep wanting more until someone puts a stop to it.'

'But we can't go through all that again; we can't lose our sons, our husbands to that,' Mother said.

'I know, we're too old; we've done our share; but I'm sure there is going to be trouble ahead for our young ones. I don't like it, but someone somewhere has to put a stop to it.'

'Oh god, I really hope you're wrong, Geordie, I don't think I can face any of that again, not after we've rebuilt our lives. It seems like we are just recovering. And it hasn't been easy.' Mother seemed to remember that her older son was still there on the sofa. 'You go to bed now, Thomas.' He wanted to hear more about this but he obeyed his mother. He got a handshake from Geordie and a hug from Eliza.

'You need a bit more practice, lad, before you'll be playing for England,' Geordie said.

Thomas walked out, a smile on his face, and into the kitchen to say goodnight.

'They're so cute, your brothers, Hamilton and Thomas; I wish I had brothers,' Emma said, getting up and hugging Thomas. 'Better than these old maids I've got.'

'You wouldn't say that if you were in our shoes,' Nicole said. They all laughed. Thomas thought he wouldn't mind having Emma as a sister; she was fun. He turned and raced up the stairs before he got hugged and kissed any more.

* * *

Thomas walked out to the outhouse. He was allowed to stay up past his bedtime; after all, this had been a huge day. A Friday that he didn't think he would ever forget. His dad had done it: he'd won the ploughing match with Topsy. His father was proud, if a little embarrassed, standing in the field and having his photo taken for the *Bridport News*; Mother would make sure it got a good spread next Thursday. Even Admiral seemed pleased when handing over the trophy.

Thomas opened the rickety wooden door, which had gaps where the old planks were weathered and Dusty kept finding her way through. There were bits of her fur caught in the splintered ends. Inside, Geordie and Dad sat on old crates with Emma. She looked out of place, with her neat hair, clean dress and faint perfume that smelled fresh like spring. She sat amongst the hanging cobwebs of the old lean-to. She held the mug to her chest.

Thomas could smell the different wine concoctions: sweet tangy elderflower in one enamel bucket, savoury sweet parsnip in another, and the ponging rhubarb in the third.

'Pull up a crate, grab a mug, young 'en,' Geordie said. Thomas still didn't know what to make of Geordie.

'He's too young, he's not allowed any,' Dad said.

'Oh, come on! You'se celebrating, ain't 'e? He can have a little taster.'

'All right, but don't let Mother know, either of you two,' Dad said, shaking his head. He dipped a fourth enamel mug down into the bucket. 'Do you want to try this?' Dad handed him the mug.

Thomas looked at the liquid and thought he could see bits of parsnip floating around. It smelled a bit fruity, he supposed.

'Go on, boy, drink it down,' Geordie said. Dad nodded.

'Don't make him if he doesn't want to; after all, it's a bit of an acquired taste,' Emma said. 'You don't have to give into them two if you don't want to.'

Thomas sat with his knees up to his chest, the mug held tightly. He looked down, then put the mug to his lips and took a gulp. The sour, disgusting taste hit his tongue; he jumped up and spat it out. They all burst out laughing.

'It might take 'e a while to get the taste for that,' Dad said.

'Are you all right, Thomas?' Emma put her hand on his back and rubbed.

'It's bloody disgusting, makes me feel sick!'

'Maybe he should try the elderflower; it's less bitter,' Dad said.

'Not bloody likely, thank you,' Thomas said, shaking his head, hopping from one foot and spitting in the corner.

'There, there. He will live,' Dad said, as helped himself to another mugful.

CHAPTER TEN

24th September 1937

Nicole walked up from Moreton Station, her hands sore from the wooden needle. She was fed up. Edna, her so-called aunt, was being a bully and giving her all the hardest fishing nets to repair. A job she hated with all her heart. It was so mundane, lonely and cold out in the yard. These nets had to be ready soon to be sent to Newfoundland or some such place a million miles away. The smell was rancid. Her hands stank to high heaven. She must have used half a bar of Lux soap and still there was the faint whiff about her. Damn Edna! Why did she have to be so nasty all the time?

She walked up the lane and watched as sparrows flew up and away. The nettles were growing strong amongst the cow parsley. She breathed in the fresh air, glad to be out of the town and away from the smell of the fish.

She saw Billy Crabb walking towards her, his shoulders wide and pushed back, his legs firm and thin. He'd filled out in the last couple of years. He towered above her. His skin was dark brown from being in the field all day. He walked with purpose and confidence. Her stomach flipped over, the butterflies mixed with guilt. Hadn't she promised her mother, hadn't she said she would never go near Billy Crabb? Lily had promised and kept her word. Lily was stronger willed. Nicole couldn't resist. It was the way he made her feel. The kisses soft. He was strong and he wanted her.

Nicole looked around. There was no one on the train with her; she'd made sure to get a later train so that no one would see them walking together and they could quickly get to the barn. How had she let it go this far? He was asking to do more and she didn't have the willpower to stop. It was a welcome release from the drudgery of the nets and from her nightmares.

He greeted her with a warm smile and they exchanged pleasantries. It was best this way, just in case anyone was watching. It wasn't the first time that she'd met him on her walk home. The first time had been a coincidence; every other one they had arranged. His smile was wide and his dark eyes twinkled.

They walked down the lane. Nicole kept her distance. She didn't want Billy to smell her hands; she was sure they still stank. When they rounded the bend, she couldn't believe it. There was her father driving the green Standard Ford, the mudguards covering both large wheels. Hamilton sat up alongside. Thomas and the Tuckers were all on the trailer behind. What the heavens?

Billy saw them at the same time. He took her hand and pulled her into the gap in the hedge. The brambles tore at the skin on her arms. Billy pulled her through. They fell together into the deep meadow and lay down. The sound of the tractor pootled up the lane. Her heart skipped. She would be in deep, deep trouble if she was seen out with Billy.

When they were out of sight, Billy laughed and rolled over. He touched her hair and put it in place. She felt his lips on hers and she filled with warmth. She yearned for more. Her skin tingled. Nicole wanted his touch.

They climbed over the gate at the side of the Farmer's Arms. The public house was empty and quiet, yet to open. They joked about being caught out like two escaped convicts on the run. They walked down the path, Billy cracking jokes as he went and telling her about his day on the farm. He was light-hearted and fun to be around. He'd already lifted her spirits and she'd forgotten about her sore hands and the smelly nets. The sun was creeping down to the west, beginning to set.

Billy took them to the riverbank. He took his waistcoat from his shoulder and placed it for her to sit on. The spot was a high bank on the river's bend. They were in a small clearing surrounded by trees to their left and right and on the opposite bank. It gave welcome shade after the heat of the day, which had been so stuffy. Her feet could not reach the water's edge; even so, she removed her shoes to let her feet breathe. Nicole held her hair and pulled it to one side of her neck. She undid the top button of her white patterned blouse. The breeze blew with the flow of the river and it was the coolest part of her day. She closed her eyes to relax and breathed in the cool fresh air. She stretched her legs out over the ledge, trying not to get dirt on her black pleated ankle-length skirt.

'What you thinking? You look like you've flown away to another world.'

'Ha-ha! Nothing so much. I was so glad to be out in the fresh air, to breathe in cool fresh air, after the day I've had putting up with my auntie and all the nets.'

'Tell me about it! We've had Theodore bloody Fox out all afternoon, barking orders like we're in the bloody army or someink.'

'Yeah. Father isn't half glad he doesn't work under him.'

'Yeah. I think he's getting worse with age.'

Nicole watched the river winding its way, pooling in the nub of the bend. It looked so inviting; she knew it would be freezing. She remembered how as children this was the best place for swimming. It was where she had learnt. They had made dams further down. Here it was deeper, slow-moving and perfect to get your head under. Even if the minnows nibbled her toes.

She closed her eyes, stretched and pulled her hair to the other side of her neck.

'You shouldn't pull your hair round like that, showing me the skin on your neck; it makes you look like a proper glamorous movie star. Your skin looks so silky and tanned, with the shine from the sun; you look more radiant than Greta Garbo.'

'Shut up, Billy Crabb, I don't look anything like Greta bloody Garbo.'

'Maybe Bette Davis then.'

She wanted his kiss, so she flicked her hair with her fingers.

'How's that?' She wanted to make him wait and earn it. The anticipation made her want it even more.

'You're not able to flatter me. I know you too well.'

'I'm glad I'm with you, Nicole; you have something about you, more than your sister.' Billy undid his boots and took them off, putting them alongside. She was conscious he had inched closer to her.

Billy leaned in and at last she felt his kiss. She put her hand on the back of his neck and pulled him in, keeping him close. His rough, large hands, gentle like before, he undid the rest of the buttons on her blouse and moved his hand inside. He touched her skin, cupping her breast. Sensations raced through her body. It felt more delicious than before. How far should she let him go? She remembered the image of her mother telling her not to, forbidding her to see him. She wanted more. Girls her age had already; Alice Dunford had and she was as sure as hell Molly Hansford had, too. They weren't pregnant and they said it was the most wonderful thing you could do and that as long as you were careful it was all right.

The guilt at defying Mother built, stronger, and intense, nagging at her. She heard herself gently moaning and Billy's breath was getting faster. He whispered in her ear. The frustration building. She could feel the strength in his body. He moved over her, his leg between hers. She could feel him. Alice had told her that it was like this, that she wouldn't be able to stop herself if she went too far. That even if you wanted to stop, you had to; the man wouldn't. Nicole wanted him and soon, but not here, not today. Not with all the Tuckers around, not after nearly being caught. She held herself back and Billy stopped and looked.

'What is it, Nicole?'

'I've to stop before – you know. One day soon; not today.'

He hid the disappointment well, but there was a small hint of it on his face.

'You know, it's funny you and me ending up together like this; I always thought it would be me and Lily and you and Romily. Why was it, then, that Lily stopped seeing me? Is it something I've done wrong?' Billy leaned over and looked at her. 'What did Lily say?'

'Nothing, really, just – well, that it wasn't a good idea, you know, for the two of you to keep talking and seeing each other. I can't say; I don't know. Not really.'

'Was it my drinking? You know I only do that for a laugh. If she had wanted I would stop that.'

'No; I don't know.'

'You know if it was my drinking, or showing off, whatever it was, I would have stopped.'

'I don't think it was that.'

'Was it her grandfather? Has he said something?'

'I don't think so; he hardly talks to her.'

'Maybe he's told her to stop hanging out with me, that he would cut her out of his Will, was that it? Do you think?'

'I don't know, Billy; it's not for me to say.'

'You do know, 'course you do; you're her best friend, her sister; she would tell you everything.'

'I can't tell you.'

'Go on, Nicole.' He leaned over and tickled her. 'We were all friends. You can tell me.'

She shrieked, laughed, giggled; he teased her, tickling her arms and legs.

'Go on, tell me; you know you want to.' He continued to tease her.

'She didn't want to disobey Mother.'

'What, your mother? What did she have to say about it?'

'She said we should watch out, you know, be careful of boys, of boys like you. That we shouldn't talk to you, that we shouldn't encourage you.'

'I can't believe that, I can't believe it! Your mother, of all people! Your mother, she said you two shouldn't speak to us?'

His voice was raised, his face turning deep red. He stood up. He looked around.

'My god, your mother! She has been like an auntie to me! My god, she said that? What about your father? He's been like a dad. Did he say anything?'

'Calm down, Billy; she was only looking out for us, you know. She wants the best for us; she didn't want anyone gossiping behind our backs.' Billy kicked at the tall thistles and paced by the riverbank.

'Sit back down, calm down; she wasn't being nasty. She only wanted us to look out, to be careful. It wasn't personal.'

'Not personal? It's like my own family stabbing me in the back. Warning you two off of me. Whatever next? And her and Mother being so close all these years.'

'Sit here, Billy. I'm talking to you. Come on, sit down. Here, like we were before.' He paced up the riverbank, then turned. He sat down, a frown on his face and ridges on his forehead. She regretted telling him; she hadn't thought he would react like this.

She felt more guilt beginning to grow. Now she'd upset Billy and she was disobeying Mother.

'I should be getting back,' she said.

'Don't! You can't go now, not after telling me that.' He touched her arm and saw the blood. 'What happened? How did you get scratched?'

'It was on the brambles back at the hedge. It's nothing.'

'It's a nasty one. Come on, let me wash the blood off.' He held her hand and they walked up the river till they came to the dip in the bank where animals came to drink. They paddled into the water together. He took his handkerchief and dipped it into the water. He wrung it out and took hold of the back of her elbow and forearm. His rough hands enveloped her and she was reminded of the temptation. He moved his hand and dabbed at her wound with the damp handkerchief.

'There, all cleaned up.'

She watched as a butterfly skipped and fluttered from tree to tree on the bank; her heart and stomach did the same. He looked her in the eye; she could see him think. He then put his hand behind her neck. The handkerchief dropped and floated away. He pulled her in. She didn't resist. His warm hand on her nape stroked at her hair. His fingers moved through her hair. His head moved in and her lips met his. She didn't want to. She put her hands on his chest and pushed him away. She walked along the bank.

'I'm going to be late, I should get back.'

'Don't go; you can't go. Talk to me some more.'

'No, I've got to go.'

'All right; say you will meet me here tomorrow. After work, the same time; our secret place.'

She was torn. The passion inside was a raging fire impossible to extinguish.

CHAPTER ELEVEN

17th November 1937

Nicole heard the church bells chime from across the valley: six o'clock. She pulled her coat tight and stepped over the stile into the pasture with the grazing sheep on her way home from seeing him, seeing Billy. Hiding in the barn with him. It was dark as night.

The pounding in her heart sounded like a steam train, or like when the cows ran for their feed across the yard. It was the noise she couldn't dampen or quell and it rang loud in her ears, like the church bells. She gulped. Why go against Mother's wishes? What if Mother chucked her out? What if she got pregnant? Why upset Lily? This was stupid. Why not turn around? Tell him no, tell him she never wanted to see him again. Why not go out with Romily? He was all right. He was decent. He would please Mother and Father; everyone loved Romily, except her. What made her this way?

She stopped by the hedge and could smell wet grass and the odour of damp sheep's wool. She put her hand on the top of the fence post and leaned down. The acid in her stomach rose and she could feel it in the back of her throat. Her stomach was empty, but it didn't stop her from coughing, coughing, coughing, till the bile came out and she retched onto the grass. This is stupid; this isn't who I am. The wave of terror came flooding over her, the terror of disappointing her family. Why was she so reckless? Her stomach cramped for the second time. She could hear Mother's voice in her head, telling her how bloody stupid she was and that she should have known better; she had let her down, but more than anything, she had let herself down.

Nicole stood up, took a breath and wanted to cry. What was she to do to get out of this mess? When with him she felt like another woman, one all glamorous and grown-up like in the pictures. He was what was good about her life; without him, it was grey and ordinary like the autumn weather. Mother would be mad as hell and Lily – that was worse. If Lily ever found out, that didn't bear contemplating. She felt her stomach cramp again. She wished to be away from the mess of her own making.

* * *

The fire was burning inside the stove. Nicole took off her beret and coat. The kitchen was warm and all her family were inside. It was the same as every other evening. Except Lily was not home, not yet. She was usually first in from helping at the village school and started to prepare the meal. Then Mother, then her, then lastly Father and Thomas would be in, exhausted from the farm. Hamilton would look after himself after school or go out with Dad and Thomas.

Nicole felt her heart racing from seeing Billy. It was always the same. Huge, uplifting joy and pleasure, followed by unrelenting, torturous guilt. Which would eat away at her if she let it. Hiding in barns, taking walks, hiding from passers-by and from her own family, from his mother, her mother, her sister, her brothers. At least the Tuckers had gone home so there was some peace and some space, though she was missing Emma. She couldn't keep on doing it, could she? She knew she shouldn't; she should end it. That's what any sensible woman would do. That is what Lily had done. But she couldn't bring herself to do it. He was the most exciting thing in her life; it felt like an adventure being with him. It was his charm, his smile, his eyes, the heat, the passion, the fire, the butterflies; it was the all of him. And hiding it made it even more so. It was hard keeping it from Mother but keeping it secret from Lily – that seemed like betrayal on an altogether different level. So many times, lying in bed, she wanted to share it with Lily. To share how he made her feel.

The door banged open. Lily stormed in, tears streaming down

her face.

'What's the matter, love?' Mother asked, looking over from the sink.

'It's her! It's her, my own sister! Ask her!' Lily went straight up the stairs. Her feet were normally so light; now, it sounded as if Topsy and Turvy had come in and raced up the stairs.

'You boys, go out and play with your football. Redver, take them out, please. Now.'

Red staggered up from the armchair. He took the boys outside.

'Lily, come back down!' Mother shouted up the stairs. 'You stay here, Nicole. I need an explanation. Lily!'

Nicole felt the back of her throat go dry. This was it; she was for it now. She should have come clean; she should have ended it. She felt sick to her stomach. Lily came back down the stairs. Nicole tried to plead with her, with her eyes. But Lily wasn't looking her in the eye.

'What's all this?' Mother asked.

Nicole could feel the acid begin to bubble and rise in her stomach.

'Ask her, ask my SISTER! I can't believe it. And after all that was said!'

'Nicole, what's this all about?' Mother turned and looked at her. Nicole felt her face drain and her stomach turned.

'It's nothing; I can explain.' She looked at Lily and saw her sister's eyes streaming with tears, her cheeks red raw. She felt the guilt build like storm waves and roll one after another to her stomach.

'You tell her, Nicole. I thought we were friends; best friends, sisters. I've always told you everything; you, you do this behind my back! When you knew how I felt!'

'What does she mean? Nicole, tell me, tell me what Lily is talking about! Is it about a boy?' Mother looked Nicole in the eye. Nicole felt the blood drain out of her and she felt light-headed.

'I... um... I don't know how to.' Nicole said.

'You better damn well try and tell the truth; that's how you've been brought up,' Mother said, pushing her hands down on the table and leaning back. Nicole felt her tears roll. She tried not to sob.

'I'm so sorry. I'm sorry, Lily. I'm sorry, Mother; I didn't mean for it to happen.'

'What to happen? You haven't, have you? What have you done?' Mother said. She felt her own tears begin.

'I made a mistake. I was going to stop it, I was; you have to believe me.'

'I don't know how I can ever trust you again!' Lily said, her tears turning to anger. 'I told you, I told you how I felt… And you, Mother, I listened to you. What a fool I've been!'

'I was… I was going to stop it,' Nicole pleaded.

'But you didn't, did you? You've been carrying on with him,' Lily spat out.

'Will one of you tell your mother now what Nicole's done?'

'I tell you what she's done! She's been behind everybody's back, carrying on with Billy, Billy Crabb, and after you made us promise not to,' Lily said.

'Nicole, tell me it's not true.'

'I can't. I'm so sorry. I'm sorry; it just happened. We haven't done anything we shouldn't. I promise.'

'By god, I hope you haven't, my girl; you promised me. I told you two he was trouble. I was right, wasn't I?' Mother looked at her, shaking her head. Nicole had never seen her mad like this, not even when Thomas had broken the window with the football.

'I'm disappointed, disappointed with you, Nicole. You've let me down, you've let your father down, and worst of all you've let Lily down. I don't know how you could have done such a thing. How can I believe your promise? It's empty words.' Mother shook her head.

'She's been doing it for months. Molly Hansford told me. I said she was lying, I said to her face there was no way on earth Nicole would be so stupid. I thought Molly was just getting back at me because Billy had dumped her. She said she had seen it with her own eyes, said they were meeting down at the hay barn, every evening. I thought it stupid, but tonight I thought I would check it out for myself and it's true. I waited, I watched, and then I saw the two of them. The two of them carrying on inside. It made me sick.'

Nicole went towards her sister: 'It was my mistake, I made a mistake. I didn't mean anything to come of it. He was asking all about you, Lily. It was you, Lily, that he was asking me about. We got to talking and then one thing led to another.' Nicole tried to put her hand out to her sister. Lily pushed her away and turned her head.

'Spare me the gory details. You broke your promise, Nicole, that is what is so disappointing to me; and you've broken Lily's heart; can't you see that?' Mother said.

'You know what the worst thing is? He's been with Molly too, Nicole; he's been seeing Molly,' Lily said. 'Oh yes! And she had great delight in giving me all the information. She couldn't help but go into great detail. He's been sleeping with her, telling her he had been seeing you but was going to end it because you were too frigid, said that he was just playing you along to get back at your mother for telling us not to see him.'

'No, he wouldn't do that, would he? You don't know him like I do. He's got a good heart. He's told me he loves me.'

'He's been using you, Nicole, using you to get at us all,' Mother said, shaking her head. 'Me and your father didn't bring you up to act like this. You've brought shame on us.'

'I didn't mean to; it happened. I was about to put a stop to it.'

'You didn't seem to want to stop it, when I saw you with him this evening,' Lily said. 'Don't try and explain it; I don't ever want to talk to you again. I'll sleep on the sofa or stay at Uncle George and Auntie Dot's.'

'You don't have to; I'll leave,' Nicole said. She was speaking, thinking on the spot. 'Yes, I'll leave.'

'Don't – what? What are you saying? Where will you go?' Mother said. 'What about work? What about the family?'

'Yes, I'll leave; I don't really belong here. I'll leave; don't worry. I'll go to France; I'll stay with the Tuckers. I can work at the hotel.'

'Nicole, that will break your Dad's heart! Not like this, not in the heat of the moment! We can work it out,' Mother said.

'I think it's a great idea. You should go and as soon as possible,' Lily said.

'Lily, you don't mean that,' Mother said.

'I do mean it. And I don't want to see Nicole for as long as I live.'

'Lily, go to your room!'

Dad walked in. He had heard the shouting. Thomas and Hamilton stayed outside, kicking the ball against the kitchen wall.

'What's going on here?' Dad said.

'Don't ask,' Mother said.

How could she leave and break her father's heart? She was ripping the family apart. She had to go. To face her nightmares, to see France, to feel close.

CHAPTER TWELVE

21st November 1937

Nicole smelled the smoke and Father ran from her. She knew she was in the nightmare. Maman appeared and gathered her up. She smelt of flowers and was warm. They went and sat on the step by the kitchen door and looked out over the stable yard. She was sad because she was no longer feeding the horses with her father. The smoke was strong and it singed the back of her young throat. The sun was hidden behind the dark grey puffy cloud. She could hear screams; they scared her. Maman wasn't Connie; she was Marie, from before when Nicole was young; and the yard wasn't Home Farm; it was a long way away. It was when she was a very young girl.

'*Ne t'inquiète pas;* don't worry, baby, Papa will be home soon,' her mother said in French. This made her feel better. Although she was too big, her mother picked her from the step and rocked her in her arms. '*Ne t'inquiète pas;* Papa will be home soon; Daddy will be home soon.' Her mother's voice was so soft and gentle. She sensed even at her young age that her mother didn't believe what she was saying, that she was trying to convince herself. He did come home; he did. How was she to know that it was Maman who would be taken from her?

She appeared at the top of the staircase in her small white nightdress. The laughter, the drinking, the whoops of delight: they had woken her. She wandered to the bottom step, her steps, where she played. She jumped around. Maman appeared; she was sure it was Maman because she smelt of roses, her dark brunette hair fell from her face and she glowed. A glow that was as magnificent and light as a midsummer sunset. She radiated light that was gold, red, green and blue as if shining through a prism.

Then she was out in the yard. There were screams, cries for help. The crow on the stable roof squawked loudly and flew off. There were tears; the tears flowed and it hurt. Her heart pounded and she could not sleep. Maman was gone and it tore, and it scratched and it itched. There was no scar to dress; there was nothing. She was gone. There were no more cuddles for a time, there was no more smell of roses. The night-time stories stopped.

There was pain from the wound. She wanted to go back. There was something to see. Nicole saw her mother again. She floated down from a high place and there she stood. Her hair was brushed and beautiful, her face perfect and unmarked. She was glowing. She pointed at the front of the hotel and beckoned Nicole inside. Her face began to bleed from her eyes and the blood poured down her cheek. There were explosions. The facade of the hotel crumbled behind her; stone by stone it fell until there was only rubble behind the bloodied figure.

Nicole woke with a scream. The nightmare: worse than before.

Lily turned over and let out a sigh. Before, she would have asked if Nicole was all right; now, she was silent. There were birds singing outside. She felt alone and couldn't get back to sleep.

* * *

They walked through the old copse below Ashcombe Beacon. Mother was ahead with Thomas, Lily and Hamilton. Her sister and mother were not talking to her. Nicole walked next to Father. The copse ground was covered in a carpet of moss and vegetation that filled in the spaces between the oak and hazel.

She touched her father's arm and said: 'I love you, I love you all so much. I'm so sorry for what I did.'

He looked at her with his dark hazel eyes. She looked at his face; she noticed more deep furrows. She really looked; she had always thought of him as being a young man. Today as she looked at him, his hair, once all brown and thick, was now thin with grey. He'd always covered up his limp as best he could but now his shoulders were beginning their descent and his knees locked. He didn't play as much football as he would have liked with young Hamilton. It was the right thing to do, to leave and give them all space. And she needed to feel a connection with her natural mother. Dad and she had never talked about what had happened, not what had happened back then; and it was haunting her more so now that she had lost Mother and Lily. She loved Connie like her mother, but she needed to fill a connection to Marie. Her flesh and blood.

'Father,' she held his hand. 'Father, I've… I'm sorry about all this.'

'Oh, Nicole, no, please, you have all of us here. All your family is here. I'm sorry. I don't want 'e to go, I want 'e to stay with us all, stay with your family. It will get worked out.'

'I love you all, I really do. But I feel I need to, I need to; I want to; I can't stay.' She saw tears run down her father's cheek.

'You two will patch it up; give it time. It will all be forgotten.' He held her hand tight and looked into her eyes. 'Mother's coming round. We all make mistakes; Lily will, you wait and see if she don't. She didn't mean what she said.'

'Don't make it harder, Dad. I have to. Let me remember a beautiful, wonderful afternoon.' She pulled her father close in and walked in silence.

* * *

22nd November 1937

Nicole's case was at the bottom of the stairs. She looked around Home Farm. They were all in the kitchen, waiting. Thomas was standing behind Hamilton, his hands on Hamilton's shoulders. Mother and Father were standing in front of the range and Lily stood adrift in the front room doorway.

'Nicole, I want you to have this; it will give you something to read on the journey.' Mother handed her a book. Nicole looked at the cover. *Pride and Prejudice*, Mother's favourite.

'No, you can't give me this; it's yours, your favourite.'

'Yes, I can and I will. I can't see Thomas and Hamilton wanting to read it.'

Nicole looked up and Lily was shaking her head with her lips pursed.

'Thank you, thank you. I promise I will look after it.' She hugged her mother. 'You all mean so much to me, you all do. Why do you have to make it so hard?' Tears streamed down her cheek. 'You bloody lot of noggerheads! Look, you're making me cry. Bloomin' heck, Romily's going to think I'm a right mess.'

'You make sure you write to us often,' Mother said.

'I will, I promise.'

Nicole cried but tried to hide her tears. She wiped them with her hand. She hugged Thomas and Hamilton. 'You two behave and try not to break any more windows before I come back.'

She looked at the range, at the mantel with the old crescent clock. The table and chairs. Everything always seemed to take place in here: all the great family meals, all squashed in, the whole family packed in, even her cousins and Uncle George and Auntie Dorothy at Christmas. It was packed full of memories.

She turned around and looked at all five of her family in the kitchen. Dusty lay out on the floor, her tail between her legs, sensing the mood. Even the old parrot was quiet for once, his cage covered with an old tea towel. She couldn't go; she couldn't. There was a knock on the back door. It was Romily. He came in with his box camera and before she knew it he had taken pictures of her and the family standing in front of the mantel. She had to go; there was no turning back.

He took her case from her hand and walked her out to the Bedford bakery lorry with its rounded cab. He opened the door and helped her up. She dared to look; everyone waved except Lily, who stood aloof. Nicole made sure to remember what they looked like. Romily started the engine. This was it, she thought; this was it, she was doing it. It all felt unbelievable.

'You'll come back, won't you, Nicole?' Romily looked over at her; she could smell his deep aftershave. His hair was swept back and his eyes were like blue, deep sea water.

'I don't know, Romily, I don't know.'

'Please say you will. It won't be the same without you; you know that, don't you?'

'I have to go. If I don't do it now, I don't think I ever will.'

'We could be good together, you and me.' Romily looked over at her again as he drove down Snowdrop Hill.

'I wish I could say I would stay and we could walk out, Romily, I wish I could. But it wouldn't be fair on you. I couldn't let you put up with me until I've… You know, it's hard for me to put into words. I can't, not while I feel like this. You don't understand; you don't know me at all. You don't know what I'm like; you don't know what I'm capable of.'

The truck bounced its way down the rutted lane.

'Thank you for driving me but I don't want you coming to the platform. Just drop me off outside. I've had too many goodbyes. I don't think I can handle any more.' Her insides felt upside down. It dawned on her that she didn't know when she would see her family again, see Bridport, see her friends.

'I will never forget you, Nicole, never in a million years.'

''Course you will! Soon as you see another pretty girl waving at you in the crowd at water polo, you will forget all about me.'

'No, I won't, I'll never forget you. You know you always put a smile on me face every morning. Every morning I would make sure I was out front waiting for you to come by, every morning rain or shine. You put a light on in my heart.'

'Don't, Romily. You don't know.'

'It's true. And you know what, every afternoon I came to St Michael's Lane and I went to Edwards netting shed, every afternoon I waited to catch a glimpse of 'e in the summer so I could see you too, but I don't know – you never came out with the other girls. I thought you knew I was out there and you must be avoiding me. I don't know why, but I thought you must have liked

Robert Paul.'

'Oh, Romily, you silly noggerhead! I worked in the Gale shed, didn't 'e know that? Alice told me she saw you over there and we both thought you must be seeing a girl.'

'Bloody hell, I've been outside the wrong shed all these months! Flipping 'eck. What a fool!'

'It was meant to be; it's best this way. Least you won't get hurt.'

'You can stay; we could go off. What if I kept driving? We could go anywhere, you and me. What do you say?'

'No, Romily, please don't make it harder. I can't go with you. I have to fix myself. I wouldn't make you happy; I would only make you miserable. I have to do this for myself. Can you understand that?'

'I do, Nicole, but I don't like it and I don't believe it. You and me: we could be great together. You like me, don't 'e?'

'I do, Romily, but in the end, I would only make you sad.'

'I don't believe that; I don't believe you could make anyone sad.'

The truck rounded the bend and approached the front of Bridport Station.

'Let me drive you to Dorchester, Weymouth, Poole or Southampton, anywhere; we could talk.'

'No, Romily, this is far enough. You can drop me off here as we planned.'

Romily pulled the truck to a stop. Nicole pulled the catch on the door.

'Wait,' Romily said. He leaned over and held Nicole's hand. His hands were large over hers. His grip tightened and he pulled gently. He leaned in. Nicole slipped her hand out of his and jumped down onto the pavement. She looked back up, put her lips to her palm, kissed and blew it to Romily.

'Don't wait for me, Romily. You find yourself a lovely girl, and not an old trollop, you hear me?'

A tear ran down her face. She walked towards the entrance, then took a look back and gave a wave. He waved. Down beneath the tears and the sadness at leaving, there was an inkling of excitement forming. She was on a journey, a journey where she could return to a connection she had never had. At the same time she felt her stomach urge. She threw up behind the milk cart.

* * *

Nicole stood outside the hotel. Relieved. It was twelve years since she'd left as a six-year-old girl with her father and Thomas, then a baby in her arms. It looked smaller to her. The sign was the same, if a little faded. The smell of fresh croissants escaped from the baker's a few doors down. The passage under the arch to the stables looked the same. The town seemed similar to what she remembered except her memory seemed faded. Her childhood in Albert seemed to be another lifetime. She could remember a lot of building work back then. The rubble sites were her playground.

Nicole looked around; perhaps she would feel more at home here. The journey had been long and slow and the train from Calais had many changes. She would write home soon as she could, let them know she was safe. She had thought about them every minute of the last weeks. The thought of not having Lily as a friend or even a sister made her feel hollow and empty. Was she forever to push away those she loved? What a mess she had made. Then there was Billy. She was surprised; without him nearby, she didn't give him much more than a fleeting thought. Of course, she missed the passion, and her fast-beating heart. But surprisingly, she was thinking how sweet Romily had been. He cared and he would have done anything. Why can't I be with a boy like that?

Emma came running out of the front of the Hotel de Madeleine.

'I didn't think I would see you so soon. Twelve years without a peep, then twice in a year! Was it because I told you how nice all the boys are here?' Emma looked so sophisticated in her long blue skirt with her dark brown hair cut short.

'We are going to have so much fun, me and you! I've been so excited since we got your letter. I can't wait to show you around.

78

You are going to love it here, I promise. Oh, the boys, Nicole! The town is full of 'em. You are going to break their little hearts even more than I can. You look so beautiful; I wish my hair was like your silky brown streams. Now, let me think who would be good for you. Maybe Marcel? Or Pierre, or Bertrand? I don't know, I think I may keep Bertrand for myself. Maybe David; he could be good. Yes, David. I think you and him might be suited.'

'What's you up to out here? You can't keep 'er all to yourself! Let her come in and at least put her case down,' boomed Geordie as he strolled out looking every bit the hotelier, dressed in a dark suit jacket that he couldn't close around his bulging midriff, and a white striped shirt with suspenders over his shoulders.

Geordie took the case from her and said: 'Cor, feels like you've ten tons of bricks in 'er. Come inside. We would have fetched you from the station if we knew what time.'

'Don't worry, I wanted to stretch my legs.'

'I want you to know you are as welcome here as any one of my sprogs; in fact, I would say better than one of me own.' He nudged her arm and winked at Emma. 'Maybe not as well as this one; she's always been spoilt. Serious like, though, if it wasn't for your father, she would never have been around.'

'What do you mean?'

'You don't remember, do you? Well, I don't suppose 'e would; were only a bairn at the time. He saved her, didn't 'e, he saved her from the fire. Don't you remember?'

'No, not much; more the smoke and the party after.'

'Ay, that was one hell of a party all right; it's a wonder I remember any of it. Eliza had to pick me up from the restaurant floor the next morning.'

'I remember the smoke, the noise, and Maman holding me at the kitchen step.'

'Ay. Well, your bloody old man is as brave as they come. 'As he never told you? He ain't said anything to you, has he? Well, we are going to have to put that right. I'm going to tell you all the old stories about your old man and me, every one of them.'

'Will you? I would like that.'

'Don't say that, Nicole!' laughed Emma. 'He's been boring the socks off us forever, telling the stories one after another; I can't believe your father doesn't do the same. My god, you've been so lucky! This one don't stop jabbering on about the good old days, how him and the lads got in that mess or won that bet,' she said, impersonating her father's deep voice.

Nicole let Geordie and Emma walk on ahead. She paused and breathed in the smell. The scent of baking was wafting on the air. She closed her eyes and thought she could see the image of her mamam in her mind.

CHAPTER THIRTEEN

25th December 1937

Lily was helping her mother to peel the carrots. They sat in silence, working together. Dad, Thomas and Hamilton were out threshing. Dad wanted it finished so he could enjoy Christmas dinner knowing the feed was in for the winter. The rhythmic sound of the Standard Ford tractor driving the thresher filtered through the window. The smell of roasting chicken filled the kitchen. She could hear Hamilton's laugh from outside. The yellow-fronted kitchen cabinet stood behind them, the drop-down shelf always left out, more papers overflowing from the top shelf. The floor was covered by lino; Mother had been so proud when Red had bought it for her after harvest, it was so much easier to clean than the flagstones. Christmas Day: and the first when the entire family wouldn't be here. Lily felt a pang of guilt. After all, it was she who had driven Nicole away.

She was missing Nicole, but she wasn't ready to forgive. It had hurt too much. Sisters didn't do that to each other. She had thought she knew Nicole, but obviously she didn't. As for Billy Crabb, he hadn't given Nicole a second thought and was carrying on with Molly: Molly now pregnant, disowned by her mother, beaten by her father and sharing a room with Billy at the station. God, that could have been her. What a disgrace that would be! Molly didn't seem to care; she held her head high, didn't duck out of sight and carried on as if it was nothing. What if Nicole had been pregnant? What if she had left because she couldn't face them? If that was me, Lily thought, I would want to be swallowed up and never be seen in public. The shame of it, the stupidity of it. Had she and Nicole lost everything because of that stupid boy who didn't give them a second thought? And now Billy Crabb taking advantage of his mum, his gran and grandad. Bringing in his girlfriend and not even married. She had to admit it: they had some front.

'I've a letter from Nicole; it came yesterday,' said her mother.

'Did you? I don't care.'

'She's well; she's arrived and she's started working for Geordie and Eliza. She's struggling with French.'

'Is this enough carrot? Shall I start on the brussels?'

'She is settling in; she says it's a bit backward.' Mother carried on peeling the parsnips. 'The weather is cold and Geordie, he traded in some old antiques for a year's supply of wood for the fire. She says that the tank that Dad was in during the war is out in the town square as a memorial.'

'Can you pass me another knife? I think this one's blunt.'

'She's picking up French again, says it's coming to her quick, but they mainly speak English when she's on her own with the family. The work is good and better than them smelly old fishing nets and working under Edna.'

Lily got up and fetched the sprouts from the larder. She returned, sat down and started peeling and putting in crosses.

'Geordie and Eliza are putting on a big party for the town. There is going to be dancing, and he's put up decorations. Nicole says it looks very pretty. But she is missing everyone and it won't be the same not having dinner with us all. She says she will even miss watching the Boxing Day football. – Lily, are you listening? She says that they don't even do a roast dinner; can you believe that?'

'Yes.'

'She's missing all of us.'

'I know.'

'Lily, we all make mistakes, don't we? You can't punish her forever. I warned you about boys like Billy; I warned you two what he could do.'

'Yes, and I did what you told me, I obeyed you. It's not me you should be giving a lecture to, is it? It was her, and she's only my half-sister; you're not her real mother.'

'Lily, I thought you should know better. 'Course I'm her real mother, who's brought her up all these years.'

'I know, I'm sorry. I didn't mean it. It just makes me so mad. I do the right thing, then she stabbed me in the back, going with the boy that I liked.'

'There's plenty more and plenty better than Billy Crabb. You only have one sister and I love you all. I may not have given birth to Nicole and Thomas, but I love them just the same. You know I love you all.'

'I do… oh, I don't know.' Lily felt the tears roll. They stood up and Mother gave her a hug. All this because of Billy Crabb; and look at him now. Thank god she had listened to Mother; but what about Nicole? Would she ever be able to forgive? It didn't feel like it.

'Lily, you shouldn't let your pride get in the way. You should make up with your sister. We're family and one day it might just be too late.'

The roast chicken didn't taste so good and Lily felt an atmosphere. Dad didn't look happy and he looked older. Thomas and Hamilton were quiet and subdued. They were all missing Nicole.

* * *

Lily knocked on her grandfather's study door, a little apprehensive. She waited for his reply, feeling intimidated.

'In.' She heard his commanding voice. She felt like she was being called to the headmistress, that she'd be going in for a telling-off, not visiting her grandad on Christmas Day. She opened the door and it smelt no less of tobacco than she remembered. It was dark and Grandfather was sitting back in his old leather chair behind the large oak desk with the green leather writing-top. Papers were scattered around and there was an old wooden cabinet to his side. In the corner the tall clock clicked out the seconds.

Grandfather leaned forward, his fountain pen in his hand. His beard was long and grey, his eyes smoky like the room. He had his glasses perched on the end of his nose. He beckoned her forward.

'Look, girl,' he said. 'It's about time we talked seriously about your future. I think as my granddaughter you should go to a good university, Oxford or Cambridge. Your father Sampson, he went to Oxford; I think you should too.'

'What?'

'Don't mumble, girl, I can hardly hear you. Speak up; project!' Admiral noted it down like he was completing an inventory for the estate. 'Yes, I think that would be a very good fit. After all, I can't have a granddaughter of mine helping at the village school forever. Yes, Oxford: they have some excellent colleges and they let women sit degrees. Yes, good. Well, that's decided then. I will make the arrangements and then you can start next autumn. Good, good, that's settled.'

'I don't want to; I've decided I will go to secretarial college. I don't want to leave and go to Oxford.'

'Don't be so silly! You don't have a say in this.'

'You can't make me.'

'What? Don't be so silly! You will do as you're told, young lady. You are not too old to have the cane put across your backside.'

'You can't make me go. The cane won't change my mind!'

'It will, my girl. I will make you go if I take you there kicking and screaming.'

'And I will just come home again; you can beat me all you want. I want to go to St James' Secretarial College. I've made enquiries.'

'What will you pay the fees with?'

'I don't know; I will find a way.'

'No, no. That's not good enough! Think about it; take the opportunity – you may never get another one. You can't be thinking straight. Look, Lily, it's what Sampson would have wanted.'

'We don't know that. I think he would have wanted me happy.'

'I've had enough of discussing it. Go away and don't come back until you've seen sense.'

Lily walked out, closing the door behind her, glad to be out of the stuffy room. Why was it she was upsetting everyone? Mother, Grandfather, Father even. How she would have liked to talk to Nicole; she would have known what to say.

She wandered in the dim light into the library. It was eerily empty; the dim electric lights buzzed and gave a false yellow light. The musty smell of old books filled the room. Large draped curtains, coloured deep velvet red, covered the windows and there was a small fire burning in the grate. Too small to heat the room. It felt cold and Lily shivered down her spine. Why did her life have to be so complicated? Why did her grandfather have to be so set in his ways? She didn't want to disobey him and she didn't want to leave her family. It was an opportunity, to go to university; there would be a lot of girls who would dream of this chance. Her mother would be sure to want her to go. Maybe it would be better if for once she didn't tell her everything. For once, Mother and the Admiral would be on the same side and she didn't think she could fight the two of them.

* * *

Boxing Day was clear and cold. The sun was low in the sky and the shadows were long, even at midday. By the afternoon the sun was moving fast and would be setting soon. The village had played the Boxing Day football match and Moreton had beaten Ashcombe, again. Thomas had played for Ashcombe and scored a hat trick; the trouble was, Moreton had scored eleven. Lily had watched and cheered him on. Billy Crabb had played and had been sent off for fighting, watched by his heavily pregnant girlfriend Molly Hansford. The talk of the two villages, her bump looked massive.

Lily went to the commiseration at the Farmer's with Rosa Colman and Alice Dunsford. It wasn't the same without Nicole.

Her two friends sipped at sherry but she stuck with lemonade. It was getting cold outside as the sun disappeared. The men inside were rowdy and boisterous; soon they were outside, running and larking about.

Billy came over and put his arms around the women. Lily smelt beer on his breath and his clothes.

'Get off, Billy Crabb. You stink.'

'Oh, come on, Lily, give I a smile, won't 'e?'

'Billy, I don't even want to talk to you, let alone smile.'

'You doesn't mean that!' he slurred.

'I do, and if I don't talk to you for another thousand years it will be too soon.'

'I want us to be friends.'

'I don't. Get off of me!' She pushed him from her shoulder; he was too heavy, he leaned further. 'Billy, I mean it: leave me alone. Go home to your girlfriend.'

She was saved by Romily Colman who pulled him away. Romily and Billy staggered off, found a ball and started replaying the afternoon's game.

'He gets more handsome every day, doesn't he?' Alice said.

'Yes, you've got to say he has something about him. That Molly's a lucky girl,' Rosa said. 'I bet he's good in other ways.'

'How can you say that, Rosa? Molly's pregnant and Billy's a drunk.' Lily shook her head.

'He's not a drunk, Lily,' Alice said, sipping on her sherry. 'He might like a couple of drinks but he's no drunk; and if he is, he's a handsome, strong one.'

'When did you become so interested in boys, Rosa?' Lily said.

'Since I had my first kiss,' Rosa said.

'Well, you want to stay away from Billy Crabb,' Lily said, looking over at Billy running wild with the boys. 'He's trouble and he's not worth it. If he was a half decent man he would be marrying that poor girl.'

'You can't pity Molly,' said Alice. 'She's as loose as they come;

we know that.'

'We might do, but it's Billy I blame. He should take more responsibility for his actions. He should learn that he can't leave a wave of destruction everywhere he goes.'

'Lily, you've really got it in for him! Whatever has he done to you?' Rosa said.

'He didn't, did he? You haven't, have you?' Alice said.

'She hasn't what?' Rosa said.

Lily blushed. 'Of course I haven't.'

'You bloody did! You've slept with him, haven't you?' Alice said, whistling through her teeth. 'My mother always said you've got to look out for the quiet ones.'

'No, I haven't. I never would.'

'I think you're protesting an awful lot. Lily, what is it you're hiding? You hate him so much and you always used to be so friendly,' Alice said.

Lily was feeling hot and said: 'Look, can we talk about something else, different to boys?'

'What like? What Mr Chamberlain is going to do in parliament?' Alice said. 'I don't think so; you're not letting on. Bloody hell, Lily. Is it why Nicole left? Is she? Shittle bum hurdle. That's it, that's bloody it! No, not Billy and Nicole.'

'No, no, no! You've got it all wrong! Don't say that; for god's sake don't spread that around.'

'Lily, you've got to tell us,' Rosa said.

'Well, did she leave because she's pregnant or not?' Alice said.

'No, I swear, no. We argued, that's all.'

'What did you argue about?' Alice asked. 'That was about Billy?'

'It might have been.'

'It was! So you liked Billy and Nicole slept with him? And that's why you can't stand him?'

'You two can't talk about this. I don't want Mother hearing gossip about Nicole. She wanted to go and visit, you know, where she lived before; that's all; and the Tuckers said she could stay.

There is no way she slept with Billy. She didn't sleep with Billy. If Mother hears this gossip, it will break her heart. So you're to stop it now.' Lily turned her back on her friends and walked down the lane in the dark.

'Lily, wait! We've not finished our drinks,' Alice called.

'I have and I will see you tomorrow. I'm tired so I'm going to bed.'

'Wait, Lily! We didn't mean anything by it, Lily!' Rosa said.

Lily was walking off too fast to be bothered with goodbye. This was the worst Christmas she could remember.

She hadn't got halfway home when she heard shouting and screaming coming towards her. It was the men of course, running laps of the village. Two or three ran past, calling her name as they did. Then the last person on earth she wanted to see came running into her. He knocked her flying to the hedge. He got up first.

'Sorry, Lil,' Billy said as he held her hand and pulled her to her feet. 'You all right?'

'Why is it always you?'

'What? I'm sorry?'

'I wish you were, Billy Crabb.'

''Course I'm sorry.' He kept hold of her hand. Then he kissed her full on the lips and ran his hand down her back. She kissed him back. It felt warm and her spine tingled. She pushed her hands on his chest and pushed him away. Then she raised her arm and slapped him clean across the face. Her hand stung.

'You stay away from me! And don't you ever do that again. Go home to your girlfriend. If you were a half decent man you would have married her by now.'

She said the words; but the temptation inside her was as powerful as the West Bay drag. She ran the rest of the way home. Maybe it would be better if she went away to university, away from the village.

* * *

14th March 1938

* * *

Lily read the *Express* at the kitchen table. Father was drinking his tea, seated in the armchair. It was all across the headlines: the Nazis entering Austria, Adolf Hitler saying the Germans wanted living space. Where would he go next? Father said this was bad. It was happening all over again. The threat of war. The sooner they stopped him doing what he wanted the better; that was the only way to deal with bullies, so Dad said. He was sure it was going to come down to England again.

Mother came in through the back door, her face frozen and white.

Lily felt a shiver run through her body. Something was wrong, something had happened. She felt her stomach roll over and put the newspaper down on the table.

'What is it, Mum?' she asked; but she didn't want to know. It must be bad for her mother to look so solemn.

'Lily, I'm so sorry. It's your grandfather, the Admiral; he's passed.'

Lily absorbed the news and didn't know what to say. She had never felt close to her grandfather but she didn't wish him bad. Mother hugged her and Lily began to cry. He was the only grandfather she had. He was stern, like an old Victorian.

'There, there; don't worry, don't worry.'

Lily could feel her throat narrow and the sound of her own sobbing. 'It's all right, Lily.' Mother hugged her and stroked her hair as she had when she was a child. 'Don't worry, Lily.'

'I never told him I loved him. I did,' Lily said.

'I know. They don't talk like that at the Manor; it's their way.'

'I love you, Mum, and Dad too; Thomas, Hamilton; I love you all.'

'We know, love, we know it.'

'Nicole doesn't, does she? She doesn't know I love her. And what if I never see her again to tell her?'

'She'll understand. Write to her. Tell her.'

'I don't know what to say.'

'Just say what you're telling me; say you're sorry and that you love her. Life's too short not to.'

'I will, I will. I'll write to her.'

* * *

The entire two villages were out for the funeral; there were over a thousand people. They lined School Hill, all the way to St Mary's, at least three deep the entire way. The churchyard was rammed full. Everyone agreed he had been a good squire: decent, hard but fair. Lily had to sit on the front bench between Grandmother and Montague; further to her side Auntie Elizabeth and Uncle Theodore sat, Theodore in his suit, holding his bamboo cane with its round silver top. Mr Grey, his hat in his hands; Miss Appledore the headmistress. Lily was wearing a black dress with a white lace collar; her mother and Aunt Dorothy had sewn it for her. It didn't seem right that she was on a pew right up front. Mother and Father were much further back, seated with Thomas and a fidgeting Hamilton.

The sermon was sombre. Grandmother sobbed and Lily wanted to soothe, so she held Grandmother's bony hand and rubbed with her other hand over the top, her grandmother's hand so cold and thin, the veins showing thick and lumpy. Vicar Wrixon gave the sermon and they sang hymns. Mr Grey got up and spoke in high regard. The singing was loud and there was much crying: the passing of a great man, a great institution. The vicar said the village would not be the same without him. Times had been hard and the Admiral had seen them through. The villages had survived better than most as depression and economic hardship had hit the country. An age had passed, he said, an age when men had given their lives for freedom. And that the Admiral had been a great steward and he looked forward to young Theodore continuing the good work his father had done. This all seemed to pass in a blur to Lily through her teary eyes. She regretted not knowing him better. There was some relief; at least he wouldn't be able to force her to

90

university.

The wake at the Manor was attended by many. Lily didn't know most of them; they were from Admiral's circle of friends, magistrates, old Navy comrades and councillors. Vicar Wrixon and Miss Appleworth were invited to the Manor. Uncle Theodore had tears in his eyes as he shook everyone's hand. Montague was by his side, looking older than his twelve years, his curly ginger hair reaching his shoulder.

Lily talked to the Vicar and Miss Appleworth, hoping this would end soon. The claustrophobic atmosphere was draining. There was much talking, with people she didn't know. She didn't like making small talk, and it was all stuffy. The wake came to an end at last. Uncle Theodore said goodbye to all and people slowly ebbed away.

'You should know: the Will reading is next week. I suppose you should be here for that. After all, he always treated you better than me and your father,' her Uncle Theodore said.

'Yes. Of course.' She couldn't imagine he would have left her anything, so she would attend and hear it out. 'What do you mean he treated me better?' Lily looked around the huge dining room at the large sideboard with the family heirlooms on it, the large oil paintings of her grandfather taking centre stage above the ornate fireplace. Her Uncle Theodore now standing alone.

'He was harsh. That's when we got to see him at all.' He pushed his hand through his full blonde hair. 'Most of the time we weren't seen; we were sent to Nanny when we were young. There wasn't much fun in this house. Then if we misbehaved like children do, or upset Nanny, he would come in with his whip. I've still the scars. That's what fathers do.'

'He whipped you?' Lily scratched her face.

'Yes, and he didn't seem to care. Like I say, he was harsh, but no more than any other father I suppose. I've never been like that with my son; I hope it can be different. But you know son takes after father, daughter like mother, and no one learns to be any different. I would do anything for my son, to be different, not to be like him or like me.'

'What do you mean?'

Her uncle looked around. He touched his face with his hand.

'It was the war. I saw things, you know, that no one should see. It still haunts me now. I try not to let it; but you are so lucky. I don't want my son going through what I did. You know, it wasn't easy for us officers; we get the blame. There were decisions I had to make, decisions I didn't want to take, friends that I lost. Not all scars are physical.'

Lily looked at her Uncle Theodore and felt a tinge of sympathy for him. He'd lost his father and she knew how she would feel. She almost wanted to put her arm around him and console him.

'Then there was the time with your father. You should know: if I'd gotten my way back then, I would have had him in front of the firing squad.'

'What! You never would. What?'

'Oh, yes; I would have had him and his mates all right. I should have.' He shook his head. 'They should have answered for that. I never did get that promotion after that. Then I had to go back again, to the front, knowing what I knew from before; that was the last place on earth I wanted to be. I never want my son going through all that.'

The air escaped Lily's lungs. Then Grandmother came in and took her hand.

'Please, Lily, come and sit with me. I need to talk.'

Uncle Theodore turned around and walked out of the dining room. Lily thought she had seen tears forming in his eyes.

* * *

Lily sat in the dining room of the Manor with her back to the fireplace. The chairs had been positioned in a semi-circle. The Fox family solicitor, whom Lily knew was from Dorchester, stood behind the desk that had been brought in from the Admiral's study. He introduced himself as Mr Cochrane. He was very tall and slim with a moustache and glasses, and he looked very serious and sombre. He lined the papers on the desk, then picked them up, tidied them, put them back on the desk, then squared the corners; precise. He talked in a slow monotonous tone. If only he could vary his pitch, make it sound more interesting.

Lily looked out of the large window. It was grey and dark outside and it didn't seem like rain was far away. She thought about Nicole and where she was. What would she be doing? How was she?

Mr Cochrane's voice droned on, not changing tone. Lily felt her eyelids getting heavy. This was all boring. She looked out of the window and wished she was anywhere but here. To be outside. She didn't take much notice as it was announced that the estate was being left to Uncle Theodore, that Gran would live on in the Manor. That there would be a trust fund for Montague; that he would get this when he turned twenty-one. This was going on and on. She thought she would really fall asleep soon. She just wanted to be away to get home so she could get ready to go to the pictures with Alice and Rosa.

'And to Lily Kingson, my granddaughter…' Mr Cochrane kept on in his monotone. Lily tried to focus.

'There will be a trust fund, in which I bequeath her Home Farm in the village of Ashcombe. This is written in covenant that she must achieve a degree from Oxford University. The trustees will see that all fees and costs are covered from the said trust fund. And without condition or covenant, I leave her the Austin 7 and fifty pounds.'

Lily swallowed and sat up straight, not believing what she'd heard. Grandfather's old runabout car, the 1931 Austin 7, the little maroon and black car, the one he loved to drive around the estate? And fifty pounds? It was more than she deserved, it was too much. And then to be left the farm if she got the degree. She would own the farm! How happy this would make her family.

'He can't do that, William, he can't!' Uncle Theodore was red in the face. Standing up he approached Mr Cochrane.

'I'm sorry, Theo, he has. It's not the time…'

'He bloody well can't! He can't leave that to her; what about us? The estate can't do without the rent.'

'Look, Theo, I'll explain later. I have to finish the reading.'

'Finish, finish! He can't do this to me. What about our future? For Montague and his family?'

'I'm sorry, Theo, see me afterwards. I've to finish this.' Mr Cochrane continued talking in his monotone.

CHAPTER FOURTEEN

3rd April 1938

Lily walked with Alice Dunsford, the waves crashing into the shore, one after another, with full force and white froth; tall, four or five feet high. The West Bay sea front: to her left the beach and to her right the rows of detached bungalows. The wind was blowing hard into their faces from the south-west. The salty sea spray landed on her face, with fine sand. She tried to turn up the collar of her coat. Winter didn't want to let spring in. She licked the corner of her mouth and tasted the salt. The air smelled of the beach.

'Why come down here in this weather?' Alice pushed Lily in front of her and pulled out a cigarette and tried to light it.

'I needed to get out, to talk to you.'

'What on earth is it?'

'I thought you'd be glad to have something to do on a Sunday morning; or did you want to go to church?'

'No, but I didn't think it would be this cold!' Lily watched as Alice shivered and finally managed to light her cigarette. She put the packet back in her handbag, smoothed down her brunette hair with her hand and then drew on the cigarette.

'How's Nicole?'

'I wanted to talk to you about something else, not Nicole.' Lily shook her head and walked to where the cliff path started. Glad the path was dry. The stones were loose underfoot. There was building work as the row of bungalows was extending up, way back from the cliff edge. Why did Alice always have to be asking about Nicole? It made her feel uncomfortable. She had not listened when Mother had read the letter, but in the night when

95

everyone was asleep she had crept down and read it on her own.

'But is she all right?'

'Alice, can I talk to you about something? You have to promise not to tell anyone.'

'What is it?'

'I've been left an inheritance.'

'I know you got the car.'

'I got a little money, and the car, but there's something else.'

'What else?'

'Grandfather has left me Home Farm.'

'What? You are joking! The farm? That place means the world to your family! Flipping heck, Lily, that's amazing.' Alice drew on the cigarette, blowing out the smoke which was whisked away by the wind.

Lily came to the gate first, opened the latch and walked into the green pasture. She looked out to sea, where white horses pranced into shore. The sea seemed less threatening from up high, where she couldn't see the size of the waves. The grass smelt lush as new shoots sprang forward. Crows flew overhead, squawking, adjusting their flight paths, mobbing herring gulls for fence post perches.

'Yes, I know it is, but it's not that simple.'

'What? Either he's left it to you or he hasn't.'

'He has; but he says I only get it if I complete a degree at university.'

'You get to go to university as well?' Alice stopped, grasped Lily's hand. 'Lily, you are so lucky, to get out of this dump, to get away! My god, Lily, to get an education! You are so lucky.'

'I know, I know, it's all so great,' Lily said, trying to sound excited.

'So why do you have a face like an old donkey standing in the rain and sound like my mother when she's doing the laundry?'

'Because… I don't think I want to go.'

'What?'

'I don't think I want to go.'

'I heard you; I just can't believe you!'

'The farm, it's all my parents ever wanted. It means everything to them to get that, to own it; that's been their dream. But I don't want to go away; I want to stay in Bridport. I love it here, I love it; I don't think anywhere can be as good. You call it a dump, but it's our dump; and they don't have the sea in Oxford, do they.' Lily felt her hands getting cold and stuffed them in her pockets. 'Why would I want to leave? I was going to go to the secretarial college; that would be good enough.'

'Lily, you have the chance of a lifetime. I don't see why you are so undecided. Go, get out of here, make a life for yourself. Get yourself a handsome man. Lily, you've got to!'

'You make it sound so easy. But what if they don't like me; what if I can't do the work?'

'Lily, don't be so bloody wet! We all know you're the smartest, the clever one; all that reading you do.' The ash on Alice's cigarette fell to the ground as they reached Eype Down, the pasture wide and flat with only a dozen sheep grazing. 'What's your mother said? She must be made up!'

'I haven't told her, not about the farm, not about the conditions.'

'Why on earth not?'

'I can't find the words. I need time, time to talk to you, time to work it out. I don't think I've the nerve to go away. What if I go and fail the degree and they find out that because of me they never got the farm?'

'Lily, you won't fail; when have you ever failed anyone?'

'I failed my sister, didn't I. I let that boy come between us. I shouldn't have reacted like I did. I should have been more mature.' Lily pushed her hair behind her ear.

The path wound its way past the old quarry. Lily watched for the puddles and walked to the side between the overgrown bushes. The hawthorn tree was bare-branched without its striking white blossom.

'You've got to talk to your mother, to Nicole.'

'I know. It's just that I don't know how to tell them I can't do that to them. Oh, I don't know; maybe it wouldn't be that bad, maybe I could do the work. I suppose I might enjoy it.'

'Of course you would, Lily, you would love it! I could see you being the head girl, or whatever they call it at university. I don't think I've ever known anyone who's gone. My whole family is as boring as anything. To think I would be friends with a woman with a degree! It's amazing, Lily; you have to; you can't turn this opportunity down. Think what you might be able to achieve and then how happy you are going to make your family.'

Lily led Alice out of the bushes and she looked down on Eype beach. There were small figures walking along the shingle, stopping, looking out, taking in the air. The clouds were dense; it was getting much darker and it was more like early evening than morning. Could she do it? She hadn't given it a thought before the Will; she had dismissed it when Grandfather talked about it. No, that wasn't true; she had thought about it and she had dismissed it as impossible; she didn't want to take Grandfather's money and she wasn't intelligent enough. Now she had it on a plate; it was there. Lily felt her legs work hard to hold her back. She wanted to be free, like the birds flying around her. It looked like Grandfather would get his way. That he would finally exert his control over her destiny. Lily thought she didn't really have a choice after all.

They walked down to the gully. Lily was careful to step on the large stones as she crossed the stream. She sighed and looked out to sea. The sea horses looked larger close up and the swell of the waves was enormous. Lily didn't have the energy to carry on to Thorncombe Beacon.

'Let's turn back, Alice. It looks like rain.' Lily touched the tip of the fence and turned. 'How can I tell them now? They will know I've been keeping it from them.'

'Don't be silly. They will be pleased for you; and for them.'

'Maybe I won't tell them about the farm. I don't want to get their hopes up because I will probably fail anyway. I can't speak Latin.'

'Lily, you won't fail. They will be pleased, won't they?'

'You have to promise, Alice, you can't tell anyone. You do, don't you?'

'Of course, Lily, I won't say a thing.' Alice brought her handbag up, held it open with one hand and took out her cigarettes before looping her hand through the straps and flicking her thumb down on the lighter. Out of the wind she lit it first time.

'And don't give that silly talk of being a failure. I know you won't give up; you will do whatever it takes. Come on, I don't know many girls who pulled their drowning brother out of a harbour. Not like you two did. Then there were all the times at school, playing games, playing chain tag, you were always the last to get caught; you would be so determined. You were always winning! Or those spelling tests, god, those spelling tests with Miss Appleworth: you were always top, Lily. You always practised and practised; I know, because you wouldn't come out and play till you had practised with your mother. There was no one else like you, Lily.'

'That was different; it was a village school. I might have practised hard but I'm too old for all that now. I could go to the local secretarial college, then get a paid job. I don't want to be away all those years; and for what? A degree: what use is that around here?'

'Lily, you would love it, all those books, the studying, the learning, and then the boys. Hmm, I would go just for the boys!' Lily felt the sweat on her forehead as she walked hard up the steep cliff path with the sea out to her right, heading back for the down. What if she could do it? What then?

CHAPTER FIFTEEN

8th October 1938

The train journey had been long, changing at Winchester. Lily was tired. Her legs ached from the inactivity. The train screeched to a halt as it lined up with the long platform. Longer and more ornate than Moreton, Bridport and Dorchester; bigger than all three put together. And there were hordes of men, all dressed in dark suits and ties, all of whom she imagined to be intelligent, clever and looking far more sophisticated than her, a plain Dorset girl. She got her battered chocolate-coloured suitcase down from the luggage rack and walked from the train to the platform. It was early afternoon. She felt alone, and approached this with trepidation. Her mother had been so excited and full of support and had said how this was the first time anyone in her family or Dad's had ever had such a chance, and that she should take it with both hands, grasp it, work hard and be thankful for the legacy her grandfather had given her. Why did she feel so bad for not telling Mother and Father that the future of the family farm now rested on her shoulders? She would just have to make sure she succeeded, for everyone's sake.

The October afternoon was cold and crisp with a clear blue sky; it could have been summer if there hadn't been a chill wind. The buildings were tall, grand and intimidating. Grandmother had made sure she knew where she was heading. To St Hilda's College. She supposed she would learn who St Hilda was and how the college got its name. She saw other students getting taxis but she wanted to walk. There were dozens of bicycles, racing through the streets. A gap appeared; she checked the road, clear; and she walked out.

A bell rang. An imposing deep voice shouted: 'Out of my way!'

Lily hadn't seen the cyclist as the bike hurtled towards her. She stood like a statue as it raced down the street. She didn't know whether to retrace her steps or move forward. There were too many people. Other bikes rode in front and behind her.

The voice bellowed, 'Look out!'

The bike and its rider were bearing down on her; she had to run. As she did she just managed to escape the front wheel. Her foot came down in the large puddle and splashed her dress. The owner of the bicycle came to a stop, got off and wheeled the bike around.

'Your stupid lump,' she said in her deep baritone voice. She stood tall, towering above Lily.

'I'm sorry, I didn't see you.'

'Didn't see me? Most people hardly miss me, dear. You should look where you are going, young lady. I guess you're new.' The owner of the bicycle was older than Lily by a couple of years, with a high forehead accentuated by the fact that she had scraped her hair back and piled it high on her head. She had steel in her narrow eyes. Her confidence seemed to belie her age; maybe it came with her height. Her skirt was full and ruffled up; she had on thick white socks. Her skirt didn't reach her ankles. Lily couldn't place the woman's accent except that it sounded full of self-importance.

'Just mind you keep out of my way. I don't want an innocent first year getting under my feet.' She swivelled around, got back on her large heavy bike and rode off.

Lily looked down at the bottom of her blue and white dress, now stained brown. She wanted to turn around and get right back on the train and go home. She walked up to the pavement, nervous, looking where she was going, noticing the top of the castle turrets over the row of shops. She walked past Woolworths, glad that there was something the same as Bridport. Who was she trying to fool? Her Latin was poor. Vicar Wrixon had coached her, but even he had begun to lose patience with her. Uncle Theodore had said it was worse than Montague's; and he was thirteen.

As she turned at the corner she saw more students, all men walking with their cases. Up ahead there was one woman, walking apart, stopping, walking a bit further, then looking. Hopping from one foot to the other, unable to stand still, she put her case down, then picked it up again. Lily caught her up and noticed she was crying.

'What's the matter?' Lily said.

'I've no idea where I'm going.' The woman's face was wet with tears. If her eyes and nose hadn't been red from crying, she would have been pretty. Her face was delicate and white, her hair brown and short and there were dimples in her chin. 'My feet are sore, I've been walking round and round for hours, I can't find it. I've blisters on my hands and all the men have told me that if women can't find their way to their college then they shouldn't be here. It feels like I'm the only woman in the city.'

'Well, you're not, and the women are just as up themselves.'

'Ha ha.' She sobbed out a laugh, coughing as she did.

'What's your name?' Lily asked.

'I'm Jean Jenkins; call me Jeanie.' She dabbed at her eyes.

'Well, nice to meet you, Jeanie. I'm Lily Kingson and I'm a fish out of water too, so you have nothing to worry about. Give me that case.' Lily grabbed it.

'You can't do that.'

'You watch me; it's nothing compared to a sack of wheat.' Lily carried the case. 'I hope you are going to St Hilda's; I could do with a friend.'

'I am! Oh, Lily, I'm glad to have met you.'

'Not half as glad as I am. I'm studying English Literature. What are you doing?'

'Chemistry. I've always loved sciences.'

Lily smiled, happy to have Jeanie to talk to. Having Jeanie to look after and think about, she almost felt relieved to be out of her own head. Jeanie reminded her of Thomas and Hamilton, having to look out for them. She took a deep breath; perhaps this wouldn't be as bad as she thought.

Lily and Jeanie stayed together and made sure that after signing in at St Hilda's they went to the dormitories together. They chose a room that looked down over the river. It was small with bunk beds, two chairs and a table that stood below the only window in the room. There was one wardrobe to share. Lily and Jeanie opened their suitcases and unpacked. Lily couldn't help but think her clothes looked old-fashioned against Jeanie's. Lily turned her back and changed her dress.

'Where are you from, Jeanie?'

'I'm from Brighton. My father has a grocery store; well, he has two of them now.'

Once changed they went to reception to await their induction tour.

* * *

Lily returned to the bedroom to check on Jeanie; she had been in bed all morning so far.

'How are you, Jeanie?'

'I don't feel any better.' Lily could tell she was still full of flu and cold. 'You will have to do it for me.'

'I can't stand up at the debating club!' She laughed. 'What the hell on earth have I got to say about the subject? It's your area of expertise!' Lily had helped her study for it but it hadn't made a lot of sense to her; and anyway, she wasn't standing up in front of that crowd. College was good in parts; she was surprised how much she enjoyed it and how well she could keep up with the work. As long as she went over the material it seemed to stay in; if she made good notes, re-read them and then copied them down, it seemed to stick. She had even been able to answer some questions at lectures. She still struggled in Latin, but she did enjoy all the books. The library dwarfed the one in the Manor House.

'I can't stand up in front, and certainly can't argue.'

103

Jeanie seemed so much more confident than when they had first met. It had only been a month. Now she was a member of the debating society, just one of the clubs she had joined along with the rowing team. Lily didn't have any inclination for either.

'Please, Lily. If you don't, I'll be blamed for not getting a stand-in earlier.'

'Jeanie, you will just have to do it! There isn't any way I could be ready. It's only in a few hours and I've all this work to do.' Lily sat down on her chair to the side of the window and looked down at the river and the busy path. She opened her books and began to read.

'I guess I'm going to have to get out and do it then.' Jeanie pushed the sheets back and stayed where she was in her full-length nightie. Her voice was deep and throaty, full of cold, unlike her normal soft tone.

''Tis only a sniffle, as my dad would say,' Lily said, and laughed. 'Look, I'll get you a dram of whisky after. I'm just glad I didn't sign up for that.'

'It's fun, Lily, you should join. The boys aren't too bad when you get to talking to them.'

'I'm not worried about the boys; it's that Mauve Layton-Lisby. She scares me; she scared me on the road that time and she scares me now. I don't envy you debating with her; she puts the fear of god in me. You and Eleanor have a job and a half going up against her and Imelda.'

There was a knock on the door. Jeanie ignored it and went to the wardrobe; Lily skirted past and opened the door. It was Celia, wrapped in her dressing-gown.

'Lily, tell Jeanie that Eleanor can't be her number two; she's in bed with cold.'

'What is it with you townies? One sniffle and you take to your beds!' Lily said, shaking her head, knowing that now she was going to have to be Jeanie's number two.

* * *

Mauve had opened up the debate: 'Is appeasement the right course of action?' The room was crowded but she commanded it with her mighty height. Mauve was for and Jeanie and Eleanor were against. Mauve spoke without a quiver, her confidence supreme. Lily knew she could never speak so eloquently. Everyone knew Mr Chamberlain's speech off by heart. It was all the talk around campus: not if, but when.

Lady Mauve recited the speech, for everyone to hear. She seemed even more commanding than Mr Chamberlain: 'This is the second time in our history that there has come back from Germany to Downing Street "peace with honour". I believe it is peace for our time.'

The oak panelling reminded Lily of the Manor House. She was worried, but at least as number two she didn't really have anything to say; she would leave it all down to Jeanie.

The debates in St Hilda's were every bit as fiercely contested as in the Oxford Union. Lily had gone with Jeanie to some of the big debates. Jeanie loved to go into the old hall and watch from the gallery above. The finery of architecture was impressive, as were the polished performances of the speakers. Most of them were too political for Lily; she liked the more humorous, and Edward Heath's the importance of not being earnest, 'liberty, fraternity, frivolity': that was much more fun than debating whether all faith had been lost in the government of the day. The term balls were fun, all the men looking so smart in their tails, and the women in their ball gowns. She'd spent some of her allowance on a gown, though she'd been too shy to accept offers to dance and had stood watching. Jeanie had no hesitation in accepting; she was a world away from the shy girl she had seemed on the first day of term. Now she was settled and enjoying life. It was taking Lily far longer to find her feet. She didn't know why. She had never had trouble making friends before, and it wasn't like she didn't get asked to dance or even to step out or go to the cinema. There were plenty of rules to adhere to, being in before ten one of the strictest.

There seemed to be more in the crowd than on previous occasions: men and women, all crammed into the study room. Lily could feel her stomach turn over. Mauve was confident and without nerves; she stood tall – she didn't really need to stand on the bench like the others. Her gaze was enough to reduce Lily to ash, and she spoke with such confidence as if her words were from the bible. Her responses were as fast as lightning. Lily didn't envy Jeanie in going head-to-head with this formidable, unmoving object. Then there was Eleanor, who didn't seem to have an ounce of fat on her body, she was so thin. Her face frozen, she seemed more masculine than the men; and she could cut you in half with her sarcasm.

Mauve rounded off her argument perfectly, to cheers and loud applause. The chairman summed up and thanked her for her arguments. He then introduced Jeanie and Lily.

Jeanie began, making a sound opening argument.

'And Churchill said that instead of snatching his victuals from the table, Hitler has been content to have them served to him course by course.' She paused, her voice cracking; she took a swig of water, then continued.

'There can be no pacifying the dictator...' Her voice broke.

'Stop, stop! This is no good. We can't hear!' Mauve boomed out.

'I'm sorry. I can... just let...' Jeanie said as her voice disintegrated. Lily watched. With gut-wrenching certainty she knew it was coming down to her. Why had she stepped in as number two? She should have known better. Lily watched Jeanie mouth the words *I'm sorry*.

'Come on then, girl, take over!' Mauve shouted.

'I don't... I mean, yes, thank you.'

Lily began, reading the notes that Jeanie had prepared. They were hard to read in Jeanie's scrawl. She didn't have the conviction in her voice; she wavered. It should be easy. Their argument was the one the whole room believed. She just couldn't do it. It was all the faces looking at her, waiting on her, staring. She wanted to run, go back to bed and be anywhere but standing in front of this crowd. She stumbled over the words and could see Mauve from the corner of her eye, shaking her head and tutting. She could feel her own face turning red. She mumbled and staggered from one point to the next, like a drunk, zig-zagging; her brain just couldn't think of the right thing to say. Words fell over themselves; her tongue coiled like a snake, unwilling to cooperate. Then she felt the crowd getting impatient for her to finish; they were fidgeting. Those sitting in the front began to play with their books, look at their watches, and talk to each other. This distracted her even more. She tailed off.

'Well, if you could make sense of that country bumpkin, you're better than me,' Mauve said. The crowd erupted in laughter, clapping and jeering. Lily didn't know where to look; she felt she would explode. She hated Mauve; she hated every one of them for laughing at her. She never wanted to speak in front of a crowd for the rest of her life. Lily pushed the notes away on the lectern and looked down at her feet. The roaring laughter continued, louder in her ears. She felt Jeanie's hand on her shoulder. She pushed it away and ran from the room, still hearing the laughter in the hall. She didn't stop until she got to her room. She slammed the door shut and climbed up to the top bunk, and got under the covers without taking off her dress.

CHAPTER SIXTEEN

12th November 1938

Thomas held Hamilton's hand. They crossed over East Street, looking out for cars. Thomas looked at Hamilton, whose smile was nearly as wide as the street. Mother and Violet Crabb talked behind. It wasn't the same without having Nicole or Lily at home. He missed them. And coming to the pictures with Mother and Violet wasn't as much fun as with Lily and Nicole. Maybe they would get a milkshake, after. Though he wouldn't show he enjoyed the film; he was too old at thirteen to like a girl's film. They turned at the town hall and went down South Street to the Palace. Nicole was happy and having fun, according to the letter that Mum read out. He hoped he would see her soon, that she would come home. She had left so quick. Was it something he had done? He knew something was off with her and Lily, probably some silly business that sisters were getting into. He was looking forward to the film. He'd seen it last year too, but it was Hamilton's first time.

There was a queue all the way out of the entrance. The noise of excited children and adults filled the air. Hamilton jumped up and down, keen to get in and get a seat. Thomas looked at the colourful poster on the wall. He had to admit it, too: he was excited. It made a change to be doing something fun; at home, the only talk was of Germany and Hitler. They inched forward and he found his feet on the polished floor of the entrance. They approached the booth and went up to the kiosk. People filtered through and the usherette showed them to their seats. The film started with a hush: *Snow White and the Seven Dwarfs*. Violet bought them ice creams and they settled down. He thought it amazing to see the colourful, moving pictures up on the large screen.

Afterwards, they walked out of the cinema and into South Street. Hamilton danced along the street pretending to be sleepy, which made them all laugh. His smile was so wide he thought his face would crack under the strain. They all walked to Rax Dairy, the women chatting and the boys playing in front. They found themselves seats and ordered milkshakes. He wished Nicole was there to share it.

He had strawberry. He sucked it up through his straw and made a big slurp at the end, which Hamilton copied. Mother told them off and said they should behave better. That only silly children did that.

* * *

Thomas had to help with the milking. He took off his best clothes, put on his brown work cords and white work shirt that was mud-splattered. He ran down to the yard and collected his stool and bucket. He climbed over the gate into Marsh Field. The cloud was low and it was dark, even though it was only three o'clock. Mist gathered in droplets on his brow. It wasn't cold and he could smell smoke in the air. A bonfire must be burning over yonder. The grass was lush and Thomas had to avoid the large clusters of reeds. It hadn't rained for a week or more but the ground squelched under his boots. He walked over the brow of the hill, then down towards the stream where the cows liked to gather in the afternoons. Dad had already made a start, with Meg, a young shorthorn. Thomas raised Fay and massaged her udders till the milk started running to the bucket.

'Good film, son?'

'Not bad.'

'Not bad? I thought it was your favourite.'

'It was, but I'm too old for it now. Hamilton loved it.'

'Good, good.'

'Dad, why did Nicole leave like that? Does she like it in France better than here? Doesn't she love us any more?'

''Course she loves us all.'

'Why did she go? Why don't she come home?' Thomas kept working, the bucket a quarter full. He could smell the warm creamy milk. He loved the smell; and the taste was even better. He licked his lips. He could still taste some of the strawberry milkshake.

'It's complicated. You'll understand when you're older.'

'I can understand now; I'm thirteen, after all. I know Lily had another father; that's why Admiral and them are related.'

'I know, son. It's women things and boys; her and Lily fell out, that's all.'

'Dad, is Connie my mother?'

''Course she is, son; you know she is. She's looked after you forever. After all, she wouldn't do that if she didn't love you, would she?'

'But is she my natural mother?'

'Why are you asking?' Thomas watched as Dad finished on Meg, climbed up on the trailer and emptied the bucket into the churn. 'Have you heard summink?'

Thomas wasn't sure if he should continue. It was something he had heard Nicole saying to Lily one day through the bedroom wall. He hadn't thought much of it again until Emma Tucker mentioned something about Nicole's mother in France. And him being born there.

'Was I in France before I could remember?'

''E don't want to be talking about all that time ago, Thomas; that's history. 'E wants to think about the future, not all about the past.'

'Is that why Nicole has gone back? Is she looking for summink?'

'No, no, it's not like that.' Dad got down from the trailer and walked over. Thomas felt his head buzzing.

'Look, it don't change nothing; it was a long, long time ago. I can tell you, it doesn't change anything, not about you and Mum or you and Lily and all.'

'Of course, Dad, I know, I'll understand.'

'I was lost in France during the war. I was in love with your mother, with Connie. But she didn't know I was alive, you see; she thought I was dead.'

'And you wasn't, you were taken prisoner, like Geordie and you were saying; you two were together.'

'Tha's right, I was lost and gone, for all Connie thought. It was a long time; and then it took me a long time to get home.'

'What's this got to do with it?'

'I'm coming to that; be patient.' Dad stroked the back of Fay. Thomas finished and took his bucket to the churn. He put the bucket on the trailer, then clambered up.

'See, by the time I got back, Connie, well… she had married Sampson and she was going to have Lily. So that's when I went to France. I fell for a French woman, Marie. She was so lovely and I had Nicole and you with her. There was a… an accident. Marie died, so that's when we all came back; and Connie's husband had died and we all became a family. You know it's like when a ewe dies, you know we give the lamb to another mother and then she takes care of it like it's her own, don't we, and she's the new mother and she loves that lamb just as much as if she had born it, don't she?'

'Yes, so my and Nicole's birth mother was Marie.'

'Yes, son. Now it don't pay to go talking about all this 'cos it does upset everyone.'

'So, Nicole hasn't gone to find our natural mother? She has passed away.'

'I think tha's enough. I'm getting a headache with all this talking and we should be getting on.'

'So, Nicole and Lily aren't friends anymore.'

'It's something like that.'

'Does that mean Lily doesn't love me anymore?'

'No, no! Tha's enough of this blathering. You knows they all love you; it will all work out in time. I hope it does anyway.'

'I'm half French and half English.'

'I suppose, boy, but you is all Kingson, like your dad.'

That made him feel better. He was like his dad.

'Dad, do you think there will be another war? Mother was reading the paper about Germany and their leader, Hitler, saying he wanted to take over more countries. Does that mean he will want England and France?'

'He might do; no one really knows, but Geordie he seemed to think so; and I ain't known him to be wrong many times. The papers say Mr Chamberlain has given in too easy to Hitler.'

'Will I have to go and fight?'

'I wouldn't think so; you are far too young and you shouldn't think about it. We've been through all that before – the last thing we want is a repeat. It don't do no one any good.'

'Dad, I miss Nicole, I do, a lot. When will I see her again?'

'I don't know.'

They sat down on the end of the trailer.

'Will I ever see her again?'

'Yes, sure you will.'

'What if I don't? You don't know. I don't think I could live without seeing her again.' Thomas could feel his stomach turn over. It was like when he was in the water, being pulled under, like he would be suffocated, and he was powerless to do anything about it. Nicole and Lily were not there to help him.

'You can write to her, write her a letter and tell her how you are feeling.'

'But writing's for girls; I won't be able to spell it proper.'

'Mother will help 'e, son, don't worry so much.'

'I know, Dad, but it ain't the same, is it, as seeing her smile.'

'I miss her too. Hopefully it won't be long; we will all be back together.'

'But what if there's a war? And last time millions died and lots in France, where Nicole is.' His stomach turned over again and again, like he was churning the butter. He even felt a bit sick.

'Don't go on like that, boy. It probably won't even happen.' He looked at Dad's face; he didn't seem to look happy or to be telling him the truth.

'I'll try and write, if Mum will help. Dad, do you think maybe I could go visit her, you know, if she stays in France? Could I go back? I'm half French, after all.'

'We will have to talk to your mother about that; and anyway, Nicole could be back soon; you won't need to.' Dad stood up. 'You can drive back.'

It wasn't often Dad let him drive the Standard Ford tractor. He hopped down and got up on the seat. He started her up. His feet just about reached the clutch and it was a lot easier to push down now than six months ago. Dad said he was nearly as good a tractor driver as him. He thought about that and the film and tried not to think about Nicole. It didn't make him feel good, thinking he would not see her smile again this week.

CHAPTER SEVENTEEN

3rd September 1939

Thomas and Dad came in from the field. They would normally have had breakfast in whichever field they were in, under a tree or up by the hedge or propped with their back against the tractor's big rear wheel. But Dad was taking much more interest in the news on the wireless. Lily had bought it for his birthday and ever since it had been on almost constantly. Thomas liked some of the shows and they even gave out the football results. There had been a letter from Nicole and she was well, as were all the Tuckers. He and Mother had been writing letters to her for two years. Still she didn't say when she was coming home; she said there was unfinished business. He just wanted to see her. He wanted her to write that she was coming home. But she didn't. He could see it: Hitler wanted all the countries for himself. He was in Poland and Dad was saying he wasn't going to stop there.

Inside the kitchen Mother and Lily were making the normal Sunday preparations for dinner. The kitchen was warm with the smell of roasting beef. Mother put the potatoes in. Thomas licked his lips as the smell of the meat juices filled his nostrils. Dusty sat up and paid attention, hoping something might drop her way. Mother closed the oven door. Thomas made do with some buttered bread and cheese. The wireless was on. Dad took off his boots and settled in the armchair. Thomas sat at the table with Lily and Mum and helped peel the carrots. They didn't talk; even Dusty seemed to be paying attention. Hamilton came in and sat down next to Dad with his comic.

'And now the Prime Minister, Mr Neville Chamberlain, after which will be King George.'

There was a crackle from the wireless in the corner.

'This is it, mark my words,' Dad said.

'Shush, Dad,' Lily said.

Mr Chamberlain talked slowly and deliberately; it was solemn.

'...I have to tell you now that no such undertaking has been received and consequently this country is at war with Germany.'

'Tha's it, then,' Dad said.

'My life is over; I'm only twenty, for heaven's sake! My life is over,' Lily said as she began to cry.

'What about Nicole? Dad, what about Nicole?' Mum said.

Dad got up and paced around the table and said, 'Geordie will look out for her, don't you worry about that.'

'I know, but she has to come home; she can't stay there; not now,' Mum said, her voice rising, her tone changing.

'Will she come home, Dad?' Thomas said.

'I'm sorry, I'm sorry, it's all my fault,' Lily said.

'It's not, dear; it's that Billy Crabb I blame,' Mum said. She chopped the carrot on the table.

'Now, now, don't get ahead of ourselves. Quiet – I want to listen to the King,' Dad said.

Dad turned up the wireless and sat back down, ruffling Hamilton's hair as he did.

'I ask them to stand calm, firm and united in this time of trial. The task will be hard. There may be dark days ahead and war can no longer be confined to the battlefield. But we can only do the right as we see the right and reverently commit our cause to God.'

'I'll go and fight; I'll do my duty,' Thomas said and continued, 'I'll go and stand calm. I'll do it for King and country.'

'Don't be so stupid, Thomas, you are only fourteen,' Mum said, shaking her head and waving the knife at him. 'Don't you ever talk like that.'

Thomas bit his tongue. He would; he wanted to do it.

'What did he mean, it won't be confined to the battlefield?' Lily said.

'It's 'cos of the planes, ain't it; they can come and bomb us now.'

'What, even here?' Mum said. 'They wouldn't ever bomb us, would they, not in Dorset?'

'Well, they have in Poland and I bet they didn't think so too. Who knows how far he's going to go? We're in it now, ain't we,' Dad said.

'It's just like Mr Churchill said in '37. What was it? Dictators on backs of tigers which they dare not dismount. And the tigers are getting hungry; something like that,' Lily said.

'I don't know about tigers, but Hitler ain't going to stop now, is he,' Mum said. 'We have to write to Nicole, tell her to come home, tell her it's time she got home. Why has it gone this far? I thought the Great War was to end everything.'

'Hitler ain't going to be happy till he's taken over all Europe,' Dad said.

'Us as well, Dad?' Thomas asked. His stomach felt upside down; he felt scared. Why wouldn't Nicole come home? What would Hitler do next?

'What can I do, Dad?' Thomas said.

'Nothing; we keep going as normal. The animals need looking after just the same and the crops need growing, more important than ever. We put a brave face on it and carry on. Hitler can't stop us from doing that! Yes, we all carry on best as normal, we don't have a choice in that.'

'Can I go and visit Nicole?' Thomas said.

'That's the last place on earth I want you, Thomas. The best thing is we all write to Nicole, say she should come back and be safe. This is the best place for her,' Mum said.

'Yes, Mum,' Thomas said.

'Can't we have some more cheerful songs on that bloody thing than all this talk of war?' Mum said.

Thomas knew that all farm workers were exempt from conscription; it was an occupation on the reserved list that had been published last year. Father was not happy. There were leaflets from the Ministry appearing most weeks: dig for victory, look at using every available piece of land. It was a shock to hear the news so clear and precise, but it had been as if the whole country had been sleepwalking towards this. Thomas got up and fed Ol' Parrot some nuts. Dusty sat at his feet, hoping for some scraps.

CHAPTER EIGHTEEN

10th May 1940

Thomas drove the Standard Ford tractor pulling the trailer, with Dad stood up behind. They were going to pick out a couple of calves for Bridport market tomorrow. The pigs all slaughtered, the sheep gone too. Dad had said calves would be fat enough this week. Thomas controlled the steering, expertly moving the tractor through the narrow gateway as it bounced over the track. He felt confident and his legs were plenty strong enough to push hard down on the clutch when he needed to change gear.

Hamilton had wanted to come out with them this morning but Mother had made sure he went to school. The air was cool; it was about seven o'clock. The familiar sound of Hurricanes came flying over. He didn't give them a second thought. Three in formation, flying low, passing on and buzzing away into the distance over Snowdrop Hill. The smell of the petrol fumes wafted back on the breeze. How ever had Dad been able to sit in that old tank breathing in the fumes? Thomas didn't think he would be able to do it. It was bad enough when out in the fresh air. 'Course, the war was going badly, Hitler's army through much of Belgium. The defence of France beginning. The worry about Nicole. Mum, Lily, begging her to come home in their letters to her. He drove the tractor on up towards the copse.

The Ford pulled on. It was effortless compared to using the horses. He knew Dad wanted more machinery. They had a disc harrow and a trailer they could attach. Thomas parked the tractor and trailer up at the top of the field. They would pick up a couple of calves; but first it was time for their breakfast.

They sat down, backs against the large tyre of the tractor.

Thomas thought he heard it first, but then Father did too. It was voices coming from the copse; it sounded like men, and a lot of them. They both got up and made their way to the fence.

Father pushed down on the top strand of barbed wire and stepped over. He made quiet, as if stalking and careful not to tread on twigs or noisy leaves. There were oceans of delicate bluebells springing forth, carpeting the woodland floor. Thomas followed Dad, who weaved in and out of the hazel. The voices were louder and if they were trying to stay hidden they were making a very bad job of it.

Thomas watched as Dad took a deliberate step, checking where to place his foot. Careful with his. He could hear the men more clearly. From behind, he heard the crack of a twig. There was someone or something following them; maybe it was one of the deer. He took in a deep breath and stood behind an oak tree; his father put his arms around him. There was a small sound, light steps. They moved from the large oak to the ash to the horse chestnut in a circular pattern.

'You!' Dad said. Thomas peered around the large trunk of his father. He shook his head.

'Should have known you couldn't stay in school.' It was Hamilton.

'You two, shush for now; be quiet as a mouse. Something be going on up in 'err and I wants to find out what 'tis,' Dad said.

Dad led the way, Thomas in second, Hamilton third. They were all careful to be quiet. A woodpecker gave out a shrill *pee pee pee* from above before flying off. They approached the voices in the clearing and crouched down behind the fallen oak trunk. Thomas got down low, burying himself in the leaves. This was fun. He could feel the excitement. It was like out of the comic. Hamilton craned his neck to look over. Dad was barely hidden, his elbows leaning on the decaying tree.

Thomas could see six men in army uniforms with shovels digging down hard into the ground. They must have been here for a while, judging by the spoil heap.

'What they doing, Dad?' Thomas asked.

'Digging a girt hole.'

'What they doing that for?' Hamilton asked.

'I've no idea.'

'Maybe they want to plant potatoes,' Hamilton said. They all giggled.

'Whatever 'tis, I don't think it's that, young 'en,' Dad said, ruffling Hamilton's hair.

'What we going to do?' Thomas said, fidgeting in the leaves.

'Watch; watch for a minute. Let's see what they's doing.'

As they watched over the clearing, two more soldiers brought up timber, tools and bricks. They waited as sparrows darted from branch to branch above their heads. Thomas watched as the soldiers continued to work, digging deeper, shoring up the sides as they went down, then widened out making out a chamber. The men laughed and joked as they worked.

'They're making some kind of shelter; ain't no clue why they be doing it all up 'err.'

'Dad, Dad, look! It can't be, can it? Look, it's the vicar!' Thomas said.

'Shittle bum hurdle, you ain't wrong, boy,' Dad said, raising his voice. 'You boys wait here, and keep 'ee's 'eads down. If the vicar finds you, there will be hell to pay. I ain't sitting 'err if the bloody vicar knows about it. I'm goin' find out what the hell is going on.'

The vicar stood in his tweeds, with dog collar, overseeing proceedings, his bald head shining in the sun. Thomas thought it funny, seeing the vicar out of church in the middle of the woods.

Dad stood up straight: 'What be going on here then, chaps?' He shouted loud and took a big step over the tree. He walked purposefully forward towards the vicar. The soldiers working didn't look up. The vicar looked over. Thomas listened.

'Redver Kingson, might have known it would be you who'd have to find us,' Reverend Wrixon said.

'So, what be going on?' Dad said.

Thomas could see the vicar put an arm around his dad and start whispering in his ear. What was all this?

* * *

14th May 1940

Thomas sat in the chair up at the kitchen table, Mother and Father in their armchairs. Lily sat opposite reading the paper, her face concentrating. She had been living with them since St Hilda's had closed to billet soldiers. There was no football today, even though there should have been. The men were away fighting. Thomas looked at the letter from Nicole in his hands. It was the best news: at last she was coming home. He thought he would explode with happiness and excitement. She would be home in less than a week; by next Saturday she would be home with them all. He couldn't believe he would have both sisters home; they would all be together again. Hamilton stretched out with Dusty on the floor. Lying on his stomach he turned over a page in *The Beano*.

Mother was the happiest he had seen her in a long time. Even with all the news on the wireless and in the paper. Knowing Nicole was coming home had lifted a cloud from over Home Farm. Things were going to be all right after all.

'Turn that up, boy, will 'e?'

Thomas moved to the brown-cased Alba radio and turned the black volume knob. The radio hissed before the voices became loud and clear. It was Mr Churchill, the new prime minister.

'I have nothing to offer but blood, toil, tears and sweat... What is our aim?... Victory, victory at all costs, victory in spite of all terror; victory, however long and hard the road may be; for without victory, there is no survival.'

Thomas gulped and felt his stomach turn over. If they didn't win they wouldn't survive. He was glad Nicole was on her way home.

CHAPTER NINETEEN

18th May 1940

The sound of artillery and mortar shells could be heard in the distance from the hotel window. Nicole ran with Emma and hid the valuables in the loft, covering them with blankets, dustsheets and old pillowcases. It was the least she could do. Coming down the narrow stairs she looked into her old bedroom; it looked so small. She didn't have time to think about all the good times they had had together in the last few years. It was a wrench to leave her French family, the Tuckers, who had all made her feel so welcome. Her nightmares now banished, she'd felt the connection to her birth mother; she could almost feel her presence when she first came. But now she needed to be home. They would have had the letter by now. She had to run, she had to go; she had to, to get back to England before it was too late. Her suitcase was packed, the same one she had brought with her three years ago; and it still had *Pride and Prejudice* stuck in the bottom. She wanted to get back, she wanted to see all the family again, she wanted to be friends with Lily, she wanted to help them on the farm; with war on the doorstep, she needed to be home. She realised now that Connie was as much her mother as Marie. She was so lucky to have her and having had Lily write to her, to say she wanted her home: that was what motivated her most to return.

She said her hurried goodbyes. It was all too rushed and she worried for them. The last three years, working in the hotel, had been a delight compared to repairing fishing nets. Well, summer never lasts forever. She chuckled to herself; at least she'd been away from Edna Palmer. Maybe she could do something in the war, be of use. Her legs and arms were strong and toned with all the fetching and carrying; it reminded her of helping on the farm in the summer. She even enjoyed the time spent in the laundry room with the huge copper, the warm and comforting steam on a cold winter's day and the smell of fresh laundry.

She even had a little romance, though she knew he wasn't the one. Perhaps she was growing up when she broke it off. David took it well. He was nice and he adored her but she didn't feel the same about him. She'd let him kiss her but it didn't feel as passionate as with Billy. Was it the danger before, or was it his charm? Emma would egg her on; but in the end she knew it was the right thing to do to let David know she wasn't interested in him in that way. Last summer had been long and it had been fun: swimming in the lake, walking free in the open fields, helping out with the harvest; all the time it reminded her of home.

'Nicole, don't go, stay with us,' Emma said, pulling on Nicole's arm. She handed Nicole a small canvas bag: 'It's a packed lunch, to help you home.'

'Oh, Emma, thank you for everything. I've loved every minute.'

The banter between Geordie, his wife and the girls always kept spirits up; but now the Germans were on their doorstep and it had all happened so fast. Geordie kept saying not to worry, that they would be held back, that the Maginot Line would hold and that the British were here; they would push them back and keep them in Belgium. He said the line was built solid. She had believed him till this week, when everything seemed to be falling apart, and so quickly. Even Geordie's confidence had fallen when the first heavy artillery had been heard and the Stukas began the carnage; then word got to them that the German Panzers were the other side of Cambrai, and the Stukas returned with more bombs. Nicole had a sinking feeling that even she had left it too late.

She ran out of the hotel, with the suitcase in one hand and her lunch swinging in the canvas bag around her neck. The Tuckers waved as she looked back. She worried for their safety. They had looked after her as one of their own. The spring morning was cool; there were clouds in the sky but looking to the east, the clouds over Cambrai were black and white. The wind blew harder. She would be sad to leave France again, but the desire to see her mother, to see her father, to see Lily and to play with Thomas and Hamilton was so deep and full she thought she would explode like a shell. Why had she left it so darn late? It was because the threat didn't seem real; Geordie was so confident that it wouldn't reach them, not this quick. She had needed to come away, and it had served its purpose. She had felt closer to her own mother. But there was no fear held for her here now. Her mind was at last free, and her sleep free from the nightmares. Now there was a much worse nightmare threatening: a German invasion hurtling towards her; and all she wanted was to be at home in Dorset, to make things right and to help as best she could.

She stopped running and began to walk. The road was straight and flat for as far as she could see, the fields on either side large and open and vast, the wheat short and green. She missed watching her father plough. She missed his easy smile and his calm way. She missed her mother and brothers; but most of all she missed Lily.

Three Stuka planes flew overhead making the sound of thunder and she jumped out of her skin. She heard artillery and mortar shells and the roar of vehicle engines. It sounded like they were in Cambrai. It wouldn't be long before they reached Albert.

The trees along the side of the road were growing taller, recovering from the total destruction of the First Great War. Now they would witness the second in less than a lifetime. She pulled her shawl around her shoulders and made sure her beret covered her hair. The wind was blowing hard in her face and she felt that she was making very slow progress. Why hadn't she left the day before? A month before, or even a week before? Why had she waited to leave until the Germans were on their doorstep? She had been afraid to face her sister. It wasn't until Lily's last letter that she at last felt like she could face her. It was five miles, that was all she kept telling herself; five miles. I can do that in an hour. She upped her pace and moved the suitcase from her sore right hand to her left hand. Five minutes later she swapped it back.

The road seemed to go on and on forever, the horizon never seemed to get any closer and the low grey blanket of cloud showed no breaks. In the distance she heard it: first, the low hum of a motorcycle engine. It appeared as a small dot; it was moving fast and straight along the road, straight in her direction. As it grew bigger in her view, she could see it was a motorcycle and sidecar. It was grey and muddy and German army. There was the rider, and in the sidecar a second German soldier manning the machine gun that was mounted on the front.

She got off the road and skidded down the embankment. The ditch was muddy and the dirty water came up above her shoes and over her ankles. It smelt stagnant. Flies and insects disturbed by her feet flew up and she waved them away. She couldn't lie down in this muck. She walked along the edge of the ditch, trying to keep her feet on the side. She slid down the bank, the angle forcing her each time to step into the brown water. Her shoes were ruined and caked in mud. This felt like being back on the farm; impossible to keep anything clean. She wondered what she was fussing for and chastised herself for being so prissy. The roar of the motorbike was not far away. Her heart quickened and she lay down on her stomach, close in to the bank. She had her papers. She didn't have anything to hide but it was best she didn't get seen. She heard the bike pass above her and could smell the sweet petrol exhaust fumes.

She got up and brushed down her coat, which was smeared with dirt, grass and mud. She brushed it down again but couldn't get rid of it.

'You won't clean that off, not with your hand; it will need a very good wash.' Shocked, she looked around.

Where did that voice come from? A voice rich and deep and comforting, like velvet. And English with an accent. She looked hard but couldn't see anyone.

'Where are you? Who is it?' Nicole said.

'You're English?'

He stood up from along the bank, breaking his cover from the opposite side of the ditch. He was tall, with blonde hair slicked back. His eyes were sharp, intelligent-looking. His Royal Air Force blue uniform was a dirty mixture of earthy stains.

'Sorry, old girl, to take you by surprise; it's best I'm not seen by that lot.' He pointed.

He introduced himself. He was a British Hurricane pilot shot down two days ago. His name was Aubrey Jones. He was flying his Hurricane when he got into a dogfight with a Messerschmitt BF 109 the other side of the enemy line past Cambrai. He had managed to bail out over farmland. Scavenging, eating whatever he could, and lying low. He'd been travelling at night up until today, when he had noticed the railway line and thought if he could get ahead of the German army he stood a chance of catching a train to Calais.

They decided to join forces to head over the fields and to the station. As they talked, Nicole found out that his family came from Wales. His father had been laid off from the mines in the Depression and had crisscrossed the country looking for work. Aubrey seemed so easy to talk to.

They came to the rear of the station. Nicole could hear the sound of engines, which were still running. Her stomach dropped; they were too late, the train was leaving.

'Damn!' Aubrey said.

She noticed Aubrey walked with a slight limp; an injury he must have sustained when he landed.

'We should lay up here, watch for movements, and wait for the next train.' He put his hand to his head and pushed back a stray blonde hair.

They came to rest behind a tall wooden fence at the railway siding. Aubrey looked through the gap in the fence, keeping watch.

Nicole opened the canvas bag and took out the baguette and the hard-boiled egg Eliza had packed for her lunch. She handed half to Aubrey. She watched as he tore a huge chunk of bread and chewed it down, hungry. His face was unshaven, his stubble dark like coffee beans; and chiselled and straight, like a worked coalface. His eyes were alive, coloured deep blue with specks of shining silver. She thought she could see herself in his eyes.

They turned and faced the fields, their backs against the fence.

When he talked, he talked in a rhythm with a lilt and a tone that seemed to sing to her. She listened as he told her of his life. He said that he must have gone to twenty different schools and that his father was a drinker, who if he worked for a week would spend most of it on drink on a Friday night. His mother scrimped and saved, as everyone did after the First War. How he never had anything. He was an only child, but his mother and father were too busy surviving to pay him any attention. He was to be seen and not heard. He had been determined to make something of himself and he saw the war as his opportunity. Being keen on motorcycles and seeing an advertisement in the motorcycle magazine he had applied to the Royal Air Force. He was a natural and took to flying like a duck to water. He'd been stationed at Biggin Hill.

They passed the time talking and finishing off the last of the bread until Nicole saw the train pull into the station. They got up and stood behind the fence.

'Let me take your case for you.' He picked it up and whistled through his teeth. 'What have you in here, the crown jewels, my dear? It weighs a ton!'

'No, only my clothes and a couple of pairs of shoes and *Pride and Prejudice*,' she laughed.

They walked around the side of the fence and towards the back of the station. Nicole looked down as they crossed the disused tracks of the railway siding. She looked up as the train finally pulled in. There were half a dozen passengers waiting to alight, all carrying their possessions with them, suitcases, packs on their backs and arms full of family belongings, all trying to head for safety.

Doors opened on the carriage. Nicole looked in disbelief. How could it be? They weren't ordinary passengers disembarking. Soldiers; soldiers, and hundreds of them, all wearing the same grey uniform: German. They filed through the doors in an ordered procession which seemed never to end.

'Oh, heavens!' She stood frozen in disbelief.

'Come on; this is no good.' He took her hand. As he pulled her, she turned and began to walk, then broke into a run. Her foot came down awkwardly on the line and twisted.

'*Halt! Halt! Halt!*' a soldier shouted as he spotted the pair of them moving away; he raised his rifle. Nicole shrieked in pain as she tried to run.

'Come on, old girl; we've got to make the fence.'

CHAPTER TWENTY

18th May 1940

The bullet whistled past Nicole's face, then she heard the crack of gunfire. Then more shots. Aubrey pulled her down behind the fence. She saw the motorbike and sidecar; it must have doubled back, now firing on them. It was racing forward, bouncing over the ground, the machine gun flapping widely up and down, with the soldier trying to control it. Shots fired and splintered the wood. The roar of the motorbike grew louder and the rider accelerated forward. Aubrey dropped her suitcase. The motorbike flew across the wasteland, jumping in the air. The young soldier – she could see he wasn't much older than Thomas – was trying to hold the machine gun straight, the *rat-rat-tat* sound growing louder. Aubrey unbuttoned his tunic. Dirt, earth and stones flew up from the wheels of the bike. The bullets came raining into the wooden fence; splinters flew up in the air and into the back of her coat. The bike closer, she could see the driver's eyes. The gunfire stopped. Aubrey placed his hand inside his tunic and pulled out his revolver. He took one shot at the biker, missed; fired again; this time hit the rider who slumped over the handlebars. The bike careered into the ditch and stalled. The young German soldier in the sidecar tried to manhandle the machine gun, but he was parked facing the wrong direction; there wasn't enough swivel for him to turn the gun around. Aubrey walked over, pointing his revolver.

'No, Aubrey, don't!' Nicole limped up, pulling the suitcase with her. 'Don't, don't do it; he's only a boy.' She reached Aubrey and pulled on his arm.

The soldier got out of the sidecar; he looked petrified. Aubrey waved the pistol at him and he fled towards the station.

Aubrey took the suitcase from Nicole and she got into the sidecar. Aubrey passed the suitcase back and Nicole put it on her lap. Aubrey then pulled the dead soldier off the seat, and got on. He kickstarted the bike as soldiers from the train fired their rifles through the open windows. The bike roared into life and he accelerated across the field.

They came to the embankment. Nicole looked over her shoulder. She couldn't see anyone following. Aubrey stood up on the bike, and rode it up the steep bank and onto the road.

'Head for Albert, head for Albert!' Nicole pointed and shouted above the noise of the engine. Aubrey nodded and turned left on the road. He accelerated fast and the bike bounced over the potholes. He got up a good speed on the straight road.

They saw it at the same time. The tanks in the distance outside Albert lined up along the road: they were not French Renaults. Nicole knew that from the pictures in the papers. The Germans had advanced.

'Go down there, take that next track!' Nicole shouted and waved her arm. She directed him to the stony track. She could remember a place Emma had shown her down by the river. The track undulated through the open countryside, Aubrey driving it hard. The stones of the track pinged off the tyres like gunshots. They splashed through deep puddles, the mud going in her eyes. She wiped it away with the back of her hand.

Aubrey saw the wooded valley. He pulled the handlebars round to the left. Nicole lent her weight as best she could and the bike turned off the track and raced down the grassland. They came into the outer edge of the woodland and found an animal path. Aubrey slalomed the bike in and out of trees until the path was too narrow. He pulled on the brake and clutch and brought the engine to a stop.

Once Nicole had got out, Aubrey searched the sidecar and found a water canteen, a blanket and some rations.

They took their time hiding the bike under bushes and

undergrowth and when it was done they found a dry spot up against a bank. Aubrey said they shouldn't start a fire. Nicole sat out with her legs stretched in front of her. It was nice to feel the warmth of Aubrey next to her.

'I can see you're good with bikes.'

'I guess I am. I was always around bikes when I could. I think we were living in Nottingham at the time; Dad had tried to get work in the pits there, to no avail. I must have been sixteen or so and I started to hang around the local garage, doing odd jobs, fetching and carrying, holding the mechanics' tools; then bit by bit I must have become more use because they took me on as apprentice. He was good, the old man at the garage. He took me under his wing, taught me and showed me; took his time explaining how it all worked. He was patient, not like my father.'

As he talked she snuggled into his side.

'Your voice is so soothing; keep talking.'

'What about?'

'I don't care; anything! Tell me a story, tell me everything there is to know about you.'

'That's not fair! I want to know about you.'

'There is nothing to know. I'm what you see: I'm a simple country girl. I've always lived in the country. I've never even been to a city.' Nicole felt physical warmth coming from Aubrey but also a warmth in his voice.

'I don't believe you're simple. There isn't a woman on earth who's simple!'

'Oh, I must be the first then,' Nicole laughed.

'Well, what's an English girl doing in France when Germany is invading?'

'I was here with friends; not friends, more my second family. I was born here. You see, my mother was French; she died when I was young.'

'I'm sorry. See, you're not simple!'

'I was on my way home; I wanted to get home and see my

family before this war took over. It looks like I'm too late now. And do you know what? Before I met you down in the ditch, I was having second thoughts; I was thinking… It seems silly.'

'No, go on. What was you thinking?'

'I was thinking I should stay, that there is some of me that is French, that I should stay here, that I should stay and fight.'

'That's not silly, that's patriotic and honourable.'

She touched his hand. 'Do you think I could? Do you think I could be of use?'

'I'm sure you could; there is no reason why not.' He touched her arm and looked at her. She felt his eyes on her eyes, and she saw them glimmer. It was the first time he had stopped and looked at her. She knew he was looking at her as a woman.

'A bright girl like you, with two languages, I'm sure you could be a great help.' He ran his fingers down her arm. 'I'm sure you could charm the birds from the trees, you're such a beauty.'

'Really!'

'Oh, yes, even with a mud-splattered face. I can see what a beautiful woman you are.' He leaned over and kissed her on her lips. His lips were soft and his hands gentle. She didn't know if it was the fact that she'd been so close to death, or the words he said, or the tone of his voice, or the danger they had been in. It felt like before. Her heart raced. She pushed on his chest with her hands but she didn't push away hard. She wanted him. She moved her hands around to the back of his neck and pulled him closer.

When darkness fell they waited till the moon was high and they walked out arm-in-arm with Aubrey supporting her weight. She led the way back to Albert. They heard the voices of German guards arguing. The tanks lined the road, and there were hundreds. They scurried down streets; Nicole limped. They made it under the passage and to the door of the hotel kitchen.

'Hey up, girl, what's this?' Geordie said as he sat at the table with a whisky in his hand. Emma sat opposite drinking coffee. Eliza was at the sink, washing up.

'I didn't quite make it home.' Emma got up, ran over and hugged Nicole.

'I've only been gone a day,' Nicole said, smiling.

'I know; but I'm glad you're safe. Does this mean you're going to stay with us in the war?'

'I don't see how I have much of a choice.'

'Do sit down, dear, you look awful,' Eliza said. 'And who is this?'

'Oh, this is Aubrey. He helped get me home.'

Geordie got up and shook Aubrey's hand.

'Good to meet you, old man. I wish it could be under better circumstances. The Germans have taken Cambrai and Albert and they're pushing on. I've heard they came through the Ardennes; I would never have believed it,' Geordie said.

'I know. They're moving so much faster than anyone even thought. I mean, they came through Poland and Belgium, but France as well? I thought they were well-prepared,' Aubrey said.

'It's nice to meet you and all, Aubrey, but you can't stay here, it's far too dangerous. France I'm sure is going to fall,' Geordie said, sitting back down and picking up his glass of whisky. 'The rate that Jerry is going they will take Britain before Christmas.'

'You're not serious?' Nicole said.

'I've seen if with my own eyes now,' Geordie said. 'They've too much power, and they have so many tanks; and if they get behind the British, then we could be done for.'

'I've got to get home, get back, to get up in the air again,' said Aubrey.

'You can stay here, can't you?' Nicole said.

'He can't, Nicole; the place is full of Jerries; he won't be safe,' Geordie said. 'He will stick out like a sore thumb.'

'But he's only just got here,' Nicole said.

'I've got to go. I should make my way to Paris; the Germans will be heading for the coast.'

'No, Aubrey, I've only just met you! I can't lose you.'

'I'm sorry, Nicole, it has to be this way.'

'Geordie, say something! Eliza, we could hide him.'

'I'm sorry, Nicole, he's right,' Geordie said.

Nicole could feel the fear creeping through her body.

'We will help Aubrey all we can, to head south, to get back in the air. Britain will need all men to do their duty now,' Geordie said.

'And women, Dad; Britain will need every woman too,' Emma said.

'Yes, ay; I forgot the goslings will want to drive the geese to pasture.' Geordie laughed.

CHAPTER TWENTY-ONE

19th May 1940

Geordie was right: the first day of occupation and the Germans were everywhere. The French had retreated and the threat was real. They hid Aubrey in the hayloft above the stables and tried to go about their business, making sure they spoke in French, as soldiers came in out of the hotel all the time; it hadn't taken them long to find their favourite haunt. Geordie pretended to be the gregarious French host. Nicole knew he was acting; he was very good at it. Nicole could feel her stomach turn over and she feared the Germans wanting to search the hotel. Thankfully in the afternoon, the Germans seemed to desert the town; they were keen to move. Geordie said they wanted to push home their advantage. They were using Blitzkrieg and there would be other soldiers moving in later to hold the town. At this point, there were much bigger prizes to move towards. It would give them the chance to move Aubrey. Tonight would be their opportunity.

The night was cool. There had been clear skies during the day and now the moon was high in the sky. Nicole had insisted she come. Geordie had gathered the maps and given them the instructions. The deep smell of smoke still lingered in the air, but at least the Stukas had moved to other targets. They were to head south and to the River Somme. Nicole pulled her beret down and first looked at Louise with her flowing black hair; she seemed so mature, the oldest and most sensible of the Tucker sisters. Her face was a picture of determination and focus. Emma in comparison was a petite bundle of perpetual energy.

Aubrey walked alongside Nicole, upright, his uniform cleaned.

'You shouldn't have come, Nicole,' he said.

'I want to, Aubrey; I owe you.'

They ducked in and out of hedgerows and ditches and kept low, keeping away from guard posts.

'I can't thank you all enough; it's more than you should do,' Aubrey said.

'I wish we had some weapons; then we could be serious,' Emma said.

'Be patient, Emma,' Louise said.

'What do you mean?' Nicole said.

'We will get some help,' Louise said.

'What?' Emma said, taking in a deep breath.

'We will be getting weapons, soon. There will be a drop; it's been organised.'

'What the hell are you on about?' Emma said, raising her voice as they walked together down the edge of the ploughed field.

'I've had some training,' Louise said.

'What training?' Emma said.

'Resistance,' Nicole said.

'What? How, my sister?' Emma said.

'It was Father; he's been plotting and scheming, making contacts in England; I think Father was talking as far back as '37.'

'Bloody hell, you get all the fun!' Emma said.

'Don't worry, I'll bring you two up to speed.'

'You better,' Emma said, shaking her head in disbelief. 'And you, Nicole, you'll want to help, too.'

Nicole didn't know for sure; but if she could slow down Germany, be of some help, that would be her duty.

'Shut up for now and be quiet. We have to get Aubrey to the river, where we can hand him over to the next cell. You know, there are hundreds of us trained and waiting,' Louise said.

'So, when are we getting the guns, weapons, explosives?' Emma said. 'I can't wait!'

Nicole wasn't surprised. Emma was full of it, just like her old man.

'Soon, very soon. And a radio; we are getting a radio we're to hide in the loft,' Louise said.

'Blimey! And you kept all this from us?' Emma said.

'We don't all have a mouth that runs away from us, but you have to watch yourself now,' Louise said.

'Thank you, sister, I can keep my mouth shut when I need to,' Emma said.

Nicole laughed and followed Louise, who was leading the way.

'I've to thank you so much, all of you; you shouldn't be having to do this for me,' Aubrey said.

'Don't be so silly. 'Course we need to do this,' Louise said.

Nicole watched her step, although her eyes were accustomed to the darkness. They could see the River Somme from the top of the hill. The moon reflected back from the stream of water as it wound its way through the landscape. There were trees down to the shore on the far bank. It was much wider than the River Asker or the River Brit. Further down the river she could see there were islands where the water flowed either side; it flowed fast, with rushing crests of white. The four of them walked deliberately and slowly, following the curve of the path as it wound its way down to the flood plain. The sound of the river cascaded up and Louise guided them along the bank to the meeting point.

Nicole couldn't help but think back to the young German soldier. He had looked so young and innocent and he had been pointing a machine gun at them. Trying to kill them. Would Aubrey have killed him? Thank god Thomas was safe at home, with the family, farming, helping Father, playing football with Hamilton. She didn't want him to have to fight. What if they got to Britain? What if they did invade? She should do everything she could to stop that happening. Would she even have a home to get back to? It didn't do her any good to think about it. She felt her stomach turn over. She tried to fight the sick back down; she couldn't throw up here. What would they think of her? Could she even kill a German soldier? What if he looked like Thomas? They were the same as us, after all, weren't they?

They followed the bend in the trees and came to woodland. They entered the wood. Immediately, the canopy of trees blocked out the remaining moonlight and it was harder to find their way. They kept walking for half an hour. Louise brought them to a stop. She and Aubrey were the only ones with pistols and Nicole was pleased. She was sure she wouldn't be able to shoot at a human being, whatever their nationality.

They sat on the riverbank and waited. This was the stop, Louise estimated. Louise and Emma couldn't sit still for long and were soon up and walking further down to check. When they came back they waved at Nicole and Aubrey to follow. There were branches strewn across the track, left over from flooding in the winter. When they got to the bridge the waiting party was there with the car.

Aubrey came to Nicole and put his arms around her waist, pulled her in close, hugged her tight and whispered in her ear.

'You will be fine, my dear.' He kissed her cheek. 'Thank you for everything.'

'Aubrey, be careful.'

'I will.' He kissed her again and she felt her face flush. The black Renault car had its engine running; the female driver beckoned to Aubrey to approach.

Above the noise of the car engine, machine gun fire erupted out of the darkness like hail on a tin roof. They instinctively ducked. Then Aubrey pushed Nicole to the ground and covered her with his body. She could smell the damp earth, the dirt clinging to her face. She breathed in as deeply as she could with his body on top. She tried to turn her head to see what was happening. Machine gun fire continued. There were sounds of the pistols firing. Then Aubrey released her. She looked up to see him standing behind the car returning fire: his pistol, Louise's, and the driver's, all firing. Nicole could make it out now: the German scout vehicle. A high mounted machine gun was firing heavy into the car. The pistols were no match; she was helpless. She counted six German soldiers as they jumped down from the back of the open-topped vehicle. They were trying to flank them as the machine gun operator kept them pinned down under fire. She was sure she was about to die and all she wanted to do was retch; her stomach turned upside down. Two of the lead soldiers were stopped in their tracks by the shots from the pistols.

The commander put his head from the window of the cab. He was in shadow from the bright headlights that shone in their eyes. He got his driver to turn off the lights and she saw his face. A dark scar was across his forehead, his hairline was receding. He had black hair and his voice was distinctive and deep, harsh and authoritative.

'Abandon! Cease! You surrender! No one needs to die,' he said in French with a deep German accent. '*Prisonniers*. Your war is *fini*.'

'Okay, yes! *Oui!*' It was Aubrey shouting. He pulled out his white handkerchief and held it high. He turned to Nicole and the others: 'It's all I can do; I don't want you to die for me.'

Before they could stop him he walked out from behind the car towards the Germans.

'And the rest of you!' the German officer shouted. Then he pulled his revolver and fired three, maybe four times in succession. Nicole watched as Aubrey fell to the ground.

She was about to run to him when Emma and Louise pulled her away.

'*Allez, allez!*' the French resistance woman shouted and waved her arms.

Nicole stood rooted like an oak tree. Then Emma pulled on one of her arms and Louise on the other. Nicole ran, with Emma and Louise alongside. The machine gun rang out, kicking up dirt and leaves around them. Nicole prayed, not daring to look. They made it to the trees; they knew the way, unlike the soldiers. How could he? How could he have shot Aubrey in cold blood? She would never forget his voice or his scar or that look on his face. They managed to get through the wood and back to the hill and the safety of the hedgerows. Nicole began to cry. How could he have killed Aubrey like that?

* * *

3rd June 1940

Nicole could see patchy thin white clouds circulating above, blown in front of the full moon. Good clear moonlight was what was needed. She hoped the cloud wouldn't get any thicker. Catherine and Emma smoked as they stood inside the tree line.

She was a simple farm girl, who worked on fishing nets at Gales in Bridport; she was no fighter. She should have dated Romily, gone with a good upstanding boy, not been tempted by Billy. She could have been at home now, on the old sofa where the springs pushed through the worn fabric, the pattern long faded where you sat, listening to Hamilton laugh at his comic, having Dusty at her feet lying waiting for attention. If she hadn't ruined everything she could have been sitting with Lily and Mother and be talking about the latest fashions. It was the nightmares; it was her urge to get away. Instead, she was here in France, with death and oppression all around her, waiting to signal the Dakota plane as it would search for the drop zone. What would she ever be able to do?

The sound of the plane could be heard, roaring over the horizon. They were miles from town, down in the valley, not far from the river. The trees in a crescent shape, the full moon above, casting shadows; the clearing in front. The women ran to their positions at the three bonfires. Nicole craned her neck and looked up, then down at the small bonfire at her feet. Catherine was at the point of the triangle formed by the position of the three beacons. Nicole was the furthest over from the tree line of the base; Emma was at her bonfire. Once lit, the three bonfires would mark out the drop zone.

Nicole felt her feet wet in the long grass. The smell of night-time dew filled her lungs. Her little pile of twigs and small branches caught, and she welcomed the heat. Catherine and

140

Emma had their fires lit; the drop zone was now marked by the three fires on the valley floor in the clearing. The sound of the hulking engines roared above the tree line; she looked up and saw the plane, low, less than a thousand feet. She tracked the plane as it roared over her head and felt her spine tingle. There was something about the beauty of the plane in the air, the power of the engines, the sheer force at which they moved the enormous machine through the air; she felt the vibrations move through her body.

Catherine stood at her beacon, her torch in her hand, waving, signalling in Morse code. They should have opened the hatch; they should be making the drop. What were they waiting for? Drop too late and the supplies would be in the rushing water of the river, lost and no good; it would be weeks, maybe months before they got any more. Why had the powers that be even chosen this site? Their signal had come over the BBC on the wireless, indicating their turn by use of keywords in the broadcast.

Nicole looked around, wondering what she should do. For sure, the nearby German patrols would hear the noise and be on them at any moment. If they didn't hear, would they see the bonfires? The plane reached the end of the drop zone, banked high and wide. Nothing delivered.

Catherine signalled to Nicole and Emma to stay put. What was taking so long? There was too much time to think. Nicole wanted it to be done, before they were found, before the Germans captured them or shot them like Aubrey.

The plane rolled in, lower, maybe only eight hundred feet above, the large propellers whirring in a frenzy either side of the cockpit. Its vast wingspan seemed to spread the width of the pasture. It seemed to Nicole that she could put her hand up and touch the undercarriage. Catherine stood, again waving her torch, giving the signal for them to drop. If it had been daylight, Nicole could have seen the pilot's eyes. Her eardrums felt fit to burst from the rumble of the engines. Again, it passed; Catherine waved and signalled with the torch, again giving the signal in Morse. Nothing happened. The plane banked again, came in for another run. Catherine waved the torch furiously. Lower, only six hundred feet above her head, the ground shuddering with vibration, it came overhead. This time, Nicole saw the undercarriage open, the payload dispatched. An enormous sheet steel container dropped, the parachute opening to slow its fall. As the plane thundered down the valley, Nicole watched as the steel canister fell in a slow spiral to the ground. She ran to the canister, to be joined by Emma and then Catherine. Relieved at last, they could take the cargo and run for the cover of the trees.

'What the hell?' Catherine said; she was still watching the plane. 'Look!' she shouted, pointing. They watched in amazement as a figure was now jumping from the side door.

'There is no way!' Emma shouted.

'They're too close to the river,' Nicole said. 'He's going to go straight in. He'll get pulled under.'

The women gave chase, running down the valley floor towards the river. The parachutist was now in the sky, with the short descent, his canopy open. He tried to control his fall and move into a spiral. Seeing the mistake, Nicole could see him pulling desperately on the strings, trying to bank his turn. The wind gusted, not aiding but taking him down to the wide river.

'Quick, try and get ahead to the bridge,' Catherine said.

Nicole ran as fast as she could. His large silk parachute would fill with water and drag him under for sure in the speeding current. Nicole, with her legs pumping hard, overtook Catherine and Emma as she sprinted for the far side of the bridge. The sound of the plane was fading into the distance. It was all the running with her sisters and brothers; at least that had been good training. Having brothers meant they were always playing chase or football; or if on the farm, there were always the cows or horses to be running after. Topsy always liked to run free when she had the chance. Nicole's father had always organised them to play games on Sunday afternoons: football in winter and spring, and cricket in the summer. He'd taught them all how to play and he was so proud of the photograph that hung in the Farmer's Arms of him and his brother and the village cricket team, the 1930 cricket match, when Ashcombe had beaten Moreton.

Her lungs screamed for air; her legs ached with the effort, becoming heavy. She looked up. He was low, coming in fast, feet from the ground. It was close; he was near the bank of the river as his feet dangled. He could almost touch the ground. As he got lower, the bank descended to the river. Each time Nicole thought he would touch down, the bank escaped him. Then he was in, struggling, fighting to free himself from the 'chute, becoming entwined in the webbing, which she was sure was made in Gales' shed. She readied her knife. She rushed into the water; it was freezing cold. It only came to her knees but she could feel it trying to rip her downstream. She watched; he came under the bridge. If he could only stand up he would be safe. He was entwined, his arms flailing at the ropes, the current dragging on him. Nicole positioned herself, careful not to lose her footing on the unseen stones under her feet. She tried to brace her feet, digging in to the river bed. The current tugged at her like ropes around her ankles, wanting to pull her under. Catherine and Emma ran down the bank, splashing into the water at the shoreline, racing to join her. The soldier held his knife in hand, his head under water. He crashed into Nicole; her feet buckled under the momentum and force of the impact. Knocked off her feet, she felt the pull of the river. She put her feet down; her foot slipped on a rock. She scrambled, pushed hard.

'Stand up, stand up!' she shouted in English. There was a tangle of webbing and bodies and silk. Nicole stood firm. Catherine and Emma reached the mangle of bodies. The three of them held the soldier. They pulled him upright and in a huddle, struggled to the riverbank. The soldier spluttered the water out of his mouth. He was in the uniform of a British soldier.

'*Bonjour! Dieu merci*. May the road rise up and meet ya,' he said, his French not good. Sounding heavily Irish. His eyes twinkled in the light. 'Blimey oh riley, that was close.'

'Close! What were you thinking? Didn't you see the river?' Nicole said.

'Thank you, my guardian angels. We weren't sure it was the right signal.'

'We didn't expect you, not tonight. We were told you were coming next week,' Catherine said.

'I couldn't wait and plans changed. Shall we go and see what Blighty has sent with me, then?'

He was tall, over six feet, his face rounded at his jawline and a cheeky twinkle in his eye. He was nothing like what Nicole had imagined. Catherine had told them to expect an agent next week, someone who was going to give them training. He seemed so young and fresh-faced, only in his twenties, for sure. She had thought he would look more like a movie star than one of Billy Crabb's drinking buddies.

They returned to the large canister, which had enjoyed a much safer landing than their instructor. He opened the three catches on the side, which was as long as he was tall. He levered the hinged lid. Nicole peered in as all four of them stood around. At one end was the empty compartment where the parachute had been. He looked in briefly, then closed the lid.

'Looks in order, ladies. Shall we?'

There were four handles, two either side. The instructor led the way, his uniform adorned with canteen, knife, torch, pistol holder, all kinds of army equipment, all in its place, attached to his belt. Nicole held her grip with her right hand. Emma complained that she was having to use her left hand. They were all right-handed, so Catherine told her sister to shut up and she would swap in a second. The weight of the canister was incredible; over a ton, Nicole thought. After twenty minutes of swapping, struggling, pulling and scraping, they reached the depth of the wood, stopped, put the canister down and opened it again. The tall Irishman put his torch in his mouth as he took the consignment list from his pocket. He handed it to Catherine to check off, then bent down over the treasure. He called out as he rummaged with his hands.

'Sten guns, Bren Gun, carbines, pistols…' It sounded like a new language to Nicole. '… smoke pistols, silencers, bullets, knives, grenades, Cordex, plastic explosives, radio set, tear gas, primers, detonators, safety fuses, igniters, charges, switches, time pencils, binoculars, torches, toolkits, bicycle repair kits, first aid kits, crimpers, nails, string cable...' He went on for minutes. Nicole was amazed at the stash of weapons and supplies.

'Don't worry, I'll have you lot trained in a jiffy; then you will be able to do Jerry some damage.' He smiled. Nicole shuddered. How on earth was she going to be able to learn all this?

* * *

Over the next weeks, they would join the instructor in the woods when they could, taking it in turns rotating their work at the hotel. Under the eyes of the German soldiers they would slip away. He showed them everything: how to hold the Sten gun and shoot from the hip, how to hold a dagger, how to slit a man's throat, how to move without noise, how to set explosives and mines. The most audacious to Nicole seemed the derailing of trains. One night, the Irishman took them to a section of railway line far from town. The new moon didn't give much light. They bent over the track as he took out the fog signal device. There was a small round pressure pad about the depth of the track; it had two metal clips. As he pushed it around the side of the track he explained that the pad would need fifty pounds of pressure to detonate. Coming from the round pressure cap was the Cordex tail which in turn went to the detonator. He instructed them to place the charges on the outside of the rail, then to place a second fog signal about a yard apart. Nicole's hands were cold and she rubbed them. He took the fog signals off and asked the women to practise; they did this, time and time again through the night.

Nicole surprised herself by picking it up fast: how to clean a rifle, how to operate the radio. She even enjoyed it. She learnt to use the Sten gun, heavy at first in her hands, with its simple pipe-like design and large side magazine; they hacksawed off the shoulder rests and hung them round their necks with the webbed straps. The Sten became her favourite, along with the Webley pistol. Her shooting wasn't bad, better than Emma's for sure. But the Sten gun was prone to jamming. The Irishman showed them how to clear it, but if it happened in a fire fight, they would have to switch to the Webley. With its bird beak-shaped handle the Webley felt heavy in her hand with the cross-patterned grip and six rounds of ammunition. The Irishman told them to keep their knives close.

'Course, there were always animals being slaughtered on the farm. Nicole was not new to that, or to the smell of blood. She didn't know if she could do it to another human. That was going to be her job from now on. If she could put up with the smell of the fishing nets, she told herself, she could do this.

The Irishman left, moving south; more training, Nicole imagined.

CHAPTER TWENTY-TWO

15th August 1940

Lily drove the Austin 7 fast down Snowdrop Hill, and looked at the wheat blowing in the breeze, her gas mask box getting in the way. She knew she was lucky and privileged to be driving the car, even if it was over fifteen years old. She passed where the signpost should have been; it seemed odd. She should really drive more slowly but she liked the speed and she loved her little car. She handled the turn with no problem at all; she'd been driving for years. Father had taught her well, and the Austin was light and easy to handle. She powered on down Yellow Lane and around the corner. She reached town and raced along St Andrew's Road and Barrack Street before turning right down East Street.

She parked on West Street outside Colman's bakers. Rosa was standing waiting for her. She got in the car with her basket under her arm; she put this on the back seat with the tea towel over the top, which didn't stop the smell of bread from filling the small car.

'I thought you were going to be late,' Rosa said through her mouthful of bread and raspberry jam.

'It was Hamilton; he wanted me to read the story from the paper out to him.' Lily put the Austin into gear, spun around on the wide street and headed up to the town hall. There was no traffic and she turned sharply at the town hall and headed down South Street, stopping outside number one hundred. She tooted the horn. After a minute Ellen came racing out, her hair tied up, her uniform clean and pressed, wearing bright red lipstick.

'You look so smart in your uniform, Ellen; I could almost fancy you!' Rosa said as she got in the back seat and tore off a corner of bread from the loaf.

'Keep that for later; we'll be starving,' Lily said, laughing.

'Have you had any letters this week from Romily?' Ellen asked.

'Nothing, not for three weeks now. Last we heard he was still on Salisbury Plain.'

'Have you heard anything from Nicole?' Ellen said.

'She was coming home she said in the letter, but she never turned up. We waited all night but she never got here; we haven't heard anything since. Thomas was distraught; so was Mother. Dad just went quiet.'

'I wish you would slow down,' Ellen said as the car bumped up and over the level crossing. They followed the outline of the coast. Lily had her window down and the breeze was refreshing and cool; it was welcoming after the oppressive heat of the afternoon.

Lily accelerated up the straight before slowing for the turning.

'I don't know why you have to drive so darn fast,' Ellen said as she squirmed in her seat. 'You're more likely to kill us than Hitler.'

'Don't you? I like it; I love the speed, the thrill of it,' Lily said, with one hand on the steering wheel, the other on the gearstick waiting to change up. She relaxed into the seat and put her foot further down on the accelerator. She changed gear and moved her left hand to the steering wheel. She wound down her window and breathed in the fresh summer evening.

Lily parked the car at Cogden. The women got out and walked down to the guns and the parked army lorries.

'Where have you lot been? It's about time you were here,' the sergeant said.

'Sorry; we got delayed, didn't we?' Lily said, as she stepped across the thick cable that ran to the generator hidden in the bushes further up the beach.

'Well, you're here now,' the officer said. He was short and sharp with his words. He went to the large Vickers gun that had been stationed on the beach. Lily knew there were pillboxes stretched out all along Chesil beach. The large Vickers guns were far more effective.

The women waved up at Alice who was already on the sound locator. They all knew what to do. Lily went on the searchlight with Ellen; and Rosa joined up with Alice.

Lily turned the large wheel which tracked the searchlight. All was working fine for a change.

The noise of roaring engines filled the air of the night sky. The machinery whirred into action. Lily controlled the wheel and turned on the huge beam of light. The second searchlight along the beach also burst into action, the two beams now illuminating the night, bright as day, criss-crossing.

'Least them in the pillbox have some protection,' Ellen said.

The noise of the Messerschmitts like a plague of angry wasps filled the night. Lily controlled the light as she had been trained to do, rotating the heavy wheel. What she really wanted to do was to have a go on the Vickers gun; but the soldiers wouldn't let them do that. The women had only their tin hats for protection.

The 109s came in low, as they had done night after night. The drone grew louder and louder. Lily could taste and smell the salt of the sea on her lip as she pushed her tongue out. The planes came roaring in and she tracked them as best she could. The anti-aircraft gun burst into life, with a large *rat-a-tat-tat, rat-a-tat-tat.* The ammunition fired off round after round, adding to the din of the aircraft; empty shell cases dispelled onto the shingle. The distinct smell of gun smoke hung in the air. The planes took no notice and carried on their path; they didn't score a hit.

* * *

The town centre was pitch black when Lily pulled up again outside Colman's bakery. It was quiet. The women said goodnight. Lily yawned; her jaw felt like it would reach her knees. The air raid siren went off; it must be signalling the all clear.

Rosa closed the door to the car and went to open the shop door. Lily heard it first: the noise of an aircraft engine, faint at first but getting louder. She got out of the car but didn't bother to close the door and ran to the house with Rosa. They both hurried straight through the house, calling for Bessie as they went. Bessie, in her nightgown, led them through to the garden. Lily could hear the planes directly above Bridport.

They fell into the Anderson shelter one after another. What use would this bit of corrugated iron be? She would rather be under the hayrick.

But then she heard it: a gentle whirring. It was like in the pictures. The noise was uncanny and it sounded as if it was directly above them. Time seemed to stand still. She was frozen; her heart paused. This was it.

The explosion came and it nearly burst her eardrums. She felt the earth below her feet shudder; dirt, earth and stones rained down. It sounded like nails thrown by the devil himself.

She got up, her ears ringing. She had to get out and see what had happened. Rosa followed. Both women ran through the house and onto the street. She looked up West Street. There was carnage and devastation where the Star pub had been. A ruin, with timber and stone strewn like flotsam.

She rushed to the lip of the crater and heard a cry for help.

'Come on, Rosa!' Lily shouted.

She rushed into the smoking wreckage with Rosa behind. They followed the sound and Lily saw a dust-covered arm protruding from the rubble. With her bare hands, she began lifting bricks and stone. She threw them to one side as she dug down. There was fire burning in what once was the snook and she could smell gas.

'Quick, quick, Rosa! Can you smell that?'

'Yes, yes! Come on!'

Lily worked as fast as she could. As she uncovered, she saw an arm. There was a huge heavy timber across the body. The two women struggled with either end, using all their strength.

'You girls, you get out of there.' It was the air raid warden. 'The fire brigade will get in there; you get yourselves out.' He walked up to them.

'There's no time to wait! Can you smell that?' Lily said.

'Is that Aida?' he said. He knelt down and started to dig with his hands.

Finally the three of them, working together, managed to clear the body from the debris.

'Come on, pull!' They grabbed at her feet and her arms and pulled. It was Aida; and she was murmuring. 'She's alive! Come on, she's alive!' Rosa said.

Lily pulled as hard as she could. Pulling Aida with them, they lifted her as best they could from the wreckage. They pulled her out onto the street, and as they did there was a second explosion which knocked Lily off her feet and into the air.

When she came to, her cheek was bleeding. Rosa was standing over her with the warden looking down. Aida wasn't so lucky; their efforts had been for nothing.

* * *

23rd June 1942

Lily ran her finger along the raised edge of the scar on her cheekbone, counting herself lucky that this and a few bruises was all she had suffered from the explosion. Not like poor Aida Burwood, who took her last breath on West Street.

When war had come, Lily had been preparing to go back to university. The memory of the debacle of a debate had faded. It had served to make her more determined than ever, and never to be a public laughing stock again; she was going to succeed at university, to prove to herself she could do it. If she ever got the chance. She loved reading, dissecting the great works of literature; she had even begun to enjoy the social life. Going to the end of term ball, she even enjoyed learning the foxtrot. Her eyes had been opened to what fun it could be. Now what? Would she ever get the chance to finish her degree? And it was all because of this damn inconvenient war; the war had ruined her life, and her family's; and now she would never be able to finish her degree and get the farm for her family. It was impossible.

Gundry's had commandeered the college, so busy were they and lacking in office space. To think she could have been coming full-time to St James' Secretarial College, if it hadn't been for Grandfather. Gundry's was a hive of activity as all the netting and roping sheds were in Bridport. They sent the girls from the typing pool and used the space in the secretarial college, there were so many orders and invoices to type. All the requests from the Ministry: camouflage nets, parachute webbing, helmet nets and ropes, hundreds and thousands of ropes, a myriad of sizes and lengths.

The college was on the outskirts of Bridport, so she could stay at home again. It felt odd but it wasn't long before it was normal, back in the old routine. She was beginning to think she was better off at Oxford; there, she was learning, and she would get a degree and the farm for the family. What good was she doing here? It was what was asked of her for the war effort. Everything was for the war effort nowadays. Having Jeanie as a land girl, helping show her around. It wasn't the same, though; all worried about Nicole. At least Dad had Thomas and Hamilton and now Jeanie to help, though he was fed up with the Ministry of Agriculture telling him what to grow and where to grow it. He was always in a bad mood when they came to survey the farm.

Lily yawned, tired from her long cold night. She looked out of the window. She should concentrate on the Imperial typewriter in front of her but the sun was distracting; the heat was distracting; the thought of all the cool American soldiers at the Manor was distracting. What a long way from Oxford and St Hilda's! Why, just as she became settled, did her world turn upside down again? The Americans were one benefit of the war; it was the way they talked, it was the confidence they had, it was the way they looked, it was the way they smelled. They were so sophisticated. She snapped her mind back to the order she was typing up: more flax was needed and with import hits, they were desperate.

There were four rows of four tables. Each one had a young woman seated behind an Imperial Good Companion Model T typewriter; each had a black surround and smelt of new ribbons.

Mrs Patricia Meredith sat behind her desk reading the invoices, collating them together, with her black hair tied back. Her lips moved, miming the words, reading and checking; otherwise, her face was set in stone. Lily had already finished the order and double-checked; it was perfect with no errors. She was easily the fastest of the girls.

The sun shone in through the large windows. Lily was seated directly in the sun; it had been warm on the skin of her lower arms. She was wearing a short-sleeved yellow and white dress, pinched in at the waist. She had on her slip-on brown shoes with slight heel. Her face was dusted with light brown summer freckles, her hair sun-bleached.

She wished to hear from Nicole, just to know she was all right, that she was safe; but no letters came. There was no chance to make amends, to say sorry, to forgive and forget. There had been no letters, not since France had been invaded and occupied. She hoped Nicole was safe, that she was out of trouble, that the Tuckers were looking after her. It was as if Nicole had been her twin, and now she was half the person she used to be. She was lucky to have Thomas and Hamilton to dote on but it wasn't the same as having a sister you could confide your every secret and every wish to.

The *click, click, click* of the keys in rhythm were like small drumbeats. Lily felt her eyelids become heavy and her head began to droop. She pushed her head back and tried to focus, to keep her mind sharp.

'Lunch!' Mrs Meredith hollered over the noise of the typewriters.

The young women got up from behind their desks and filed one by one past Mrs Meredith.

'Half an hour, that's all,' Mrs Meredith dictated.

* * *

Lily and Ellen went to their favourite spot under the large canopy of the old yew tree. The shade was welcome and the breeze was cooling. The sun was past its midpoint high in the cloudless light blue sky. The weather could not have been any more perfect. Lily unwrapped the greaseproof paper and took out the buttered bread and piece of cheese. She breathed in the odour of fresh bread; it always seemed so much more powerful when the sun was out.

'Oh, I'm so tired from last night.' Ellen let out a yawn. 'Lily, you're so lucky to have butter and eggs and everything; I wished I lived on a farm. We can't get anything in town.' Ellen stared at Lily's lunch. Ellen was dark-haired with full lips and dark hazel eyes. She wore a chiffon scarf round her neck. Lily always thought her older than her twenty-three years: Ellen, the mother of the typing pool.

'I think Father keeps some behind in his secret stash. The Ministry of Food take everything else. We don't have much and he keeps trying to get me to eat rabbit. I tell you, I'm not eating that! He keeps saying it tastes lovely, like chicken. Chickens don't go hopping and skipping through tall grass looking all cute, do they? And – well – Mother doesn't like him… you know, skinning them and all; he has to do it in the shed.' Lily stretched her legs out in front. 'Hamilton: he don't seem to care! He will scoff down anything. And Father's not the same, not since Nicole went, not since he was told to slaughter all the sheep.'

'We had spam fritters again last night. I reckon rabbit would be better than that any day of the week.'

'Spam fritters? They sound disgusting.' Lily screwed up her face.

'Not as bad as rabbit fritters though, eh?' The girls laughed as they stretched out yawning.

'Do you think this war will ever be over?' Ellen asked.

'I don't know. The Great War lasted four years; who knows how long this will take? Five, ten or whatever.'

''Least we have the Americans on our side, and they're handsome and dashing; and I don't know, they have something, don't they?' Ellen smiled. Taking her red Max Factor lipstick from her handbag she applied it, looking in her rose-patterned powder compact.

'Where on earth did you get that?' Lily shrieked.

'Ask no questions and I will tell you no lies.' Ellen smirked.

'Is he American?'

'He might be!'

'Did he give you that?' Lily whistled through her teeth. 'Can he get me some stockings?'

'I don't know about that, Lily; I've only just started seeing him.'

'You lucky devil! They're so sophisticated,' Lily said, taking a small bite of her bread. 'And don't they seem able to get just about anything.'

'We should be getting back and I don't know how I'm going to stay awake. I hope we don't have another night like last night,' Ellen said.

'We can have ten more minutes, can't we?' Lily closed her eyes and breathed in deeply and felt herself begin to drop off.

Her nap was disturbed by the sound of rustling in the bushes.

'What's that, Ellen?'

'I don't know; it's probably just birds or something.'

The rustling became louder and Lily said: 'It's coming from the wall over there in the corner.'

She pointed to the wall and the large shrubs. They got up from the bench and walked to the side, past the yew tree, and followed the border of shrubs and bushes. 'Look, look, it's...' Lily whispered. Lily took her flask and flung the iced tea and half-eaten sandwich at her target. The women ran together across the lawn and straight into the arms of another soldier who appeared from the opposite wall.

Lily looked around. They were now surrounded on three sides by soldiers and the gothic bay windows of the college on their left. There was nowhere to run, even if they could pull away from the hold they were now in.

The first soldier caught up with them, wiping cold tea from his moustache.

'Don't be alarmed; you have nothing to worry about, nothing at all. We are friendly.' He smiled from under his elegant trimmed whiskers. Lily liked the drawl of his accent. He was taller than her; he must be six feet tall or more. He was imposing and she thought he might be a little handsome, although his ears stood out from the side of his head and he had a gap between his front teeth. His uniform trousers were covered in dust and a bead of tea resolutely clung to the hair above his lip.

'What do you think you're doing here?' Lily said, trying to sound confident.

'I'm sorry, ladies, we're on exercise; everyone was supposed to be told we were coming. This is German HQ.'

'This is nothing of the sort! This is St James' College, St James' Ladies' Secretarial College, I will have you know.' Lily pushed her shoulders back.

'Well, thank you for the introduction! I'm Sergeant Perry Andre-Kearns of the 2nd Canadian Division.' He stroked the droplet from his moustache, obviously irritated by it. 'And you are?'

'We can't possibly tell you that. There are spies everywhere. Careless talk costs lives, don't you know,' Lily said.

'Why is that an official secret?' the soldier said.

'How do we know you are who you say you are? You might be the invading German spies impersonating Canadians,' Lily said, as Ellen still clung to her arm.

'And why would I be capturing the secretarial college?'

'You might have heard we were working on something top secret, like breaking your submarine codes or writing lots of propaganda with our typewriters and it was imperative that you stopped it,' Ellen said.

'And are you working on top secret codes?'

'No, we are typing invoices for nets,' Ellen said.

'Don't tell him that, Ellen,' Lily said. 'You might be here to take all the women prisoners, being you know how valuable we are.'

'Look, ladies, what do I have to tell you?' He smiled. 'I'm not German; we are not German. Well, I don't think I am; I do have a great-uncle who emigrated from Austria, years and years ago, so I suppose I might have a bit of German blood in me somewhere. We are not here to take you prisoner or try and break the code or take your typewriters; we are just on exercise.'

'Ellen, I think Percy here might be telling us the truth, as they haven't shot at anything and their English is pretty good,' Lily said.

He shook his head and said: 'Thank you, ladies; at last. Now, where does a man go to have a smoke? And it's Perry, not Percy.'

'You have cigarettes?' Ellen said.

'Come with us; we've got a couple of minutes.' Ellen and Lily grabbed him and pulled him under the yew tree.

Perry took out a packet of Players. Lily's green eyes lit up. He took the first cigarette and passed it to Lily and the second for Ellen before taking the third for himself.

Lily held the cigarette delicately between her fingers and bit her lip as she waited for it to be lit. Perry took out his small pocket lighter and leaned over and lit it for her before doing the same for Ellen.

'Thank you so much, Percy.' She dragged on the cigarette, then held it in her fingers before blowing out the smoke over her shoulder.

'Oh. You should know it's Perry, Perry! Not Percy.'

'Is it? Oh well, you will always be Percy to me. My favourite pet rabbit was called Percy,' Lily said, as she held her lips from breaking into too wide a smile.

'I still don't know your names.'

'I'm Lily Constance Kingson, if you must know.' She felt her lips parting and she stood closer to Perry.

CHAPTER TWENTY-THREE

11th July 1942

Lily thought of Perry. His charming accents, his funny words, the way he walked, the way he stood. When would she see him? Since their first meeting he had come when he could; he would write; they had walked out on the cliffs together, shared time on the farm. Everyone liked him. He would lend Dad a hand. He was good with the tractor, though he wasn't used to the cows or horses. Lily typed out the letter on her desk and took it to Mrs Meredith.

Another letter: this one about the number of camouflage nets that could be produced in the next three months. There was no stimulation in the work, just monotony. The numbers were huge. She was lucky to be in the office and not in the netting shed, from what Nicole used to tell her. Even so, she wished she could be outside in this weather. She was relieved when it was time to go home. She walked out arm-in-arm with Ellen.

They walked out to the front of the college building. Her lips parted and formed a smile: he was there. Standing by her car, smoking, standing tall, all smart and dressed to perfection, his boots shining. His lopsided smile wide, full and welcoming.

Perry pushed his hand through his hair, extinguished his cigarette under his boot, then made his way to her.

'Perry, what a surprise!' She could feel the excitement tumble over in her tummy. He held her elbow as he pecked her on the cheek. There was a rush that ran the entire length of her body.

'I see you have a lot to talk about,' Ellen said, smiling, as she went to catch the bus home.

Lily drove the two of them to town. Perry got out and put his arm through hers and took the short steps to the front of West End Dairy. The window, once full with its display of fresh meats, cheeses and butter, was empty, all the produce kept close at hand on the shelves. They walked in past the counters of woman queueing, holding their ration books open. Each was allowed one shilling and tenpence worth of meat. The aroma of fresh milk and cream filled the shop. Lily led Perry up the three steps and to the tables and chairs which were squeezed into the old store room, where there was a makeshift counter serving teas, coffee and handmade cakes made by Mrs Martin, the owner's wife. It had been her idea to open up the café, years before the war. Perry ordered two strawberry milkshakes. They sat down. Lily looked at the sunflower-patterned tablecloth.

'Don't go. I don't want you to go! Can't you get out of it?' Her neck ached from being hunched over all day. She toyed with the edge of the tablecloth, then moved her hand to the back of her neck and used her fingers to massage the knot.

'I'm glad that at last we can do what we've been training for all this time; it's about time we Canadians showed what we can do.'

'I love it when you tell me about your country.' She looked into his dark blue eyes. Her lips parted and her tongue flicked at the corner of her mouth.

'It's such a lovely town near Calgary; it's so beautiful. Wide open spaces so vast; this little place makes me yearn for the freedom. There are lots of farmsteads, large, bigger than Home Farm.' He stroked his hair back even though it wasn't out of place.

'What about your family?' she asked, her eyes blinking. She held his gaze. He looked into her eyes. It felt like he was looking deep inside her, that he could read her thoughts.

'My father died in the First War; Mother has brought me up. She's a dressmaker. I've a brother; he's younger than me. He's in the army too, stationed near Portsmouth. I write to him every week. We even caught up the other day. I think that's why I've a soft spot for young Hamilton; he reminds me of Patrick at his age.'

'He's lucky to have you.'

'He is, but he won't ever admit it. You know what brothers are like.'

'I do, that's for certain. Mine aren't too bad; give them a football and a comic – that keeps them quiet. I don't know how I would feel if they were in this war, I really don't.'

'You have to believe; all we have is our belief. We will make it through.'

'I know. It's so hard. My mother is in pieces about it, says it's a waste, it's all a waste that no one has learnt anything, that normal people are the ones that suffer.'

'That's what mothers do, isn't it? I make sure to write back to mine, but it takes so long for letters to get there.' He sipped through his straw. 'It's so hard for that generation, don't you think? My mother lost her husband, her own brothers; and now she is having to face it all over again, all over again with her sons.'

'That's it exactly, how Mother feels.' Lily sipped on her straw, holding her head down. She looked up and saw Perry was watching her. 'I wish this was all over. I wish you didn't have to go.'

'I'll write to you, I promise; and I'm sure this year it will be the end of it.'

She sipped her milkshake and looked around. She hadn't noticed before but there were other soldiers with their girlfriends packed into the small cafe. She was one of the same of dozens. She pushed her gas mask box to her side.

She tasted the sweet strawberry on her lips, and made sure to dab at the corner of her mouth with the paper napkin.

'Come on, Lily, let's finish these and go for a walk. It's too nice to waste being inside.'

She finished, being careful not to slurp at the end. She thought of Hamilton and how he would gurgle up every last drop. Perry left a tip for the waitress, then got up and led her out. They reached the Austin 7, the car with the black roof and maroon panel sides.

'You can drive, Perry.'

'Are you sure? It's your pride and joy.'

'Of course! Surprise me.'

Lily handed Perry the keys. His rough hands consumed hers and she felt the charge flow from his hands to hers up through her arms. The feeling spread rapidly along her shoulders to her neck, down her spine, spreading the warmth down her legs; even her toes tickled. She moved to the passenger door and got in, happy to sit down, feeling her legs might buckle: the feeling that she would melt in his arms, like ice cream in the sun.

'Where are you taking me?'

'I thought you wanted the surprise, ma'am.'

'I do… I don't… I don't know.'

'I think I can remember how to get there. You might need to help.'

He drove out of town, then followed the lane down the hollow to the coast. Lily knew it was the mouth of the river onto the beach, with the steep cliff paths on either side.

'However did you remember to get here?'

'Don't forget, we're Canadians; we never forget.'

'Oh, I see.'

Perry stopped the car and they looked out over the coastline. The sun was beating down. In years gone by, there would have been many walkers and bathers; now there were just the pillboxes, barbed wire and tank traps.

'You never forget, but you're not too clever to leave milkshake on your moustache.'

'You must think me so uncouth.' He tried to brush it with his hand but missed.

'Let me.' Lily took the napkin she had stowed from the café and dabbed at the corner of his mouth. She thought it endearing; for all his smartness and his control, she could still see the boy in him.

'You will be all right, Lily; you have your family.' He sat back in the seat; he looked so in control.

'I do know that; but I miss my sister too. We parted on bad terms. I may never get to say how sorry I was.'

'I'm sure that she will feel the same; and once this is all out of the way, you can make it right.'

'I so hope so. I can't bear the thought that we will never see each other, that I can never say sorry to her, that I may never share her laughter again.' Lily looked at Perry. He looked so wise and handsome in his uniform, with his stripes.

'What did you do before the war, Perry?'

'I was a mechanic in a small garage. I'd signed up as a reservist, into the Calgary regiment; that's how I got into the tanks.'

'It must be worse for you, being so many thousands of miles from home.'

'It's not so bad; I've seen something of the world, I've met you, and you light up my world.'

'That's not true.'

'You do! You're the most interesting woman I've ever met, and your accent is just perfect. You're the only woman I've ever been able to talk to like this.'

'Shut up, Perry! You're embarrassing me with all your compliments. You had lots of girlfriends.' She felt the blood rush to her face.

'Maybe one or two, but none as sweet as you.'

'What were they like?'

'Local girls, plain. You seem so cute and smart.'

'Perry.'

'You better learn how to take a compliment, Lily, because, honey, they are all true. And you are going to get a helluva lot more.'

'I like talking to you,' Lily said, looking over. Perry's face was wide in a smile.

'Do you have to go?' They got out of the car and walked down to the pebbled beach. There were two other couples walking arm-in-arm. She put her hand through Perry's. 'I feel so safe with you.'

'I have to go; it's why I'm here.'

'If it wasn't for this war, we would have never met,' Lily said.

'I know, but now I've found you, I don't want to lose you. Lily, trust me, I will come back.'

'But you don't know.'

'None of us do, but I will move heaven and earth to make sure I do, I swear.'

'How long will you be gone for?'

'Not long; we should be in and out.'

'Where are you going?' It was a stupid question; she should have thought. 'Don't answer, I'm sorry. I shouldn't have asked.'

'Oh, Lily.' He stopped walking, turned to her. Put his hand on her healed scar. 'You be careful, too. You put yourself in as much danger as anyone.' She felt her blood move slowly through her body as if time itself would stand still. She didn't know how she knew: woman's intuition, a feeling that he was the one. His fingers moved lightly down her face. The feeling of anticipation moved through her, like an energy she had never had before. The sun seemed brighter, warmer. The sound of the waves gently breaking on the shore sounded more vivid. The smell of the beach and Perry's musky aftershave mixed to give a deep, pleasant aroma. His hand moved to her neck and pulled her in close. His lips met hers, soft; his moustache soft, too; he kissed her and she felt like time had ended.

CHAPTER TWENTY-FOUR

12th July 1942

Lily accelerated up Snowdrop Hill, the Austin struggling to make the crest. She wanted to make it better at home, to make everyone smile and laugh like they had before, when they had all been together. She felt guilty and torn in two. Was it fair that she was so happy that Perry was in her life, whilst war raged? The hills looked barren and bereft of life, her father not the only farmer to be ordered to slaughter the sheep; Dorset Horns gone. Food was needed to feed the country; the sheep could be sacrificed. Where there had once been acres of green pasture there were now patchy fields of wheat. The wheat should be golden and full; instead, the new fields were not suited; there were weeds, couch grass, wild oats, rye grass, a tangle, the red and green of the odd poppy. This war was doomed to make everybody miserable for eternity. She would try and do her best to raise the spirits. It was so hard, the longing for family, the longing to see Perry, now he was going on the mission to god knows where, to face god knows what; would she even ever see him again? To think he would be fighting, like the reports on the radio and in the paper. She tried to bury the thought and stay positive. Her family needed her.

She focused on the road in front of her. The smell of summer was in the air, a time when smiles would come back on people's faces; but not this year.

When she got to Home Farm she pulled up outside, surprised to see Mr Grey the estate manager's car parked in the yard outside. Thomas and Hamilton played with the football, kicking it against the yard wall. She smiled and tried to kick the ball to Hamilton. She mistimed her kick.

'I've done what I can, young 'en, but he ain't listening to me any more.' She overheard Mr Grey's deep voice as she came through the door. He was dressed in his black suit with white shirt. His hair was thin and wispy. It wasn't often he was without his black hat. He stood in front of the range; he looked tired and drained. Mother and Father sat at the table, their faces sullen.

'He's struggling, since Admiral passed; it was the death duties, see, and then this war.' Mr Grey nodded at Lily. 'Me, I think it's more his ways; the estate is not being run the way it should, not the way Admiral would do it, or I would if I had my way. But he don't listen to me, not that Theodore. Since old Admiral passed over, ain't never been the same.'

'It's more than you needed to do, more than we could have expected,' Father said.

'Yes, thank you, Mr Grey; thank you for everything,' Mother said.

'You know, this is the last straw for me; I don't think I can work for him any more. I ain't doing his bidding, not like this; I won't be part of it,' Mr Grey said, as he put his hat on and went to the door. He apologised and left through the back door.

'What's Mr Grey doing? Why was he here?' She saw Mother and Father look at each other with an expression of concern, her father's eyebrows raised. She could see they were deciding what to tell her. 'Tell me, go on. I'm old enough.'

'We don't want to bother you with this, Lily,' Mother said. Her eyes darted back to Father, avoiding Lily's gaze.

'I'm twenty-four, for heaven's sake! I'm a grown woman! Tell me.' Mother and Father looked at each other and they nodded.

Father spoke, his voice slow: 'Lily, dear, it ain't been easy these last few years, having to plough up pasture, slaughtering the sheep. Sowing more and more wheat and potatoes for the War Ag; and you know, the rent has near on doubled from what it were ten years ago, and Theo has kept on rising it and rising it. He's putting it up again; that was what Mr Grey was 'ere for. He's putting it up, and Mr Grey has told us he's going to keep on putting it up for all us tenants right up until he has us evicted; that way he will then be able to pick and choose which farms he can sell.'

'I reckon he wants us out so he can give this farm to Montague; that way, he won't have to go and fight,' Mother said.

'He can't do that!' Lily ran her hands through her hair and scratched the corner of her eye, then ran her finger down her scar.

'He can, love, and he will; we all know him; he will do it, I've no doubt; and it's us he wants out. We should have known better,' Mother said, shaking her head.

'Mother's right, I should have seen it. I should have made other plans but it's always chasing our tails to stay afloat, there's always been other things to think about.' Father's eyes widened and he looked down at his feet. Dusty slunk to the corner.

'You can't give up so easily; you have to fight! You can't let him get away with it.' Lily's voice was raised. She felt her stomach flip over. She felt sick. 'You must protest, take him to court.'

'He is the court; he's on every damn committee from here to bloody Timbuktu,' Father said. 'And if he ain't, one of his cronies is; he's got it all tied up, all ways. I can't see any option. He's got us. He's going to ruin us if it's the last thing he does.'

'Come on, Dad, Mum, you can't let him; I won't let him.' She looked at them. Their mouths looked slack and their eyes dull.

'I've still got some money left from my Trust fund; I can sell the car; I'll pay you more for my lodgings.'

'It won't be enough, Lily; we're already behind,' Father said.

'And we don't want you to; that's your money and you are to spend it as you want, not have to bail us two out,' Mother said. 'You'll need that to go back to university.'

'No, I won't let him do this to us; not to you, to me or to Hamilton.' She put her shoes back on and rushed out of the house before they could stop her. She drove straight to the Manor.

She rushed into the kitchen and saw Aunt Dorothy and Mary. They tried to calm her down. She breezed past and went to the library. Her grandmother was sitting in her window seat, draped in her black shawl and hunched over, much as she had been in the time since Grandfather had passed away. She looked up and a smile flickered and faded before her sombre look returned.

'Hello, dear.' She spoke slowly.

'Grandmother, did you know about this?' Lily's nostrils flared.

'No; what is the matter, dear? Sit down.'

'Where is my uncle?' she snarled. She felt heat move from her stomach to her face.

'Whatever is the matter? What is going on?' Grandmother fumbled with the book in her lap, trying to close it and put it on the side table.

'You don't know?'

She shook her head. 'He doesn't discuss anything with me, dear.'

'He's putting up the rent and he wants to evict us! What have we ever done to him?'

'I don't know. Calm down; sit here.' Her grandmother patted the seat next to her.

'Where is he?'

Her stomach was filled with fire. She stormed out of the library, not waiting for her grandmother to answer. Dorothy was waiting in the corridor. She pointed towards the study. Lily opened the door without knocking. Smoke filled her eyes and the deep musty smell of tobacco engulfed her.

'My niece! I'd like to say what a pleasure it is but I don't think you would believe me.' He puffed out another wave of smoke, which hit her in the face.

'What do you think you are doing?' She stood straight.

'I'm sitting here having a nice cigar, thinking about how much I'm going to sell Home Farm for.' He threw his head back, his chin up, and relaxed in his chair.

'How can you do that to us?'

'So easy, you wouldn't believe. It gives me pleasure to see you all squirm. You are all going to get what's coming to you and I can sit back and watch. You don't realise how much joy that gives me.' He rolled his eyes.

'But I'm your niece! They're my parents!' she said in an uncertain tone.

'That makes it even more joyful for me, my dear.' He leaned back in his chair and smiled, taking another drag on his cigar. 'I've been thinking: it wouldn't be right to see you all homeless after all, and seeing you here, Lily, I don't want to upset Mother unduly; so you can tell your father that if he makes it nice and easy for me, if he gives up the tenancy without any trouble, he can come back and work for me. Hell, I will even throw in the old tied cottage he used to live in with his parents; it's empty up there. Mind, I think it's got a leaky roof been so empty so long; but yes, how does that sound? You can tell him yourself if you like.' He raised his eyebrow.

She felt as if all the air had escaped her. She had come in brimming with fire, hoping to reason with him. She had hoped to achieve something, to fight. She could see from his face and from his words that there was no argument; she had no weapon to rally with. He held all the power.

'Yes, what are you waiting for? Go and tell your old man. Such a shame you didn't have the chance to finish university like Father wanted you to; then you would have been given the farm. To think, the war came along just in time.'

'I can still go back.'

'Oh, I don't know about that. As a trustee of your fund, I'm not even sure there will be anything left. – Look, I'm a reasonable fellow; your father can come and work for me. It will be just like the old days! 'Course, I won't be able to pay much; but then you will have a roof over your heads. I'll get that seen to just as soon as I can, of course. It will have to go on the list, and the list is very long; it's all these old properties we own, you see. You're an intelligent girl; you understand it's just business.'

She turned and left the study. She bit down on her tongue and rubbed her eyebrow. Had she just made things worse? She had wanted to stand up to him; but her confidence had left her.

CHAPTER TWENTY-FIVE

17th July 1942

Thomas made his way indoors. The kitchen made a welcome retreat from a summer scud. The smell of boiled onions greeted him. He hung up his coat; he took his time. He sat on the bottom of the stairs and undid his bootlaces one at a time. Father was already in the kitchen. Thomas pulled off his boot from his left foot, then his right. He had to say it; he couldn't wait any longer. He'd put it off so many times already he had lost count. He couldn't hold it in anymore. He sighed. It was time that he did his duty. There were many boys his age who had already signed up. He could spend the war working on his father's farm. But with his friends all going he couldn't stay, not when they were fighting for his country. Billy Crabb had gone, leaving Molly and his daughter. Romily Colman, too; and hundreds more. He couldn't stand by and watch. After all, his father had done his duty in the First War. It was time he did his. He couldn't look people in the face if he didn't. He had to do it, he had to do his bit. God, if anything happened to Nicole, he wouldn't be able to live with himself.

Lily was at the sink peeling potatoes. He pulled out the wooden chair and sat at the table. The warmth from the stove and range radiated out. His father and mother were sitting in their two chairs. Mother was reading out sections of interest from the *Express*. Her lips formed into a grimace.

He waited for Mother to fall silent. He pursed his lips. He coughed from the back of his throat. He sipped from the mug of tea. He coughed, louder. Mother and Father looked up, Mother from behind the paper.

'I'm going to sign up and I don't want you to stop me,' he

whispered. He touched his ear and felt his chest tighten. 'Um…
I'm going to sign up,' he said more loudly.

Mother put the paper down very deliberately. The colour
drained from her face. Lily dropped the peeler in the sink and
faced the table.

'What did you say?' Mother said in a hushed, calm tone.

He coughed again; his throat wouldn't clear. He wanted to go
out to the shed, up to his bedroom or out and milk the cows. He
wanted to be anywhere but in the kitchen. His fingers were cold
and he felt them tingle. He avoided looking Mother in the eye. His
breathing quickened.

'I've decided. It's time I signed up.' He tried to swallow without
Mother noticing. His hands began to tremble; he didn't dare pick
up the mug. He tried to sit up straight, but felt himself slide on the
wooden chair.

'I don't think so, Thomas,' she said. Her mouth opened and
closed. 'No, no, I'm not having that.' She raked her hand through
her blonde hair. He looked up; her green eyes didn't blink. She
held his gaze. He looked away. Lily was shaking her head.

'I'm to leave tomorrow…'

'You are not! They won't have you. I won't let you go!' She
slowly shook her head. He watched as his mother's face turned
white. She put her hands to her temple. 'You can't, Thomas, you
can't go.'

He fingered his collar. His chest tightened. He felt the colour
drain from his face, like water pouring through a sieve. This wasn't
going well; but then he hadn't expected it to. He wanted to say
more, to say how much he loved everyone; but he couldn't find the
words.

'You're not to go. We've seen Nicole go; we've been through
enough as a family. You can't go; I won't have it.' His mother stood
up and pushed the chair in. 'The worry of not knowing if she is
safe: it's killing me inside. I can't have two of you away, I just can't.'
He stood up. He wanted to hug her and say it was all going to be

all right. He wanted to say sorry, but he couldn't move his mouth. He was still shorter than her and he felt intimidated.

'Thomas, don't do this to me. To your father. Please.'

'Mother, I don't want to argue with you. I don't want you to be upset; I don't want you to worry.' He tried to hold her arm.

''Course I worry, 'course I bloody worry! You have no idea, do you? You are too young, for heaven's sake! You can't do this to me, you can't do this to your family. You know how Hamilton looks up to you; if you don't stay for me, stay for your brother, stay for your brother's sake. Stay for your sister, stay for anything; just don't go. You've no idea, you've no idea! They won't even take you. You're just a boy.' She walked past and went up the stairs.

'Mum, wait, don't go up like this.' He felt worse than when he'd broken the kitchen window. He regretted saying it; he should have waited till they had eaten. How could he stand back and watch?

He turned to his father. 'Why not me? I can't stay; I've to go.'

'I know, son, I know. It's hard for your mother to take, 'cos of before, 'cos of me, 'cos of Nicole, 'cos of this lousy war.'

'I don't understand: 'cos of the last war?' he stuttered. His hands felt warm and sweaty and his stomach was spinning round and round.

'It's not that easy, young 'en. We had our hopes and dreams and all; we lost good friends, close to us. It isn't all what they make out in the paper. It will be the hardest thing you have ever done. I made your mother worry so she thought she lost me; and to think she might lose you now… For a mother, that's ten times worse. We've lived through a war, and this one isn't any easier.'

'But, Dad, you understand, don't 'e? I've to go; it's my duty and all.' He touched his lips with his finger.

'We do all 'ave our duty. I was the same back then and I was older than you. But don't think you're gonna be a hero and everyone will remember 'e, boy, 'cos it doesn't work like that. I do know why you feel that way. You can stay 'ere, work the land; it's good, honest and valuable to us all. I know that look on 'e's face. It only brought heartache and this old foot to me and I was one of the lucky ones.' Dad got up. 'I'll go speak to your mother, but I don't hold out much hope.' His wooden foot echoed up the stairs.

'Lily, you understand, don't 'e?' Lily put down the peeler. She walked over and hugged her brother. 'Oh, Thomas, I'm sorry, I love you so much; I don't want you to go.'

She turned and Thomas saw she was crying. She wiped it away with her sleeve. Why had he upset his family? He should have kept his mouth shut and left in the dark of the morning.

* * *

T.W.R Kingson T175555
No 145 Coy. No 6 D.T.C
R.A.S.C
Herne Bay, Kent
22nd July 1942

Dear my own dearest family,

Hullo you Dorset darlings. I am in Herne Bay and note the address as this is where you are to write me. I am ok, the train journey was long and I was on my own I didn't much like it. I have been billeted in a bungalow with five other chaps who all seem nice. We have been given towels, razor blades, shirts, socks and boot brush. Sergeant Major is good and he is like a second father to us all. We are up at six, it's parade at seven, breakfast at eight, dinner at one and tea at five. I am proper tired at the end of the day and I am in my bed by ten.

I started this letter a couple of days ago but had no time to finish. Sorry it's written in pencil the fountain pen did pack in. Mother forgive me if its untidy but I write this leaning on my knee. Meals are at the seafront and we have to march a quarter of a mile. The food is bloody good, we had roast dinner and rice pudding and were served by the W.A.T.S they looked like you Lily in your uniform and they were very kind to us.

The boots are darned heavy and many chaps had to give in to their blisters, I kept going and I think I look very smart in my uniform. Us chaps in the bungalow are going to try and get our picture taken in the garden I will send you it when I can. I like it when it rains cos we get under cover and have our

173

smokes. We have inoculations coming, many boys faint. I hope I don't. Oh, I should tell you I'm as fit as a fiddle with all the parade and physical training. We have to constantly polish our boots and buttons for inspection there is lots of red tape err. There is a proper hot water system in the bungalow, my bath night is Thursday and the water runs hot straight away, it is proper soothing to my aching muscles I think I'm like an old man, like you Dad!

I'm going on so, how is everyone? How are you mother and father and Lily, Perry and is there any news from Nicole. The hardest thing is missing home. Being so far away it looks impossible to get back, I would only have ten hours then have to come back. How is Dusty? And Ol' Parrot. And of course, what is Hamilton doing playing football and reading the Beano I spec. We are in good spirits, please write it will lift me even higher.

Your loving son, Thomas xxxxx

31st July 1942

Dear my own dearest family,

Thank you Mother and Lily the letters are coming thick and fast, that's one thing you can say about the army the post does run efficient. It did proper lift my spirits hearing from you all. By the sounds of it Ashcombe sounds like everything is happening more than here. You think of so much to write, I think my letters are so short when you send me eight full pages.

Herne is nice and is bigger than Bridport they do have a Woolworths just like town. On Saturday we had a proper half day. I needed the rest, but a proper half day there was no milking to do in the afternoon. I will think this a luxury life. We are doing one months training which the regular army does in three, Sergeant says we are a fine group one of the best he's had, I really like him. There is no news of leave so I'm sorry if I disappoint you mother, father, Lily and Hamilton. I do so miss you. We had prunes and custard for desert yesterday and it was lovely. The sausages you had from Connick's sound lovely and sweet. One day we had pear and apricot with creams. I think I will be very fat when you see me next.

On Saturday night, we walked down the front, we got some chips for supper then went to the pictures. The film was Summink like 'French without tears' and I didn't like it much at all. Lily might like it but don't take Hamilton he will not like it at all. Most of my chums are married, and I don't even have a sweetheart, they tell me I'm better of without the earache.

I should tell you father that we did proper training on Friday with the Bren gun, we went to the target range and had practise at three hundred yards, lying down on my belly, the Sergeant came over and said: 'very good work'. I think he was impressed. Then we had gas mask drill, running with our respirators on and had to carry our ninety-pound kit, with water bottle and ground sheet.

Sergeant is good to us chaps. I did my guard duty in the night. It was a moonlit night and I thought it would be boring but we had a good chat about being back home and it went quick.

There is word we are moving soon but we don't know where I hope it will be closer to home and I get some leave to come back and see you all. Hope all is well, please write back I want to hear from you. I miss and love you all even that old parrot.

Your loving son and brother, Thomas xxxxx

CHAPTER TWENTY-SIX

4th August 1942

Dear my own dearest family,

Thank you, mother and Lily, for writing me I was glad to hear you are all well and I am missing you all a thousand times over. I hope I get back soon to see you all.

We have been moved on to Margate and we are billeted in the Royal Norfolk hotel there is about one hundred of us. It did proper pour down. I came back and we did look like drowned rats one and all of us. It was good to take a hot bath. I think five bob was missing. I forgot to take out my money. The conscripts came in, they are allowed to do that in the rain. The money has been pinched or it is missing. I am still with my good pals from Herne and my chum is Jack Mason, he is all the way from Penzance in Cornwall so like me he can't get back. He married a month before he came away so he is missing his sweetheart and he writes her every other day. There is another man with my name, so you have to make sure and write all my initials T W R on the envelope it will then find me we are Section 3 put that on as well it will help.

Have you been to the pictures, Lily? I went up on Saturday night with my pals and saw 'Each dawn I die' a very good picture with James Cagney and George Draft course he dies as usual. We have to get their early cos there is a very long line to get in and if you're late you don't make it. I went to the dance that was put on and there were some very pretty girls. I was too shy to ask them, my pal James stayed in and wrote home because he promised his new wife he wouldn't and he says he's going to stick to it. When we went back we said it wasn't up too much to make him feel better.

Don't worry about me mother I'm in the pink, fit as a fiddle and ok. I've been out in the lorry the steering is proper heavy but it's not much different to the Standard Ford. The lad I was paired with was only used to motorcycles

176

and he was done for, said he'd lied to get on the lorry's as he would do anything not to be in the infantry. There has been lots of driving and I do like it, I'm glad Romily suggested it. We have lots more practise, with parades. Mother you will be proud of me I'm sure. I went to the church parade and they played there will always be an England, we all had proper lumps in our throats. Thank you for the parcel it came through on Friday and I have plenty of ciggs.

I seem to write a long list of what's happening to me every day. The food is still tops, we had chips and eggs there is plenty of it.

How is Dusty and Ol' Parrot and of course all you family. I wish there was news of Nicole, I guess there is nothing?

The inspections keep coming and if you don't look smart you get put on spud peeling duty. I make sure there is plenty of spit and polish on my boots and buttons and make them sparkle. Word is we have to be ready to move again at half hour's notice. But I have no clue where I will be, I hope it's near Dorset and I can have a few days to see e all.

Your loving son and brother, Thomas xxxxx

* * *

12th August 1942

Dear my own dearest family,

It sounds so much fun you all did have on the weekend. Hope you are all well, I was sorry to hear that Auntie Dorothy was not so well and I hope she is up and about soon.

I have been doing lots of driving and I have passed as first-class driver. My pal Jack Mason didn't pass and he has to stay back. We clubbed together and got Sergeant a silver cigarette case. We all had lumps in our throats and he said we were the best group of lads he had. As you can see I'm in Bournemouth and you are to write to this address. We are in good spirits and I have to tell you something. We went on parade for a big inspection and told there was a special guest. I could have thought myself dreaming as I paraded I could have put out my hand and touched the King, he inspected us all and there were about a thousand. After we went and sat on the grass and told there was another special visitor. She didn't get out of the car; the Queen drove past and she waved at us all. We were told to give three cheers as she went by and we all shouted as loud as we could. I think she was impressed as she smiled as she went by. It was a proper good day.

Lily how is Perry? Please let everyone know that asks I'm fit as a fiddle and doing ok. The food is great and still plenty of it. Roast Beef today prunes and custard for afters it was proper good, I had extra roast spuds. I'm writing this from my room. Hope you are all well and I guess father is out late in the fields, say Hi to Jeanie? I think of you always and what is happening on the farm. I do miss it but I do love driving the lorry. I was sent up to Woolwich, Arsenal with Chris he's a good mate and married I think I is the only single man in the army sometimes. The Arsenal is a special place I ain't never seen the like of, its huge and all line with ammunition, machines and arms. We set off at eight and didn't get back till eleven at night I was very tired and went straight to me bed.

This afternoon we had a game of football, it was so much fun it reminded me of back home and playing with you all in the yard with the Tuckers. Would you believe the opposition had a player who plays for Arsenal! My team won four nil and I scored twice, like Tommy Lawton. Dad you would be proud one was a screamer from outside the box into the top corner all my pals jumped on me in a bundle I thought was going die before facing the enemy. Some of the chaps have talked about transfers to the Tank Corps, well you should know all about that Dad, what do you think? They say there are better chances of promotion? Training would be at Bovington and isn't that where Rom and Billy are perhaps you can ask and see what their word on it is?

I love you all and I miss you, I hope to get leave soon. I'm sorry to disappoint you mother, maybe you can come down for the day Sunday. Send me a telegram and let me know. I hope to see you all.

Your loving son and brother, Thomas xxxxx

* * *

18th August 1942

Dear my own dearest family,

It was go good to see you all and we were so lucky to have the sun all day. It was a shame to part like we did but it was best. I must say to walk away on my own looking back down the street was the hardest thing I have ever done.

Thank you for the chocolate and ciggs, they were much enjoyed.

We have moved to Salisbury plain and the camp is the best. We are billeted in a mansion would you believe; the gardens are as good as the manor and we share a room but we all have our own space. I was sent up to Gloucester and had to drive one hundred and fifteen miles and through four counties. We are going to set up our own canteen, the officers have chipped in for us. For our meal, we have to catch the bus in to the town.

Some of the lads who also applied for transfer have heard back and have not been successful I hope I will be, thank you Dad for the advice. I'm sure I will love it if I get in. I've seen the Churchill tanks and they look a proper good bit of kit. I'm hoping I will and make you all proud.

I wish you all love and hope to see you again soon, after three months I should get seven days so hope I see you all for longer. Tell me all that is happening on the farm, in the village, and in Bridport. Have you been to the pictures Lily, there in only a small one here and I couldn't get in.

Your loving son and brother, Thomas xxxxx

CHAPTER TWENTY-SEVEN

12th October 1942

Thomas walked out, in khaki shirt with short sleeves, shorts and desert boots. His shorts came much further down his legs than the rest of the crew's did. He was lucky to have got transferred to the tank corps. He loved training as a driver in the Churchill tank. He and the four other crew had become a tight unit. Now they had travelled south, to Africa. He had never been anywhere so hot. The sun was high up in the desert sky. The landscape was desolate and he missed the hills, the streams, and the colourful landscape of Dorset. It was a suffocating furnace of heat that burned into his skin. He was used to be out working all day on the farm with his dad in hot summers; this was different, oppressive. His mother hadn't approved, of course, when he left school; he couldn't seem to do anything right for her. He'd hated sitting in the classroom on sunny afternoons. She'd argued and argued he should stay on. He wanted to be outside doing something, being active, being of use. He knew he could help Father, be of use ploughing, sowing – anything. He liked the tractor best; he'd always liked the tractor pulling the harrow. Whatever, it was better than sitting still doing nothing.

He wasn't going to sit aboard ship all day, either; he wanted to see some of the town.

The others had told him to catch up with them at a small local bar they had found. They told him to make sure that he didn't tell Sergeant and to come alone. They were going to show him the sights and sounds. Already he could hear the noise coming from the bazaar; there seemed to be the funny people everywhere with their funny-looking clothes, the smell of spices, foreign to him.

They were sitting outside, all dressed as he was with large hats down over their faces; they'd all been told this is what they should wear to keep the sun off the tops of their heads. The British Army didn't need any more of them taking to their beds with heatstroke.

'Young Tom, young, young Tom,' Billy Crabb said from above his pint. 'Glad you could join us.'

Thomas thought it wasn't his first, given the way he slurred.

'How many has he 'ad?' Tom turned to Romily and asked.

'It ain't the first, put it that way,' Romily said as, more cultured, he sipped at his.

'I'm glad you're here, Tommy lad, glad you got out. Sergeant didn't see 'e, did 'e?'

'Nah, course not; slipped out without anyone noticing.'

'Good, good, glad you got out. Now the games can begin.' Billy clicked his fingers and asked the waiter for another beer.

'I'm not sure; not a pint, maybe a half,' Thomas said. 'They don't do cider, do they?'

''Course they don't do bloody cider, Tommy,' Billy said.

'Maybe he should only have a half; he ain't a drinker like 'e be, Billy,' Romily said.

'Get on with 'e, we'll all have a beer, if that's what you can call this rat's piss they're serving.'

'It's all right, Romily, I'll have the beer,' Thomas said, wanting to fit in.

'Good, good! That's settled.'

The waiter brought out three warm beers. He put them down on the table in front of them.

'Come on, down these; we've got places to be,' Billy said.

'Where's that, Billy lad? Not the Italian lines, that's for sure,' Romily said.

'No, we ain't going there, not today.' Billy put the neck of the glass to his lips, tipped his head back and downed the beer in one.

'Oh, Billy, slow down there, slow down!' Romily said.

Thomas sipped at his beer.

'They don't call me Billy the Tank for nothing.'

'Don't think I've heard 'e called that.'

'Look, drink up; I've another place to take 'e.'

Romily looked at Thomas and nodded for them to drink up. Thomas struggled but managed to drink it down, trying to keep up with the men. Billy got up and led them through the crowds, the people, the goats tied up. They filed down narrow streets, turning left and right and turning down darker passages. Thomas tried to remember his way and keep his bearings but there was no way he could. He began to get fed up with the heat, the crowds, the smell. He could do with resting his feet. He saw animals large as shire horses and knew they were camels. He'd only ever seen them in films and they looked much scarier in the flesh.

'Where you taking us, Billy?'

'You'll love it; lovely little place, 'tis.'

'How the hell did you find it in the first place?' Romily said.

'It found me, I think, if I remember right.'

Thomas watched, surprised how quick on his feet and how straight Billy could walk, given the beers he'd been drinking.

'Not far now, not far.'

Billy turned the corner; Thomas followed on in tow, scared he might get separated from Billy and Romily with no idea how to get back to the ship.

'This is it,' Billy announced. He leaned on the wall of the daubed building that looked the same as every other. There were no tables outside. Billy walked straight through the door; Romily, then Thomas, followed.

It was dark and cool out of the sun. Billy walked in and was greeted by a woman dressed in a long gown. They got taken further down in the building, which had rugs hanging from the wall and on the floor and cushions scattered, all patterned with colours of the rainbow. Thomas liked the bright red and yellow flowered designs.

'I don't think this is a bar,' Romily said.

'No? What is it?' Thomas said. Then three girls came out and began to belly dance for them as they sat on the cushions. The girls were dressed in light-coloured dresses. After the dancing, they came and held the hands of each of the men.

'No, no, I'm not! Come on, Tom; think we should leave Billy to this.' Romily got up to walk out.

'Oh, come on, Romily! Leave the lad. He's got to lose it sometime, ain't 'e?'

'Not like this! It should be special, not in the back of some downtown dive. And you should leave too; you've Molly at home, and young Charlotte, for god's sakes,' Romily said.

'Get on! I ain't doing no harm.'

Thomas was given another drink by the host; he stayed stuck to the spot, shuffling his feet.

'I'm off back to ship, Thomas; you should come now, before.'

Thomas wanted to stay but couldn't; it wasn't right. He left Billy and went back to the ship with Romily.

* * *

Thomas was glad to be sitting outside the Churchill tank. Billy and Romily were seated with their backs propped against the big tracks. He was glad to be breathing fresh air and out of the confined space. They had suffered a breakdown; the Bedford engine had been out of action for an hour or more. They were all trying to stay cool out of the heat of the day. Thomas took a swig from his canteen to quench his unending thirst.

They'd struggled trying to clear the engine; dust had been sucked in through the fuel pump. It was easier to repair a link on the track than search for a blockage. The heat had meant they soon had to take a rest. It was so much harder fighting the German tanks; the small six pounders on the turret were no match for their armour and if they took a direct hit, that would be it.

Dust flew up on the horizon as the battle raged. Trucks raced up to the British lines to supply more ammunition, food and water. The driver of the last truck pulled over.

'You lads all right? Need anything?'

'We should be all right,' the commander shouted back. 'Maybe we could do with some water.'

'I'll see what I can bring up next trip; I've only ammunition.'

The truck drove away leaving a cloud of sand. The planes appeared and dived in to attack. The sky filled with dark menacing shadows as they darted and bombed like buzzing swallows, diving, pitching, dropping their bombs on the battlefield. The Spitfires came in for combat, driving the German planes back. A stray plane, German, moved on its own through the sky. Thomas watched as it came in low, flying straight at the truck. It dropped its deadly cargo and scored a direct hit. The truck exploded in a fireball as the ordinance went up.

The Messerschmitt looped around and came in menacingly low with machine guns firing on the other side of the tank. The crew dived for cover. The plane came back around to make a second pass. They were stranded and could make no reply. The Messerschmitt came in again lower. Thomas covered his ears. Then from the horizon a Spitfire came hurtling through the air, its machine guns rattling, close in on the tail of the Messerschmitt. The air was full of the sound of deafening machine guns. The planes fought in a dogfight: first the Spitfire on top, then reversed, taking the enemy fire. Then a second Spitfire returned and joined the fray. The Messerschmitt, hit in its engine, burst into flames and crashed to the desert in a ball of flame.

Thomas punched the sky and the crew, Billy and Romily jumped up, and they all hugged. All the while transfixed by the noise and the action in the sky, they didn't notice the truck approaching. The truck came to a stop opposite. Troops dropped down from the rear tailgate and surrounded the tank.

The German soldiers pointed their rifles.

'*Kapitulation, Kapitulation!* You surrender!' the German officer shouted.

CHAPTER TWENTY-EIGHT

4th November 1942

The bar was packed to the rafters with German officers. It was their favourite haunt and it had been like that for the last two years. Nicole flittered from table to table serving more beer. The soldiers were well behaved as long as the beer kept flowing – up to a point before they got too friendly and their hands began to wander and their eyes became too intense. The trick was to water down the beer before they got to this point. Nicole smiled at the memory of Geordie and Emma coming up with that one. She looked over to the bar and saw Geordie smile; takings were up. War was good for business.

She was amazed at the calmness of the others. Geordie, he could lead a double life, it seemed, without a second thought. Louise – who lived in Geordie's old house, in her early thirties, married to Patrice – led them like a mother hen. Patrice fighting and alive, unlike a lot of the men from the town. Serving the same table with her was Catherine: late twenties, second eldest of the Tucker clan, earnest with pursed lips, short black hair, beaky nose, quiet since she couldn't ever get a word in.

Nicole gathered up the empties, her arms full, and raced to the bar. Catherine followed behind, bumping into soldiers as she did. Edith was at the bar waiting for Geordie to fill her glasses. To her disappointment she was the shortest of the Tucker sisters; but Nicole knew she was no less brave. She was the daughter that looked most like her mother Eliza with her mousy blonde hair. With her glasses refilled, Edith spun around; Nicole dodged her but Catherine was too slow and bumped right into her sister. Glasses smashed on the flagstone floor

'*Zut alors*,' Catherine muttered under her breath.

Geordie passed her the dustpan and brush over the counter. It wasn't unusual; Geordie swore at them all for costing him money.

The Major with the scar on his forehead sat in the corner. It was worse because he had the best manners; if he was horrible or he pestered the girls she could hate him even more. Being nice to him wasn't hard; he was so polite and he tipped well. He looked hard and she knew what he was capable of. This scar-faced Major, the commander of the main garrison in Cambrai, who lived like a lord in the château.

The German headquarters were set up in the château four miles out of town between Cambrai and Albert. There was a large garrison at Cambrai, but only a small detachment in Albert; nevertheless, word had got out that Hotel de Madeleine offered the best food and beer. Nicole had scoped out the garrison on one of her early patrols: six Panzers, a couple of half-tracks, three sidecars, about fifty soldiers in total. It wasn't large but they kept the place under control.

Tonight would be the first mission she was to run. She hoped she wouldn't let anyone down and she wouldn't freeze. Louise had been training her up to take command and this time she would be leading with Edith and Emma, and Louise would be with Catherine, taking one of their strays south. It was common for them to help airmen or escaping prisoners move on to the next contact. To see what the Germans were capable of; she didn't want them to reach England. She wanted Thomas to be safe, for all of her family to be safe. She couldn't save Aubrey but she could make up for it now and they had, they had caused a lot of damage. She was proud of that, but tonight was a big step up and she felt the nervous thoughts begin to form in her mind. Would she remember everything the Irishman had taught them? Nicole pushed the thought to the back of her mind and returned the drinks to the table.

She finished at twelve; Geordie and Eliza gave the girls the nod for them to leave. She went upstairs and got changed into trousers and shirt. She pulled on her old beige coat and her beret. Emma and Edith were waiting in the kitchen. Louise and Catherine had already left, taking the airman from the hayloft. The women didn't say anything. They went out of the back door and into the stables. The stables didn't give her any nightmares any more; she had faced them; she had looked them square in the eye and overcome them. It had been hard at first. The first day back had been the worst; coming to the stables she had remembered it all. The blood, the screams and her mother and grandfather on the floor in a pool of blood, the shotgun lying on the hay. She couldn't believe that she had buried it that deep that she hadn't remembered it before. She supposed that was because her life had been so wonderful in Dorset.

She had new nightmares now, with the occupation one huge living nightmare every day. You didn't know who you could trust. There were so many factions, so many working for the Vichy government, the *gendarmes*, and even more atrocious the *Milice*: the French military police, who were vicious. Those that did it openly and those that did it surreptitiously. Then of course there were the *réseaux*; far from being unified they were split too, the Communists being the worst. Yes, the living nightmare was all too consuming to have nightmares when sleeping. At least again tonight they would get to make a difference.

She pulled the old ladder and put it up against the wall. Her hands grabbed each smooth wooden rung one after the other and she climbed into the hayloft. She crawled over the musky-smelling dusty floor and the threadbare mattress that smelled of stale sweat; it still felt warm. In the corner, the hay smelt mouldy. She pulled out the large loose stone using both hands and took out the rag-covered parcel, careful not to brush her hand against the spiders' webs. She untied the string and took out the three Webley revolvers and ammunition. They would soon need more. She folded the rag and string and put them back neatly before replacing the stone. She joined Emma and Edith in the stable cubicle. The smell of horse manure evoked memories of home.

The three women, all dressed in berets, trousers and coats, left the stables with their pistols stashed in their coat pockets. Nicole led the way out along the passage, their footsteps light on the cobbles. The half-moon shone down providing some light; but they knew their way around, and Nicole could see as well in the dark as in the day. They made their way down the cobbled back streets, careful not to be seen. She looked around to make sure they hadn't been followed. The sound of male tomcats fighting over territory filled the night.

They climbed over the town wall and entered the rear of the cemetery. It being Thursday they went to the fourth row and the grave of the old mayor. Here she found the stone covering a small hole; she picked up the rolled-up message. She read it before tearing it up. They all knew it was Geordie leaving the messages. Louise insisted they follow protocol like she learned in training. It brought it home to Nicole that she was in charge this evening; she just hoped everything went to plan. Tonight, they were to go out of town and derail the train. It was down to her to shoot the guards and she hoped she could do it. Yes, she'd shot at soldiers before; but to go on an assassination, that was different; that was planned. She was always much better when she didn't have to think, when she could just act. It was her imagination: if it had too much time to ponder, it would run away with her; she would start thinking of all the things that could go wrong. Her brain started to whirr. She tried to think good thoughts and remind herself why she was doing this.

She whispered to Edith and Emma and the women nodded their heads in agreement. They walked faster and headed back out the way they had come. The walk to the woods was quick; Nicole didn't have time to think. They had their objectives and they would have to work fast before the sun came up.

They entered the woodland from the north and followed the

old badger path. It snaked its way through, around trees, over humps, and down into dips. After twenty minutes of walking they found the spot, one that had been used before. Nicole, Edith and Emma knelt down and scrummaged at the leaves; further back, they found what they were looking for. One of the cache of supplies they had hidden. Nicole took a Sten gun and put the strap over her shoulder, picked up the fog signals, and stashed in her pocket more ammunition for the Webleys, along with the wire cutters. The sisters took Sten guns and ammunition.

The ground was damp underfoot as they made their way out of the south of the forest and headed for their target. The women whispered as they went. Least if they were causing a disturbance here, it would hopefully keep the coast clear for Louise, Catherine and the airman to get to the River Somme.

'Father says I'm not to flirt with the Germans; but you know what, I can't help myself, not when they're so tall and blonde!' Emma said as she tossed her head back.

'Emma, come on! You know they have killed so many French and English, don't you?' Edith said, shaking her head at her sister. 'They're trying to kill Patrice, Bertrand, Pierre, David – boys we knew in the town.'

'I know, I know! But it isn't their fault; not some of the young ones, is it? They're just like our French and British; they don't want to be here any more than our boys do. And – well, I still need a man in my bed! I haven't had one for so long I'm beginning to think I might freeze up.'

'Shush, you two; be quiet,' Nicole said. The path came to a stop as they came to the edge of the wood. They could see the fence at the railway crossing. Nicole knew there would be two guards in the signal box.

'I'll take the guards out. When I wave, you set the fog signals,' Nicole said. The two women nodded.

Nicole crawled up the embankment and looked up and down the line. There was no sign of trains. She would have to move quickly. She took out the wire cutters and cut the bottom two strands of fence and crawled underneath. Out of sight from the guards, she walked to the far side. The wooden staircase led up to the first floor and the signal room. Nicole took one step at a time; the noise seemed to be deafening. She neared the top and took a deep breath. Her mind flittered and she tried to quash it. She thought of home; and at least she had sent a letter with the airman. Hopefully he would make it the length of the freedom trail. The network ran all the way to the Pyrenees. In Paris, he would get the train all the way to St Girons, then he would have to walk the route through the mountains. She hoped the others they had moved had made it home.

She took out the Webley and double-checked it was loaded, then placed it in her pocket. She put her hand on the trigger of the Sten gun and held it at her hip; the Sten jammed all too often for her liking. She put her free hand on the doorknob and went to turn it. She put all thoughts of fear out of her mind and turned the brass. The door released from its catch, and she felt it free and light in her hand. No longer held, Nicole pulled gently. A small gap. She moved her feet so that the door would open, with her on the gap side. Time slowed and she held her breath. There was no reaction from inside. The sweat on her hand dripped onto the trigger. She moved her hand up and held the door, ready to fling it wide open. Could she kill them? Her shooting was good. The time out practising in the woods, Geordie helping all the girls. Taking them out in the evening when they weren't on missions. Firing at tins, bottles, targets that Geordie made. She checked that the safety was off. Turn off those thoughts, stop thinking, do it, do it, do it. She flung the door open and in one movement was inside.

CHAPTER TWENTY-NINE

The soldiers had coffee mugs in their hands, sitting at the controls. She saw the look of panic first in their eyes, then across their faces. Dropping their mugs, one soldier made for her, the other for his rifle. Nicole held the trigger, and a burst from the machine gun filled the quiet. Bullets rained into the soldiers. The first fell to the ground, screaming in agony. The second soldier grabbed his rifle and moved it to his shoulder. Nicole kept the trigger pulled; the bullets found their target and he fell to his knees, then to the floorboards. Still he reached for his gun, gasping for air. He screamed, rolling to his side; his arm went limp and he succumbed to his wounds. Nicole looked down at the pools of crimson blood on the wooden floorboards. It flowed from both their bodies. It was a job, her job. She didn't look at their faces. She turned and ran out through the door.

She whistled loudly and waved. Edith and Emma ran onto the line below from their cover and began setting the fog signals, each one three feet apart, just as they had been shown. Nicole ran down and joined them. With the explosives set, they ran back to the edge of the embankment.

'Do we wait for a train?' Emma said.

'We should. To check it works. You know how unreliable these are,' Nicole said.

Nicole could feel the tension; the adrenaline was coursing through her body. Half of the mission was complete and the hardest part for her. This was a delay they didn't need.

Nicole could feel the vibration through the ground. It must be a very long train. The noise of the train became louder as it hurtled along at high speed.

The train came roaring in. It hit the pressure switches; the explosive went off with a crack. At full speed the train careered off the mangled rails. The engine twisted in mid-air, its momentum taking it full on into the signal box. It smashed through it like it was paper. There was a huge explosion as the boiler exploded. Fire raged through the box. The engine lay on its side. The rest of the train consisted of open-topped wagons, carrying tanks, and a carriage. One after the other concertinaed, like a blacksmith's bellows under pressure. A series of explosions boomed out. Nicole covered her ears and forced herself to her feet, even though she was transfixed by the scene unfolding in front of her.

She pulled Emma and Edith with her and made for the woods. Behind her she heard shells set off, fired up into the night sky. Nicole couldn't prevent herself from stopping and looking around. The sound of shells numbed her ears. She saw soldiers pulling themselves out of the mangled wreckage. Twenty huge tanks lay on their sides. She saw a soldier get to his feet; he put down his rifle and pulled his comrades out through the smashed window.

'Nicole, come on! Come on, Nicole!' Emma said urgently.

'Yes, yes,' she said. She focused back on the job in hand. They ran to the woods.

'Quick! It won't be long before this is crawling with soldiers.' They ran back along the badger path heading for the lane. Edith came to an abrupt stop. Emma and Nicole stopped behind them.

'Can you hear that?' Edith said.

'No; my ears are still numb. I can hardly hear you,' Nicole said.

'Jerry boots, and lots,' Emma said.

She was right. Nicole looked past Edith and could see marching soldiers ahead and coming their way. They dived into the bushes and hid. There must be twelve, more than they could safely take out. They would have to wait for them to pass. She tried to hold her breath and hoped they would not be spotted. The women clung to each other. The sound of the heavy boots on the track passed.

They waited, then followed the path to the eastern edge of the wood. It would take longer but it would be better to take the longer path back to town rather than the direct route; there were bound to be more soldiers.

They soon approached the lower end of Albert. It seemed quiet. Nicole looked to see if the coast was clear. They came onto the canal path and headed for the bridge at the wharf. They kept to the edge to keep from the light of the half-moon reflecting up from the water. Soon they reached the bridge, only to see there were three soldiers keeping guard. They got to the bushes and crawled into the undergrowth. It was too close to home to take out the soldiers and it would look odd if they were to approach them. There was only one thing to do and that was to swim across and avoid the bridge altogether.

Nicole beckoned the women to follow her on the path down the canal and away from the bridge, further down out of sight of the bridge. She took her pistol and held it above her head. She dropped from the bank as quietly as she could, holding the pistol above her head. She felt the icy cold water cut through her clothes and take her breath away. With one arm held high she swam the short distance across and scrambled out on the opposite bank. She watched as Edith and Emma took turns to follow, working to cover each other as a team.

Drenched and with their teeth chattering, they made it back to the stables where they stashed their pistols away before entering the hotel. They stripped down in the kitchen and dried themselves with clean towels from the laundry. Nicole put her clothes in the laundry basket and wrapped another towel around her chest, happy to be inside and warm. She wrapped her hair in another towel.

The women chatted under their breath, excited by their

triumph. They hadn't managed anything as effective as that before. They'd blown up tracks, even several pylons, but never a loaded train. It did give Nicole a great sense of satisfaction and a real buzz. She wanted to do more. She had even been able to shoot the soldiers when she had to. The women giggled and talked excitedly as they dried their hair wrapped in towels and sat around the large table drinking hot coffee. They just needed to have Louise and Catherine return.

CHAPTER THIRTY

5th November 1942

Nicole, with bags under her eyes – which were growing deeper purple with each passing day – sighed as she thought about the day ahead. The restaurant was packed with German soldiers. Louise and Catherine were there, their mission successful too. Their path had been clear and without hiccups, the airman successfully passed on. They waited on tables all afternoon and into evening.

When he came in, the restaurant fell quiet. The scarred officer leading his men. This wasn't pleasure and the atmosphere was cold and tense. The soldiers sensed it and Nicole could see it on his face.

'*Raus, raus, ihr alle*. Out!' he ordered.

The soldiers drinking beer put their glasses down, picked up their hats and got out of his way, quick.

'*Vous, la famille: restez.*' He paced up and down through the tables. 'You are doing very well here, aren't you?' he said in French. 'I expect you want the war to continue for a long time.' He looked at Geordie. Nicole stood by Emma. Edith and Catherine stood either side of their father at the bar.

'Yes. I have to admit it's not bad for business.'

'And you must be the age, too old for now, but old enough for the last war?'

'I was there; it was no good for any of us.'

'Yes, my father also. You do a good job keeping my troops happy; it's not always easy, I know that. Some don't know how to behave. I'm sorry for their behaviour. And the way they treat your daughters sometimes.' He looked from Louise to Catherine, then finally to Nicole. His blue eyes seemed to dwell on her longer than the rest.

Nicole felt frightened. She knew what he was capable of.

'And of course, if you heard anything, anything that was of use, you would tell me, wouldn't you?'

'Yes, of course. I want you to be happy, all of you. Like you say, I'm a good businessman; I want you all to keep spending,' Geordie said.

'Yes, I see, it makes sense. That's for all of you: if there is anything… You must hear it all here, the centre of the town.'

'Not so much, not really; but I will look, and listen,' replied Geordie.

'And your daughters: they must speak to people, friends who know things.'

'You can see we are all too busy, but if there is anything…'

'Good, good; we have an understanding then. I'm always reasonable, you see. Lothar is so polite, they all say; I was brought up right.' He nodded and smiled to the girls. 'And this daughter, she is not married yet?' He pointed to Nicole. She felt herself blush and looked down at the ground.

'Her boyfriend is away, but I'm sure he was going to ask for her hand, Major.'

'You don't need to call me Major; are we not all friends now? You must call me Lothar. Although that is very observant of you.' He stood tall; his scar seemed to inflame. He put one palm inside his grey tunic.

'Look, you look after me, I look out for you all.' He paced further down as if he was on inspection. 'I'm very happy to have reached this understanding.'

Nicole hoped her face didn't give anything away. All the secrets she knew. It felt like he could read her mind. He walked up to her. The image of the dead soldiers lying on the signal room floor came into her mind.

'You are embarrassed, because I like you.'

Nicole moved her lips, but nothing came out. She mumbled

under her breath and tried to clear her throat.

'I know you can talk.'

'Yes, I'm not embarrassed; I'm quiet.'

'I don't believe that, not when you have sisters and he's your father.'

'I don't know what to talk about,' Nicole said.

'Don't worry; be quiet for now. But you will tell me if you hear any rumours, won't you?'

'Yes, sir.'

'You call me Lothar, as well.'

'Yes, Lothar.'

Lothar walked back to the bar.

'You see, last night there were some busy activities. I'm surprised you haven't heard. No?' He leant over the bar and looked at Geordie. 'Some very big explosions, from the resistance; you see we cannot tolerate.'

'No, we hadn't heard; not yet. That is terrible,' Geordie lied.

'Well, I want you to put out a message, a strong message to the town: I will come down hard. You know it's not in my nature; but like in other towns, there will be reprisals, you know. If you don't send this message I will send my own.'

'We will all send the message; you will have no need,' Geordie said.

'Good. Because I don't want to spill blood; not if I don't have to. You understand, don't you, all of you?'

Nicole nodded with the sisters and Geordie. The Major brushed down his tunic and stood up straight.

'Good, good, I'm glad we all have this understanding; and if this is the last of it, then we can all enjoy our time here together.' He smiled, looking around at Nicole, and nodded. 'Go on, open up; get everyone back in. I think this is worth celebrating.'

Nicole ran out to the square with Emma and they called the soldiers who were smoking by the wall to return. The restaurant soon filled. The Major went and sat at his normal table. Even when she went to the bar she could feel his unwanted eyes on her back.

Emma and Nicole worked their tables together, Catherine and Edith theirs, and Louise made sure to keep the officers happy. It suited Nicole. She made sure to bring the weakest beer to her table. The six soldiers seated around it had had more than enough and were getting to the point of being leery. When a soldier touched her bottom as she glided past, she thought nothing of it. It wasn't until later in the evening when they were clearing down that Emma told her she had seen the Major take the soldier outside and hit him across his face with the back of his hand. How was she ever going to deal with his advances? It made her stomach turn.

* * *

They all sat around the large table in the kitchen. It was late and Nicole was glad to rest her feet. There was no mission tonight. And she thanked the lord for that. She was far too scared after the Major's warning.

'You can have a night off, all my girls, tonight,' Geordie said, sipping at his mug of coffee. Eliza busied herself, washing down the surfaces. Nicole wondered if she ever stopped working. Her pinny was stained with food and red wine.

'We can't carry on with what we're doing, can we?' Nicole asked, looking to Louise.

'Oh, I think so; we can't let him worry us. We have too much work to do,' Louise said.

'But how can we? He's too close.'

'You let me worry about him; there's plenty I can do to divert his attention,' Geordie said. 'And you could take a leaf out of Emma's book and flirt with him a little; you all could.'

'Geordie, don't,' intervened Eliza. 'You don't have to, girls. Nicole, don't listen to him; he's old and losing his mind.' She stopped wiping down the table, stood looking at her husband and then punched him on the arm. 'You girls don't do anything you

198

don't feel comfortable with. Be pleasant; but don't lead them on, don't make them angry.'

'I'm just saying oil the wheels a little, keep everybody happy and smiling; and it doesn't do any harm to be friendly to keep the heat off,' Geordie said.

'Don't you think we should stay quiet for a little time?' Emma asked. 'It doesn't have to be for long. Nicole has a point.'

'Yes, she does; but we have the escapees; we have the drops; there is too much, and we can't stop now. We shouldn't even be talking here like this. What if the Major came back here? What if he did come looking? We should keep to the protocols,' Louise said.

'Sometimes I don't even think you're my daughter with all these rules and protocols. I was never one for them in my time,' Geordie said.

'I know; but we have to do this right! We have too much to lose, don't we?' Louise stated, standing up to make her point. 'We need to be as professional as them, don't we, if we are going to succeed.'

'All right, dear. Watch how you talk to your father,' Eliza said.

'Yes, Mother. I just mean we have to survive, and to survive we have to be better; we have to be at least as good as the Germans if not better. They would have us up against the wall and shoot us all if they knew what was going on.' Louise wandered to the sink and looked out into the darkness.

'I know we are all risking so much; but if we don't, there is no one else who can do what we can,' Geordie said.

'That's why I think we should cool off, just for a short time,' Emma said.

'I've said… Emma, are you not listening to me? We can't! There is too much to do!' Louise lost patience with her young sibling.

'Don't take it out on me, just because you haven't heard from Patrice,' Emma said.

Louise spun round from the sink and said: 'Emma, you have no idea how it feels to love someone and be separated, not knowing. You're too young; you've never committed to anyone longer than a week.'

'That's not true.' Emma looked up at the ceiling. 'There was Bertrand; and it must have been a month.'

'I'm not talking about your casual hook-ups, I'm talking about a committed, long-term relationship where you put yourself before the other person, where you would die for that person, not someone you have a quick roll in the hayloft with and forget the next day.'

'Girls, girls, please! Don't you know how it makes your mother feel, arguing between ourselves? We've a war to fight. We all want our friends and family home soon; that is why we are doing what we're doing,' Geordie said.

Emma got up and hugged Louise.

'I'm sorry, I'm sorry. I forget what I'm saying,' she said. Louise hugged her back and kissed her on the cheek.

Nicole had tears in her eyes, thinking of herself and Lily. She wanted to hug her sister and forget everything, to be home, to be together, to be as close as before.

CHAPTER THIRTY-ONE

19th December 1942

Lily was dressed in her brown cords and white shirt; Jeanie wore a green shirt and tie and a thick dark green jumper, all tucked in under her brown dungarees. Being Sunday they should have been in church. Hamilton had been helping out on the farm all week, the school having closed early because of the outbreak of scarlet fever in the village. With all the years on the farm, Lily would have thought herself more than able. But the wind was driving the rain into their faces and if they didn't get the wheat threshed and in soon it would all be ruined. At least Perry was alive. The mission had been a total disaster: all but one hundred men captured or killed, from a force of a thousand. Nothing like what the papers were saying, that the mission had been a huge success; it was an utter disaster. He had been lucky to make it back but now he felt guilty that he had and his mates hadn't.

Father looked over the huge threshing machine. He was missing Thomas. This year there were no men coming to the farm gate looking for work, not like in years gone by, when working men like Bob Pritchard would turn up year after year knowing that a good worker would be needed. Now there were no men to help; the shortage of labour was chronic all over. Father's face had changed over the war. Threshing time was always so important, but now the war agriculture committee were on his back, his face was etched with concern. Even though he tried to hide it, Lily knew he was not happy.

The Standard Ford chugged on with the thresher's belt wrapped around the spindle, stationary, the belt turning and flapping as it turned the cogs on the machine. Father atop, loading with pitchfork; the girls racing to feed him the stooks from the cart piled high with sheaves. Jeanie was sweating, her brown hair tied up, her brown dungarees dirt-stained. She was keen to help, but like all the land girls, she lacked experience. There was still half a rick left to thresh. The smell of corn was full and reminded Lily of summer. She drifted off in her mind as she pitched the sheaves over to Father.

The relief of seeing Perry return, to hold him in her arms again, to smell his deep musky aftershave: that was so intoxicating; it could make her tingle. To have his hands touch her face, to caress her and to whisper in her ear. He had been so distraught to see men cut down. He felt the guilt of being alive, of not being able to help more, of failing, when they had gone with high hopes. It went wrong from the first landing to the last; more opposition than they had ever thought, the lack of air cover, the lack of organisation, the lack of co-ordination: a horrendous shamble. It had taken weeks for him to return to anything like his old self. But slowly he was coming back to her. It was just they never got any time to be together.

She looked down into the yard as the sound of the car reached her. It was her uncle's car, the big black Rolls Royce that he'd bought after Grandfather died. Her uncle got out of the car and walked over to the thresher, leaning on his cane. He was the tallest and most imposing man in the village. His hair was still blonde when many other men's had turned to grey, even her own father's more so now. Her cousin Montague, seventeen and learning from his father, got out of the car and walked at his father's side, his curly ginger hair tossed by the wind. He was tall like his father but yet to fill out. He was gangly and awkward, she thought; he was the same as Thomas.

'I'm surprised you're not finished with this yet!' her uncle shouted.

'We would if all the men weren't fighting,' Father shouted down.

'I'm here about the rent.'

'Doing your own dirty work for once? Guess you have to, now Mr Grey has retired.'

'It was his time to go.'

'I… well, if it wasn't so unfair, so high, you could have it; you'll have to wait till I get this in.'

'How long will that take?'

'Longer if you keep interrupting.' Father stood on his pitchfork looking down, failing to hide the contempt on his face. Lily looked to her uncle and could see a wide smile on his face.

'I've mouths to feed and the welfare of my family to think about, and if I let one off, all the other farms will want the same!' her uncle shouted.

'I'm only asking we pay a fair price.'

'Look, I've put up with this for far too long. You're lax, Kingson; you're a bad farmer, you're a bad payer; your debts are mounting.'

Lily could see her father turn red. He pushed his pitchfork down into the corn, twisting the handle. She saw him bite his lip.

'Uncle,' she said, 'he's a good farmer. We are short of men, that's all.'

'Oh, she speaks! The Oxford drop-out. Montague, when you go to Oxford, be sure to finish your course. Has she told you, Kingson, you could have owned this farm, if she had finished her degree? It was all in the Will; did she ever mention that to you?'

Lily blushed. She had been going to tell them; but she didn't need the pressure, and it seemed so pointless, now. Father looked at her with a quizzical glance.

'It don't much matter, not with the war on,' Father said.

'Well, it does, because given that you are breaching about every line of the tenancy, I am giving you notice that I want you out. You don't pay on time; you don't make it work. The land looks awful.'

'You can't do that!'

'Watch me!'

'But your father promised the tenancy to me for life, in the thirties!'

'I don't care what the old man might have said to you in the thirties; I live in the present and I've no use for a lazy old timer who can't make this place pay.'

'You can't do this,' Lily said.

'You can spout all you like, young lady; you didn't finish your degree, your father hasn't kept to the tenancy, your family are going to be out of Home Farm just as soon as I get my day in court. Good day.' He spun around, followed by Montague, and they got into the car. He spun the wheels as the huge car turned around in the yard. Topsy and Turvy whinnied in the stables, looking out.

'Is it true, Lily?' Her father looked at her. 'Admiral said you could own the farm if you got your degree?'

Lily felt herself getting warm; she rubbed the nape of her neck. There hadn't been any point telling them. She hadn't wanted the pressure of her family knowing; they would probably have tried to talk her out of it. She was stupid for thinking her uncle wouldn't use it against her if he could. There were no secrets in the village; the gossip got around in the end.

'Yes; I was going to tell you. I thought what was the point if I failed, if I let you all down. And now I have. I wanted to tell you and Mother but I never felt there was a right time. I didn't want to get your hopes up; I wanted to surprise you when I did get the degree. But the war put paid to that.'

'You know, Lily, your mother and me only ever want you to be happy.'

'Can he take the farm, like he says?' Jeanie said.

'He thinks he can. The Admiral promised, didn't he? First the tenancy and then with this 'err degree business; it shows me he wanted us to farm it, don't it? Trouble is Theodore has all the power and the connections; I'm sure he's connected to the War

Ag. Him and his cronies.'

They stared over, putting the wheat through the thresher. 'I hope you didn't go to university just because of the farm, Lily. We only want you all to be happy in what you're doing.'

'I loved it there in the end; maybe not at first, but I was getting used to it, beginning to enjoy it when the war came.'

* * *

Lily rushed out and met Perry in the yard as he got out of the green army car, its red maple leaf on the door. The light was fading; there was a clear sky and this added to the chill. She didn't stop to think to put on her jersey. She thought her hair a mess and she would stink to high heaven having worked on the farm all day.

'Perry, I'm so glad you got leave.'

'I'm sorry I didn't give you more notice…'

'Don't be silly; the telegram was fine. I'm just glad you're here now.' She hugged him, feeling his warmth through the thin shirt.

'I would have written sooner, but I think they wanted to give us some time before we are posted again.'

'It doesn't matter. Come here. You've forty-eight hours?'

'Yep, only a couple of days. I'm lucky; it's more than some.' He shook the cold from his shoulders. 'I want you to come to Bournemouth for the weekend.'

'Perry, what?'

'Come to Bournemouth! I've organised a bed and breakfast. It's lovely, looking out over the sea. Just you and me. We can forget the war, forget the fighting and the drudgery. Please.'

'I can't, Perry; there is too much to do here on the farm. I would love to, but I can't leave Father, and the threshing isn't finished.'

'Lily, it will be so much fun.'

'I know, I would love to! I can't. You see, I've to make it up to father.'

'What?'

'I do; I've to pay them back.'

'What can I do to help?'

'You can't, not on your leave.'

'I'll work with you all day and take a room at the Farmer's Arms.'

'No, don't be so silly; you can stay here. We will put up a camp bed in the living-room.'

'I don't want to impose on you all.'

'Don't be silly! Mother will love having you; she's still cooking as if Thomas was here.'

After making up Perry's camp bed in the front room she turned in on her own. As she lay in bed she wished Perry was with her; if they had gone to Bournemouth, she would have been with him.

* * *

Father loved having Perry work, helping to load the thresher, carrying bags of corn and storing them in the barn; he was much stronger than Jeanie and Lily. His easy smile was never far from erupting on his face. They would sit together eating lunch in between the hard work. Just having him close made Lily's world brighter, her smile larger; her face felt as if it would crack, so happy he made her. His jokes no funnier than her brothers', but coming from him made all the difference.

The day passed, her father happy that they had finished the threshing.

'This deserves a celebration! Turn that wireless up,' Dad said.

Vera Lynn's voice crackled from the speaker:

There'll always be an England while there's a country lane,
Wherever there's a cottage small, beside a field of grain,
There'll always be an England...'

Dad fetched the parsnip wine.

'Here's to 'ee, young 'ens, to Thomas, to Nicole, and to finishing the threshing.' He ladled out the wine into glasses from the old enamel bucket.

'And thank 'e, Perry; you made all the difference.'

'Dad, what about Jeanie?'

'Oh, and 'e too, Jeanie, I forget 'e! Seems like you've been with us forever.'

'I don't mind, Mr Kingson. I know I'm not that much help.'

''Course you are dear,' Mother said. 'It's nice to have you with us; you've been more help than you know. And Dad would never have tried making that silage if it wasn't for you.'

'I guess my chemistry came in handy for something,' Jeanie said.

'Who would ever have believed them cows would love that smelly fermenting beet tops covered in black molasses?' Dad said.

'Yes, well, you love that fermenting parsnip wine, so it's not that hard to believe!' Mother said. 'Jeanie, you did well; it's not anyone who can change an old farmer's mind, is it?'

'Thank you, Connie.'

Father handed the mugs of wine out. Lily held her nose, knowing what to expect; the pungent sweet stink of wine would be far better than the taste.

'Here's to Nicole and to Thomas,' Dad said.

Lily looked at Mother; she felt her own tears in her eyes, looking at Mother weeping tears of love for Thomas. Dad, too, with a tear in his eye. Perry put his arm around her shoulder and squeezed her to his chest. She wanted Nicole and Thomas to be in the farmhouse as they had all once been. To have Mother happy, she put on a brave face; but she knew it was killing her inside.

She watched as Perry took the glass and downed the first mouthful. He winced, tried to stifle his cough.

'Ay, the first one's the best, ain't it, young 'en,' Father laughed.

'Oh, delicious, sir.'

'Call me Red or Dad. I ain't never been a sir and ain't never going to be.'

There was the drop of a letter on the mat as the last post arrived. Lily watched as Mother put the mug down and rushed to the front door, her hair trailing in her wake. She could still move fast when she thought there would be a letter from Thomas or Nicole. When she returned, her face was sullen and sombre. Still with tears in her eyes, she opened the envelope. Lily feared the worst.

'What is it?' Lily gasped for air.

'It's… it's a notice from Uncle Theodore. He's going through with it; he's taking us to court.'

Lily shuddered and her spine shivered. Her parents' faces registered the shock. To lose the farm… Living and working there was all they had ever wanted.

'I ain't giving it up,' Father said.

'We will fight him all the way,' Mother said. 'He can take us to the highest court in the land. I was there when your grandfather gave the word; I can remember the time, the place, the exact words. I'm not standing for Theodore to treat us like this. – Come on, let's have some of that wine.'

Later, when everyone else had gone to bed and Jeanie had left for her lodgings in the village, Lily helped Perry make his bed.

'Do you have to go, Perry? Can't you stay longer?'

'I just have to; you know that.'

'I do, but I miss you so much when you're not here.'

'I miss you too, Lily, more than you will ever know.'

How could she tell him she wanted him to come to her? She wanted to feel his body next to hers in bed. She wanted him to hold her, to take her, to be her first. Only it just wouldn't be right.

He turned to her and gave her a peck on the cheek, then moved his lips to hers. He kissed her so gently she thought herself begin to melt. Was it the heat of the wine or the heat of his passion? She didn't know which; she just knew she didn't want to be alone. She put her hand out to his; her fingers stretched around two of his. She walked out, pulling him gently with her as they delicately stood on the first step. They smiled at each other as they synchronised their steps. Despite all the years in the farmhouse, she'd never worked out which steps creaked; now she wished she'd been more observant. They stepped together, their bodies close; it just made her want him even more: the touch and smell of him seducing her.

They stepped as one until they reached her bedroom and she led him in.

* * *

The sun was shining through the kitchen window and Lily looked over at Perry, who was smiling. The shards of light filtered through the window catching dust particles in the air. The stove was throwing out a heat, but that wasn't the only warmth. There was a volcano erupting in her heart, the blood pumping like lava. The sun seemed brighter, the birdsong more tuneful. It was wrong for her to feel this happiness, when Nicole and Thomas would be in danger, when they could all be evicted. When there was war raging. How could she be feeling this range of emotion?

Dusty sat at her feet, hoping for scraps from the breakfast table. Hamilton was reading his comic, lying over the faded patterned rug. The smell of fresh tea wafted on the air mixing with the cooked bacon. Father walked in, followed by Mother.

'Mum, are you all right? You don't look well,' Lily said. Her mother's face looked red, white and blotchy. Her mother sneezed.

'Yes, yes, fine.'

'You don't look fine,' Lily said.

'I'll be all right.' Her voice was weak and nasal sounding. 'It's that parsnip wine; you know I don't drink. I shouldn't have had it; it never agrees with me.' She went to the yellow kitchen dresser, where Dad had stuffed all the farm paperwork. 'Lily, can you help me with these?' She pushed the plates to one side. 'You will have to do the washing up, dear,' she said, looking at Dad.

'We need to make sure we are ready for court,' she continued. 'I want to be well prepared. Theodore has so many friends in high places; if we don't put up a good case, he will walk all over us.' She sneezed.

'Are you sure you're all right?' Lily asked.

'Mrs Kingson, that isn't just the wine,' Perry said.

'Shush, will you? It's nothing; I'll throw it off in no time.'

Returning to organising the farm's paperwork, she continued

speaking. 'Look, what it looks like to me is we have to prove that your grandfather the Admiral gave his word. I'm sure he would have put it in writing. I think I know who the judge will be; and from what I've seen when I've been reporting in court, I'm sure he will give us a fair hearing. If we can just explain.'

'Is it true? Are you behind on the rent?' Lily said.

'Don't you be worrying about that,' Father said.

'But if you are, it makes a big difference,' Lily said. 'Mum?'

'It's only a couple, I think, isn't it, dear?' Mother said.

'It's three, actually,' Dad said.

'Three months? I didn't think it was that many,' Mother said.

'It's only till we get paid for the wheat,' Dad said.

'But it gives Uncle Theodore a reason, it gives him leverage,' Lily said.

CHAPTER THIRTY-TWO

5th January 1943

Lily returned to the farmhouse in her Austin 7. It was freezing. The lanes had been treacherous and she had only just made it up Snowdrop Hill, the white flowers having been in full and striking bloom. She seemed so emotional; with Perry, it seemed she could never be happier; then when he was gone it was like life itself had left her: the wanting to know he was safe, the waiting for him to return. And now there was the court case hanging over them. They could all be homeless in a matter of days.

When she got into the farmhouse she was surprised to see Father indoors, standing over the stove, trying to cook tea.

'Oh, Lily, is Mother going to be all right?' Hamilton ran to her and held her hand.

'What on earth is going on, Dad?'

'It's your mother; she's taken to her bed. That's no cold; it's more like flu.'

'Are you sure?' Lily said. She didn't wait for an answer and ran up the stairs without taking off her coat, her shoes banging on the steps, which creaked one after the other. She went straight to her mother's bedside, and looked down. Mum looked pale, with blotchy skin.

'Have you had the doctor?'

'No, Lily, it's just the flu.'

'I don't think so; you look awful.'

'Don't fuss,' Mum whispered. 'I made you go to school with worse.' She coughed, clearing her throat. 'You should leave me be. A good night's sleep and I'll be up and about.' She pulled the blanket up and around her. 'I'll be fine in the morning. I've got to be. Your father can't stand up in court; you know what he's like with public speaking.' She coughed, weak and hoarse. 'You shouldn't be in here; I don't want you catching it.'

'Don't worry about me, not now.'

Lily looked down at her mother who was wrapped tight in the blanket and slowly pulled it back.

'I don't like the look of that.' She saw the red rash on her mother's neck. 'I'm getting the doctor.'

'No, Lily, don't waste his time.'

'No, Mother, you're to listen to me for once. I don't think this is any cold or flu.'

Lily ran down the stairs as fast as she could, called to Dad and ran straight down the lane. Snow had begun to settle. There was no time. Her breath escaped her. She scrambled down the path through the valley and up across the fields, cutting out the dogleg of the lane to the doctor's; it would be quicker then faffing with the car. If it was what she feared, there was no time to delay.

It all happened in a blur. Doctor Tatlow drove Lily to Home Farm in his car. When he came downstairs from examining Connie, he said to Lily, 'We have to get your mother to the hospital; it's imperative it happens now.'

'Is it... Doctor, is it scarlet fever?' Lily asked.

'I'm afraid it is, Lily. Your mother is very ill and if we don't treat her soon, I fear this could turn very bad.'

Lily stood, shocked. She had thought her mother invincible.

'There's not time. Help me get your mother ready. We'll take her in my car.'

There was snow falling when they had Mother in the car and it was starting to settle. Lily sat in the back, Hamilton on Father's lap in the front. The doctor's eyesight was not so good in the murky gloom and with the blizzard blowing heavy into the windscreen, the wipers just coping to clear each new layer. Lily cradled her mother's face as the car slid down Snowdrop Hill, the tyres struggling for traction. The doctor fighting for control, they skidded to the bottom of the hill, bumping the opposite bank.

'I can't do this,' Doctor Tatlow said.

'Let me,' Dad said.

'Go on, Redver.' The doctor got out and he and Father swapped places. When the door opened the wind blew in soft white snow, such fun to play in, now a trap. The road was covered in the white blanket which was getting deeper by the second.

Father took the wheel, then expertly feathered the accelerator, applying the right amount of power as he did. Mother slipped into sleep. Lily caressed Mum's hair; it was moist. She worried for her. The car wheels acting like runners, her father gently guided the wheel, applying small power to assist the turn, feathering the brakes into the bends, keeping the momentum up the hill, using the banks and opposite lock to negotiate down the hills and into the bends. When they reached the outskirts of Bridport, Lily thanked God that she could see the tarmac of the road.

* * *

6th January 1943

Lily rushed to the town hall. She and Dad had stayed at Mum's bedside all night. It was touch and go, but Mother seemed to be through the worst. Dad stayed with her now. She ran in through the large door under the brick walk and up the echoing stone stairs. The magistrate sat high up, looking down on the courtroom, his face distinguished, with his full grey and black moustache. Lily would think him in his seventies with his deep craggy forehead lines. He wore a plain black gown, his hair high at the sides and bald in the middle. He had a look of power and authority, of education, of experience and control. The sort of man who was used to having his every word listened to and obeyed.

The wooden panelling made it look dark, even with the light pouring in through the tall oval windows. She sat on her own at a desk in front of the oak-panelled bar. To her right her Uncle Theodore sat at a similar desk with his tall, thin solicitor, Mr Cochrane. Lily could smell the courtroom: its taste of officialdom, of rules and regulations; something to be intimidated by. The threat of punishment for rules broken seemed to cry out from every corner.

There was no solicitor for Lily or her family. She wished her mother and father could be with her. She felt alone. The nerves flooding her body, she hoped she wouldn't sink. She tried to put out of her mind the disaster at Oxford, and she tried to gather up all the confidence she could find in her slim body. The trouble was everyone seemed so intimidating: the Justice of the Peace, Harold Rudyard; her uncle; her uncle's solicitor, Mr Cochrane. The building, the smell of fear and nerves. Then there was Auntie Elizabeth seated on the benches behind with Montague and the villagers, looking on with a fixed glare, not hiding her disdain. There were friendly faces too; Gran, for one, dressed all in black, nodded and smiled at her. The vicar, in tweed suit and his dog collar.

The Justice of the Peace started addressing the court, his voice controlled and authoritarian.

'This shouldn't take long; it's pretty clear to me, the matter of Fox versus Kingson: unpaid rent and subsequent termination of the tenancy.'

The JP finished and the clerk of the court nodded at Lily to begin the defence.

Lily stood up, pressed her pleated green dress down and said: 'Sir, we were promised the tenancy of this farm for the rest of my father's life by the Admiral, my grandfather, before he passed.' Her voice was calm and clear, if a little quiet. She tried to speak louder.

'He promised it to us in 1930 and as my father is alive; we see no reason why that promise should be broken.' Lily fiddled with the paper on the desk in front of her; she tried to summon up her confidence. She was doing this for her family. There was no option; she had to be confident. Their livelihood depended on her.

'I am of the understanding that you are three months behind in your rent and you don't have proof that the promise was ever made.'

Lily coughed and cleared her throat. She tried to push her shoulders back and not to slump. She stood tall and looked the magistrate in the eye.

'It's true, but there is a war on. As soon as the Ministry of Food pay us for the corn…'

'I'm sorry; you make a good point, but the fact that you are behind means that your landlord has every right to serve you with the eviction notice.' He scratched his beard. 'We need good farmers who can pay their rent on time, and produce food for the war effort. If I was to overlook this it would set a precedent that could lead to anarchy. Without full payment and proof of the lifetime tenancy I'm afraid that I can't look on this kindly.'

'I'll pay it,' a voice called out from the room.

Lily looked. The voice was familiar. A voice she heard on a regular basis, yet she couldn't place it. She looked over her shoulder. It was Vicar Wrixon. Her jaw dropped.

'I'll pay it for them; they can pay me back.' The vicar stood in his suit; his voice was loud and confident as if he was talking in church.

'This is very irregular. I'm not sure I can authorise this,' the magistrate said.

'Does it matter who pays, as long as they get it?' The vicar walked down the centre of the court approaching the bar. 'Redver has done more for this country than you will ever know. He is one of the men who came back from the Great War, who gave his everything, like others are now doing, He has a son and daughter who are away. This is no way to treat our heroes who fought so that we could live our lives as we want. It is about time people woke up, looked around and valued these ordinary men who are heroes.'

'He was no hero; he did nothing, nothing compared to what my friends did!' Theodore shouted. 'I want him out, whether he's paid or not. I'm fed up with him and his family. They're a nuisance;

poor farmers and useless to me. They will only be behind again. I want that land back and I have every right to have it.' Theodore looked over, his face full of disdain. 'I'm sure the Ministry would agree we need efficient farmers.'

'I'm to agree with the plaintiff,' the magistrate said.

'But sir, we had that promise. Does the Admiral's promise count for nothing?' Lily said.

'It does. Look, I'm sorry. You need to show me something in writing; otherwise it means I can only make one judgement. It is with regret that...'

'Harold, please.' Lily looked around. It was her grandmother, standing frail in the aisle, now approaching along with the vicar.

'Mrs Fox, it's so nice to see you; but this is not the time. We... I have a way of doing things.'

'Yes, yes, I know; but this is important. Look, there is proof. I know my husband was nothing if not meticulous. I can speak for him. You can take my word, can't you?' She approached the bar, walking slowly, raising her tone. Lily felt goosebumps on her arm.

'I can take your word, Mrs Fox, but I'm ever so sorry: the court can't. It has to be written; it has to be in writing. You do understand, don't you?' He nodded at her.

'Well, the least you can do is give us time,' Grandmother replied, standing by the bar with Vicar Wrixon. Lily looked on, holding her breath.

'I've to finish this case; I've a busy agenda.'

'For an old friend, surely you can give me till the end of the day.'

'Please, sir, these are good people, good farmers; they deserve every chance,' Vicar Wrixon said.

'Well, this is out of the ordinary for something so mundane, but as it's you, Mrs Fox, I will give you until the end of the day. We need the written proof; and Vicar, I take it you will still be happy to pay.'

'Yes; you can take my word, can't you?'

'Well, yes, of course. All right, Miss Kingson, you have until five; not a second late, mind.'

* * *

They went into the study. Her grandmother showed her the big cabinet where Admiral stored all his documents. It was made of oak like all the furniture and stood as tall as Lily. It looked huge; wherever was she to begin? They had less than an hour until the magistrate's deadline. The strong smell of tobacco hung in the study. The large grandfather clock clicked out the seconds.

'You start from the back; they should be in date order. Don't worry, I'm sure you won't have to go through all the papers. Admiral was nothing if not efficient, dear.' Her grandmother looked on. 'I'll start with his desk.'

Lily tried the first drawer of the tall wooden cabinet. 'It's locked, Grandma.' She felt her stomach sink. She couldn't help but think about that morning and how little time they had left.

'Let me see; the key should be here.' Gran opened the top drawer of the large oak desk. 'No, nothing.'

Lily waited impatiently as Gran checked the second drawer; she moved some papers.

'Yes, yes, it's here; I have it.'

She handed the key to Lily who placed it into the lock of the large cabinet. It opened.

The smell of old paper greeted her, in the organised file. But as Gran had said, they were in date order. She searched for 1930 and found it halfway back. There were hundreds of sheets; she grabbed them all out.

Gran cleared the desk and Lily put them down.

'Dorothy, Dorothy!' Gran shouted and rang the bell. Dorothy came running in and she began to help. The three women took a wad each and began sifting through them.

'What are we looking for?' Dorothy asked.

'Anything that confirms that we are to have the tenancy of Home Farm,' Lily said, pushing her hair behind her ear. 'Anything at all that can give us proof.'

217

'There is sure to be something here, I know it, Lily; there will be, you have to trust me,' Gran said.

Lily hoped with all her heart that they could find something that would be good enough for the judge. That there would be evidence that they could have the tenancy on the farm. That they didn't have to leave their home, that they could carry on farming and they could for once in their small lives beat her Uncle Theodore. The grandfather clock showed twenty to five.

Lily searched, trying to read the handwriting, trying to see something official. There were tenancies for other farms but nothing to show for Home Farm. All three of them scoured and Lily hoped and prayed they would find it soon; after all, Gran seemed so sure and trusting that there would be something for them to find. Even if Grandfather had made a record, what if Theodore had gone through the file before them? What if he had found it and destroyed it? What if there was no record? They would have been wasting everybody's time. The grandfather clock ticked on; it sounded louder and louder. It was all Lily could hear. She was concentrating so hard she couldn't make conversation. She read and read, paper after paper; and then to her surprise she began reading… This was it! This was the one, the agreement. She doubted herself, thinking it was wishful thinking. At last there was hope! The second read through confirmed it. This was their salvation. The judge wouldn't be able to refute this; even Theodore would not be able to argue against this.

She read it a third time to make sure. It was true; it was all there, all that her father and mother had said was true. The Admiral had promised them the tenancy on the farm for the rest of her father's life. She read it again just to make sure. If only the war hadn't happened, she would have been the owner; they wouldn't have had to answer to Theodore, or go to court, or pay rent; it would all have been theirs.

'I've got it, I've got it!' She held the papers up. 'Come on, let's go.'

'You go, dear; I'll get Spencer to bring me in.'

She drove as fast as she dared in her Austin. She made the courtroom with five minutes to spare and handed the papers to the clerk. This was it; at least now they would be able to farm the land and live in the family home. She would help with the rent and she would help more on the farm and so would Hamilton. They would be able to live without Theodore's threat.

She sat down, relieved that she would be able to listen to the magistrate's verdict happy that she had done her bit to keep the family where they wanted to be. If only the war could be solved in such a way. If only Perry could stay with her.

'Miss Kingson, you make a good case and I have listened to the arguments.' He shuffled the paper and looked at the tenancy. 'Yes, the agreement is here. But his beneficiaries: they have rights too and it's very serious when you don't pay him what you owe. You do understand that. I am heartened to see that your spirits have not been damaged by the war and I commend your father for doing his duty. There are many farmers who have not and I have sat on many of those cases, too.'

He paused and took a deep breath before continuing. 'Quite extraordinary; I have never known anything like it. There is proof that they have their rights. The rent arrears are to be paid; therefore I am to find in favour of the Kingsons.'

Lily looked over at her uncle's sour face. It looked as though he'd been stung by a thousand wasps.

CHAPTER THIRTY-THREE

7th January 1943

Lily put the fruitcake down in the middle of the kitchen table. She cut four pieces. The smell of cooked cake filled the kitchen. It was a shame Mother hadn't been home. The house had been fumigated. Hamilton didn't show any signs, but the school had been closed as infection was spreading through the children. Mother had looked more like herself, but she wouldn't be coming home to recover; she was going to stay with relations in Southampton to recuperate. Lily would be spread thin, working at Gundry's, going out on the searchlights, helping feed Hamilton and Father, helping where she could on the farm.

Father beamed at her. They were all relieved Mum was on the mend, and even if she wasn't at home at least she was recovering. Hamilton tucked into his slice with gusto. Dusty looked up and Lily threw her a piece. Jeanie shook her head.

'You an' that old dog, Lily; spoilt she is.' Jeanie shook her head. She seemed to love her life on the farm: so different from studying or working at her father's greengrocers.

The rain beat down on the windows, a winter storm; raindrops seemed to bounce off the yard. Father got up, having only popped in to dry off and have some cake to celebrate their day in court. It would only have been better if Perry was on leave. Lily would go and help Father later. She was still tired from the night on patrol; it was far more boring now that there were fewer German aircraft to worry about. She hoped it would all be over soon. Father put on his long coat, hobnailed boots and his greasy brown cap. Hamilton went with him, glad that school was closed, dressed in shorts, a macintosh, wellington boots and with his gas mask box hanging from his neck to his knees.

Lily made quick work of putting the cake away, sealed in the tin with the Snow White and Seven Dwarfs lid. She looked at the letter from Perry and hoped he would visit soon. He was stationed on the Isle of Wight: too far for her to visit in a day, and too far for him too unless he could get a week away. She would make sure she wrote to him that night. She pulled on her coat; then she heard Father call urgently from the yard. She put on her wellingtons over her brown dungarees. She rushed outside; and what she saw made her jaw sag.

Old Topsy, her father's favourite shire. She must have been nearing twenty. She had collapsed on the cobbled yard, half in, half out of the stable, having slipped on the yard floor. Topsy's head turned in on her side, snuggled to her shoulder. If she could have talked, Lily thought she would have been saying, 'Leave me be.' Lily didn't need to be told twice; she joined her father at Topsy's flank. They worked together with Jeanie and Hamilton to try and push the horse to her feet. Lily pushed the old mare as hard as she could in unison with her father and friend as the rain poured down. She gritted her teeth and tried to push old Topsy to her feet. The shire was not helping herself; she didn't budge an inch.

Lily felt the rain soak through her coat and reach her skin. She pushed her damp hair from her eyes. The four of them paused to catch their breath, then tried again and again; still Topsy didn't get to her feet. Father nodded for them to stop. He went and fetched the large rope and thick chain. Jeanie jumped on the green Ford and backed it up. Lily rubbed Topsy's ears and the back of her neck as she had done as a child. Topsy didn't move her head. Lily knew then it was her last day.

Jeanie backed up and Father tied the chains and rope around the fetlocks. Jeanie jumped down, the *put-put-put* of the tractor's engine hardly heard above the pounding rain. Father drove forward, pulling Topsy from the door. Turvy, Flotsam and Jestam, inquisitive, stepped around Topsy: their old matriarch fallen. They were not keen to leave of their own accord. Lily encouraged them and called them out. She herded them through the gate and into the marsh pasture. She heard the noise of the shotgun. She closed the gate behind her and returned to the yard. She saw Father standing over Topsy, his face set in a grimace. Mud, sweat, tears and rain mixed and ran down his cheeks. She watched as he wiped them away with the back of his hand.

As he did so, Mr Milton, the Ministry man, walked into the yard; he was back. Did he have to be here, today of all days? He was dressed in smart coat, trilby and black shoes and he tiptoed around the muddy puddles.

'Mr Kingson!' Mr Milton called as he wandered in, trying to avoid more pools of dirty rainwater. He didn't remove his hat. He was thin and short and his eyes seemed ferret-like: small, broody, darting from side to side. 'Mr Kingson!' He called louder, still not removing his hat.

'Ay, tha's what they call me, Mr Milton.' Her father rested the shotgun up against the wall. 'I'm a bit busy at this time. If 'e wants to do another survey, you can bugger off.'

'There is no need for profanity, Mr Kingson. Will you stop and listen to me!' Her father was heading to the parlour. 'It's important you stop.'

Lily felt rain penetrate the gap between her coat and neck. It was cold and ran down her back, making her shiver. Her father stopped and turned around.

'It ain't the best day for 'ee to be here.'

'Look, it's never the best day, not with this war on, and I have ten farms I have to get around, so the sooner you stop and talk, the sooner we can both get on with what we need to do.' He walked after Father. 'I'm doing my job, just the same as you are.'

Father looked around. His eyes were focussed on the short thin man. Lily came over.

'Can't you come another day? It's not convenient,' Lily said.

'It's convenient for me. And who are you?'

'I'm his daughter. It's not the best day.'

'I'm sorry, dear, but we don't come at your convenience, do we; we come when we can. Now don't you have somewhere you should be?' he snarled at her.

'Look, there is no need to be rude, is there?'

'That's not rude, dear; I've a job to do and I don't have time for this discussion.'

Lily couldn't abide the short rude man with his hat pulled down over his forehead and his beady eyes looking out, his snarling tone.

'I've my survey to do. You can come with me, Mr Kingson, or I will go through it with you after.'

'Lily, you go on to work.' She didn't want to leave.

* * *

When she got home, Father was in from the cowshed. Hamilton was upstairs. She got the kettle on. Father's head was in his hands, his elbows on the table, his face taut with strain. She wanted to ask what had happened after she'd left. Father shuffled the papers in front of him. He moved one page behind the other and then back again, looking at the report that Mr Milton had left. Father shook his head as he read the first page again.

'Gave me a bloody C grade. A C on his bloody survey and he only wants us to plough up Marsh Field, don't 'e, the silly bugger.' Father shook his head from side to side, deliberately. 'He ain't no idea, has he; how can he? It needs bloody draining before we can touch it. That field ain't no good for nothing; didn't he see the reeds and how boggy it is down by the stream? Blimey, today of all days; this ain't what I needed.'

'I know, Dad. Do you have to do it? Can't we do something else?'

'There ain't no way I can grow wheat in that field. It just ain't right for it. Pasture is all that is good for.' Propped up on his elbows, Dad rested his face in his hands, staring down at the paperwork. 'And I don't have your mother with me, to even help.'

'I can help. And Jeanie and Hamilton; we can cope,' Lily said as she peeled potatoes at the sink, looking out at the yard.

'Who the hell does he think he is coming 'err and telling me what I has to plant where and when?' He chewed on his lip and scratched his head. Lily went and stood by his shoulder and looked down at the paper. It was official, signed off by the Ministry.

'I ain't going to do it; it will cost thousands. We can't afford that! There is no money in it.'

'Can't they help, Dad, with money or machinery?'

'He said not; 'e said there was plenty in the same boat, that it's for the war effort. That there was no money, there was no help. 'E said it's down to me and if I don't then he will put someone in who does.' Dad pushed his hand through his thin hair. She thought it looked much greyer in the low light. He rubbed his hand down the side of his nose and sighed. 'They won't get no wheat out of that boggy old pasture, mark my words; even if I 'ad the money to drain that marsh, it would never be worth it.'

'But Dad, if you don't, he's said he will put someone in who will. He can't do that, can he?' She touched him on his shoulder, holding her mug of tea.

'They can and they will. The War Ag have all the power, they can do whatever they think is right.'

'That's not right! We won in court. We beat Theodore; we have the right to the tenancy.'

'The War Ag have been give the power to do whatever they want. And he's behind it, ain't 'e? This has Theodore Fox written all over it.'

'But we can go back to court! We did it once; we can do it again, can't we?'

'I don't think so. The War Ag committees have even more power than the court now, Lily; what they says goes.'

'That's not fair. We should fight them, appeal against this.'

'He said we were a badly run farm, that it was a mess; it was poor and the yields should be much higher.'

'But Dad, we've just won the tenancy. What happens if he goes through with it? What if he keeps his promise?'

'I don't know. Theodore Fox wants us out one way or another, regardless that we beat him in court.'

* * *

5th February 1943

The wind blew the mixture of straw, hay and dust into her face as she ran across the yard. The parked car was big, black and important looking; she knew the owner. Lily went to the gate and climbed it, wearing her wellingtons over the brown dungarees.

It wasn't going to be good news, that was for sure; it never seemed to be where the War Ag was concerned. Their demands were exacting. When she came to the brow of the hill, they were standing in the hollow. Lily walked through the unwieldy marsh foxtail and the abundant rye and couch grass.

She dodged the wide patch of common rushes standing two feet tall, slowed to a quick walk and made her way to Father and Mr Milton. The morning had been cold to start, but as the sun rose over Ashcombe Beacon, it was beginning to warm the winter air. The fresh breeze carried with it the last scent of morning frost.

Dad and Mr Milton were standing pointing at the land above the stream.

'You can argue all you like, Mr Kingson; I've given you fair warning: this land is to be drained, ploughed and sewn with wheat. I've my targets to reach…'

'I've told 'e, it can't be done; I've not the money, the labour or the time. And the wheat should have been sown in the autumn like we always do.'

'Mr Kingson. It can be sown in spring; it's been done. And if you don't do it, I'll just get a capable farmer in who can.'

'That's not fair,' Lily said. 'This is our farm; the court said so.'

'Well, we are higher than any court; don't you know there is a war on?' Mr Milton said.

'Wheat won't be worth having from here, I tell 'e, man. I know

225

only too well there's a war on: my son's fighting in it and my daughter too. This is ours, it's our livelihood, it's our home, our way of life.'

'I don't like doing this; it's the only way. It has to be done. We need more wheat, we need to have sufficient; with convoys being destroyed, we need this wheat like never before.'

'What about flax?' Lily said looking at Mr Milton. 'I see the orders all the time in Gundry's. They can't get enough and it used to be farmed around Bridport.'

'I guess that would work better than wheat,' Father said.

'Would you be happy with that, Mr Milton?' Lily asked.

'I don't know,' Mr Milton said.

'It would help the war effort; you can't argue against that,' Lily said.

'It sure would give a better crop than wheat. You only had to look at all the couch grass in them new fields last year,' Dad said.

'I suppose… I can't argue. It's needed; I could give you the concession to grow flax.' Mr Milton paused and pulled out his diary. 'You've still got to get on with it. I have to tell you if you ain't got flax sown by the twenty-second of March, you will be out, do you understand that? The twenty-second of March. On the next visit if I don't see the signs of flax, you will be out.'

'What about help: money, labour, machinery?' Lily said.

'You've got that land, girl; I've compromised on the crop. You've a tractor; what more can I do? You're not big enough for anything else. You've had the time. It's not my fault you've been sitting on your hands when you could already have made a start.'

* * *

Lily stood with her father. They looked down over the stream. She could see her father thinking; he stood with his cap held in his hand. He was missing Mother who was still in Southampton recuperating. He didn't have her to talk to, to mull things over, to work out how they were going to get out of this mess. Lily could sympathise; not having Perry with her at this time made it feel like she was only half a person, whereas when her soulmate was with her she felt whole. Is this how Father and Mother felt about each other?

'It will take a lot of clay pipe; not hundreds of feet, thousands. We would need a channel down both valley sides –' he pointed with his cap '– coming to the stream, then many spurs off the two main drains.'

'Like a herringbone pattern?' Lily asked.

'Exactly, girl, that's what's needed.' He shook his head. 'It would take months, even if we did have the money.'

* * *

Lily stood at the kitchen sink, peeling onions. It seemed she was attached to this as much as she was the farm, keeping Father and Hamilton fed. Hamilton helped where he could but he was missing Mother as much as they all were. There was no chance she would be back before the weather got warmer. At least with her cousin she would be well looked after, as her cooking was the best. They'd managed to fit in a visit, seeing the trams and the city. Lily was glad to get back from the busy port bustling with cargo, with men and ammunition. Seeing the large ships in the harbour, ships like Thomas would have been on. They all hoped and prayed they would hear from him soon, and hear from Nicole. To have lost touch with both of them – the not knowing was the worst.

Lily tried to shut it out of her mind. Now she needed to work out how she was going to keep this farm. It was good to have Jeanie with them; what she lacked in experience she made up for in enthusiasm and effort and brains. Father was all but resigned to losing it; the toll of Thomas, Nicole, and now Mother away was eating at him from the inside. She knew it; he wouldn't admit it, though. He was retreating into his shell, keeping the farm ticking over; he was hiding it from her. Everything she had ever known as a child seemed to be falling apart. The house empty, the atmosphere cold. What could she do? Who could help?

Lily put the potato peeler down, grabbed her long coat and

went for a walk. She walked down past the Farmer's Arms, taking the short cut across the fields, not sure where she was heading, just wanting to clear her head, to try and work things out. What could she do to help Father, to help her family, to get things back to how they had once been? If only Perry could be here to help her; he always made her feel better. She walked down to the river and watched as it carried on its way, with no hindrance; there was always flow.

She took the path to the church and found the vicar in the vestry. She knocked on the door, and when he answered she walked in.

'Miss Kingson! What a pleasure to see you. Such a shame you had to leave Oxford. I'm sure they will welcome you back when this is all over.' He got up. 'Why don't we take a walk? It's such a nice morning. It's not often we get a chance to talk; I miss our little Latin sessions.'

'I miss Oxford, and I never thought I would say that.'

'It is a truly special place. I think they were the best days of my life. You must return if you get the chance.'

'I will.' They walked out of the church together and took the path back down to the river.

'You know, it gave me so much pleasure to see you at Oxford. You know I'm sorry that I stood in your mother's way at the school; she was a fine mistress, but rules are rules and when she married I just couldn't allow it.'

'That's all in the past. I wanted to thank you so much for helping with the rent.'

'I meant every word: your father is a hero; and your brother too; all the men who are doing their duty, and you too.'

'It was nothing, really; we all do what we can.'

'You make me very proud; to think one of the girls in the village made it all the way to Oxford. You've done well, Lily.' He smiled at her.

'It was nothing. I would never have gone if it wasn't for

Grandfather.'

'You should be proud; he would have been.'

'Vicar, can I ask you…'

'Why, what is it?'

'We've been told by the War Ag we have to drain and plough Marsh Field; we need to put in thousands of feet of pipe.'

'How stupid.'

'Could I use my trust fund to pay for the drainage?'

'I'm sorry; you have done so well, but there are rules, Lily. That trust fund is for your education.'

'But Vicar, it's for our home. What if I never make it back to Oxford?'

'I'm sorry, Lily, it just can't be used for that.'

'Please, Vicar, it's our only hope. And I know we could get a good price for the flax; Gundry's are desperate for it to make all their orders.'

'There is just no way I can let you dip into the trust fund. – I've known your father and mother all their lives, and their mother and father. And I believe in you. I don't do this lightly; I have faith: I will invest the money.'

CHAPTER THIRTY-FOUR

5th February 1943

The night had been very cold and the thin blanket gave no respite so Thomas huddled with Romily and Billy, glad to share their heat. Dust flew up from the carriage floor as the train rattled and creaked. It was midday and the stench of human waste was sickening and the heat suffocating. The abundance of flies annoyed him. He didn't know where the train was or where it was heading, but they were on the move from the last prison camp. He sat on the floor with his back against the wooden side. In one corner prisoners played draughts with stones on a sketched board on the floor. His stomach roared with hunger and gnawed at him, feeling like it was eating itself. He sat with his knees folded to his chest, his arms resting on top. When hadn't he been a prisoner? It felt like a lifetime. He couldn't remember straight. His head ached, his back ached, his legs ached and his throat ached.

'Drink this, young 'en.' Billy passed him his canteen.

'No, Billy.' He put his hand up.

'You need it.' Billy forced it into his hands.

Thomas took it at the third time of asking. He put it to his lips and took a swig back. The water was warm and tasted of dirt, earth and flies. Briefly, it was the best thing he had ever drunk. He took a second swig and handed it back to Billy. He could feel the warm liquid trickle down his parched throat like rain down a dried-out river bed and fall to the empty cavern. The next second he ached for more. His thirst unquenched, his hunger raw. If only they could catch another rat, like yesterday. It was Satan's inferno; he was in hell.

The *thud, thud, thud* of the large wheels on the tracks pierced his head. He flittered in and out of sleep and his dreams came and went. He stroked his stomach and hoped the diarrhoea would not come again. The stink in the carriage was from two dead men. The living's mess festered in the corner; flies, fleas and bugs flew and crawled all over. When the carriage stopped the guards came in and took away the two dead bodies. Thomas didn't know their names, but they were British and they had died in the night. He hid his face behind his palms and could not look as the Germans carried the bodies out and threw them down by the side of the track.

'We bury.' Romily stood up, pointing at the desert ground, his shoulders pushed back, his ribs showing through his open shirt. 'Let us,' he pleaded.

'*Keine Zeit,*' the closest guard shouted, jumping up into the carriage, pointing, prodding men with his rifle. '*Raus!* Line up!' He shoved the first prisoner out of the carriage and down into the midday heat.

The sun glared down and Thomas's hands trembled as he put them up to shield his eyes. He stumbled. The officer walked down the line. He tore off bread as he went and threw it into the sand. Thomas watched as prisoners dived and fought over the tiny morsels. The officer reached them. Thomas prayed for food. The officer smiled. Thomas thought he enjoyed his power. He tore off a chunk of bread and threw it. Romily reacted first. Thomas had no energy and watched as soldiers dived on top of Romily, all fighting for the scrap. There was a huge scrum.

The guards ordered the men back onto the train. The dead bodies lay on the ground, awaiting the vultures. Inside the bare carriage, the smell was rancid but the shade a relief. Thomas returned to his position and propped himself between Romily and Billy. Romily opened his palm and showed the morsel of stale and mouldy bread. He tore at it and broke it into three pieces, handing one to Thomas and one to Billy. Thomas put it in his mouth. It tasted bad, like decayed fungus. He retched. He stopped himself from vomiting and forced the bread down. He folded his arms over his stomach, hoping the aching would stop, hoping he would keep the food down.

The monotony of the train began, the *thud, thud, thud*; the vibrations rattled the carriage. He'd once loved the sound of the steam engine; now, he hated it. There were all kinds of noises from the prisoners but none of them were of conversation. If he wasn't dead and in hell, this wooden box could soon be his coffin.

* * *

'Wake up, Tommy lad, wake up.' Romily poked him in the rib. 'It's stopping.'

They were made to march from the railway siding. There was no shade and the sun shone down without mercy. He could hardly lift one leg after the other. His head slumped. His body sweated out what moisture he had. He hoped the march would end soon; his feet were blistered, his socks damp. His captors showed no mercy. They shouted, ordered and whipped. He couldn't muster his energy. He knew he should keep going. He lifted his foot and put it down. It took all of his concentration. He sagged; his head felt like a heavy bag of wheat and his chin met his chest. He fell to his knees and before the guards could whip him, Romily put his shoulder under his; Billy did the same. They hobbled on together, limping in the long column of men. Thomas hoped with all his heart that the pain, the marching, the emptiness would all end. The smell of sand, sweat and the dirt of human life assailed him. He stumbled, and Romily and Billy propped him higher; he was hardly walking himself as his friends kept his feet above the dust. When he didn't think it could get any worse, the wind whipped itself into a frenzy, and the sand came into their faces like nine inch nails. The march continued for hours.

When he woke in the morning, he couldn't remember having stopped. After parade and some bread for breakfast, they were allowed to sleep. He slumped on the prison camp bed of the hut. This was luxury compared to the train. Days passed. He recovered a little. Then they marched to the boats. The harbour smelled like West Bay, but it was full of large ships. They were herded on and stuck in the hold. It was dark black and stank of tar and oil.

* * *

It felt like a spring day in Dorset. The nights were warmer and the days cooler. It was a relief to Thomas. They were on a different train; there was a new beat over the sleepers. When they had landed at the port it was hot, but a different kind of heat. The stone walls of the harbour and the buildings looked different. It wasn't home; Thomas knew that, but it was no longer the desert. There were snow-capped mountains in the distance. More educated men than him said this was Italy. It didn't look like Dorset and it didn't feel like home.

Every day now seemed to be cooler than the last. It was bearable; but the scraps of bread the Germans fed them tasted of sawdust. He was used to the pain of hunger. More men died, more than he could count on his hands. He was accustomed to the smell of death. They kept to their corner, him, Romily and Billy, surviving. When they could muster energy, they worked together, saving the odd breadcrumb from the black bread. They laid up traps made from wire pulled from the carriage. They hunted rats, mice, spiders and insects like they were manna from heaven. This sustained them until the rats became scarce. There was more water now and there were fewer flies in his face.

Light flittered through the wooden slats of the train as it continued on, to the monotonous beat, yet if he could find the rhythm and time his breathing he could doze off and think of better times.

He woke with a start. At first, he thought himself waking up at home, with the sun creeping through the window and the sound of lambs bleating in the pasture. It dawned on him that it was men crying. He was still in his living nightmare. He shut his eyes and tried to blank out the sound. He couldn't and sleep would not return and rescue him. Billy and Romily were in the corner with

233

their backs turned. They were being furtive. Thomas crawled along the floorboards, scraping his knees. The train started to pull uphill; gravity pushed him into resting soldiers who called him out. He clambered over legs and arms and struggled to Billy and Romily. He found them ripping and tearing at the loose plank on the carriage side. He joined in. They had thin sharp stones, and shards of wood. The board was loose; they got it off in one piece. Thomas could see that if they removed the second row, there would be enough room for them to squeeze through. They worked at it together. They needed it off in one piece and they would need to get it done before they stopped again.

It took them more than an hour to loosen the half dozen nails holding the plank in place. Each time Thomas thought it would come off, they would see one more nail; always one more nail. At home and full of energy they would have ripped it off in no time. Now every effort seemed to drain him of all his life. In time, using the other plank as a lever, they pried it off, with a satisfying crack. There was now a rectangular window of light pouring in. They could see fields, rivers, bridges and buildings all pass by. When should they go? Romily insisted Thomas go first and Billy agreed. Romily argued over who should be last. They both said the other should go first. In the end, they picked dried grass from the floorboards and picked straws. Romily won; he was to go second; Billy got what he wanted and would be the last of the friends to escape.

Thomas looked out, seeing the countryside pass by in a flash as the carriage bounced over the sleepers. Other prisoners, alerted by the light, took an interest.

A burly Scottish prisoner who fought for every scrap of bread stumbled over and said: 'Ay, lads, what 'ave 'e 'err then?' He was tall and burly with a moustache and beard, his clothes soiled. Thomas cowered up against the corner. Billy stood up tall, his head coming to the Scot's shoulder. It would have been heavyweight against middleweight before the war; now it was more lightweight against flyweight.

'You can shove off back to your dark corner and let us be, Jock,' Billy said.

'Shut up, ye fucking skinny shit!' The Scot shoved Billy hard in the chest and sent him sprawling into the carriage wall. 'Them mutton fists of yours ain't no match for I, is ya.' The Scotsman had a deep scar running from the corner of his mouth to his ear. His eyes looked hard and showed no sign of kindness.

'There's no need for all this!' Romily stood up; he stammered, 'We… we… we are all in this together; we're on the same side, remember?' They would need to get out before the next stop and away from town, away from people, away from soldiers.

'Ay, that's true laddie; but I'm the one getting out of 'err first.' He looked down at Romily. 'Ain't that the thing.'

The prisoners murmured in their groups. The light seemed to have energised them. Given them a ray of hope.

The train rattled on. Billy got to his feet. Thomas could see the colour was rising in Billy's cheeks.

'We made that gap; we are going out first. Our mate here, he's going first; then Rom, then me. We don't care who follows after that.' Billy rolled his shoulders and pushed his chest forward. Thomas looked as he clenched each fist in turn.

The train began to slow. It couldn't be; not already. It was pulling for a stop, Thomas thought. He looked at the burly Scot who was facing off again with Billy. He looked at the gap. There were rolling fields of green. He went for it with his arms outstretched in front of him, as if he was going to dive into the River Brit. There was no take-off; just two burly hands grabbing him, pulling him back, flinging him; he landed on his elbows and side. Thomas struggled to look round. As he did, he watched as the Scot first pushed at Billy, then dived forward and out through the gap. As he did so the countryside changed from rolling hills to blue sky and the sound of the train over sleepers changed to an echo. Thomas got to his feet and looked out. The Scot had jumped out just as the train came onto a bridge over a high ravine, the blue sky replacing the green pasture. The Scot had gone right over the edge; there was no way he could survive that. Thomas counted his blessings and crossed his heart.

The train came off the bridge. Billy nodded. Thomas poked his head out and checked up the line; they were in fields of pasture. He took a deep breath and dived out of the gap. This time he glided through the air. He landed awkwardly on his elbow. The pain was shocking and he forgot his hunger. He rolled over and over, laughing, clutching his elbow. The smell of sweet spring flowers reminded him of home. He felt more alive than he had since capture. The sun was hot but it was not oppressive. The air was fresh and clean and he was free; he felt relieved. He'd survived. He should find the others. He kept to the bank, following the track. He couldn't run, but he walked as fast as he could manage. He could see the white tentacles of smoke from the engine rise high in the sky. The train was picking up speed and moving into the distance. He was concerned for his friends. How far would they be up the line? He didn't want to be on his own.

Gradually the euphoria of freedom faded and new worries took hold. What if Romily and Billy hadn't made it out? What if he couldn't find them? He was in the middle of god knows where. He dodged over a fallen tree blocking his path, keeping out of the sun where he could. The path he followed soon led him from the track and into the fields. He didn't want to be far from the track. He didn't want to miss the others by veering too far off course.

CHAPTER THIRTY-FIVE

5th March 1943

He ran but couldn't sustain it. He didn't have the energy. He should have found them by now. Thomas felt his shoulders tighten. What if Rom or Billy had jumped at the wrong time, like the big Scot had done? What if they had made it out but got injured? What if he'd missed them further back when he had to take a detour further in from the track? He walked on, rubbing the back of his neck.

He came to a high bridge over a valley. If he walked over the bridge he would be out, exposed on the line; if another train came from behind or in front there would be no cover. It would take him hours to take the valley floor route and then there would be that river to cross.

The valley: a huge plain with steep wooded sides full of pine trees, the river bending and coursing over the flood plain. He decided to descend. He found a path that snaked its way through the wood and down to the valley floor. There were farmers out in the fields. He gave them a wide berth and headed for the river bank. It was large and wide. His eyes bulged and he breathed in; it made the River Asker look like a stream. The panic began to build, the memory of playing polo. He hoped his swimming was up to it; this was huge and racing. He picked the spot that he judged to be slow and shallow. He waded out. The water came up to below his knee, then deepened; he had to swim. It was cold and took his breath away. He had to continue. He tried to control the acid feeling in his stomach.

He was halfway over when the current became stronger and pushed him down river. He paddled as hard as he could but he seemed not to make progress. He tried with his remaining energy, his face falling below the surface. He took a mouthful of water. It was just like playing polo against Lyme when he got sucked into the harbour; and this time he didn't have his sisters to drag him out. There was no choice; keep going, keep going, keep going. His head came up and he gasped for air. Using the last ounce of energy in his arms, he made a grab for an overhanging tree branch. He held on tight as water raged against him. He felt cold. He rested. He pulled as hard as he could muster and pulled himself up and out. He crawled out on his belly, turned over and breathed in.

He was tired but he got himself to his feet and took one step, then another, heading for the shade of the wood, looking for a path. When he found the path it wound its way through the pine trees. There were old brown cones littering the forest floor. The pine needles were deep and spongy. His feet felt comfortable as he went, as if walking on hay. The birds rustled leaves as they searched for food. He stopped and watched the blackbirds hunt for worms and insects and they sang out loud, welcoming the spring. At least the birds were the same. He found wild berries and ate as many as he could find. His thighs screamed at him as the gradient steepened and he fought to continue.

At last the climb ended. He was now on the ridge. He headed towards where he thought the railway line should be. The light of the day was fading and the sun was beginning to descend. There was maybe an hour of daylight left. He wanted to find the others. He came out of the trees and found the railway line. He continued to walk, glad he could not hear any trains up ahead or behind. His head bowed, he walked on, glad his clothes had a chance to air. His feet were sore but he knew he had no choice but to continue. He could see the line up ahead snaking around the hillside and heading for a town below. He would have to decide: should he keep following the track and into the town, or should he stay in the countryside? He knew what he preferred: stay in the countryside, away from people and troops. He carried on, only stopping to let the berries out. What he would do for a proper hot meal. He knew why the men fought between themselves. It was the desire to survive. He had to survive and his best chance was to stick to what he knew. He would have to miss the town. Perhaps he could catch up with the line on the other side. There was perhaps another mile of line he could see before he would have to split away.

Thirst and ravenous hunger consumed his mind. Then he heard muffled voices. He contained his excitement; he didn't want to be let down, not as he had before when he thought he saw them only to be disappointed that it was a farmer and his son. He heard male voices coming from the other side of the tall trees. He couldn't make out if they were English or not. They were arguing and raising their voices. He was careful to sneak up, watching his feet and branches.

He let out a huge sigh and his shoulders dropped.

'What took 'ee so long?' Thomas shouted.

Romily jumped, then looked around, bewildered. A smile appeared on their faces. All back together, they hugged each other.

* * *

6th March 1943

He fell asleep easily and slept well. The birds woke him at sunrise. The sky was clear and the air was pine fresh. Billy and Romily were asleep. Thomas got up and went for a walk. They had camped in the clearing where he had found them, all relieved they were together. He clambered up the bank to the railway line. He hoped Billy and Romily had a plan. Their uniforms of light brown shirt and shorts, dishevelled as they were, would make them stand out; and if that didn't do it, their British army boots would. His time working with his father on Home Farm seemed so long ago. What would he give now to be sat down milking a cow? Back then there was the promise of adventure; now all he wanted was to have his mother hug him, and a plate of hot cottage pie.

He looked out over the line and walked up to get a better view of the town below. He shouldn't wander too far; he didn't want to lose the other two, not after finding them. He looked out over the town. It didn't look so different to Bridport looking down from Colmer's Hill. Maybe there were more houses, but he couldn't really tell. He turned around and retraced his steps to camp. They were gone. There was nothing, the fire scuffed out. There was no Romily or Billy. He felt the acid surge in his stomach.

'Ha, caught you there!' Billy said.

'Cor, don't you ever do that to me again!' Thomas said, playfully punching Billy on the arm. 'Where's Rom?'

'Having a dump down at the stream.'

'Bloody hell, he could shit for England at the Olympics! Don't know how he can when we have hardly eaten a thing,' Thomas said.

There was rustling in the trees and Romily appeared. His hair wet and slicked back, he looked more like his old self.

'Tha's better,' he said.

'I hope you washed your hair before you dumped in the stream?' Billy said.

'Ay, 'course; what do you take me for?' Romily looked annoyed.

'What's the plan?' Thomas said.

'Fucked if I know,' Billy said.

'Go and ask for help; a farmer,' Romily said.

'And get handed over to Gerry or the Ities? Not on my life,' Billy said.

'What are we going to do? Wander round getting nowhere? We have no maps, no compass,' Romily said.

'We should follow the line. See where it takes us,' Billy said.

Romily gave in and they set off. Thomas walked behind Rom and Billy. The older men continued to bicker. Thomas watched the blackbirds and sparrows, happy to see a familiar sight. They followed the line up the crest and he looked down over the ridge to the town. They headed what they thought was north-west.

They kept to the trees and bushes of the woods for miles, and that took most of the morning. The sky was cloudless and if their bellies had been full he would have been happy taking the walk. They came to a field of white long-haired cows that didn't look well cared for. Billy and Thomas grabbed hold and Thomas milked into old cans they'd found. The milk was warm and tasted of home, but there wasn't much of it.

They kept their distance from people and still didn't see soldiers. Keeping to the fields, woodland and pastures they made slow progress. They kept the railway line in sight as much as possible.

In the afternoon, they found an orchard. But the tree's were only beginning to bud. There was no fruit. He wanted some bread and some good cheese, or even some bacon. What he would do for a bacon butty or a big roast dinner from the canteen at Herne Bay.

They walked up a hill path into the woods. They found a clearing in the soft pine needles. Thomas liked the smell; he felt safe. Billy and Romily continued their bickering.

'What is it with you two? Why do you keep on at each other so? We're on the same side, ain't we?' Thomas said, looking down at the pine needles.

'He's being a noggerhead, ain't 'e,' Romily said, pursing his lips together.

'He's all right; what's he done?' Thomas asked. They stretched out their legs.

'Why do you think your sister left like she did?'

'You still pining for her? That's it, ain't it? It's not my fault you didn't do anything about it when you had the chance.' Billy shook his head and pointed his finger, jabbing it towards Romily.

'How could I? Billy Crabb steams in again! It ain't good enough for you to have one girl on your arm, you have to have two or three, don't you? And what about poor Molly at home, when you've been with others? And a child an' all. You should act like a grown-up.' Romily's face was flushed.

'This is it, isn't it? This is it! You're bloody jealous! I knew it, I bloody well knew you were jealous. It's only taking all this time for you to say it.' Billy snorted loudly.

'Jealous? That doesn't even cover it! It's bloody you, Billy Crabb! He's the one, Thomas, he's the one why your sister left like she did.' Romily stepped back from Billy, his head down.

'What do you mean, Romily?' Thomas stepped forward, scratching his chin and looking in Romily's dark blue swirling eyes.

'Bloody Billy Crabb! He wasn't satisfied chasing after Lily, he wanted Nicole as well. When your mother put her foot down, that was like a red rag to a bull. Billy Bull Crabb: that's what they called him at school, always has had the gift of the gab when it came to the ladies. He's only chased after Nicole, ain't 'e, after she's promised your mother. Well, I don't blame Nicole, but course you can see why her and Lily fell out. Nicole felt so guilty, thought it best if she left.' Romily's hair fell down over his eyes and he pushed it away.

'You can't blame a man for trying. They're so pretty; and like I say, it's not my fault. You had every chance the same as I did. You can't go blaming me for your lack of effort.' Billy stood straight and still.

'Don't you blame me, Billy; Billy Crabb, who can't control his temper. Always fighting, always after whichever piece of skirt he ain't had. Trouble is, soon as he's had 'em, he dumps 'em, not worrying about the aftermath. That's what's torn your family apart, Thomas: bloody Billy Crabb.'

'Is it true, Billy, is it?' Thomas said, his voice rising. He moved his hand to his temple.

'It might be! Look, you don't understand women like I do. There could be a thousand other reasons them two fell out. You can't put it all on me, Romily.'

'I can; I know. I was taking my time with Nicole, getting close. God dammit, you knew I liked her; you knew it! You bloody knew it, you did; and you still stomped in with your size bloody tens and stuck where they weren't wanted.'

'She wanted them all right. You should have heard her. Purring like a kitten in the palm of my hand.' Billy opened his fist.

'I don't understand you, Billy,' said Romily. 'Why do you have to be like this? I know why: my god, you've had people around you all your life. People who have given in to what you want; oh, poor little Billy, he doesn't have a father! Get 'im that football, give him an ice cream; that's it, ain't it? You've had no father of your own, no father to show you how to behave. Well, you're not the only one, are you!'

'Don't you bring that into it.' Thomas could see Billy's face boiling. He couldn't believe what he was hearing. To think his sister had left because of Billy! He'd had no idea.

'Don't you bring up my father like that! It has nothing to do with us. You're just jealous because I was with Nicole and you weren't.'

'No, Billy; I'm fed up with you, fed up with you always getting the girl and not caring after, always getting your way and never thinking about the effect you have. It's always the same; you want something, you get it, you throw it on the spoil heap. If your old man were alive he would despise you. I bet he's turning in his grave.'

In a split second Billy got up and jumped down on Romily, beating on him with his fists. Romily retaliated, hitting back. The two men rolled over between the pine needles and cones. Stones and loose rock rolled out from them as they tussled. Thomas tried to pull them apart but he was too weak.

'Stop, you two! Stop, for heaven's sake!' Thomas screamed. He had tears in his eyes.

'He has it coming to him!' Romily shouted out.

'You're a twat and a cunt,' Billy said. 'Don't have a go at me for you lacking the guts to get the girls. All *sweet Romily*, it doesn't work, mate. Girls like a man, not a weak mouse.'

'For fuck's sake, stop it!' Thomas tried again, his arms feeble.

A gunshot rang out, echoing around the hillside. All three

stopped. Thomas looked round. They were surrounded by a company of soldiers, dressed not like the Germans: these were Italian.

CHAPTER THIRTY-SIX

7th March 1943

The truck bumped over the rough track. Thomas was thrown from side to side, Romily on his left, Billy on his right. The smell of stale sweat came from his armpits. If he could have a wash it would make him feel more human. There must have been fifty prisoners in the rear of the truck. All smelt the same. He was lucky he could sit. They drew up alongside the tall wire fence, the top lined with sharp barbs. There were green towers at the corners. The mountains provided the rear boundary, with sheer climbs leading to the snow line. The air was spring fresh, cool, and the smell of eucalyptus trees made a welcome relief from the smell of men.

The captured soldiers stretched their aching limbs as one by one they got down from the truck. Thomas struggled to his feet. The white sign on the sheet metal gate indicated Campo 78. There was a screech of metal on metal as the large gate was pulled to either side on its runners.

Inside the camp they were given a bowl of watery rice soup. The bread had a nutty taste; Thomas found out later that it had been made from chestnut flour.

Roll call, parade, physical activity, work detail, discipline and order. There was a hierarchy between the prisoners with the officers taking charge. Thomas had time to think and to write home. Was Nicole safe? It tore him up inside. He hoped they were all well at home. He wanted to be with Mum, Dad, Hamilton, Ol' Parrot, Dusty. He missed that dog as much as anyone. He prayed to be home safe, for the war to be over, and to be reunited with his family. He wanted to be back in Dorset, to settle down, to work in the fields. To be free. To have a good meal and never to have to travel again. Would this ever end? He would write and ask for a thick jumper; maybe the Red Cross could get it through.

Billy and Romily stayed his closest friends, on beds next to his in the wooden hut. 'Course, there were games, draughts and even a chess board turned up in a parcel. Billy talked of escaping again and the officers dissuaded him, but talk went on between the men.

Out in the spring sun, he wandered the camp taking the morning air before lunch. Romily walked next to him. The guards lounged, smoking at their posts; even up in the large green tower, the machine gun was left to loll, looking down over the camp. It was good to take a deep breath; there seemed no worries here. They walked the camp, Thomas happy to be in silence with his friend. He surveyed the mountain in the background with its loose scree and gravels, leading to the sharp, near vertical face; above this were the snow-capped peaks. Such a huge sight, the like of which he had never seen before. It made Ashcombe Beacon look like a dimple.

They turned underneath the mountain and round the back of the huts, now with the mountains on their right-hand side. The perimeter fence in front of them, high criss-cross fencing, was topped with razor sharp barbed wire. Yes, if he got that knitted jumper, it would do for him. They carried on; it would be normal for them to do two laps of the camp, then back in time for their bowl of rice soup and stale bread. What he would do for a small piece of meat. There wasn't much food around; anything growing in the local fields had been burned to the ground.

Thomas looked at the huge metal gate. It was in two parts, so heavy it took two soldiers to pull either side on its tracks. It was locked with a huge chain and a mighty padlock. It was often opening and shutting for lorries and trucks of all kinds, bringing in more prisoners, or changing the guards.

'Rom, will we ever get home?'

'We have to think so.'

'What if we don't? What if I never see my family?' Thomas said.

'You can't think like that,' Romily said. 'We've made it this far.'

'But what if we don't?' He kicked a stone into the air with the toe of his big boot. 'I hope so. – Romily, what's it like to be in love?'

'Bloody hell, Thomas!'

'I was thinking I might never be in love. I might die before I've ever been in love.'

'Stop it! 'Course you bloody will.'

'Tell me, Romily; I want to know, in case I never feel it.'

'It's wonderful, amazing; you feel light as a feather and like you're the tallest man in the world. You feel like your heart is as big as the moon, and that if you had to you would walk to that moon and back for her. Then there's other times, that if she don't love you back you feel like you're living in the worst kind of hell, where the devil has you on a leash and you just want to surrender and curl up and die.'

'Flippin' 'eck, Romily! And you tell me to keep my chin up!'

'You asked; you should know that when you get that feeling, it's like the whole world is more alive, the birds sing louder, the sun shines hotter, the colours seem brighter; life just seems to roll on more vivid, more complete.'

'And that's how you felt with my sister?'

'I do.'

'Is that what keeps you going, too?'

'It is, Thomas; so much the thought of seeing her again.'

'Should we try and escape, like Billy says?'

Thomas looked through the wire fence on his right, where the lane ran alongside. There were women and girls walking from the village. The girls were walking slowly behind their mothers, pointing, giggling under their breath. He watched them as they looked in. The girls approached the fence, dressed in bright skirts and tatty coats. Their faces were inquisitive, curious, dark and dust-covered.

'It's not worth the risk,' Romily said.

Thomas looked at the girls, who were playfully poking their fingers at the fence. He waved at them and they waved back. The mothers turned around and told them off. The girls, drawn back, ran off up the lane.

Romily and Thomas stopped talking. Thomas looked down at the hard earth and they continued to walk in mutual silence. What would love be like for him? Who would ever love him? Why didn't this war end so he could have a life? He didn't want to be here; he wanted it to end; he wanted to be home; he wanted to have his loving companion; he wanted to feel the good things Romily had felt.

CHAPTER THIRTY-SEVEN

7th March 1943

The written message was clear. Nicole read it to the sisters, twice, before destroying it. Though she omitted to tell them who the target was. It would only make them more nervous. She swallowed hard. She could smell smoke; it triggered bad memories which she had to fight down. It was only the smell of a bonfire. Tonight, she was with Catherine and Emma. Louise and Edith were on another rendezvous to collect a prisoner of war escaping south. She looked through the windows of the derelict warehouse. The frames were empty, the glass long ago smashed by gunfire. As she paced to the next window the glass crunched under her boots. The warehouse smelled of damp. Blowing up railway lines and pylons was pretty audacious, but an assassination was a whole new level. Nicole looked at Catherine and Emma and they shook their heads.

'We can do this,' Nicole said.

'Can we? I'm not sure I can,' Emma said.

''Course we can! Look at everything we've done; we can do this.' She had to be strong, she had to convince herself as much as she had to convince her friends.

'I suppose Dad thinks we can if he's given it to us,' Emma said.

Nicole's boots splashed in the puddles through the building as she returned to the first window. She looked down over the canal. She turned around and faced Catherine and Emma.

'I can do this on my own. You two go home; it will be safer.'

'No, Nicole, we can't let you do that,' Catherine said.

'We're all in this together,' Emma added.

Nicole was starting to think this might just be more than they could manage. Sure, they had pulled off successes. Blown up that train. Got POWs away, collected drops; all sorts. And did it make any difference? The Germans seemed to have an infinite amount of men and weapons. Was this ever going to end? Then tonight there was that niggling feeling in the bottom of her gut. How long could their luck hold out? And Major Lothar Ziegler: he creeped her out. Always smiling and being just too nice. Being too polite. The warning still scared her. It still rang in her ears. And now she was charged with his assassination. What if they messed up? What if they made it worse? What if he was true to his word? What would he do to them and the family, the village? It didn't bear thinking about. She didn't want her imagination running wild with this thought. They would have to do it right; she wanted revenge.

* * *

The three women walked the path from the wood and out into the open land, all with Sten guns hanging from their shoulders. They crawled up to the château and hid by the moat. It was a cool damp evening and the air smelled of smoke. There wasn't a night that didn't seem to have the smell of burning or sound of explosions. The long grass was wet; it wasn't long lying there before the damp took hold of her clothes and chilled her skin.

They lay and watched the entrance. Cars arrived, dropping off soldiers with women from out of town on their arms. A car with flags on its wings approached and Major Lothar Ziegler got out. Looking smart and self-important, he walked with confidence – that way he had about him when he held court in the hotel. No, it was more than confidence; it was the arrogance of power that he strutted with. He waited by the side of the car for his two female companions. His gait was upright, straight, tall and true, his shoulders pushed back and his chest forward. Nicole thought him young. His attractive women companions wore glittery dancing gowns, one red, the other green. Tall and beautiful; and it was obvious how they were surviving the war.

Nicole's teeth chattered so loudly she thought it would give them away. They waited as they lay flat on their stomachs. She watched as car after car turned up. The cars lined the drive for half a mile. She reasoned there were many German officers there, but they had been instructed to take out only one. Why, when there would be so many in one room? If they set off a pencil charge, or detonated some plastic, they could take out hundreds. Of course, if they did, the Germans would run rampant with their rerprisals.

When the cars stopped arriving, the women ran half a mile up across the field to where the road met the long drive. They hid in the cover of the tall trees and watched. They could see the exit of the château. Nicole hoped they were far enough away to make an escape. It was just a matter of waiting for the party to end. If the plan worked and the information was right, he would leave early at the suggestion of his new friends on his arm.

'Do you ever think what would happen if we were captured?' Emma said, rubbing her hands together and moving from foot to foot.

Nicole pulled her coat close around her; the temperature was dropping fast. Looking out from the trees she could see there was low cloud rolling in. She hoped it didn't turn to thick fog.

'Have your fingernails pulled out. Sent to Ravensbrück. I'd rather be lined up and shot.' Nicole said.

'He wouldn't do that. He's so polite and well mannered; he's not like the ordinary soldiers, is he?' Emma said.

'What on earth, Emma? How could you? Have you forgotten how he shot poor Aubrey?'

'That was different, wasn't it?' she replied.

'How's that different?' Nicole said.

'He was escaping.'

'He had a white flag; he had his hands up,' Nicole said. She felt her hands freezing and tried to warm them in her pockets.

'I know, but I've seen the way he looks at you; he wouldn't do that to you or any of your friends,' Emma said.

'I think he would, Emma; don't be so naïve,' Catherine said. 'He would torture us and kill us as easy as kissing us if he knew everything we'd been doing.'

'Don't call me naïve; I know how men work. You don't, you're so frigid. We have more power than you think. There is no difference in how their brains work; they're boys at heart,' Emma said.

'They're the enemy; I wouldn't even think of it,' Catherine retorted.

'You wouldn't sleep with him, a handsome man, who likes you? The way he moves, dishy-looking, like a movie star; it wouldn't be so bad,' Emma said.

'No, not for anything; I would rather be shot than sleep with him. He killed Aubrey in cold blood; and who knows how many more?' Catherine said.

'Will you two stop arguing? It won't make a difference after tonight. He's the target. The bloody target. Your dishy Major Ziegler, Emma, is the target. So get your mind on the job; it can't be long now.'

The fog seemed thicker and from the trees it looked as though the château entrance was shrouded in cloud. There was a dim yellow light emanating from the stepped entrance. He came out, adorned by the same two women, the yellow light glistening from their dresses.

The timings were accurate. The plan was to the minute. The large car with flags on the wings moved to collect him and his entourage. The car moved up the drive. Nicole checked the Sten gun and put her finger on the trigger. When the car was fifty yards away, they stepped out into the road. Her fingers felt numb on the metal trigger and her senses seemed heightened. She knew it was the adrenaline in her body. The car engine seemed to roar. Nicole's breath escaped in a white cloud from her mouth, in front of her face. Emma and Catherine were alongside her. The roar of the guns as she pulled her finger back and the sisters did the same. The kick into her hip. Bullet after bullet riddled the car; crashing glass as the windscreen shattered. The tyres burst out. The car was shredded. Steam escaped from the radiator in a huge cloud. The car careered from the drive and came to a stop in the ditch. Nicole ran over. She went to the passenger door. The driver and his front seat passenger were slumped dead in their seats.

Catherine opened the rear door on the driver's side. Nicole and Emma stood facing the rear door with guns raised. Emma opened it and Nicole took aim. She didn't want to kill the women, who were shrieking and crying, shaking their heads. They might be sleeping with the enemy but she wasn't going to shoot them for that; they were useful.

She looked at the target, seated between the two women, and gasped. It wasn't the Major. It was a bloody Colonel! What the hell had gone wrong? What should she do? They couldn't shoot a bloody Colonel; the repercussions would be massive. It was too late. The noise of the attack would have been deafening. The Colonel sat between the dark brunette in emerald green and the blonde dressed in the red sequin dress, their makeup pristine: dark red lipstick, foundation and blusher. Both had their hair arranged in long wavelets. She went to pull the trigger.

'Stop, Nicole, stop!' Catherine shouted. 'We can't! Have you seen his uniform?'

The Colonel, given the split second, pulled his revolver from the holster inside his tunic. Nicole watched as he aimed his gun. She felt her eyes bulge. He fired.

The gunshot rang out.

CHAPTER THIRTY-EIGHT

Nicole watched in disbelief. She pulled on the trigger of the Sten gun and fired. Catherine screamed in agony as the bullet from the Colonel's revolver hit her in the lower arm. The bullets from Nicole's gun found their target; the Colonel slumped forward, dead.

'Quick!' Nicole said.

The brunette pulled the belt from the dead man's waist and handed it to Catherine who wrapped it as a tourniquet on her arm. Nicole took off his boots and socks, then ran to the bonnet. Opening it, she put her hand in the sock and undid the hot radiator cap. The metal was scorching, even through the thick sock. She plugged the holes with the socks, then took her canteen and poured in. She went to the driver's side and helped Emma pull the soldier from his position and dump him in the ditch. The two escorts removed the rest of the Colonel's uniform.

Nicole got into the driver's seat and drove across the fields, heading for the woods. The car struggled for grip, making a horrible screeching and clanking as the rims hit the ground. But it was moving. Nicole looked at Emma and Catherine, her heart pounding hard. Catherine was holding her arm in pain. She drove fast and without care. The car hurtled over bump after bump. She stopped and let out the glamorous women, who took the uniform with them to burn. She knew where she wanted to head. Across dips and hollows, she was amazed that the car kept going. She came to the deserted wharf. They took rubble and debris and loaded the boot. When the car was fully laden, Nicole opened the driver's door and loaded the accelerator with bricks; she put it in gear and dived out of the car. The car plummeted nose first into the canal and the engine died.

The three women took the cobbled passage, looking out for guards. Nicole was pleased to make it to the safety of the kitchen. They heated the coffee on the hob and slumped in the chairs.

'How's your arm?' Nicole asked Catherine.

'It's only a graze, nothing really; it will be fine.'

'Put some iodine on it. Here, let me.' Emma went to the cupboard where Eliza kept all the medicines.

The women sat and talked for thirty minutes. Nicole didn't think she would be able to get to sleep; her body seemed too alive, coursing with images and with thoughts of the danger they had been in. She jumped when the back door opened with a thud.

'It's you; thank God,' Emma said.

Louise rushed in, pulling the escaped prisoner with her. Edith was behind her, removing her coat and beret. 'Get me a cup of coffee, will you? There is bedlam out there; I never thought we would get back.'

'I don't know what's going on, but there are Germans everywhere,' Louise added. 'I've not seen it so bad since the first days of the war. They look like they are going house to house. We need to be quick.'

Edith reheated some soup for the soldier. Nicole and Emma went to the stables and made sure there was fresh hay and blankets. When done they collected him from the kitchen and shifted him up the ladder.

'I'm so thankful to you girls; you don't know; just hearing an English voice… I'm so grateful,' the soldier said.

'Shush, be quiet. We will come back tomorrow. Take this bread and stay quiet,' Emma said.

Nicole could smell his body odour, a mixture of sweat, damp, blood and mess. Like the worst decayed eggs. She tried to brush away woodlice crawling over the mattress. It was the best they could offer. Emma threw up more hay to block the entrance to the hayloft. The soldier was cocooned behind. Nicole padded in the gap from the top step of the ladder.

After finishing her coffee, Nicole went up to her bed, undressed and got in. Her mind whirred with all the thoughts. She waited for the noise of the soldiers coming, knocking down the door to wake everyone, getting everyone into the square where they would be lined up and shot. She tossed and turned to her side and tried to control her breathing; but sleep wouldn't come. She wished the soldiers would come. She listened out but there was no noise. The light became stronger through the thin curtains; she would have to get up soon. But she was now tired. She dropped off to sleep, only to wake with a start half an hour later. It was time she got up.

* * *

She served lunch: onion soup, fries and eggs. At the large round tables sat soldiers in their uniforms. She looked from face to face and couldn't help despising them. She lingered at the wall, hoping not to be noticed as she listened in on their conversation. She knew some German and it was enough, she could understand the gist. They were discussing last night and the attack they had made on the small village to the north of Cambrai. The fun they had had taking the women and girls, taking them as they wanted. Shooting the remaining men of the village and dumping their bodies in the gravel pit before burying them. Nicole rushed to the kitchen to find Catherine and Emma. They had heard the same; they hugged each other.

Geordie rushed in with a look of raging thunder on his face. He didn't stop and rushed out into the yard. Nicole watched as he went to the stables, before he headed out under the arch and out of sight.

Her heart felt heavy. She placed her hands on her head. They should never have taken on such a mission. Was it her fault? Should she not have killed him? He would have killed them all if she hadn't. She was sure it had been the Major coming out. She walked out into the yard to gather her thoughts. Dead leaves were whipped up and tossed in the wind, before falling to the corner. She walked over to the stables and looked in from the door. He was up there, hidden and quiet, and they would have to move him soon. The images of her mother lying dead in the corner came to her. The current nightmares were too fresh for childhood nightmares. The smell of hay rekindled her thoughts of home. The long summers, glorious picnics, at school playing games with Miss Appleworth telling all the young girls they should take off their dresses and run about in their vests and knickers; of course, she had run wild and free, smiling and loving it. Miss Appleworth told them it was good for their constitution, but Lily wouldn't; she had insisted on keeping on her dress. But Nicole and Alice: they had run around free as birds. Screaming and laughing in their underwear. Long summer picnics down by the river, with Mother's fruit cake, fancy little cakes from Colman's. The trips to the village shop with Lily, looking at the tall glass jars full of sweets through the shop window, being so tempted; then once a week, Mother coming and treating them both to a quarter each of their favourites. Mother had always been fair like that, hadn't she.

Where was Romily now? For sure, he and Billy would have signed up. And what of Thomas? He would be of an age now. God, she hoped he was safe at home with Mum and Dad, working on the farm. She didn't dare think of him being in danger.

She looked up and saw Geordie rush back into the yard, his boots clipping on the cobbles.

'Hey, young Nicole, what's that look for?' His face was relaxed and his mood seemed to have lifted.

'Nothing; I don't know. It's war, that's all. Missing home, I suppose. Wondering what they're all up to.' She looked down at the cobbles.

'Don't worry. I'll make sure you get through this, back to your family and your old man and that brother of yours.' He put his arm around her shoulder and they walked back to the kitchen together.

'When we weren't fighting, we used to have a laugh for sure. I'll never forget the look on your father's face when I blew up all them trout in the lake.'

'When's it all going to end, Geordie? There seems no end to it. Germans everywhere; we will never beat them, will we?'

'Don't talk like that. We won last time and we will do it again.'

'But Geordie, at what cost?'

CHAPTER THIRTY-NINE

8th March 1943

Nicole took a minute from serving and looked out of the restaurant window. Today was Monday. What a day yesterday had been! The contrast with Sundays in Ashcombe was stark: going to church with the family, then back to the warm kitchen. The smell of roast beef cooking slowly in the range. The thought of roast potatoes, and apple crumble and custard for afters. Watching Thomas and Hamilton stuff their little faces. They must have had hollow legs! Then they were out playing football in the yard, calling for Dad, asking them all to play. It all seemed very far away.

German soldiers walked across the square. The town was quiet. The relic of the old British tank still stood rusting in the square. It looked tiny against the huge German Panzers. There were great holes in its side. There was a memory far, far back. It used to be a climbing frame for her and Emma when they were young. It was missing the old machine gun that Geordie had ripped off and hidden in the woods, and then he had given them target practice. The German tanks roared into life with huge plumes of white smoke. Their tracks rumbled on the road and they rolled out in convoy, their defensive line to be set miles from town.

Nicole threw off her daydreams and returned to the busy day of the hotel. She went to find the others. Geordie was all smiles in the kitchen. Eliza busied herself, cooking on the range, dishing up food onto plates.

'Soon be over now; don't doubt my word, they're going on the run, those bloody Hun.' Geordie smiled. His black hair was standing on end, with wispy pieces of white hair mixed through.

Nicole walked back with full plates and served the hungry

soldiers. As she was about to return to the kitchen, the Major and six of his soldiers stormed in. She went and stood next to the bar. His face was stern and his scar was flaring. Emma, Catherine, Louise and Edith stood with her. Geordie stood behind the bar.

'I'm sorry for storming in like this, but I can't let it continue.' He paced between the tables and looked at Nicole and the sisters, who were all dressed the same in white blouses and black skirts.

'I've given you fair warning, Monsieur, you and your girls; but I don't think you have been helpful to me.'

'If I could have helped I would; you know that, Major Ziegler. Give me time; I am sure I will have something for you,' Geordie said.

'You say that, Monsieur, but it doesn't happen, does it? You look after me well, and the men; the beer, the food, yes, you are very hospitable; but what I really want is information and that is not forthcoming, is it?'

'I can't tell you what I don't know, but I'm sure I will soon.'

'I'm thinking a man of your position and influence in the town, you should have something, especially after what I've found in the canal.'

Nicole could feel her face beginning to heat up. She had to control herself, to keep it deep down. To not give herself away, or the family. She dared take a look at the Major; his eyes were on hers. His brow was furrowed.

'I really don't know what to do, if you don't give me something. I mean, we wiped out that small village. I could do that here; I don't want to, mind, not when I thought we were all friends.'

'There is no need; I'm sure I can help. I just need more time.'

'That's it, though; I don't have the time.' He whistled through his teeth. 'Not when he was so important.'

'I don't know what you mean,' Geordie said.

'I get this feeling, I'm not sure where from. Maybe it's the whispers I've heard and don't want to believe.'

'Give me a couple of days,' Geordie pleaded.

He turned to his soldiers and addressed them. 'Go on, search the place. I mean, look everywhere: under the beds, up in the attic, down in the cellar, the stables, the wardrobes. Turn it all over; go on! What are you waiting for?' They obeyed and ran off, not waiting to be told twice. Nicole's stomach did somersaults and she gulped. She tried to stay confident.

'Well, see. Are you sure there isn't anything you want to tell me?'

'No; I don't want to tell you any lies,' Geordie said.

She couldn't believe how calm Geordie and the sisters were. Her insides felt as if they would come up to her throat. The bile began to rise.

'And you, what do you know?' The Major paced in front of Nicole. 'Your eyes look darker; maybe some late nights?'

'Yes, it's always late nights in the hotel, the clearing up,' Nicole whispered.

'Yes, of course; the clearing up.'

The restaurant was silent, the atmosphere turning cold. Nicole felt goosebumps on her arms and heard the soldiers banging around upstairs.

'And you,' he said, turning to Catherine: 'how did you hurt your arm?'

'This? Oh, this was a burn from a scalding pot; always the clumsy one,' Catherine said, touching her bandage.

'You see, some women talk; you know, you should choose your friends carefully. We've found women in other towns very cooperative, but not so much here. Why is that?' The Major spun round. 'You, Nicole: I'm sure I could be good for you. If you joined me for dinner.'

'I have too much work here.' She looked down at the floor, not wanting to look into his eyes.

'I'm sure your father wouldn't mind giving you a night off.'

Nicole looked from the Major to Geordie.

'They're all needed; my daughters are all needed here. You see how many of your soldiers we keep fed and watered.'

'I do, but for one evening: you wouldn't say no to that.'

'No, I need them all here.'

'Well, if that's the case, if you're certain you couldn't spare this one to join me for a nice meal at the château, then I will have to continue with my questioning.'

The soldiers conducting the search breezed out to the yard. Had she hid the ladder when they hid the POW? Was the radio out of the way?

This was torture, standing here, not wanting to move. Not going with him: wouldn't that have been easier, if she'd said yes? He would have gone away happy; he would have left them alone. This was agony. If she went with him, she could take the pressure away from the family. Take the Major's mind off the assassination. Wasn't it her duty to do it, for Geordie and his family? They were taking far too long outside; they would find it, and then the Major would get what he wanted one way or the other.

'There is nothing, nothing,' the sergeant reported back.

Nicole sighed with relief.

'That's sad and good.' He paced back to Nicole, stood in front of her. 'You look so innocent, so sweet.' He traced his finger down her cheek, then pushed her hair behind her ear.

Nicole felt repulsed and her skin crawled.

'This is all so bad, this war; the things it makes us do. You really give me only one choice. If you don't give me information I will have to take it from you.'

'Look, there is always a deal to be made,' Geordie said.

'I don't think so. I'm bored here; I think it's time that I did more questioning at the château. Let me think.' He scratched his jaw, looking at the sisters. 'Who would be most use to me? I think your eldest to start with; there should always be order. Yes, in age order; that I think is the best way.' He pointed at Louise. 'Yes, take her.' Two soldiers took Louise by the wrists and stood behind the Major. 'And who's next? Oh yes, of course; you with the bandages.' Two more soldiers took Catherine and stood with

Louise.

'You can't! No!' Geordie shouted.

'That's the thing; I wonder when they will start talking? That is the fun part for me.'

'Don't, don't take Louise; take me,' Emma said. 'She has a husband; I don't. Take me, please.'

Emma walked forward, standing up to the Major.

'I'll go instead of Louise; I'm next,' Edith said, pulling Emma back.

'Oh, what spirit; it makes me weep! How endearing!' the Major said. 'No, these two will talk, I'm sure, when I'm finished with them.'

Nicole fought the sickness down in her throat. She wanted to speak, to say she would sleep with the Major to make all this stop. But she didn't; her mouth stayed shut.

'No, no more. You.' He pointed to Nicole. 'You don't want to change your mind and have a nice supper with champagne and candles?'

Nicole looked at Louise and Catherine, who shook their heads at her.

'Okay, this is good; I enjoy giving torture just as much.' He turned and beckoned the soldiers to follow.

Eliza hurtled in from the kitchen, rubbing her hands on the food-stained apron. Nicole looked at her; there were tears in her eyes. Eliza was restrained by soldiers nearest the door.

'You can have your daughters returned, just as soon as I get what I want.'

CHAPTER FORTY

8th March 1943

The sun was out, shining down on Marsh Field. Lily looked at the early marsh marigolds, the yellow flower reflecting the sun; its large green leaves fluttered in the breeze. Father drove Turvy out with the cart, full of everything they could get their hands on, begged and borrowed from neighbours and friends: spades, shovels, scythes and crowbars. Lily watched as Dusty stood looking out over the edge of the wagon, impatient. The enormity of the project dawned on her. With the three of them digging with spades it was going to take not just hours and hours, but days and weeks. Mr Milton had set the deadline to have the field planted with flax as Monday the twenty-second of March at nine o'clock sharp. She didn't dare think about it too much or else the panic would form in her stomach.

They got into a rhythm. The order for the clay pipes, one foot long and six inches wide, was placed with Mattick's in Bridport, to be delivered on the following Friday. Lily, her father and Jeanie dug for hours, mostly in silence, sometimes talking about the war, thinking of their absent families; then someone would think of something interesting to ask, or to gossip about someone in the village. There were fewer aircraft flying over the coast on her night time patrols; Lily wouldn't be needed so much for the following two weeks, up until the unfair deadline set by Mr Milton. Turvy stood forlorn, with the feedbag draped under his nose, lonely, his brown and white mane brushed out, flowing down his back. Dusty looked bored; she rooted in the grass looking for grubs, intermittently rolling in musky odours. Mr Milton had even put on his survey that Dusty should have been put down, that she was an unnecessary mouth to feed and that she should go the same way as the sheep; Father didn't give it one moment's thought.

Lily kept on digging in the red-black soil, which stuck to the spade. The ground was heavy and waterlogged. The smell of earth filled her nostrils. Her hands – not used to the handle of the spade, more used to turning pages or typing – began to blister. She thought herself fit and healthy, but soon she felt herself beginning to tire. Her father kept going for longer, more determined. They followed the stick markers that Father had laid out, which reached down the valley and up to the other brow of the hill; they seemed to reach for miles. Lily took out the sketch she had made for Father; it looked so daunting. He had told them they were lucky it wasn't clay, or they would have had to load up the wagon with gravel for backfill, making the job twice as hard and twice as long.

Father moved ahead, cutting reeds and rushes, clearing the turf and stacking it neatly to the side as he went. Then Jeanie and Lily would dig down, judging the distance with Father's notched stick: four feet down. He would come back and check their work, often saying they hadn't got deep enough. It was soul-destroying to have to dig out another six inches, as soil collapsed and rolled to the bottom. They were still on the first, centre channel; they would have to repeat this on the other valley side. Both would lead into the stream, off-centre. Then after that they would have to do the spurs, every ten yards apart and angled into the main drains. It was a huge, thankless task; Father was no more convinced it was worth it, and he was worried at having the vicar's money in the farm.

They ate lunch of cheese and bread on the back of the cart with earth-stained fingers. When school was finished, Hamilton came and helped too, dressed in wellingtons and shorts; he seemed to have boundless energy. He would have liked to have skipped more school but Mother had sent a letter saying that on no account was he to miss any schooling to help dig the ditches. In the letter, she had said she hoped to return to the farm in a week, although her cousin Mildred was happy having her stay as the conversation was so much more interesting than with Albert, her husband. Mother felt she was outstaying her welcome and she was sure the Ashcombe air would do her more good than the air in Southampton. It was far too busy with army traffic, loading onto boats. She said she would be far more use at home, and she felt strong enough to be here with them.

Was there any chance they would be ready in time? It seemed impossible. They just had to keep their heads down and keep inching forward. Lily prayed for miracles. Would Mother come home and find they had lost the farm?

Uncle George came to help when he had finished with the sheep for the day on the estate, but it was such a short time before the sun went down.

When they returned the next day after feeding the horses and milking, their progress seemed so small. It was overwhelming how much was left to do. Not one quarter of the first drain dug. Lily calculated that they would never be ready on time. They needed to speed up, but how? They were going as fast as they could. Her hands were bandaged to cover the blisters from the day before. At least Perry had some leave on Saturday and would be able to help.

Today was overcast; the threat of rain hung in the air. It was mild and warm. Lily soon discarded her coat and got back down in the ditch, her father moving on ahead.

'I don't think we will ever finish this, Jeanie.'

'We can; don't worry. I've asked for some help.'

'Where from?'

'The old girls' network.'

'What? You're joking! No!'

'You wait and see! You've more friends than you think.'

Lily carried on with spade in hand. Her whole body ached and her back cried out for her to stop. Yesterday had been hard, but now with the soreness from the day before, her body was in agony. She hadn't wanted to get out of her warm bed at the crack of dawn. There was no choice; she had to get on with it; she had to help Father get this done. The first hour was always the worst, when the body was cold and every ache from the day before screamed. When lunchtime came the sun came out from behind a cloud and it felt good on her face. They all sat up on the wagon and watched as Dusty jumped in and out of the ditch, splashing in the water; Dad would throw stones and Dusty would chase after, searching, splashing, covered in mud, barking as if the stones were sheep, trying to get order.

'Shit! What the hell does he want?' Dad shouted, with his mouth full of bread.

Lily followed Dad's gaze as he looked up to the horizon. It was the figure of her uncle, standing in his tweed and carrying his cane. He took ten minutes to walk down to where the cart stood.

'You have time for lunch, Kingson? It will make such a difference to the new tenants.'

'We will finish,' Lily said.

'I was so surprised you went to the vicar cap-in-hand; more fool him for wasting his money.' Uncle turned and faced Lily, staring at her with his cool gaze.

'It's not a waste, it's an investment,' Lily said.

'I doubt that; not when I get this farm back when you've failed. You have no chance of being finished.'

'I think we might surprise you, sir,' Jeanie said.

'I doubt it very much; the three of you have no chance.' He stood surveying what they had done. 'And I'm sorry I can't spare George; he's not to be coming here helping you. He has too much to do. And make sure you get the right depth, won't you? I want them to last for years and years.'

'Don't you worry; we're doing it properly,' Father said.

'I'm sure you are, Redver; such a shame that you won't benefit. But don't worry, I will find work for you on the estate. 'Course, it won't be with the horses, and you will have to start at the bottom. I've still the old cottage for you and I won't be able to pay you much.'

'I won't be needing it.'

'Really? Are you sure you're going to get all the pipes you need? I heard from my friend that there is a terrible shortage.' Theodore turned around and stomped away up the hill.

'He will bloody do it.' Father shook his head. 'You just can't beat him.' He looked resigned.

Lily felt a foreboding. Her stomach sank. She tried to not feel resigned to losing the farm. But Father was right: Uncle had too many friends, too many people in high places; he had so much control, so much power. Was he destined to make their lives a misery at every step?

She looked up at the sky. Clouds covered the sun, the temperature dropped and the rain came down. She picked up her coat and wrapped it tightly around her. The rain poured down; the bottom of the ditch filled with water, making it twice as hard to dig out. They didn't stop; they kept going, on and on.

What were they going to do? What if Theodore was right and the pipes they had ordered didn't arrive? She couldn't bear to think of it, of Theodore winning, of evicting them, of making Father work for him. What would she ever say to Mother, to say she had let them down, again?

On Friday with only ten days left until the deadline, they finished the first main drain. Then went to the top of the brow and started on the second main channel. After lunch, they began to make better progress: the soil seemed lighter, or maybe she was accustomed to having the spade in her hands, which were becoming hardened and adjusted to the manual labour. She began to enjoy the task, looking back on the progress that they had made. It was good to be in the fresh air; and the banter with Father and Jeanie was fun. Perhaps if they could get this ditch dug quicker they stood a chance. Mattick's in Bridport, the large agricultural supplier, had promised the pipes for three o'clock. They'd supplied Father for years and years and he thought Mr Mattick a friend: all the harnesses and tack, feed, everything for the farm. Lily was worried the delivery wouldn't come, that all the toil wouldn't be worth it, that the ditches would be left without pipes. Uncle Theodore would no doubt be scheming with his cronies, trying to thwart them. What if he did? What if he had got to Mr Mattick? What if he let them down? Dad trusted old Francis Mattick and said you could set your mealtimes by a Mattick's delivery.

The afternoon began to drag and the temperature dropped. It was fast approaching three o'clock, and there didn't seem to be any sign of the lorry. She must have asked Dad five times what the time was, and each time it was only a minute or so later. There was a feeling in the pit of her stomach which refused to go away. She prayed for the sound of trucks.

At last she heard the sound of a lorry coming up the lane and she heaved a sigh of relief. They were here, the first delivery! She would feel better when they could start getting the pipes in, getting them covered. There was a slim chance, but at least some hope that they could actually do this.

The lorry parked at the top of the field; Lily walked up with Father and Jeanie, glad to see the pipes in the back, the first of many lorryloads that would be needed. Francis Mattick, dressed smart in his tweed suit, got down from the passenger door and met them. He was a rotund Dorset man, educated, with glasses, his accent lost; he had an honest look on his round face and his pocket watch was in his top pocket. He was on time as he always was. For a man in his seventies, he was still sprightly.

'Redver Kingson, it's good to see you.'

'And you, Francis; thank you.'

'No, don't thank me. I'm sorry, I've let you down.'

'What do you mean?' Father said.

'These are the last pipes I can get you for a month; they were the ones in the yard. I've been trying all week; I hoped not to let you down. I've been all over Dorset; nobody has any, no one. Not my normal suppliers, not in Dorchester, not even in Poole. I'm sorry; I've never known anything like this in all my fifty years in business.'

'What on earth are we going to do? This won't get us very far. We need to be finished in ten days, or we're finished,' Lily said.

'I'm sorry. It's to do with the manufacturers; they say they've other more important projects that the War Ag have prioritised.'

'Oh, I bet they do,' Father said.

'What do you mean?' Francis Mattick said.

'They're bound to have more important projects; it all makes sense. I've no doubt who is behind this.'

Lily shook her head. Father was right, she knew it: her uncle was stacking the cards against them. He would do anything, ask any favours of his cronies to get them out. Francis Mattick shook his head, apologised, then helped them along with his foreman to load what pipes they had into the cart pulled by Turvy. They all worked in silence through the afternoon. Winter seemed to return as it became cold, the sun hidden by deep grey clouds, and it began to drizzle. Lily tried to think it could still be done; but they had no hope now. Even if they did all the digging, got all the ditches, all the channels completed, there would be no pipes.

CHAPTER FORTY-ONE

13th March 1943

Lily prayed for a miracle but she knew there couldn't be any. Even the thought of Perry turning up didn't raise her spirits. Hamilton joined in, happy to be free from school, but even he was downcast. Dusty skulked around with her tail between her legs, sensing the depression that surrounded them all.

It was lunchtime when Perry came with six army mates who he had convinced or bribed, Lily wasn't sure which. She hugged him hard, pleased to see him, happy with the help and the effort he was making; but it was all so pointless. She explained the problem and he tried to soothe her, to tell her everything would work out, that they just had to keep going, that she had to keep her hope alive. She tried to put a brave face on it, but she just couldn't see how this was going to work. Later the vicar came with his wife and four more from the village. Lily's heart was full as she contemplated their helpers; they seemed to come from all over. When she heard a lorry in the lane and she saw who it was, she gasped out loud. Standing tall on the back, with a lorry full of women, were Lady Mauve, Eleanor, Imelda: all the old crowd, all dressed in green jumpers, white shirts and ties with dark green cord trousers and boots, with Lady Mauve leading the way, all of them armed with their weapons of choice: spades and shovels of all types and shapes.

'What?' Lily said as Lady Mauve led her army forward.

'Now, don't go all wishy-washy on me, dear girl. When Jeanie here put the word out, I couldn't stand by and let one of us down, could I?'

'But…'

'Don't! Tell us where you need us. It's all I seem to have been doing since I left Oxford. I think we can even have a wager with those soldiers of yours; I'm sure we can dig faster than them.'

'Well, I'm up for that,' Perry said. 'We ain't going to let the side down.'

'Good; that's clear, then. Let's get cracking!' Lady Mauve said.

Lily showed Lady Mauve and Perry her hand-drawn sketch and they each began with their teams on the herringbone-angled channels each side of the first ditch. Saturday afternoon, and the sun broke through the grey thinning cloud; the first patches of blue came through. The progress was soon much faster. Earth was piled everywhere and the small Marsh Field was full of laughter, of voices shouting, joking, the Canadian soldiers of the Calgary regiment flirting with the St Hilda's girls over hot tea. Lily wished Mother was here to see it. Father was flabbergasted, and speechless; overwhelmed by the help from strangers, disappointed that more from the village were not there.

At break, Lily went to Lady Mauve, who was covered in sticky wet Dorset mud with her sleeves rolled up and her hair out of place; she didn't seem to care one bit.

'It's all a waste, Lady Mauve.'

'Call me Mauvie; my friends do.' She wiped the sweat on her forehead with the back of her hand, smearing it with mud. Lily would have laughed if the situation hadn't been so grave.

'We don't have the pipes, and we're told there are none in all Dorset.'

'Well, it's a good job I'm not from Dorset, my girl; I'm sure I can get some pipes. We had some on my father's estate and I'm sure our supplier will be more than happy to help when I ask him; he's wanted to take me to a ball forever.'

'I can't ask you.'

'You're not asking; I'm telling you.' Lady Mauve turned around and walked briskly up the hill, which only seemed to take a second with her huge stride. She got into her lorry and drove off.

Lily's body felt lighter. They were working hard but now there was more than hope; she could see the progress being made. Everywhere she looked there were soldiers, land girls, male and female working for one cause. It was uplifting. The spade seemed to cut through easier and quicker. She watched as Perry made friends with everyone he talked to. She watched as she worked, seeing Perry and her dad talking standing by the cart as Perry was asking about the field and what was needed to be done. She saw them pointing; they should really be getting on with the work; there was not much time. They seemed to be laughing. Dad even put his hand on Perry's shoulder, bending over double. She would have to get Perry to tell her the joke. If only Perry and his crew could stay past Sunday evening; but of course he was going back, he'd be travelling most of the night.

The sun was fully out, even though they only had an hour of daylight left. Typical for the sun to come out just as it would be heading in again, the best part of the day.

Then she arrived without fanfare, walking slowly and carefully between all the spoil heaps. It was Mother, looking fresh, a smile huge on her face.

'I'm so proud of you, Lily; I know your father would never have been so organised.'

'Of course he would,' Lily said.

'Not a chance; I would never have got this many people 'err,' Dad said.

'It's so good to have you home,' Lily said.

'How could I let you cope on your own?' Mother said.

Perry came over and put his arm around Lily. Then Hamilton came running over in his wellies and hugged his mother. Lily knew he thought he was too old for hugs now, but it didn't stop him.

'We've missed you like you can't imagine,' Lily said, her smile so wide, feeling so much more relaxed now that Mother was finally well and home.

'Oh, shut up, will you?' Mother said.

'Now everyone is here, I think it's my turn,' Perry said.

'Have you had something to do with Mother being home, Perry?' Lily said.

'Well, we've been hoping,' Perry said, looking around. 'Haven't we, Dad? And now we are all here.' Perry got down on one knee by the cart, facing Lily. Her heart fluttered and all the blood rushed to her face. 'Will you marry me, Lily?'

'Perry! What? Yes, yes, of course!' She thought she would explode.

Perry smiled broadly. 'I've the licence in my pocket, and the vicar is going to do it tonight.'

'But what… Dad? Mum?'

'It's all right with me, if Perry wants the trouble,' Dad said.

'He's a good man; don't keep him in the mud for ever,' Mum said.

''Course! Come here,' Lily said, grabbing hold of Perry. He picked her up and swung her around. 'But what am I to wear?'

'Don't worry; I've thought of that, too. I hope you like it,' said Perry.

'I will love it; it's from you,' Lily said.

'Well, Mum has checked it over too,' Perry said.

'And you, Hamilton: have you known, too?' Lily asked.

'Yes! Perry kept me supplied with *Beano* and chocolate and made me!' Hamilton said.

'He did; and he drives a hard bargain, I can tell you,' Perry said, ruffling Hamilton's hair.

'You lot!' Lily exclaimed. Her happiness was only tempered by thoughts of Nicole and Thomas.

* * *

It was as if the whole village was in the farmhouse: in the kitchen, through the front room, even spilling out into the yard and the stables. What with the land girls and Perry's army buddies, it was a heck of a party.

Lady Mauve led the land girls; Lily joined in, singing:

'Back to the land, we must all lend a hand,
To the farms and the fields we must go.
There's a job to be done. Though we can't fire a gun
We can still do our bit with a hoe...'

When finished, and it was quiet, Dad made a toast: 'To absent family and friends, to Nicole and Thomas; we pray for them.'

Everyone stopped. There was silence as they raised their glasses. Lily felt tears in her eyes, both of happiness for herself and of deep sadness that her sister and brother were missing the best day of her life. It was also the worst night: now a married woman, having to say goodbye to her new handsome husband in only a few hours; a few hours together as a married couple, then he would be gone for who knows how long. Not knowing if she would ever see him again or for how long. He was sure to be posted with all that was going on.

When the party subsided and Dad had got rid of all his homemade wine, she retired with Perry.

'When will you be back?' she said as she held his hand, leading him up to bed.

'Don't, Lily; you are not to worry. I will move heaven and earth to be in your arms again. Let's just enjoy tonight.'

'Oh, Perry, I've never felt like this.'

'And me; I love you more than you can ever imagine.'

'I love you, Perry. I don't want you to go, not ever.'

'I don't want to but this will all soon be over and then we will have every day together for the rest of our lives.'

'I hope so, Perry, with all my heart. But I'm worried: what if you don't, and what if we don't finish the field?'

'Look, I will be back and you will finish. Keep going; the hard work's been done.'

'But my uncle – you don't know him like I do.'

'Don't worry, not tonight, Lily. Mark my words: everything will work itself out.'

'I hope you're right, Perry.' She melted into his arms. Holding his head in her hands; she'd never felt more complete than when she was holding him, smelling him. Feeling his body warmth so close; it made everything tolerable. She tried to savour every second, but time seemed to move so fast. Soon it would be morning, soon the day would be gone and he would leave. And how would he survive? Life was so tenuous in battle, he would be in so much danger. How could he sound so confident? She tried to dispel the worrying thoughts that were trying to push her enjoyment of the night away.

They slept together. It was more passionate, more intense; she felt at one with this man from another world. It was his everything she loved: his smile, his moustache, the whole of him. She didn't want to let him go; but she did on the Sunday.

CHAPTER FORTY-TWO

15th March 1943

Monday seemed so quiet to Lily, after the wedding, the hubbub of activity. The soldiers now gone, it was just the land girls and herself, Father and Jeanie – and no sign of Lady Mauve and those cursed clay pipes. Tuesday came; six days left. Still no pipes. Whatever would Lady Mauve be able to do? What if her man couldn't get enough? What if they were left to look like idiots with the field all dug up?

After lunch Uncle Theodore came to gloat, with Mr Milton at his side. Mr Milton was dressed in his pompous style with his tall hat. They stood in the gateway, looking down over the field, pointing, laughing. Lily had enough of it. She walked up with her spade, followed by Jeanie and Father.

'What do you want, Uncle?' Lily asked.

'I'm just checking on progress,' her uncle said.

'I see you've brought your lapdog,' Lily spat.

'Don't talk to me like that, young lady! I can always change the deadline, you know,' Mr. Milton retorted.

Lily's blood boiled to her cheeks; Father put his arm on her shoulder to calm her.

'We'll be ready,' Dad said.

'We will know if you don't put any pipes in; don't think we haven't thought of that,' Uncle said.

'Don't worry about that; we keep our word,' Father said.

'Really? And where are you going to get them from?' her uncle said.

As he spoke, the sound of roaring engines filled the countryside. The first lorry came into view around the bend, its horn beeping. Lady Mauve was waving from the cab window for them to clear the gateway. Lily, Uncle and Mr Milton struggled to reach the safety of the field edge. Lady Mauve drove straight in through the deep puddle, splashing Uncle Theodore and Mr Milton with the dirty brown water. The lorry was stacked to the brim with glorious clay pipes laid end to end. Theodore and Mr Milton frantically brushed at their splattered trouser legs, swearing under their breath. Lily waved up at Mauvie with a huge smile. A second lorry appeared, and a third, and a fourth, and a fifth; and finally a sixth lorry, all following Mauvie in through the gate and parking up in a long line at the top of the field. Lily and Father shook their heads in disbelief. Mauvie came and joined them.

'I said I would! Will this be enough, Mr Kingson?' Mauvie said.

'I sure as bloody hell think so.' He smiled.

'Who the hell do you think you are?' Uncle shouted as he approached, wet through. 'How dare you!'

'I'm Lady Mauve, the daughter of the Duke of Wiltshire, the third cousin of King George and something like twenty-ninth in line to the throne. That's who I am; who are you? No, don't worry. I'm far too busy to talk to riff-raff and no-good busybodies; we've work to do. Don't you two know there is a war on? Perhaps you might like to roll your sleeves up and give a hand, old chap.'

'I… euh…' Uncle Theodore said.

'Now don't waste our time.' Lady Mauve turned away. Lily felt elated; she grabbed her father's arm and walked over to inspect the lorries loaded with pipes. Her heart soared. She looked around to see her uncle skulking off with Mr Milton trailing in his wake.

They cracked on. Lady Mauve formed them up into a chain gang, handing pipe after pipe, laying first the main channel, then the second. In the herringbone ditches the first pipes had a corner knocked off so they could abut to the main pipes. The shards of clay left were used on top of the pipe before the soil was filled in. The filling in was completed by Friday. Father ploughed all day, using the Standard Ford; on Saturday he finished the ploughing, then hitched up the disc harrow and cultivated. He used the horse-drawn drill to sow the flax.

Lady Mauve and her team took no thanks and Mauve told Lily to be sure to look her up at Oxford and be sure to finish her degree. She left as quickly as they had turned up, driving the trucks away. Lady Mauve waved theatrically from the back of the last truck as the convoy made its way down the lane.

On Monday morning after feeding and milking, Lily went with Father and Mother to meet with Mr Milton. Dusty chased birds. Lily stood at the gate looking down over the drained and planted Marsh Field, so proud of all the work. The warm sun shone down through the clouds, spreading shards of golden light.

Exhausted but elated, they had finally done it: completed the order from the War Ag.

Mr Milton drew up in his car, with a passenger. They both got out and walked over to the Kingsons. Mr Milton was looking sheepish. He walked two steps behind the tall, distinguished gentleman, who stood straight. He had an oval face with a short nose and the biggest white and grey handlebar moustache Lily had ever seen. His large, honest eyes gleamed.

Her father stood up straight, and saluted. What on earth was he doing?

'No need for that, Kingson, not these days.' He spoke in a calm, authoritative but kind tone. 'It's good to see you.'

'Yes, sir, Brigadier Billington.'

'I must say, this is terrific work,' the Brigadier said, looking out over the cultivated field. 'I've never seen anything better. You know, I would never have found out if it wasn't for the fact that you were planting flax. I was so surprised when I saw the survey.'

'That's Lily; I never thought of it,' Father said.

'Well, she's a credit to you and your family. I need to apologise,' he continued. 'You should never have been given such a demanding timescale.' He came close and shook Father's hand. 'I must admit that as Chairman of the Dorset War Ag I've neglected this side of the county. I thought, wrongly, that I could trust those in command. Not like the army, eh? And I will have to reconsider Mr Milton's position as I've found him to be a little over-zealous and easily influenced,' he whispered as Milton stood by the car door.

'Don't worry, Brigadier; come and join us all for a cup of tea,' Mother said.

'I would love to, Mrs Kingson. You look every bit as radiant as you did in 1918; and you, my dear, are the spitting image! How could I turn down such an invitation?'

Lily stood tongue-tied.

'You've done such good work, all of you Kingsons.' The Brigadier laughed, holding onto Father's shoulder. He seemed so much full of life, and so happy to talk to Dad about the old war years. They were miles apart in class, but he was not bothered; and he made Milton wait in the car all the time they chewed over stories as they sat in the kitchen drinking tea and eating fruit cake.

* * *

17th July 1943

Lily walked down the esplanade at Weymouth, hand in hand with Perry. The beach was unrecognisable compared to what it had been before the war. The large expanse of sandy beach was covered in rolls of barbed wire, great steel crucifixes up on end, scaffolding and fences. Concrete blocks and pill boxes stood at either end of the wide beach. The huge searchlights she knew so well stood positioned with the huge Vickers anti-aircraft guns. There was no room for lounging in the sun. She wondered what strings Perry must have pulled to get their passes. There were guard boxes every hundred yards. The road was packed with army lorries. Trucks ferried soldiers back and forth on the road. Still, it felt so romantic, just to be holding his hand again. The sun began to cast shadows, but there was still heat in the air.

She twisted her wedding ring and couldn't quite believe it; she was now married, and at last they had the chance to celebrate with a honeymoon. It was the first time in her life she had stayed in a hotel. She had missed them all at breakfast, looking round to feed Dusty a scrap. They walked towards the pavilion. Lily looked out at the calm sea and wondered where her brother and sister were. There was the noise of artillery fire, carried on the wind from Portland. She felt so grateful that Perry had returned but she was still missing her sister and Thomas; she couldn't be whole until they returned.

Perry smiled at her and she felt her heart melt again. She regretted the wedding taking place so fast, that her sister and brother were not there to see it.

'They will come back, sweetheart, the same as I did,' Perry said. She thought he was reading her mind.

'How did you know?' She looked into his blue eyes that looked glassy and smooth like the calm dark sea.

'You have that faraway look, looking out to sea; I guessed that was what you were thinking. I do the same.' His lips parted as he held her eyes. Those beautiful shaped lips she wanted to kiss again.

She had forgotten that he was away from his family too, that he must be missing his family as much as she was.

'You can share my family too, you know; you're one of us now.' She reached out and touched his arm.

'That's so cute! I do love them. I can't wait to meet the others. They will be back; you have to believe that.' He pulled her in close as they walked arm in arm.

'I do, I do; I pray for them every day. I wish there was more that I could do.'

'Don't worry. I'm sure if they're anything like the rest of your family, they will find a way.'

'I do hope so.' She looked longingly out to sea, glad to have Perry close. They wandered to the Gloucester Hotel, with its white facade and its tall pillars at the entrance.

* * *

Lily brushed her blonde hair, which fell in ribbons around her shoulder. Looking in the mirror her eyes looked tired and old. The bedroom of the Gloucester Hotel seemed so large with its huge bed, the bedding so ornate and patterned, and a huge dressing table with gilded mirror. Perry must have spent a fortune for the one night. Lily stood on tiptoe and looked over her shoulder at her back, checking on her figure; she hoped she would be attractive to Perry. Her body was still as it had been when she was a teenager, her hips just wider than her slim waist that led to her long shapely legs. All the exercise on the farm certainly made sure there was no weight being put on her slender frame. Lily picked up the red silk gown that Perry had bought for them to attend the dinner and dance. It felt so soft in her hands; a perfect wedding present. She slipped it on and felt the soft fabric against her skin. She looked so daring in red. It fitted her perfectly and it gave her confidence. Her tongue darted to her lip.

'Perry, do you still find me attractive?' she called out. He came into the room in his vest and trousers, wiping the last of the shaving soap from his chin.

'Are you kidding? You're the sweetest, prettiest girl I've seen in all England!' He came to her and lifted her up, his hands strong on her waist. His touch sent shivers racing through her body. 'That's wrong: you're the best in all England, Canada, and the Commonwealth; and I'm pretty much sure all the world, but I haven't been there yet for me to say.' He put her down, then kissed her on the neck.

'Join me, Mrs Andre-Kearns.' He put out his hand; when she took it, he pulled her close and began to dance with her.

'What, Perry?'

'It's practice.'

'You old fool!'

'Less of the old.'

'It sounds so exotic, Mrs Andre-Kearns; it's a bit odd, isn't it? So different to Miss Kingson.'

'It's true, honey; Mrs Lily Andre-Kearns; nearly regal. My

mother is so going to love you.' He whispered in her ear.

'When do you have to go back?'

'Monday. Let's not talk about that for now.' Perry leaned over and kissed her with his soft lips. He had the sweetest, softest lips, and he was gentle. She could kiss him all night.

'How long will it be before I see you again?'

'I don't know; and even if I did I couldn't say.'

She leaned into him, kissed him and put her hand on his chest. She felt his taut body and his heart was beating fast. She felt his hand in her hair. He put his hands on her belly and stroked it; it sent ripples of desire through her.

'I'd like a strong Canadian boy one day,' he said.

'Canadian and Dorset. And I want a girl!'

They made love, with Perry very gently whispering in her ear as he lay to her side. Afterwards, she dressed again and they went down to dinner. The night went by in a giddiness of pure delight as they danced the foxtrot to the big band.

* * *

As the band finished the last song, Perry took Lily by the hand and walked out of the large ballroom and down the corridor. They went into the hotel where they could hear a large amount of talking, shouting and merriment. There were many tables under dust sheets. At the far end, there was one table in use, from where all the noise was coming. A crowd of onlookers was watching those seated at the table.

After Perry had a small whiskey and she had her glass of water, they wandered down to see what the crowd was watching. The shouting reached a crescendo as they joined the throng. They squeezed a way in. Looking down at the table she could see they were playing a card game. There were men in their dinner jackets, drinking whiskey and smoking cigars, and a couple of men in uniform. As she looked around the table she caught sight of one man she knew. Uncle Theodore was seated at the table with a large cigar in his mouth and cards in his hand. She made sure she stood hidden in the crowd. She watched with interest as the dealer pushed out cards. The stakes were made. Her uncle seemed to be placing the highest bets. She watched as her uncle lost hand after hand; each time he lost, he would raise the stakes in the next. She stood transfixed. He was losing, and losing big. She looked at Perry, who shook his head. Her uncle's face grew redder and redder with each losing round, his temperature rising. He began writing IOUs on napkins and placing them in the centre of the table. The dealer announced the last hand of the evening. Her uncle had nothing left.

'Do you know who I am? I own the great estate in Ashcombe; I'm the bloody squire and you should give me more credit, more credit! I'm bloody good for it!' her uncle slurred. The dealer looked round to the manager of the hotel, a burly man and ex-military, who had a huge belly, moustache and receding hairline.

'You've not paid off your last debts yet; what can you promise us you haven't already?' the general manager said.

'I'm good for it, man, good for it, I tell you! I've money coming in; I've plenty! You have no worries about that. I've plenty to sell, and my luck is about to change.'

'I don't much know about keeping estates for sure, but I do know we're in the middle of a war and that prices are low,' replied the manager.

'Don't tell me what's good! What do you know? I'm good for it, I promise you! I'll have plenty of cash soon to pay you off, I've no doubt.'

Her uncle gazed around the crowd, his eyes wild and challenging. She hoped he wouldn't see her.

'Come on, love, we don't need to watch this,' Perry whispered. He took her hand and pulled her away. 'We don't need him spoiling our night.'

'Shouldn't we help him?' Lily said.

'I've seen men like that before; they're beyond help.'

Lily seemed frozen to the spot, watching her uncle so out of control, all his reasoning gone. It was a shock to see. She was tempted to stay and watch, to help in some way, to break him out of his despair, to keep watching. How long had her uncle been doing this, and what did he mean he would soon have the money? She let Perry pull her out of the crowd; it was their honeymoon and Perry was right, she wanted to get to bed and to have Perry's body close to hers.

CHAPTER FORTY-THREE

One afternoon, Thomas had lined up as usual to play football for the POWs against the guards, when a huge uproar broke out. All the prisoners were out, watching or playing.

'It's over! The war is over!' the shout went up.

Three cheers went out. Thomas was caught in a huddle of jumping, cheering, crying, shouting men. His tears ran down his face. He was going home, he was going home, he was going home! He didn't dare believe it. Men cried; he cried. He found Romily, and they hugged.

'Romily, thank god! We're going home!'

The Italian guards began to congregate; others from the furthest guard towers were running to join their line. Guards in the high towers were climbing down the ladders. There was one hell of a commotion. Then without ceremony or warning, trucks arrived. In less than an hour, they were all gone.

There was a small party, a celebration; at last their war was over. The officers told them to wait. The routine stayed the same; they were to stay put. The big metal gate was pulled shut. It was only a matter of days before the Allies would be there. It was eerie and quiet. There were no more guards to keep them in; it was like a training camp. The officers were in charge and the routine didn't change. There were a few dissenting words and of course Billy was speaking out. He said they should walk out; they should go and meet the Allies. The officers clamped down on this talk; it was stupid talk and it would no doubt get you caught. No, the war was effectively over for them. The sleep at night seemed even deeper, the dreams more vivid in the mountain air. He was going home;

very soon he would be back home in Dorset. Around camp, rumours and gossip spread. Six prisoners from hut G decided to go against the officers. They prepared with haversacks and after a breakfast of stale bread walked out of the camp, saying they were not going to starve to death waiting. They had a point: rations were running low. If they weren't rescued soon, there would be no food. There might not be any guards but they might as well still be convicts. Billy got fidgety and couldn't settle, said they should go too, like the six from G hut. There were arguments and bickering, but still they waited. What Thomas didn't realise until later was that it was the Italian surrender.

One morning he woke to the sound of trucks coming up the lane to the camp. Everyone got out of bed, dressed quickly and ran to the parade. He glimpsed the first truck as it swung into camp before he was mobbed: first Billy, then Romily, than a pile of mates, all cheering, shouting. He was jumping up and down, his arms around shoulders of who he didn't know; one big melee of celebrating men. At last his war was over! He felt the relief flood through him and his body seemed rejuvenated.

Then murmurs began, then silence; the atmosphere changed in an instant, like a branch snapping; it was cold. Thomas looked up; what was wrong? Their war was over, surely! He broke free from the melee; he looked back at the truck and saw the large swastika painted on the truck door. Energy drained from him; he felt the colour go from his face. His head drooped, his shoulders fell; all his old aches came flooding back to him. He felt as though the life was being squeezed from his body like an old rag being wrung out.

* * *

14th September 1943

Thomas settled down on his bed and looked up at the ceiling. This time the camp was in Germany. They'd been put on cattle trucks and slowly brought to this camp, which was much the same as the previous one. He soon fell asleep. He woke in the morning and found men up, washing and shaving and ripping open the Red

Cross food parcels. They shared out chocolate and cigs. It was like Christmas. The parcels were handed out, shared around. Thomas missed out on the best; those were the Canadian ones. He got a parcel; he should be thankful for that; but this one, it was from the Old Ladies' Knitting Committee. Perhaps he would get that jumper after all. He undid the knots in the string and pulled away the brown paper. He was expecting a woolly hat, some gloves, or even better than that, a warm jumper.

'Bloody hell, it's only Monopoly!'

'Great! I love that,' Romily said.

They gathered around, opened the box, and Romily showed them how to play and explained the rules. They played at the end of the camp beds. Romily took out the pieces: the old boot, the iron, the racing car, then to everyone's amusement a small compass, hidden. The soldiers were drawn from their beds, excited. Romily found more secret compartments with miniature tools. Slicing open the lid he discovered, folded very tiny, a wondrous silk map.

'Blow me down!' Romily said. 'An escape kit!'

They played on, not wanting to arouse suspicion, whispering. They spoke of those others who had been with them, waiting and waiting in Italy. For Thomas, that was the hardest thing to take: that split second of believing he was free; the best feeling of hope, ripped away. Just one split second when you were so relieved that it was finally all over – having that hope ripped from you was what he couldn't take. If there was a chance, a slim one... And now they had got it, they should take it.

At last being a private had an advantage; they were out on work details, helping farming; no one would suspect them. The officers reminded them of their duty: they were not to kill anyone or hurt anyone during their escape; they were British, after all, and they were not to make the position of those staying any worse. It was decided they should go for it. They had more opportunity going out to the farms.

Thomas looked at the map when the others became bored and the plan had been hatched. It covered the entire route to France and he could see Cambrai and the town of Albert. His heart fluttered and an inkling of an idea took place. If they made it, if they could escape when on work detail, then why not? Why not head for Nicole, for Geordie and the Tuckers? He smiled secretly and kept it to himself. There was something more valuable than a jumper; those old maids had given him the gift of a glimmer of hope.

He sat on the cart, leading the horses to the fields. The guard sat next to him. Billy, Romily and three other soldiers who were up for the escape sat spread out in the rear of the cart. The sun was hot. Thomas felt sick to his stomach. What if this went wrong? Billy had convinced them that it would work; even Romily thought it had a chance. To just run for it, when they were out in the fields. The guards often took cigarette breaks, normally towards the end of the day. Where they had worked yesterday was near a small group of trees. The plan wasn't complicated; Romily would call up when he thought best, they would group together, then leg it for the trees.

Thomas fidgeted on the wooden bench seat. He tapped his foot against the wooden board. He looked at the horses and thought how thin they were. He noticed his foot tapping and hoped the guard wouldn't. His throat was dry. They were Dorset born and bred; no one took much notice of them. They did their work; they got their heads down and they kept out of trouble. Thomas had even been able to supply a couple of rabbits for the table, which earned him some grudging respect. Hell, they even got on with a couple of the nicer guards. Some were old, the others young like him. There didn't seem to be any middle-aged; it was the young and inexperienced or the old and past it who guarded them. Thomas didn't want them to get into trouble. The guard was older than his father.

The gang worked all day loading carts with the sheaves of

wheat. There wasn't much of a harvest; it was thin, and Thomas thought of poor quality. Nothing like Dad's. He enjoyed working outside. There was a thin veil of white cloud. The heat of the sun was on the wane. The ground was earthy stubble. They were dressed in their dull grey overalls, still with their original army boots. He motioned to the guard; he needed to answer a call of nature. He went with Billy and Romily. The guard nodded and took his cigarette and stood by the cart, his rifle propped against the cartwheel. The other three POWs were further down the field, watched by more guards. Thomas followed Billy and Romily and they faced the tree line; they made as if to relieve themselves but instead just kept walking quietly away. There was no reaction from the guard; he was too busy in a world of his own, or he just didn't have the stomach for a fight. It was so easy; it was like a walk to Moreton on a Sunday afternoon. Billy even started whistling as they made it to the trees. As soon as they could they all began to run.

Out of breath, not used to the exertion, they soon resumed walking. It was two hours of walking when they were hungry and tired. They needed food, they needed clothes and they needed some help. When they came through the wood, it opened out to show a farmstead on the outskirts of town, near a crossroads. Thomas could see a German checkpoint on the road. Tired and hungry, they agreed to head for the farmstead. They came to the back of the barn. Billy peered around and motioned that the coast was clear. As the three of them wandered around, the farmer saw them first; his pitchfork was in his hand. Then behind the farmer, there were German soldiers in a cart taking food. The look of shock on the farmer's face… They shook their heads at him: no, no. Thomas hoped. Then the farmer called out, began pointing at them. The soldiers stopped the wagon and readied their rifles.

Thomas didn't wait. He ran for the ditch. He dived in, got to his feet, kept his head down and ran as fast as he could. There was running behind him but he dared not look back. He heard gunfire ring out and the cries of men. He didn't stop to look. He ran as fast as he could, heading for the woodland on the horizon, away from the gunfire. His legs were screaming at him. The lactic acid in his thighs was intense. His arms pumped. He kept his legs moving up and down. He ran and kept running all the way to the first trees. He skidded round the large elm tree and collapsed on the dry earth. He was next to a badger's sett, with earth and sand excavated by the animals. His breathing slowed as he recovered. He looked up. It was Billy; there was no sign of Romily. They sat waiting; they looked at each other as their breathing eased.

'I'm going back to look for him,' Billy said.

'The place is crawling with Jerries.' Thomas tried to slow his breathing, his heart pounding in his ears.

'I ain't leaving him; I can't leave him.' Billy placed his hands on his hips, bent over double, taking in deep breaths.

'You what?' Thomas raised his voice.

'I ain't leaving him to Jerry, do you hear me?' Billy looked around and pointed.

Billy took off and ran back out of the wood; Thomas followed. They needed to find Romily; they couldn't leave him. They ducked down and found the ditch. They could see over the farm. Germans were scurrying from building to building; there was a party of six heading towards the ditch. Three soldiers called from the checkpoint were holding barking dogs.

They inched their way along the ditch and Thomas saw Romily lying on his back. He rolled over and greeted them.

'What's up?' Thomas said.

'I saw you two running fast as rabbits; I thought I would keep Jerry occupied. I didn't expect 'e two stupid noggerheads to come running back.'

'You all right?' Billy asked.

'Yes; I'm a better swimmer than a runner; always has been,' Romily said.

'Will you two give over and follow me? They think we've made it to the woods. Why don't we cross over the road and head for the town? Jerry won't think we're that dumb, will 'e?' Thomas said, looking over the top of the embankment.

'That idea's so bloody stupid it might just work,' Romily said, nodding.

They saw the troops enter the ditch back at the crossroads. They moved over the brow of the hill, running together. They crossed the road and moved into the far ditch. Water and mud came over their old boots. The smell was rancid. Thomas crossed the field; Romily and Billy followed, looking back. They could hear the dogs barking. Thomas hoped they would follow their scent to the woods.

The three men clambered through a makeshift fence. Thomas saw a barn across the far end of the field and headed for it. They bent down, keeping their profile as small as possible. Thomas came to a brook. He jumped in and followed it away from the barn for fifty yards; the others followed. He clambered out on the bank, then double-backed before reaching the barn. They squeezed in through a rough hole.

There was hay, glorious-smelling hay. It catapulted his mind back to home. Long hot summers haymaking and rick building, up on top of the rick, with Father throwing up the hay. He fell over and lay on his back. Romily and Billy came and sat next to him. He could taste chaff as the dust hit his lips.

'We will have to take guard. I ain't getting captured again; I ain't making that same mistake twice,' Billy said.

'That will make a change, learning from your mistakes,' Romily said.

'Will you two stop arguing?' Thomas said.

'I'll take first watch; it's bound to be the most dangerous,' Billy said, getting to his feet.

'Have it your way, if you insist. I'm going to get some rest; all that exercise ain't half tired me out,' Romily said, lying back and closing his eyes. He turned over and snuggled into the hay.

Thomas went and sat with Billy.

'You should get some rest, young 'en,' Billy said.

'Is it true, Billy? Were you and Nicole seeing each other?'

'Ay, I was. I'm sorry, Thomas; he has a point. You know I didn't want to hurt anyone. Guess I don't think has always been my trouble. You'll understand when you're older. I liked her, I didn't want to hurt her; but I guess I didn't like her as much as 'im over there.' He pointed at Romily. 'I never knew he liked her, not like that. It's 'cos he never acts; he's always talking round it. Mark my words, you never get a woman by being a shrinking violet. That's what I know from life; you got to go out and take what you want before it's taken from 'e.'

'Do you think we will ever make it home?'

''Course we will, son; I swear I'm getting us all home in one piece. Now, go and lie down; I'll be wanting my kip in an hour.'

* * *

18th September 1943

Romily was closest, though by the sound of his snoring he would be no use. Thomas spun on his heels. The murky darkness made navigating the barn dangerous. Another barn, another day of freedom on the run. There were all sorts of implements and scrap metal under the hay. He moved to the noise. The sound of an upset bucket. He was sure it was men crawling through to pounce on him and Billy from behind. He passed the sleeping Romily. There it was again, louder this time. Thomas looked at Billy, his expression the same, neither of them knowing who or what it was. Thomas reached the end of the barn first and then saw. It was an old goat, escaped from its tether, rooting around for food. He breathed a deep sigh of relief and picked up the bucket.

'Look, 'tis only an old billy goat, eh, Billy!' Thomas said, laughing. 'He looks like you, all grumpy.'

'Shame it ain't female,' Billy said.

'What! You wouldn't! Not even you!'

'No, stupid, for milk.' Billy laughed.

'Ha-ha! Maybe there is one; let's go look,' Thomas said.

'You go look. I better keep guard over sleeping beauty 'err.' He rolled his eyes.

Thomas crawled out through the gap in the wooden slats, seeing the white goat hair trapped on the splintered wood as he did so. The smell of manure filled his nostrils. The moon was out and he could see as clearly as if it was day. The barn was about three hundred yards from the farmhouse. The henhouse was quiet, the chickens put to bed.

He looked around. He could see that there was another goat in a small enclosure. He headed over, looking around as he went. He didn't want to wake anyone from the farmhouse. The smell of hay mixed with the odour of animals was strong, and it was like home. He wanted to see his whole family, to feel their arms around him. To talk to them, to tell them all how he missed them.

He found the female goat and began milking into the bucket. She was used to it and she stood still for him. He patted her tuft of mane. He talked and soothed her as he worked. He finished up and returned to share the warm milk with Romily and Billy, who were both watching the front of the barn. It tasted rich and a bit tangy, creamy; not as pleasant as cow's, but he wasn't complaining.

'Maybe we should move tonight, you know, under cover of darkness,' Romily said, brushing the last of the milk from his top lip.

'Or we could stay here, rest for the day, then make a move tomorrow night when we're stronger and can make more of a plan,' Billy said.

'There is more chance of us being found, ain't there, if we stay put,' Romily said.

'Yes, but if we're rested, we can move faster and might not make any mistakes; make quicker progress,' Billy argued.

'There must be hundreds of barns we can rest in. Let's make a move; get moving as far and as fast as we can away from here. The more distance we can put between us and that German camp the better,' Thomas said.

'When the hell did you get so bloody wise?' Billy said.

'When you two went and got us caught last time,' Thomas said as he wiped the milk from his face.

'He's a point, I suppose, ain't 'e,' Romily said.

'Before we do, though, I spotted the henhouse; it's worth a check. Might find some eggs we can half inch,' Thomas said.

The three of them crawled through the gap in the barn and Thomas led them out. He opened the wire door to the coop and found his way through the narrow gap. He went to the rear and lifted the lid and pushed the hay to the side. He was in luck: two tan freckled eggs. He picked them up gently and put down the lid so as not to wake the birds. He tiptoed to the door, turned and put it on the latch. As he did so, the cockerel let out a shrill *cock-a-doodle-do*. He saw Billy and Romily jump out of their skin and all three began to run. He held the eggs in either hand. He smiled and laughed as the three of them ran out of the farm and into the field.

They could hear the cockerel singing its morning alarm in the distance as they headed for the brow of the hill. They laughed and smiled.

'They don't half get up early over 'err, don't 'em?' Billy said, laughing.

'Gave me the fright of my life,' Romily said.

Thomas felt the dew on his boots soaking through to his socks. There must be holes in his boots. He shook his head. Glad to be alive. They walked for hours, keeping to fields, following hedges, steering clear of roads. Thomas began to enjoy the countryside. The houses they saw looked funny, with their steep pitched roofs. His mind began to wander as hunger came back with a vengeance. How long was it since they had had a proper meal? They walked through fields, crossed rivers and tramped through thick woodland.

Afternoon was drawing to evening. The darkness was about to

take hold, the time when he wondered if they would ever find a place to sleep or something to eat. He became more anxious. His stomach called for food, and his head felt like a dandelion being blown by the summer breeze. They searched for a farm with barns. The first they spotted looked too busy with a farmer and his children unloading a cart of potatoes. The second, further on the other side of town, was too close to German tents. Keeping low to ditches and culverts they pushed on. With night coming, his stomach was screaming at him to be fed. They waited to cross a road. Six huge German Panzers roared their way past. They kept their heads down. They had to detour round a detachment of soldiers. Thomas shared the raw eggs. It did nothing to satisfy his ravenous hunger.

They found a secluded farm, far from the soldiers and the town. Thomas could only think of finding eggs, milk, vegetables: anything. He went to the barn, the door ajar, and slipped through without pulling it wider. He should have taken more care; why hadn't he thought before entering?

She looked up and saw them straight away. She didn't move from her stool where she was milking the cow. He looked at her and they stared at each other in shock. Her face was round like an apple and it went out of focus, becoming all fuzzy. This is funny, he thought; his legs buckled. He concentrated and moved forward. He felt his head go dizzy, and put his hand out to rest on the post. It didn't work; he fainted and fell to the ground.

* * *

He woke up in bed with the girl looking down at him. Romily was sitting nearby on a chair. The room was bare except for a dresser under the window on which stood a bowl and water jug in front of a small mirror.

'What happened?' Thomas said groggily. His throat sore, he felt hung over.

'You bloody bugger, you went and fainted, right in front of the girl,' Romily said.

'Where are we?' The girl handed him a glass of fresh milk before leaving the room to the two friends. He sipped it down; it was delicious – fresh cow's milk. He emptied the rest of the glass.

Thomas smelled the clean sheets. He felt warm and comfortable.

'We're in France. Don't know how or when; sometime back there we got over the border. Not that it makes much difference.' Thomas felt his heart lift. It might be possible after all; he might get to Nicole; for sure Romily would agree.

The girl came back in. She looked the same age as Hamilton, with a round ruddy complexion. She had a plate piled high with bread, cheese, onion, garlic and ham. Ham! Thomas would keep that to last to savour. He pushed it to the side of the plate. He sat up with his back against the headboard.

He took a bite of cheese, followed by the raw onion and bread, and finally the glorious ham.

'They've taken pity on us, they have. You slept all day yesterday. They've given us as much food as they can spare. They don't have much; bloody Germans arrive with a cart and take it away. Leaving 'em with hardly a spud to spare. They're due back soon, we're told, so don't 'e go getting used to this luxury of staying in bed.'

'Where's Billy?' Thomas said through a mouthful of food. He looked at Romily, who was dressed in clean white shirt and brown corduroy trousers.

'He's been out scouting, looking for the best route out of here.'

'You better get yourself up and out when you've finished with that lot.' Romily left.

Thomas finished the food and wanted to turn over and go back to sleep, so tired did he feel. He forced himself up and found a clean white shirt and green trousers hung over the chair with his boots underneath. He was glad to be finally out of the prison overalls. But where was the map he'd had in his pocket? He went downstairs and to the kitchen. It was much the same as at home: a wooden table and chairs in the centre. A range that was warm and comforting. The French farmer and his wife sat in old armchairs in the corner. Thomas joined Romily at the table.

'Where's the map?'

'Don't worry, I've got it.' Romily pulled it out and unfolded it silently and put it in the middle of the table.

'Here, drink this,' Romily said, handing him a mug.

'What's this? It stinks! Ain't they got tea?'

'This is what they drink. Don't you like coffee?' He smiled.

'No, never have.'

A tall woman in her early twenties came through the door, followed by Billy. She had striking looks with narrow cheekbones and long black hair. Her eyes were dark and brooding. She held a haversack over her shoulder. Billy was grinning. The mother and father got up from the corner and left. The girl went up to her vacated bedroom. They nodded good night.

'You leave tonight, yes,' she said in English with her French lilt. She put the haversack on the table with a clunk. 'Head for this town –' she pointed; 'there is a safe house. You should then head for Paris, many safe houses, then head for the Pyrenees, the mountains, Spain, safety.'

'Um… I've been thinking: I would like to go here, to Albert,' Thomas said, pointing it out on the map.

'What? No, no, no. *Non.*' She shook her head. 'There is a route; it's organised, it works; there is a plan.'

'Why, Thomas?' Billy said.

'Is that where Nicole is?' Romily said.

'Yes. I'll go on my own if you let me have the map.'

'You won't be on your own, 'cos I'll be with you every step,' Romily said, smiling. 'Why on earth didn't you tell me?'

Thomas sipped on his bitter coffee. There was silence. He swallowed hard.

'I ain't letting you two on your own. I've promised young 'en to get him home safe and if he wants to see his sister then that is where we go,' Billy said.

'*Zut alors*, you British!' the woman said. '*Tout ce que vous voulez*. If you must; it makes no difference to me if you want to kill yourselves.'

She opened the brown canvas bag on the table. Thomas raised his eyebrows. There was a Webley service revolver, grenades, and cordex.

'Supplies.' She put the contents back in the bag and handed it to Romily.

Romily stuffed in the food the family had prepared for them.

'Ain't she the one? Always so serious! I know there is a heart in there somewhere,' Billy joked. He stepped closer to her and went to put his arm around her shoulder. She backed away.

'No room in my heart, not after...' She looked wistful. 'You are lucky to have found us, so do not joke. You are wearing the clothes of my brothers who will never return; so do not joke, please.'

'We're not; we're sorry. 'E don't mean it,' Romily said.

'What's your name?' Thomas asked.

'No names; we don't have time.'

'Of course, sorry. It's that you remind me of my sister, Nicole, so much; and of my other sister, Lily; you have spirit.'

Her face softened. 'I'm sorry I snapped. It's if you get captured, if you talk. It's all of us, the whole family. I've seen the Germans do it.'

They sat around the range and Thomas drank the bitter-tasting coffee and screwed up his eyes.

'It's time we left.' The woman stood up and led the men outside. 'I'll take you to the woods; from there, you are on your own.'

They walked across farmland and followed the stony track, led by the woman. The night was chill with a cold breeze. But Thomas felt better than he had in a long while; his belly was full. He was heading for Nicole. There was new hope. The woman came over to Thomas.

'I hope you see your sister soon. My name is Véronique' She

whispered in his ear. '*Bonne chance.*' Her lips kissed his cheek and he felt blood course through his veins and go straight to his head.

CHAPTER FORTY-FOUR

19September 1943
They trudged through the night, speaking only the odd word. Smoke and cloud floated, blocking out the moon. Before morning came Thomas, Billy and Romily made camp in the wood. They fashioned large branches into a lean-to; it was tricky in the darkness, even though their eyes were accustomed. When the branches were tied with strips of thin bark, they interlaced them with bracken. The sound of a stream filtered through the night. Thomas breathed in the smell of the sweet bracken. It made a pleasant change from the smell of men. In the early morning he went to the stream to fetch water in an old can. They dared not light a fire. He walked up the path from the stream and looked at the shelter; good, it was almost invisible, so well hidden. The first birds began their morning song. He walked to the shelter. Romily and Billy were still dozing. He thought he had best keep guard. He drank the cool water from the can; it tasted rusty. After a while of sitting, his eyes grew heavy. He tried to keep his head up; he tried to poke Romily but his arm was tired and relaxed; he was already giving in to sleep. His head fell forward.

He woke with a start. The noise of huge engines surrounded the woods. He could hear men shouting, the distinct sound of German soldiers going about their business obeying their barked orders. It sounded like they were nearly on top of them. He couldn't have been asleep for long. He crawled out of the makeshift shelter. He could see up on the ridge above, through the trees, three huge Panzer tanks reversing in. Soldiers with spades, shovels and axes were clearing out scrub, digging the tanks into camouflaged positions.

He crawled back to the shelter. He prodded Romily and Billy. God, they could sleep through a thunderstorm.

'What do 'e want my darling? Not now, I be asleep,' Billy said. He turned over and a fart escaped into the air.

'Bloody hell, Billy! Talk about blowing a trombone to give our hideout away,' Thomas said.

Romily rubbed the sleep from his eyes. Billy sat up.

'Wos all this, young 'en? I was dreaming of that sexy French resistance lady; all mine she was,' Billy said.

'Shut up, will 'e! It's three bloody tanks setting up right above us, ain't it!' Thomas said.

'Oh, shittle bum hurdle. Trust our bloody luck to camp under that bloody lot,' Romily said.

'Jerry is everywhere; they're digging in,' Thomas said.

He squeezed in between Billy and Romily.

'What the hell! I need a bloody good shit,' Billy said.

'You ain't doing it in 'err,' Romily said.

'No bloody way,' Thomas said, shaking his head.

'I've got to go; always do, first thing in the morning.'

'You'll have to wait,' Romily said, tutting.

'I can't bloody wait; it's so far out it's touching me pant cloth. I can't wait, not no longer. Jerry ain't making me poo meself; I ain't a bloody baby.' Thomas tried to hold one arm and Romily the other but Billy was too strong for them as he made his way out of the shelter. Thomas got up and Romily followed.

'What do you two think you are doing? I don't want a bloody audience.'

'We better keep guard; we don't want 'e getting taken out whilst you're shitting, do we?' Thomas said.

'Is nothing private? You know, I could do with having me paper to read; I always study the football when I'm having me first crap of the day.'

'I'm sorry, Billy; shall I nip over and ask Jerry if he's the *Bridport News* for 'e?' Romily said, laughing.

'Will you two keep your bloody voices down!' Thomas said as they followed the path down to the stream. Billy dropped his trousers and squatted. Thomas and Romily turned away; taking cover behind two large trees, they kept watch. The noise of the engines was loud above the sound of birds. A large fart echoed up from Billy.

'Bloody 'ell, if he don't hear 'e, I reckon he will smell 'e,' Romily said.

'You don't know how good that feels; getting that out don't half make me feel better,' Billy said, wiping his arse with a huge dock leaf. 'Think you boys should take a turn.' They both did so before setting off.

The stream wound its way down a gentle slope. The sound of the tanks behind them grew fainter. After an hour walking through the woods they came to an opening out onto farmland. Keeping a steady pace, they walked into the open. Thomas felt his heart rate increase; they would need to find cover quickly or risk the chance of being spotted. In the distance they could hear more tanks, trucks and cars. How close they had been to being discovered! It was so good to know there were strangers like Véronique and her family who were there to help them. He thought they might even be able to make it. He seemed to have the spring back in his step. He tried to practise his walk like a Frenchman, like Véronique had said: try, try not to look like you're still in the British army, marching up and down.

The land was flat and stretched to the horizon. The wind blew hard out of the shelter of the trees and into his face. It was afternoon before they found a secluded farm. They kept watch; a farmer and his wife went about milking. Night was coming in. Should they chance making contact?

The three of them crawled on their bellies to the outskirts of the farm for a closer look. The farmer took in the milk from his two cows. Thomas could hear his wife telling him off in French.

'Come on, they will be fine,' Billy said. He got up and strode across the pasture. Thomas and Billy followed, trying to keep up.

They walked into the yard.

'*Allez-vous en! Allez-vous en! Vous n'êtes pas bienvenus; on ne vous veut pas ici!* ' the woman shouted, waving her arms. She looked formidable. Thomas didn't understand. The farmer came out with his shotgun. His eyes blazed in stubborn defiance. It was clear he meant it.

'Come on, we are friendly; friends of yours,' Billy tried to say, smiling. The farmer took his shotgun and put it to his shoulder.

'Something tells me he ain't messing around, Billy,' Thomas said.

'You think?' Billy said. 'I'm getting out of here.' He turned and ran. Thomas and Romily followed. Thomas looked over his shoulder at the farmer who was still waving his shotgun.

'Do they know we've been fighting on their side?' Billy said.

'I guess they don't want the trouble. You can't blame 'em, can 'e,' Romily said.

* * *

The light faded quickly. Thomas was hungry, his stomach roaring at him. He felt weak and light-headed. He hoped they would stop soon. He could do the walking if he was fed. His legs were beyond tired; each step was heavier than the last. His head hung down from his shoulders which were rolled forward. He could smell his own body odour. They dodged road blocks and checkpoints and hid in ditches with dirty water when vehicles passed. He hoped to find shelter: a barn, woodland, a derelict house. If they had headed the way Véronique had wanted them to, there would have been safe houses. They came to a railway line and followed it for half an hour. His feet were numbed; the sole of his right boot flapped loose as it had done for miles; the water crept in. He felt a new blister forming and it made him limp. He looked at Billy and Romily and they looked in the same sorry state.

Thomas lifted his head, which he found difficult. Soon they came to a German checkpoint where the road crossed a level crossing. They would have to detour. The three men nodded in agreement. They crossed the line and skidded down the far embankment. Thomas felt his feet give way in a muddy bog. He tried to lift his leg; his boot and foot were sucked in under. He strained, pulling harder. He pulled with his hands. His foot came free with the sound of a sucking squelch. Just like at home with wellingtons in mud. He sighed and looked at the others. They leant back on the embankment. The smell of black fetid mud emanated from the bog. There was no way across; they would be sitting ducks. They retraced their steps across the line. They could hear the sound of a train in the distance, getting closer. They lay down together and watched the checkpoint. There were six guards, three either side, pacing up and down, guarding the barrier. There was a small wooden hut for their shelter.

There was no way through the bog. There was the train coming and all around them was open flat farmland. Thomas couldn't face heading back the way they had come. There was nothing.

'We will have to take them,' Billy said.

'How the hell do you suggest we do that?' Romily said. 'And it's against our orders to hurt anyone.'

'Fuck that; we don't have much choice. We've got the grenades, we have the gun.' He held up the canvas bag that they'd been taking turns to carry. 'Let's fucking blow them up. There is no way around and I ain't walking back on myself. And there ain't no officer here to help us.'

Romily shook his head. Billy continued talking.

'You two walk down the road, taking their attention. I'll blow them to kingdom come then take out any from behind; they will be too busy with you two to worry about me.'

Thomas didn't know if he could go through with it. He felt anxious, but he was so tired and he had no better idea. He wanted to keep walking so he could get to Nicole.

'Billy, I don't like it,' Thomas muttered.

'I don't like it; but don't worry, they won't know what's hit them.'

'I suppose. Don't think we want to walk any further.' Romily caved in, too tired to argue. Thomas lay out on the embankment on the cold wet grass; he looked up at the grey moody sky and prayed to get through this.

CHAPTER FORTY-FIVE

20th September 1943

Thomas walked down the centre of the road with Romily. He could see it stretched for miles. He tried to control his breathing; his chest felt tight and his palms were clammy. His heart was beating faster with each step he took. In the middle of the plain, the checkpoint and barriers stood, guarded by six German soldiers. There was a red and white barrier on each side of the railway line at the level crossing. Two guards stood at each barrier and two took it in turn, resting in the hut. One soldier was positioned on the concrete counterweight to make it rise. Thomas tried to slow his breathing but it wanted to run away with the speed of a steam train. The guards hadn't spotted them yet. He could still dive into the ditch on his right-hand side. The road in front of him dipped down to the level crossing and the guards; the other side eventually ran up to a tree-lined ridge. He had no idea if this would even work. They were in desperate need and it was the best the three of them could come up with. He took his dirty white handkerchief and held it in his hand. He put his hand above his head and waved; Romily did the same. He kept walking towards the guards. He prayed they wouldn't shoot him. His heart jumped as the first looked, then reacted.

He didn't shoot. He ran to his commander in the hut and pointed up the road. Thomas walked more slowly, his hand still held high waving the hanky. He felt every stone under his boots as he neared the enemy. The road could have been anywhere; it could have been the walk down through Ashcombe. The rain came down from thick grey clouds which were so low they seemed to touch the ground. It smelled smoky and there was a fire in a brazier near the hut. What on earth were they thinking?

The first soldier returned with the commander and they all raised their rifles and pointed them at Thomas; they stood frozen, pointing, their fingers on their triggers. Thomas and Romily inched and shuffled forwards.

He wanted to turn and run for his life. He pushed himself to continue. His shoulders tensed. It would be all right, he prayed. What was Billy waiting for? Throw the bloody grenade. He got within feet of the first guard, who had sharp eyes. It would be too late. He saw the arc of the grenade, a graceful lob up in the air, its metallic clank on hitting the ground. The guards, startled, looked. Tried to run. The grenade rolled along the road. The explosion went up with a huge thunderball of fire. Although expected, Thomas was taken by surprise at the sheer ferocity. He part dived and was part blown into the ditch. His ears numbed. He heard muffled gunshots, cries and screams.

He pushed himself up the bank. He looked on at utter destruction. Romily was getting to his feet. The German guard with the blue eyes staggered towards them, his right arm hanging loose, blood gushing from the wound, his face distorted in pain. He screamed, his blue eyes pleading for mercy. The soldier stumbled and Thomas watched Billy as he came rampaging through the smoke and the remains of the barrier, his pistol raised. Billy fired two shots into the guard, who fell. Thomas screamed.

Billy ran to Thomas and took his arm. He pulled Thomas with him. Thomas found his legs running, heavy, like in a bad dream. The three ran up the road and towards the small group of trees on the ridge, quick to escape the scene of carnage. Thomas took one look back. The guardhouse was a splintered mass of timber; it looked as if a box of matches had been turned out and set on fire.

The three friends reached the ridge and the shelter of the trees, their breathing deep, heavy and laboured. Thomas bent over double to catch his breath, his hands on his waist. If Billy hadn't thrown the grenades when he did, he would be dead now, he was sure. The other two were speechless. He gathered his breath and looked up. In front, not more than two hundred yards away, was tank after tank after tank. There must have been one hundred or more. All on the ridge, lined in a crescent, all pointing their guns to the huge fields below. Thomas swallowed.

'We're fucked,' Billy said, shaking his head from side to side.

'Too right,' Romily said, and nodded in agreement. 'We will just have to take a detour.'

* * *

They had found the farm as dusk drew in; and — thank the stars — the farmer was friendly. His wife and three children took them in. Thomas was glad to get out of his wet clothes. The farmer heated water and filled an old tin bath. He left the three of them to wash. The water was tepid and dirty but was a welcome relief from the cold rain they had been walking through all day. They were given clean farmer's clothes and Thomas felt he was right at home. He could have stayed for days but he knew they had to move on. Morning came too soon.

The farmer took them out to the yard. His two horses were harnessed to his old cart, filled with potatoes. Thomas savoured the earthy smell. In French and broken English, the man indicated the plan. He would drive them seated in the cart with the spuds; he knew of a safe house and gave them the address. He would get them to fields out of town on top of the pile of potatoes. From here, they would have to make their way on foot.

Thomas sat up on the potatoes with Billy and Romily, glad to be off his feet. This could work. He smiled at the others.

The farmer kept to his tracks and fields away from roads. Thomas rested against the side of the cart. The earthy smell of fresh potatoes filled his lungs.

The farmer brought the horses to a halt. Thomas, Billy and Romily got off the back. They hugged the farmer and shook his hand. He shrugged, turned around and headed to market. They

309

hid up against the hedge. There were nettles, dock leaves and brambles. They crawled in as far as they could. It was cramped, but they were out of sight. The outskirts of the town were less than a mile away. The plan was to wait until darkness, then try and make their way to the safe house.

Thomas tried to sleep; it came fitfully to him. He came out of dozing, woken by the loud snores of Billy.

'What you going to do after this is all over?' Thomas asked Romily.

'I'm going to ask your father if I can marry Nicole.' He smiled at Thomas.

Thomas noticed the colour in Romily's cheeks when he mentioned Nicole's name.

'You know she can be a right pain, takes forever to get ready to go anywhere,' Thomas said.

'You will learn, Thomas, that's what women do. Makes 'em special, it does. – Come on; we better wake up sleeping beauty here and make a move,' Romily said.

Thomas crawled out, careful to look from side to side. The three of them stooped, part walked, part ran, following the hedgerow for the mile up to the town. They picked their way through dark lanes and passageways looking for the alley that led to the safe house. Thomas looked hard at the blue street signs high up on the stone town houses at junctions. It was hard to make them out. They walked past the local hotel; its doors open, he could hear shouts of laughter, music playing and German voices. There were motorbikes and sidecars parked outside with German staff cars. He walked quickly past with the others.

They found the road and turned. It was then that Thomas saw three German soldiers come staggering along at the far end of the road. They looked drunk. They couldn't turn back; it would look odd. They had to keep walking. All the doors of the houses were shut tight; there was no side alley. They kept walking straight. The drunken soldiers staggered and walked past in a zigzag, paying them no attention.

Thomas came to the safe house and knocked on the door. It seemed an eternity before the door opened with a creak. He entered, and Billy and Romily followed. The door shut with a bang behind them.

* * *

21st September 1943

She spoke in the sexy French way, the tallest of the three women. The leader was twenty-three and the oldest by some margin; the other two only girls. She looked sophisticated and had long black hair. When she talked to the girls she spoke fast and he couldn't understand. Every once in a while she would look up and speak in broken English. She explained how they had been helping all kinds of soldiers escape. He understood some of the town names. He dared not let excitement build in his stomach. She had mentioned the town, Cambrai; he was sure she kept saying Cambrai. That was where Nicole was near, he was sure. It was near where he had been born. That was the largest town near her. He looked at Billy and Romily. He touched Romily's arm and whispered to him.

'Rom, that's near Nicole. That's the town near Nicole.'

'You sure?' Romily whispered. The two of them were like a pair of naughty schoolboys.

'Yes, I'm sure; it's on the map. We must be near her.' He felt his face break into a smile; his eyes felt like they were glowing. 'I'm going to get to see my sister! I can't believe it, we're near her!' He got the crumpled map from his pocket and put it on the table.

'Shush, you two; can't you see I'm trying to listen to these gorgeous girls?' Billy said.

'You know one of the women, in the resistance?' the lead woman asked Thomas in English.

'I don't know about the resistance. I've a sister near Cambrai: dark hair, petite, very pretty.'

'There are many who do this. It's all we can do. We hope people are doing the same for our brothers, our husbands, our boyfriends.'

The lead woman got up from the table and pulled up a small canvas shoulder bag. She handed it to Romily.

'Some supplies; a little food and ammunition. You have pistols?'

They nodded. She marked the map for them.

'We will take you to the edge of town; you're on your own from there.'

It was the same drill as before. This time, could it be true? Would it be his sister next that took him in? He wanted it to be true.

* * *

He didn't sleep well. He tossed and turned. This time, it wasn't worry; it was the hope and excitement that he might be reunited with Nicole. They were woken at three and taken out into the early morning mist. They were left in fields and pointed in the direction they should head. He felt more of a spring in his step. He couldn't remember the last time he had felt this happy. He looked at Romily, who was also smiling wildly. They found the river marked on the map and followed this in the valley. After hours of walking they entered a wood. The tall trees gave them shelter. The sun was out and there were shadows in the clearings. He rested and drank fresh water. It was then that he heard the first dogs bark, faint at first but then louder.

'Are them dogs after us, or what?' Billy said.

'I don't know but I ain't staying to ask,' Romily said.

They got up and ran. After a hundred yards or more they stopped running and began to walk. They crossed in and out of the river to try and lose their scent. Still the noise of barking was in the background. Thomas kept his pace as fast as he could. Billy strode on in front, the bag around his shoulder. Thomas thought he heard more shouting from higher up and from behind. There was more than one group tracking them.

The river wound its way slowly down. Thomas looked ahead and saw more light penetrate the forest, the trees thinning out.

The sun was bright and directly overhead. He could see a road crossing through the wood and then out to open land. The road was busy with constant German army traffic, armoured troop carriers, Panzers, sidecars, motorbikes and cars. There was a small bridge. There was no way across the road. The noise of soldiers got louder from behind. They headed up the hill, away from the road, away from the noise of the dogs. They kept moving, afraid to stop. Soon Thomas felt his legs get heavy and start to give way. He would need to rest; he couldn't keep moving. His legs bowed under him. He forced them straight and kept walking.

Their pace was slowed by the steep gradient. The woodland path dwindled to nothing. They were walking through bracken with its sweet scent. Perhaps this would deter the dogs. They tried to keep low; they stooped their heads down. They were in an open clearing, walking slowly.

Thomas looked up ahead and saw the German army uniforms of six soldiers coming their way. He pointed them out to Romily and Billy. They veered off to their left keeping low and as silent as they could in the vegetation. They found the cover of trees and scurried down the pine-covered bank. Thomas stumbled and fell to his knees. He put his hand down, feeling the soft mattress of pine needles on his palm. He picked himself up and followed Romily and Billy. The fragrant smell of pine wafted around him. He ran and stumbled, following Billy and Romily. He then heard the dogs, barking more loudly. They sounded close. He began to run, fast, powered by fear, chasing Billy and Romily. There was more than one dog. He ran faster. They returned to the valley floor. He was sweating hard. His shirt was stuck to his skin. The dogs were barking for all they were worth. They were close to the road. Trucks kept passing; then one stopped and a dozen soldiers jumped off the tailgate, heading in their direction, rifles primed. The dog handlers were closing in. They ran towards the river. The shouts went up from Jerry. Thomas took his pistol and turned and fired; he had no time to take aim. Billy grabbed his hand and pulled him running for the river bank. He pushed Thomas down onto the gravel shore. Romily pulled Billy with him. Shots rang out from the German rifles. Romily joined Thomas on the beach. They watched helplessly. Billy took his pistol and fired. He ran along the beach; he was heading towards the dogs.

'We have to try and save him!' Thomas shouted.

'We can't; he's drawing cover for us. He'd doing it for us,' Romily said.

Thomas watched. Billy ran up the river bank, shooting his pistol, running straight at the dog handlers. He made it to them, firing as he did so. He took down two. He turned, then jumped down on the shore further up. Thomas saw his plan. Billy tried to leap over the boulders, trying to reach the water, trying to make the rapids. Gunfire rang out: six, seven bursts; then machine guns, all on Billy. He kept moving, but the crescendo of shots increased. Thomas watched as Billy was mown down feet from the water's edge. Billy didn't move. Thomas shouted. Romily covered his mouth and pulled him under the bridge. They ran as far as the shore allowed, the white water raging to their side. Romily pushed him forward.

'Go, dive in, dive in and swim for your life.'

Thomas heard machine gun fire ricochet off the rocks and stones around him. Romily was beside him, pushing him away, looking back and firing his pistol. There was no time to think. He ran and dived in. The water was freezing cold; his breath was strangled from his lungs. His face plunged under the water. He came up and gasped for air. He glanced up and watched Romily as he dived for the river. His own head was pulled under by the current. He heard bullets pepper the water around him. He swam for all he was worth, trying to keep his head below for as long as he could. The current pulled him under and down, and he gathered speed. He bumped into sharp rocks, his arms and elbows were ripped. His knee banged a boulder. He couldn't see Romily; he looked for his friend. He knew Billy was dead but he hoped that Romily was alive. If he could survive, so could Rom. He kept swimming away from the soldiers; but the power of the water which had moved him out of range was now his new enemy. He couldn't feel his hands; the cold was fierce. His mind was numbed. He tried to swim for the safety of the shore. The sound of rushing water was all around him. His mouth filled with water. His nose filled with water. His lungs screamed as water found its way in. He tried not to panic. He summoned every last bit of strength he had and swam for the bank. He grabbed out at passing branches but couldn't hold on. He began to despair. His mind travelled over his life; and then there was darkness. There was no one left to save him. He opened his eyes and with one last effort he swam for the bank. He stretched his feet down; they didn't touch the bottom. He had to keep swimming. He gasped and pushed his head up and took a breath. The river took him where it wanted. He prayed to live. He cascaded and buffeted into rocks hitting his ribs hard. Then the river took him on and around. There was no energy left in his body.

* * *

23rd September 1943

He awoke on the stony beach, with water lapping at his feet. He shivered uncontrollably and his teeth chattered. His clothes clung to his body. He rolled over and screamed out in pain, his ribs red-raw and purple bruised. He heard the river lapping at his feet. He could smell the fresh water. His memories came flooding back to him. He staggered to his feet, no idea how long he had been there. He felt like he'd had ten pints of beer at the Farmer's Arms. His boots were waterlogged. He pulled himself up the bank by the roots of an ash tree. He sat there and took off his boots, pouring the water out. Billy was dead, and it was more than possible Romily was too. He had to get moving. He couldn't go back; that would be certain death. He would have to move down river and hope with all his heart that Romily made it.

He took off his socks and wrung them out as best he could. Water ran from them as he scrunched them in his hand. With socks and boots as dry as he could make them, he gingerly got to his feet. He followed the river. His ribs cried with pain when he coughed. His knees were bruised. It was agony to draw breath. The sunshine filtered through the canopy of trees. One friend dead and one friend missing, and he was more than lost with Billy having insisted on holding the map. He followed the river for the rest of the day. He sheltered under a bridge for the night.

The next day he felt no better, his mood low, his hunger beginning to pain him as much as his ribs. He coughed hard and flinched in pain. He drank straight from the river. He walked until the river came to the outskirts of a town. He could hear the sound of gunfire coming from the streets. He took the detour and picked up the river on the far side. He walked deep into the night, through farmland and over hills. He walked until his legs gave way. He slept where he fell. He dared not approach strangers.

The sound of troop movements could be heard above him. He thought about surrendering, giving himself up; at least he would be fed. He dismissed the thought; it wouldn't have been what Billy would have done. He lay on his back and tried not to cough; it would be painful and it would give him away. Where was Romily? Was Romily dead as well? He waited for the sun to set and the traffic to stop. He followed the long straight road. He walked up the embankment and onto the road, his mind too tired to think.

He heard the car behind him but couldn't move his legs fast enough. The car screeched to a halt. He turned slowly and raised his hands to surrender. There were no gunshots. A figure got out of the car, a woman.

'*Entrez, entrez dans la voiture et quittez la route.*' She pointed and he didn't hesitate to obey her hand signal.

She put the car in gear and accelerated. His head dipped; his eyes shut. He forced them open. She sped the car down the straight and through the S-bends. He thought it fast. They raced through the countryside. He was thrown against the door and he couldn't stifle the scream. She took no notice.

She saw the roadblock before he did. She didn't touch the brakes and to his surprise kept driving. The small car struggled for acceleration. She drove for the barrier at high speed. She motioned for him to get down. He put his arms around his head as if this would make a difference and crouched down low in his seat. The first bullets smashed through the windscreen and he felt the broken glass shower down on his head. He kept low and prayed. The car didn't slow; he felt it swerve off the road and hit the field, hard. He bumped and jumped; he screamed as his ribs hit the inside of the car door. All the time he could hear machine gun fire above the sound of the engine. He tried to protect his injuries with his arms. He could hear shots ripping through metal. He held his breath, waiting for the pain of gunshot wounds. It didn't come. The car swerved and he braced. The wheels of the car touched the road, the woman corrected the steering and they were back on the straight. He stayed low. He popped his head up. There were lights shining on them. They were now being followed. The machine gun fire ripped into the trunk. There followed the sound of breaking glass as the back window was shot out.

The woman took her focus from the road. She turned to Thomas and then pointed to the rear seat. He looked and saw the machine gun. He squeezed through the gap between the front seats, gritting his teeth. He got into the back, picked up the machine gun. He aimed towards the lights and opened fire. The car following swerved; realising they were being shot at they turned off their lights. In the moonlight Thomas could still see his target. He kept firing. The small machine gun was no match for the armoured car. It drew up alongside and fired bullets that rained into the car.

Thomas kept down low, firing the gun from above his head and through the side window. He dared to look up. He took aim at the wheels. He hit. The armoured car barrel-rolled into the ditch and exploded. He breathed heavy and clambered back to his seat. He relaxed.

'*Très bien*,' she said, and smiled. She looked so young and cute, his age; and she didn't seem to have any fear.

The car jostled and bumped along and he fell asleep. He awoke when the car came to a stop. She got out and lit a cigarette; she leaned with her back against the car and drew heavily, blowing out smoke. Her face was dimpled, yet she seemed so sophisticated.

CHAPTER FORTY-SIX

30th September 1943

Up in the hayloft, with the POW washed and dressed in Geordie's old clothes, Geordie showed Nicole how to operate the radio.

Geordie said: 'You need to know in case anything happens to me, if our plan doesn't work.'

'I can't do it.'

'Yes, you can, you and Emma; you will do fine.' Nicole scratched her check. 'It will work.'

'I don't think I can do any of this any more. Why don't I sleep with the Major? You've all done so much for me.'

'No, don't even think it! I wouldn't want one of my girls having to do that and you are like one of my own. Blimey, Eliza would string me up if she even thought I put the idea in your head.'

'I would, Geordie, for you, for Eliza, for the girls. It would just be so much easier,' she said with a long face. Geordie put his arm around her shoulder like her father used to.

'After tonight, it won't even matter. We will sort all this out once and for all and the Major won't even see it coming.'

'What if he doesn't take the bait?'

'He will. The women, they work for us; they will tip him off. Don't worry, he will be there and he will think it's all his own idea.'

'Geordie, this is just too much. I can't ask you to do this.'

'I've set that old machine gun up above the clearing. You get there after you've dropped him off.' Geordie pointed to the escapee who had propped himself up on the hay. 'Then we'll see what Major Lothar is made of. You just make sure you get down low and don't move. I was always a bloody good shot, better than your old man.'

They didn't have much time to make the rendezvous; they would have to be quick. They ran out of the cemetery, heading for the canal. The wharf was crawling with soldiers. Six armed guards stood on the bridge, three at either end. They used their knowledge of the lanes and passages to take them further down the canal and to the hidden rowing boat that they had made sure to put in place. She didn't want to be swimming in icy cold water.

Nicole and Emma got into the boat with the British soldier and rowed down the canal, away from the town. After a mile, they got out on the opposite bank and made sure to tie up the boat. They followed the path for a hundred yards before crossing the field and making their way to the level crossing. Here they waited in the ditch alongside the road. Emma jumped when an owl hooted.

'Calm down, will you?' Nicole said. 'You're making me jumpy.'

'It won't be long.'

'Do you remember what it was like before the war?' Nicole asked. 'It's been going for so long, I think I'm beginning to forget what life was like.'

'I know. We just have to get Louise and Catherine back; Mother is distraught. I've never seen her like this. I thought she was the strong one.'

Nicole thought of her own family at home. Would they remember her? She looked up at the edge of the road and wished for the Dorset lanes in summer. She remembered how she and Lily had watched as the workmen came, scraping back the overgrown edges. Laying the hot, stinking tar, then putting down the chippings and rolling backwards and forwards with the big steam engine, the tar fumes wafting on the air. Then when all the workmen had gone, she and Lily finding pieces of cooling tar on the verge and stepping down and popping it with their rubber soles. 'Course, Lily watched her first to make sure Nicole didn't burn her feet. Then day after day they would return to check their footprints were there until the next year. When had they stopped and Thomas and Hamilton taken over? She craved for home.

Where had all the years gone? Was this to be her life forever?

The small Citroën appeared on the road above and they could watch as it wound its way down the lane with its headlights off. They lay out in the ditch.

The car drove over the crossing and pulled onto the grass verge. The two members of the resistance got out and came to the side. Nicole and Emma got up and pulled the escaped POW with them, relieved the waiting was over. That was always the worst part, the amount of waiting around all the time.

'*Nous avons quelquechose pour vous*,' the driver said.

'*Quoi?* No, we are making the drop,' Nicole answered.

'*Regardez, nous savons que c'est hors de l'ordinaire* for one to be coming back, but he was very insistent even in the state he's in,' the driver said.

'But why on earth would he want to come back this way, when freedom is to the south?' Emma said.

'All he kept saying was, he must come to Albert. He must get here. Something about a sister in the resistance.' She shook her head. 'Damn fool, I said he was wasting his time. I've no time for this; he's your problem now.' She pulled the seat back and pulled the man from the rear passenger seat. The blanket covered his head and body and he looked like an old monk. He sat down on the verge. Nicole pushed their POW forward and did the swap. This was not good, not part of the plan. They were no better off, one for one. She always felt her teeth on edge, when they were hiding escapees; there was no time to relax or breathe.

The women in the car, their job done, closed the doors, started the engine and drove off, spinning the wheels on the loose gravel. Nicole looked at the blanket-covered man, thinking how frail he was. What now? This complicated matters. They waited for the car to leave and then approached. She walked up to the man. He was listless. She looked down at him. His face was bruised and the skin stretched and thin; his cheekbones showed through. She gasped. He looked so old. He looked so weak. He looked nothing like the brother she remembered.

His light blue eyes looked into hers without life. She could see those once sparkling eyes; now they were dulled and weathered. She hugged him close, afraid he might snap in her arms like a twig.

'Nicole,' he said weakly. 'Is that you? Tell me I'm not dreaming; tell me I'm not seeing angels in heaven; please god, tell me it's you.'

'It's me, it's me, you daft noggerhead!' Nicole hugged him close through the blanket. She could feel his bones and there seemed nothing of him. He smelt so bad, like rotten vegetables in the compost heap. She and Emma got either side of him and helped him to his feet. They slowly made their way across the field.

'He used to smell better,' Emma said.

There was no way they could head to the clearing; she had to get him safe, safe and hidden in the hayloft. They trudged, like in a drunken three-legged race, their pace slowed by Thomas who was too weak to walk on his own. They slowly made their way towards the boat. Nicole looked down to pull it in from its mooring but was disappointed to see it was not there. She looked around and saw it floating in the middle of the canal, far out of reach.

'Blast! I thought that was secure,' Nicole said.

'It was; someone's been and untied it, I'm sure,' Emma pronounced. 'We should head for the woods. There's no way we can make it through with Thomas.'

The women retraced their steps, headed into the field, then picked up the path that led to the wooded valley. They traced the path thick into the centre, under the tall beech and ash trees. They found a secluded spot far from the clearing. It had been so long; all she wanted to do was sit and talk, to stroke his hair, to feed him and take care of him, to hold onto him, never let him go. She looked at him; he looked so ill, so thin, so breakable. Like he was a baby again. She'd looked at and held him before and always thought she should be a mother for him until they'd made it to England and thankfully Connie took him as one of her own. Why had she ever thought Connie wasn't her mother? She had been the best mother she could have wished for. And now she was having to leave Thomas here when all she wanted to do was hold him hard in her arms and be with him. She remembered the times she had walked home with him from school, how she and Lily had ordered him around playing games, dressing up in old clothes and making little plays. He was always so good, playing with his sisters. How could she stop the plan? Maybe go up, tell Geordie; no, take the long way back to the hotel. This was flawed; this was only going to make matters worse. There was no way Geordie would be able to take out the squad.

'Nicole, I know you don't want to leave him,' Emma said. 'Let me go.'

'No, Emma, we go together. I know it's time,' Nicole said.

'Nicole, don't leave me. I don't want to be on my own. Take me with you,' Thomas said.

'I can't, Thomas, I can't. There isn't any time,' Nicole said.

'But we have to get Romily,' Thomas said.

'What?' Nicole said.

'Romily. I think he's alive.'

'What! Romily is with you? Was with you?' Nicole said.

'Yes, him and Billy. Billy, he saved us.'

It didn't make any sense. How long had he been in this war? How ever had he made it all the way to her?

'Why did you ever come for me?' Nicole said.

'I had to; and when I said, Romily insisted too. I wanted to make sure you were safe, and I remembered where I was born,' he whispered.

'You daft Dorset boys!' She shook her head.

Nicole turned to Emma. 'We can't go through with this plan, not now. It's too dangerous. Run to your dad now, before he lights up the woods like bonfire night.' She added, 'That's an order.'

'Cor, listen to you! When did you suddenly get so bossy?' Emma said.

'Since I've got this one. I've to get him home in one piece; it's how I make it up to Mum. To Connie, to my mother. If it's the last thing I do.'

'What about the Major?'

'Don't worry; I've an idea for him,' Nicole said.

CHAPTER FORTY-SEVEN

30th September 1943

Nicole gathered her thoughts. Geordie, Emma and Edith sat with her; they held their coffee cups up close to their chests, seated around the hotel kitchen table, late into the night. Eliza busied herself, washing in the sink. Nicole breathed in deeply and let out a huge sigh. Her brother Thomas was safe, sleeping like a baby in the hayloft; she'd taken him another warm brick wrapped in a towel and when she changed it he hadn't moved. Her heartbeat was fast; she tried to calm it. The adrenaline of the evening was still coursing through her veins. Her joy at having Thomas safe was reined in by the fear for Romily and the loss of Billy. Thomas had said he'd been with Romily days ago at a river; and by the sound of it, it could only have been the Somme.

'You should have let me go through with it; that old gun would have ripped through them,' Geordie boasted.

'I have to go and look for Romily.' Nicole spoke out loud what she had been thinking.

'You can't go; there will be soldiers everywhere,' Eliza said, looking over her shoulder. 'Not when you're here; you can't risk it.'

'I can't leave him out there. I have to go and search, even if it's only his body I find. I can't leave him on his own. He would do it for me.'

'It's too dangerous, Nicole; you don't have time. Your brother has only just made it back. Stay with him; he will want to see you when he wakes,' Emma said.

'I want to, more than anything. I can't rest, though, knowing that Romily is out there. It's not far, is it? I can make it to the Somme. If I don't find him I will come straight back, I promise.'

'Nicole, don't do it; stay with us, stay with your brother. Tell her, Geordie,' Eliza said.

'She's her own woman,' Geordie said to Eliza, then turned back to Nicole. 'If it's what you want, if you think you can do it, I will help you all we can; and you know we will look after Thomas.'

'I'll go with you, Nicole,' Emma said, her dark green eyes staring.

'No, Emma; it's too dangerous. I can't ask you to do that.' Nicole shook her head and forced her hand through her hair. 'I can't take you with me and put you in danger, when this is personal.'

'And what we've been doing for the last four years, that's not dangerous, or put us at risk?'

'Well, no, but this is different.'

* * *

'Thomas, I love you. I have to,' Nicole whispered in her brother's ear as she sat next to him in the loft, with the wind rattling the wooden shutter. She kissed him on the cheek. She stood up, her back arched under the eaves. She pushed the canvas bag with her food and supplies around her neck.

'You will be safe; they will look after you. Just make sure you stay out of sight.' She kissed him again. He looked so frail. She remembered how his body looked when they washed him down: deep purple bruises, ribs shining and transparent skin. At least he was clean now, and smelled of soap.

Thomas stirred and said: 'Nicole? Is that my sister Nicole?' His voice was a whisper, his throat hoarse, and he was barely able to open his eyelids.

'It is, Thomas.' Tears came into her eyes and ran down her cheek. How could she leave his bedside and go out into the night? After all the years fighting she wanted it over, she wanted to stay with her brother, she wanted to make him better and for him never to leave her sight.

'Stay, Nicole; sit with me, read to me.' He forced himself to raise his head and look over. She could see the pleading in his eyes.

She swallowed hard and felt her throat contract and said: 'I can't, I have to see if I can find Romily. I have to look for him. I can't leave him out there, knowing what they are capable of.'

'I don't want to ever lose any of you, not ever. He's a good man, Nicole; he's never stopped loving you; he was always telling us that. He said that he did all the bloody time, him and Billy. Well, you know Billy. He was so brave; he saved us; he did, Nicole. Poor Billy. He saved us and he died for us.' She watched as her brother began to cry, his whole body shaking.

She sat back down and put her arms around his shoulders. She felt Thomas's shaking body as he sobbed into her arms. She had left Romily behind before. She couldn't leave him out there. The not knowing was the worst.

'It's over for you, Thomas; the war is over for you. You don't have to worry any more; you're going to be safe now.' She wished she believed it.

* * *

She walked for an hour out of the town, taking the southern route. Nicole was well-armed: the Sten gun hanging from her shoulder, the Webley in her pocket, a couple of grenades, stashed, her knife and a canteen.

It was something deep within her. Intuition. She knew she was being followed long before she heard it. That sense that there were eyes on her. Her teeth wanted to chatter so she walked faster, getting heat into her body. Soon she wouldn't notice the cold. The breath escaped her mouth in a plume of smoke. The scuffling in the bushes confirmed it. She kept going, not letting on until she found a spot where she could hide above the track. She waited for the hooded figure to come into view, then she pounced, diving down on the figure with her pistol drawn. She wrestled the slim figure to the ground.

'Bloody hell! Let me breathe, will you!'

Nicole got up, pointing her pistol at the figure. The figure turned around. Nicole laughed.

'You, Emma Tucker! What the hell?' Nicole smiled.

Emma waved her machine gun.

'Couldn't let you come on this mission alone; I might miss all the fun.' Emma touched Nicole on the shoulder before pushing her hand through her hair.

'I nearly shot you! What the hell are your mother and father going to say?'

'It was Dad told me that if I wanted to go I should, that if it was his best friend he wouldn't let them go on their own.' Emma stuck out her chin in defiance.

'You bloody Tuckers! You are all the bloody same, aren't you? Can't let a girl do a thing on their own.'

'That's right, girl; you should know us by now.' She nodded.

Nicole laughed as Emma slipped her arm into hers. They followed the animal path in and out of the trees. Nicole knew their chances of finding Romily were slim; still, it didn't stop her praying that they would. The bravery of the Tuckers never ceased to amaze her: two daughters already in prison and Geordie telling Emma to go and help her friend. She had to repay them. It was down to her to get Louise and Catherine home.

'You know that brother of yours? I bet he won't be bad looking when he's put some weight on.'

'He's lovely; he's my little brother.' She wished she could have been with him, combing his hair and reading to him.

''Course, we will have to feed him up; he's all skin and bones. I prefer to have more to hold onto,' Emma whispered.

'Emma, you're bloody incorrigible!' Nicole shook her head and tutted under her breath.

'Has he ever had a girlfriend?' Emma asked.

'Not that I know of.' She parted her lips.

'He might need a girl to show him the ropes then.' Emma grinned.

'Oh, Emma, don't! He's my baby brother!' She shook her head.

'So, better a friend shows him then.' She giggled. 'You must like this Romily?'

'I do, Emma, but I made a mistake with another boy.'

They wandered down through the slopes of the wide valley. Shards of morning light fought through the low cloud. They kept to the hidden paths, out of sight of German outposts. Nicole remembered the last time she'd seen Romily: him looking so sad, sitting in his delivery truck. Dropping her off at the station. She'd had no idea then that it would be so long before she saw him again. She thought then she would be able to return at any time. Having to stay, having no choice, made it all the worse. When she'd had the freedom to return she wasn't ready; now she was and she couldn't. It frustrated the hell out of her.

Nicole led Emma to a crevice they found in a rocky bank, covered by woodland, looking down over the valley floor. They tried to sleep and rest. They got a short nap, twenty minutes. When she woke she looked down at the River Somme in the valley below. It looked like a gigantic snake, slithering its way in the moonlight. A large serpent. Where on earth would she start?

What was her plan? She hadn't really thought it through. She knew she wanted to search for Romily, but where? Thomas had described the rocks and the bridge. She thought she knew the place; but the river was long and there were hundreds of bridges. She would need to be careful of the guard towers every three hundred yards out in the open.

Would it be so bad if Thomas and Emma got together? She laughed to herself. She watched as deer grazed below, a mother and her fawn straying from the herd to graze on the lush grass on the bank below. Nicole watched the beauty of the animals, so lithe and carefree. She wished for home, for Ashcombe Beacon, for the shorthorn cows, for the pigs, the chickens, and most of all her family. She pushed the thoughts out of her head.

The deer wandered away, its fawn following. They joined the herd and moved on. Nicole fell in and out of sleep. Nicole and

Emma shared the bread, cheese and garlic. When dusk fell they began to move. They walked down the slope where the grazing deer had been. It didn't take them long to reach the river. They followed it downstream. Nicole kept watch. They found rocks, sandy inlets; they searched under bridges and looked down from the river banks. They found the rocky boulder outcrop. Nicole led Emma and they walked over the moss-topped stones. The odd rock was bald; she stopped when they came to one that was blood-stained. She said a prayer under her breath for Billy. She crossed her heart. She heard the crescendo of rushing water and she prayed for Romily.

They made their way onto the river bank and followed the path. The river wound its way down. They followed it for hours. They went under bridges and scrambled down waterfalls. They searched disused mills and farm buildings. They dodged around the guard towers, kept to ditches when in the open. She'd all but given up hope and resigned herself to not finding him. It was time they returned. They were pushing their luck.

The first light of early morning came up with the moon still out. They came to another old mill, with a large water wheel turning. The sound of rushing water was annoying to her; it always had been. The spray cast a shower, and the air smelled of spring. They watched from a safe distance. The water wheel turned over. They approached, creeping through the lush green vegetation, through bracken, rushes and ferns. Alder trees stood tall. The smell of bracken was fragrant and earthy. They ducked down when the sound of a car engine approached.

The Renault car drew up and three women got out. They were dressed like her: dark trousers, berets and beige coat; they entered the mill. She got up and crept to the edge of the stone wall adjacent to the main house. She got within earshot.

They were talking in French. Discussing how much the prisoner would fetch. There was a good price on English POWs on the run. She leaned up against the window and looked in through the dust panes. Her jaw dropped. It was Romily: tied, slumped up against the wall. He looked weak; his bones glistened through his skin, just like Thomas.

Her heart lifted and then sank. Why were there people like this, people who would do anything for money? She beckoned Emma over and whispered in her ear. Emma went and took up a position opposite the door.

Nicole walked in.

'I've been sent by the network; they want me to go with the prisoner. Plans have changed; they think he's more use to us now,' she said in French.

'Who are you? Why?' the tall woman said quickly in a thick accent.

Romily couldn't move his body or his head. He was bent over, with his head down between his knees.

'It's true; I've been sent. My patrol is in the woods; they're waiting for me.'

'The code?'

'I don't have time for this! They didn't give me a code. I got sent the normal way, with a dead letter drop. You know it's right.'

The sound of gunfire roared out from above the mill. It was Emma, firing down on the mill as planned.

'Look, I'm not staying,' Nicole said. 'I don't have the time to fight your battles.'

The three women crouched below the window. Nicole undid the ties on Romily. He looked up. She could see a faint sign of recognition deep in his eyes. The three resistance fighters stood up, took cover, smashed the windows and returned fire. While they were preoccupied with Emma's fire, Nicole took her pistol and shot the traitors in the backs of their heads, one after another. She had no regrets.

She took Romily and supported him. Emma ceased fire having heard the three shots. Nicole staggered out and between them they got Romily into the car.

Nicole drove as fast as she dared in the small Renault. It wheezed up the steep hill. Romily was groggy and incoherent.

'I love you, Nicole,' he whispered.

'Yes, Romily, and I you. Now shut up, rest and be quiet; I've to concentrate.'

'You love him?' Emma quizzed with a smile on her face.

'Yes; and don't start.'

They ditched the car on the outskirts of the town and made their way on foot to the hotel. They cleaned Romily up, the same as they had Thomas, and reunited the two of them in the hayloft with hot bricks.

'Now for Major Lothar,' Nicole said to Emma, as they crossed the yard to the kitchen.

CHAPTER FORTY-EIGHT

3rd October 1943

Nicole stepped out of the hot bath and wrapped herself in the towel. She dried herself down and tousled her hair. Her body was lithe and fit, with no fat at all. All the activity kept her body toned. Her brunette hair fell across her body and over her full breasts. Emma had picked out a dress for her; it was Louise's, a present from her husband. It was a long red silk dress. Emma had insisted that Louise would want her to wear it; if she was going to seduce the Major, then she should look like a film star. Nicole dressed in the loaned silk underwear; the dress hung over the back of the chair. The texture was exquisite, so soft and gentle. Nicole looked at the knife and the strap on the seat; she picked it up and tied it around her inner thigh. It was uncomfortable. She tied it off tight. She stepped into the soft silk, so light she felt naked. The neckline was embroidered with lace; it wasn't low but it showed a hint of skin.

When she went downstairs, Emma gushed at her, but more importantly said she couldn't see the knife. Nicole took a deep breath and got into the car with Geordie. He dropped her at the top of the drive and she walked down. It didn't take her long to reach the entrance; she wished it was longer. Sometimes, when she had been going to meet Billy, she would walk the longer route because she was nervous, a delaying tactic; a longer walk to get her breath, gather her thoughts. She wanted to delay the inevitable. But there was no delay; the guard had seen her; she was expected. The Major had made sure of that.

He pulled out the chair for Nicole as she was ushered in by the guard.

'I'm not a beast, am I?' the Major said, smiling.

Nicole pursed her lips, unsure of how to reply, so she said nothing.

She looked around the dining room of the château before taking her seat. Once, years before the war, it would have been magnificent. Now it was a dusty shell, with sheets covering the antique furniture. The German occupation didn't take much care or put a high priority on keeping the dust down. The smell was of working boots, of the traffic of war moving through the husk of a room. Chairs were lined along the wall. Tonight, two were positioned: one at the head and one to the side of the long table. Close enough to be intimate.

His deep voice echoed from the huge ceiling and he spoke deliberately slowly, speaking his second language but not losing his German tone. Nicole knew he was trying to soften his voice, but it still crackled with authority. What would he do to her if he knew her other language? The table had been cleared for tonight's dinner; that was obvious, as the tablecloth didn't quite reach to the middle. It was make do and done in haste. She wondered where he would have found the cook; no doubt he would have pulled in a chef from one of his favourite eateries in Cambrai – for sure, a place where there was low light, a comfortable ambience and where he would have entertained many an elegant lady. Perhaps a lady who didn't have high morals and who would be more than pleased to have some light in her life, a relief from the mundane drudgery, and the security of knowing she was favoured by the commanding officer of the local garrison. He wouldn't be short of women to be entertained by. He would be younger than his looks suggested; years of war did that to everyone. His black hair was smooth, his hairline receding; his hard-flat nose didn't match his slim jawline. He was tall and he accentuated every inch of his height when standing by pushing his shoulders back square. Tonight, he was in a clean pressed uniform and smelt of aftershave. Looking at his eyes she saw they were hazel, soft, with a piercing intensity.

'*Vin?*'

'A small glass,' Nicole said in French.

'It's a great vintage; the cellar is full of it.' He flashed his white teeth through his wide mouth. He held the glass delicately in his hand before taking a second, longer sip.

'Why did you do it?' Nicole said.

'Do what, Nicole? – I hope we can be friends.'

'Why did you shoot him?'

'Who?' He put his glass down, thought better of it and returned it to his mouth, taking another drink. She looked him in his eyes. His eyes narrowed; he was thinking.

'I've shot a lot of people; it's war, of course,' he said. 'Let's not talk about it tonight; let us have a calm, reasonable conversation and forget the conflict. Tonight, let us be two friends having a nice meal. I've gone to a lot of effort.'

'And where are Catherine and Louise? You need to release them; I've kept my side of the bargain.'

The guard who had shown her in returned, bringing the first course. Two delicate china bowls filled with thick onion soup. He placed them down and left the room. The soup was piping hot with steam coming off it.

'Your sisters are safe; don't worry. I will return them, when we've had our time together. You think me an ogre, don't you, like in the fairy tales? What am I, the wolf?'

She forced down the soup. It tasted good but she had no appetite.

'We have all done things we are not so proud of; war does that, doesn't it? You see the best and worst of people; it's an exaggeration of us as humans. You put us in awkward and pressured positions and that's what happens.'

'You shot him when he was giving himself up to you, and you don't even remember.'

'Oh, I remember! I think of it all the time and it doesn't please me. I was young, inexperienced, trying to lead men, trying to show the men I was the big man, the Major. Don't you think I regret those things? There are far more worse than me.'

'What about Catherine and Louise?'

'They are safe. – Drink up; have another glass of wine.'

'I want to see them.'

'That is not possible; they are not here.'

'I want them released.'

'I'm not going to do that.' He paused, took a spoonful of soup, dabbed at his mouth with the serviette and sipped from his glass of wine. 'You know the SS, don't you, and the Gestapo? You've seen them about in their long black leather coats.'

Nicole knew them; they all did.

'I've to act like I'm in control, that I have the situation… I don't know how to say. What shall we call it? Managed.'

'Managed?'

'Under control.'

'What?'

'You don't make it easy, none of you.'

'I don't?' She forced another spoonful of soup in her mouth.

'I don't want this war, I don't want this life, I don't even want to be here.' He stopped. 'Gunter!' he called.

The guard, who must have been standing outside the door within earshot, came in.

'Take these away.'

The guard took up the soup bowls. He had done it before; perhaps in another lifetime he had been a waiter, or in service.

The Major took his glass and continued to talk, to tell her of his life before. When he was young, maybe seven, he had lived in the hills; his father and mother were not rich but they were content with their lot. They subsisted on a small plot of land, a few cows, goats and a couple of horses. And when he was seven it all changed. His father died of a heart attack in front of him in the fields; he just keeled over. And he had stood watching him, helpless, not knowing what to do. His mother ran to him but there was nothing she could do; his father was already dead. It was horrific for him as a little boy, to know already that bad things could happen, that the world wasn't safe and that your mother and father were not invincible.

'We were so poor; the soup we had then was not much more than water. The reparations Germany was repaying crippled the country; we were destitute. Me and Mother couldn't survive. She couldn't survive and she couldn't cope. She passed me off to her brother in Munich, thinking he would do better with me. I hated it; he was hard and mean, and I had to fight in that family to survive. In his family of seven children, he said an eighth wouldn't make much difference. He was right; it made no difference to him. He was a watchsmith, good and intricate with his hands, but the three other boys were already his apprentices; there was no room for me. He was wicked, too, because any money he made, he spent on Friday in the *Bierkeller*. He beat my auntie incessantly, and she was a wreck. I never saw my mother again until she was dead. Unknown to me, she had been working as a whore for what little money she could get.

'So, when I was twelve, I ran away from that diabolical city house. I wanted to be free of that tyranny, free from the smog of the city. I wanted to make it on my own, and I did. I worked on farms; I saved every penny. I spent afternoons at the library, I got books, I read and I read and I learnt everything I could; and I was good at maths, my brain was good. I saved enough; and the librarian – a kind, grandfather figure – took pity on me. He gave me lodgings for a small price, he and his wife who had no children of their own. They were like grandparents to me. He helped me a lot and in the end, I got to university; I got my degree and I got a good job for the time. At the railway. Not an engineer, but close; I was working my way up.

'She was a beauty, my wife. Long blonde hair, large generous lips; she was perfect for me. She was my soulmate; I never thought from where I had come that I would be so lucky. Of course, I worked hard. We had a rented room. Lotte worked in an office as a secretary. We were blessed to be working at all, renting the house. All we wanted was to have enough for our own place, out of the city, maybe some small land. She was patient for me to work my way up. On Sundays we would escape the city and cycle to the countryside; it was so beautiful. Lotte would plan where we would live. As we cycled with the wind in our hair through the forest, we were free from day-to-day monotony, the smog and the grime and the desperation. The time was like no other in my life. We were so happy; that little piece of freedom was enough to power our dreams. We didn't ask for Hitler… but the suffering… I've seen it: the begging, people living on the streets, in shop doorways, everywhere. German people were down; they wanted better for their families.

'Slowly, I got the promotions. We were not long to leave the city. To be out; to have our dream home. Then the war, and this. It wasn't long after I got the letter; yes, we suffer too. The letter, you see; the British bombs: they did for my pregnant wife.

'So maybe if I wasn't thinking straight…' His hazel eyes glistened with moisture.

The guard brought in their main course. It was roasted duck in thick plum sauce, with potatoes cooked in cream.

'I never asked for this war; you see, I never wanted to be here at all. I'm a man who wanted to have a family and live with his beautiful wife. I'm not the enemy. I've been protecting you, you and the family. I know what you've been up to; I saw you back in 1940, in the woods. You were unmistakable to me. But if I didn't make your lives hard I wouldn't have been doing my job; I would have been replaced by far worse.'

'You've been protecting us…'

'In a way.'

'Why take Louise and Catherine?'

'I needed to be seen to act.'

'So, what now?'

'There is no way we can win this war; we're holding on. Hitler won't let us go without a fight.'

She cut into the duck with the silver knife. It was tender and cooked to perfection. She pushed it around her plate, then put it on the end of her fork. She'd never had such heavy cutlery in her hand.

'You should never have killed the Colonel,' he said. 'I didn't like doing what we had to do after that.' He drank his glass empty and refilled it from the decanter in the centre of the table.

'It was meant to be you.'

'I'm glad it wasn't.'

'Why bring me to dinner?'

'You have spirit, and it's nice to talk, isn't it? And to have some beauty in this dreary war.'

'What do you want from me?'

'You should stop your activities and those of the family. I can't continue to cover for you.'

'That's all?'

'I'm still in love with the memory of my wife. I don't think I can forgive the enemy for that, but I don't really want to take you. If times were different, if we had met under different circumstances, you are a woman I would like to know. You have to stop; I can't keep the SS and the Gestapo away for ever. If you can get out, you should go now, before they destroy everything.'

'What about Catherine and Louise?'

'You can stay here tonight, in my room. I will sit in the chair. It will look good for the men. They will think I've had my way. You can leave in the morning. I'll release the sisters, as the bargain.'

Nicole touched the inside of her leg. The strap holding the knife itched on her thigh and she couldn't scratch it. She let out a sigh of relief.

CHAPTER FORTY-NINE

4th October 1943

Lily woke, restless, tossing and turning, without Perry who had left on an operation in August; he was sure this was the big push; it would be more dangerous than ever and he hadn't sugar-coated it. He had been brutal and kind as they had walked together down Weymouth esplanade in the morning sun back in the summer. It had been early, just after dawn, and the town was beginning to wake.

'Don't wait for me.'

'Of course I'll wait for you.'

'I don't want you to; you're too young. If I don't come home, don't cut yourself off. I love you and I want you to have the most fantastic life ever. I don't want you being an old maid. I want you to have a large family, to remember the good times, this time, our honeymoon, the time in the field; but don't hold a flame forever; you're too young for that.'

'But Perry, I want to have you and only you.'

'I know, but that will pass in time. You're so bright; I want you to get your degree, to get the farm.'

'But we will be together, Perry! Don't talk like this.'

'I hope so, Lily, I really do; there is nothing more that I want than to be with my Dorset girl. But I can't promise, only that I will move heaven and earth to come home.'

The moon was shining through the thin curtain of her bedroom in Home Farm. She wished for Perry to be with her, to be in her bed, to feel his warmth. To hear his voice soothe her. The first birds were yet to sing. Unable to return to sleep she got up and looked out of the window. At least they had got a letter from

Thomas, even though it was six months old, the whole family so relieved he was alive, and Mother and Violet busy with knitting needles, making jumpers for the boys.

She opened the window to air the room and was met by the thick smell of acrid smoke. She saw there were thick tendrils of smoke clouds on the horizon, coming from the Manor House. There wasn't a moment's hesitation. This was bad. She dressed quickly in her uniform and tied the belt around her waist. She rushed to Father's room; it felt odd to be in here waking him. He was always the first up. She shook him. He woke with a start. She saw the panic on his face before it set. He tried to persuade her to stay in the house but she was insistent. Mother told them to go; she said she would raise the alarm. She rushed out of the door, grabbing her coat as she did. She couldn't help but think of the bombing raids and the nights spent on Chesil Beach.

When she rounded the corner of the lane, she saw the great plume of smoke rising up high in the sky. She had to run to the Manor, as fast as she could.

'You should get back in the house with your mother,' her father shouted after her, struggling to keep up.

'I've seen worse, don't forget!' Lily shouted back as they ran up the lane, heading for the drive. Running with her father trailing, she headed for the source of the great tail of smoke in the air. It was fanning out across the night sky but its source was obvious. It was coming from the Manor. She swallowed hard and tried to remember her training. She couldn't help but remember poor Aida Burwood. She prayed for her grandmother but she hadn't heard the bomb drop or the planes in the sky.

The smell of smoke filled the air. She tied her hair up. When she came around the bend the sight of flames greeted her. The fire crackled and windows exploded as the fire raged. But there was no bomb crater, there was no explosion; there was just a huge wall of fire engulfing the Manor House. She felt the heat hit her hard in the face. Her father was somewhere behind her. She didn't think twice. She ran, dodging falling stone, tiles and timber. Her grandmother was in there. She went in through the kitchen door. The smoke was suffocating; she held her breath and ran up the stairs to the landing. Fire licked the ornate oak panelling.

She rushed down the corridor and found her grandmother's room. The door was ajar. She entered; the fire hadn't spread here, thank god. Lily approached the bed, shouting for her grandmother. She got to the bed. Her grandmother was unconscious. How would she get her out? Would she be able to manage her on her own? What the hell had she done, coming running in here without a moment's thought?

She pulled the sheets back, tried to wake Gran: but nothing. She put her ear to her grandmother's face. She couldn't hear anything, but she felt the faintest breath on the hairs of her earlobe. She couldn't stop; she had to act. She knelt down, half-lifted and dragged her grandmother from the bed and onto her shoulder. The smoke and heat were all around her. She pushed down through her feet with Gran slumped over her shoulder and stood up. There was not the weight she was expecting; she could do this. Where was the rest of the family? What about Elizabeth, Montague? And her Uncle Theodore? They would be in here somewhere. She stumbled out of the bedroom, keeping her feet, wanting to reach out for support. She kept her hands around Gran's legs as she lurched down the stairs. She met her father coming in and handed Gran to him; he took her without hesitation.

She went back up the stairs, searching the bedrooms. There was no one there and the beds hadn't been slept in. She ran down the stairs. The fire was more intense. The smell was acrid, the heat unbearable. She jumped the last step of the stairs. She went to escape through the kitchen, but the way was blocked by the inferno. She turned and headed for the library; she would be able to escape through the large windows. The books were burning all around her. The bookshelves were ablaze; they fell like dominoes as their footings burned away. What a waste: all the great works, the first editions her grandfather had collected… She tried to keep low out of the smoke. She headed for the bay window at the far end, running the gauntlet of falling shelves and burning embers. She ran past the stone fireplace and decorative mantle.

She saw him. It was her uncle, cowering, sitting in the corner on the floor. The fire seemed to be chasing her to the end of the library.

'There was nothing left, no money; I've gambled and drunk it away. I'm ruined; I have nothing.'

'Where's Elizabeth and Montague?' Lily asked.

'I'm ruined; all the money's gone; I've nothing.' He sobbed, his head in his hands.

'Where are your children? Listen to me, where is your wife?' She shook him.

'It's gone; I have nothing, do you hear? Nothing; it's all been taken from me.'

Lily looked at him but there was no recognition on his face.

'I wanted to stop so many times. I wanted to run the estate better, but I've never been able to stop. I thought I would get the money back, make it all back, but my luck never changed. If I could have got the farm, I could have sold it, paid my debts.' He suddenly snapped out of his trance. 'It's your fault! If you'd given up, let me win, my luck would have changed. I would have paid my debts. I would have been all right.'

'Uncle, what about your family? Where are they?'

His eyes cast down, he succumbed to his inner demons. He was lost again in an incoherent babble. Lily looked at the fire approaching, then turned back to her uncle. She slapped him hard across the face, making her hand sting. 'Where are Elizabeth and Montague?'

'What, them? They're not here; they're in Weymouth.'

'Thank god! We have to get out.' She pulled at his arm.

'Leave me, leave me; I'm done for, I have nothing.' He pushed her away.

Lily looked at the library filling with smoke, at the fire: a gigantic torrent heading their way. She climbed onto a chair and went to open the window. She put her hand on the catch; it was hot to the touch and scalded her fingers. She put her finger in her mouth. She tried to release the iron catch. She couldn't get it to budge. She felt her lungs filling with smoke.

'You have to help me. Forget yourself for a moment; help me, help us get out of here.'

'I'm dead already; there is no point.'

'I'm pregnant, for God's sake! Pull yourself together, if not for me, for my child!'

Lily took off her jacket, wrapped the sleeve around her hand and tried to force the window catch. It didn't budge; it was stuck firm. She looked back at the fire which was engulfing them. She felt her lungs struggle for clean air.

'Help me, Uncle, help me!'

'I can't; I want to die.'

She looked for something to break the window with. She found a paperweight on the desk and threw it as hard as she could. It bounced back, like the regrets in her mind. She was going to die without seeing Perry for a last time. She was going to die and her baby inside her too, and she had told no one; no one would know. Perry would lose them both. And she would never be able to say sorry to her sister. He was going to be the death of them. Her uncle's selfish, thoughtless actions were going to kill them and ruin all their lives.

She looked around as the fire approached, a wall of red and orange flame. The heat was intense. She scanned the library for an alternative exit, or something. Her eye drew her to the fireplace, to the fire-making implements hanging on the stand: dustpan and iron shovel, the large log grabber, and the heavy iron poker with its twisted grip. She dashed for the poker and picked it up; it was long and heavy. She ran back to the window catch, jammed the poker underneath and levered it as hard as she could. At first it slipped away. She could feel the smoke reaching her lungs. She jammed the poker in again. Looking through the window she could see Father and Mother looking at her from the other side of the glass. They were only feet away, trying to get to her; it could have been a thousand miles. It became harder to breathe; the air was fast disappearing. If only she could get the poker in at the right angle. She tried again; could this all be in vain?

Uncle whimpered, cried out. Lily grasped the poker again, concentrated, then jammed it right into the catch. She pushed down hard; then with a crack, it released and was sprung. She pushed the window ajar and clean, fresh air rushed in. Her father was there before she could move, pulling her out, pulling her with ease, with no care, getting her out into the night air. She collapsed onto the lawn, her father holding her, her mother cradling her head.

Smoke clung to her lungs, like limpets on rocks at West Bay. However much she coughed she couldn't seem to shift it.

She turned her face to her father and said: 'I can't leave him, not even after all he's done. I couldn't live with myself.' She tried to stand up, to clear her throat of smoke. Ashes fell onto her hair, soft like snowflakes, and she brushed at them with her hand.

'No, you don't, Lily,' Mother said.

Her father reached out and held her shoulder.

'Not you, me.' He said.

Her father pushed her back and into the arms of her mother. He left them and climbed in through the window. She watched as the fire blazed through the roof. Its once rich architecture was now smothered in smoke and flames. The minutes seemed to last for hours. Then he was there, climbing through the window, hauling her weak uncle over his shoulder. Her uncle's body was limp. Her father dropped him on the lawn, next to her grandmother who was being tended by Dorothy.

Lily stood over Uncle Theodore. She bent down over him and

loosened his soot-covered shirt. She knelt down lower; she put her hand over his lip. She could feel his faint breath. She loosened his tie and undid more of his shirt buttons. He murmured, incoherent.

CHAPTER FIFTY

5th October 1943

Lily, hand-in-hand with Mother, meandered towards the Manor. The sounds of birds could be heard, rustling, searching for food in the hedgerow. The leaves were gone from the oak tree, revealing its naked skeleton. The Manor had been destroyed, burnt to a cinder; now a pile of rubble. It was all the talk of the village.

'You should never have run in like you did,' Mother said.

'I didn't stop to think; I had to try and save them.'

'But in your condition: the baby.'

'I know, Mum, but I had to; I couldn't leave her to die, not like that.'

'I love you so much, Lily. I couldn't bear to think of losing you, to lose any of you.' They walked through the avenue of tall pine trees. 'Life wouldn't be worth living.'

'I'm sorry. – Nicole and Thomas will make it home, won't they? There is so much I want to say to Nicole,' Lily said.

'All me and your father ever wanted was for you to have a good home and a life without war. It's so bloody awful, it benefits no one. And then there are people like Theodore who want to make a profit out of it.'

Lily stepped through the needles and cones littering the tarmac drive. She breathed in the scent of pine, but it didn't soothe her.

They came out of the pine trees and ambled past the row of cottages, one for the butler, one for the gardener and one for Cook, all the cottages built by the Admiral for his staff. There would be no chance of Uncle Theodore being so caring, not like his grandfather had been; a time when the estate had flourished. It showed the Admiral's compassion. He could have disinherited her after Sampson's death, ostracised her, but he didn't; he took great care and interest in her life, and that he continued to do even on his death.

Gran would be in bed, moved to the butler's cottage; they would call in afterwards, for she was sure to ask for a report.

The ruin of the Manor House stood in front of them. Rubble was piled twenty foot high, timber was strewn like matchsticks, still smouldering. Lily gasped. She knew Mother hadn't visited the Manor since the day they had both left, when she herself was five years old, after Sampson had died. Mother and Redver had married a year later.

They walked on to the gardens and looked at the flowerbeds, dug and clear, neat and tidy, attended to, in stark contrast to the devastation.

Her uncle was standing surveying the scene in front of him. He walked over with his cane in his hand.

'What are you doing here?'

'I… I… I wanted to see.' Lily thought he might even say thank you. 'We were going to see Gran.'

'Lily, we shouldn't bother; he's not worth the effort,' Mother said, pulling on her arm.

'You and your father should have left me,' Uncle Theodore said.

'What were you doing back here? It's not like you, coming back in the night; why was that?' Lily said. 'I know what you've been doing in Weymouth. It doesn't seem to me…'

'I was worried about my mother; you know she's been suffering with such a cold.'

'That would be the first time you thought of someone else in your life, wouldn't it?' Lily said.

'I think of my family all the time.' He tapped with his cane. 'I can't trust those servants to do anything right.'

'Why did you come back, Uncle?'

'I don't answer to you two.'

'Tell us, Theodore: why were you here?' Mother said.

'There was a problem with the car.'

'What about all you were saying?' Lily said.

'There was a fire raging, Lily; how is a man meant to think? I was incoherent, not thinking straight.'

Mother said, 'It will make a very good article for the paper, don't you think? A lot of people will be interested to hear how a Captain and squire has fallen so far, so desperate, so addicted to gambling, out of control, running the estate into the ground, destroying every last piece of his father's creation. Yes, it will make a great front page.'

'Don't you dare!'

'Readers will love to know how he lost it all. You are not even a tenth of the man your father was, or even your brother,' Mother said.

'Don't you compare me to my father, or that little shit of a brother of mine! None of them had to go through what I did, did they? They didn't face the onslaught, the stench of death, the constant barrage, their friends blown to bits, did they? They didn't have to order their friends to death! They didn't see men missing arms and legs, men with holes in their heads. They didn't have to live with the smell of shit and death and disease, did they? You have no idea.' Her uncle looked up at the grey clouds. Lily studied his face; there were tears in his eyes.

'All we wanted, Elizabeth and I, was to have children. It nearly killed her, my poor wife.' Uncle Theodore banged his cane down on the stone paving; it let out a crack like a gunshot. 'And you're not perfect, Constance, are you? Didn't take you long to go and marry Redver, did it?' he said viciously.

'I did it for love,' Mother said.

'Did you? If that's the case, did you ever love Sampson? Or was it a great convenience? He came along at the right time. He was always such a sap for lost causes.' He glowered.

'I did care for him. He gave me so much,' Mother said. 'And after he passed I wanted the best for Lily.'

'And that's what I've been trying to do for my family: the best.'

'You don't seem to be making a very good job of it. And you don't have to do it by making other people's lives a misery,' Lily said.

'I'm trying, for Montague's sake. We went through so much trying to have him; you don't know, that do you? I could have lost Elizabeth and him. I couldn't lose him to the war.'

'I know the truth…' Lily said.

'It's your word against mine! And who will they believe, a magistrate and local squire or some low-paid waif? Your mother tried to break free once, but that never lasted. Who's going to buy your father's produce, if I put the word out it's damaged goods?'

'How can you be so…' Lily bit her tongue.

'So… ruthless?' he said.

'Yes,' Lily said.

'If I had my way I would have had your useless father court-martialled when I had the chance. You know he should have been shot.' There was silence between them, interrupted only by the screams of the crows as they flew overhead.

The three of them paused as they looked over the debris of the burnt-out shell of what had been the splendid sixteenth century Manor House.

It was such a waste. Much of Europe must look like this, ravaged by war; and here she was sure it had been done by one man. Was it because of what he had seen, of what the war had done to him? What would Thomas and Nicole have seen? What would they have had to do? And what about her poor Perry, what effect would war have on him? Would he be the same if he ever made it home?

The remains smouldered; soft and light smoke clouds rose to meet the grey of the sky. The smell itched and scratched in her throat and lingered in her hair.

Montague walked into view and joined his father. His thick mop of curly ginger hair, buffeted by the breeze, looked like autumn leaves. His skin was pale, with many and various shaped freckles. His moustache was not yet quite taking root: thin, the colour of wheat stubble after harvest. To think he was the same age as Thomas, who was god knows where, while Montague stood here under his father's protection living a life of luxury, cosseted from danger. She couldn't help but feel antagonistic towards her cousin; he hadn't grown up, he hadn't done his duty; he was here and Thomas, Nicole and Perry weren't.

'We're done!' her uncle shouted. 'Come on, Montague; let's go and find your mother. You two have gloated long enough; and don't even think of printing one single word.'

'I'll print what I like, when I'm good and ready,' Mother said.

Uncle Theodore placed his hand on Montague's shoulder and turned away, then turned back and said: 'You'd better have a good harvest, because someone's going to have to pay for this.' He pointed with his cane at his ruined home.

Lily and Mother turned and left. They visited Gran who was sitting up in bed, looking frail; she could only manage to talk for short periods, and when she fell asleep they left her. They returned through the pine trees.

'What will you write?' Lily asked Mother.

'He's right, that's the problem; he's always right, and he won't be happy until he has us out of Home Farm, will he?'

'But, Mum, he started the fire; I know it, you know it. And Gran was in there; he knew that too. We can't let him get away with it.'

'I know, Lily, but what can we do? If I print any allegations he will come after us more ferocious and harder than ever. I can't put our home, our farm, our livelihood, our whole way of life on the line to risk it all for some headlines that will end up as chip paper.'

'If we don't, what if he takes it all anyway?' Lily looked her mother in the eye. She felt her own eyes beginning to water with the wind blowing. 'What about if it wasn't in the *Bridport News*? What if it was another paper? You've plenty of friends and contacts; couldn't they help? What about the *Dorchester Gazette?*

* * *

Lily woke to the sound of loud banging, fists on wood. She hadn't been in a deep sleep; she had been tossing and turning and thinking of Perry, hoping he was safe, hoping she would get word soon, hoping above all things to get a letter, a letter that would say he was safe and would be home with her soon. She touched her wedding ring and then caressed her stomach; their baby together. Sometimes she would wake from a fitful sleep and before she was fully conscious, she would think what a great life she had; that there were no worries, that everything was perfect. Then as morning slipped into her mind it would dawn on her that they were still living through the war, and that there was nothing she could do to bring her husband, her sister or her brother home.

The banging got louder and she heard Mum and Dad chatter through the bedroom wall. She got up, picked up her dressing gown and, wrapping it tightly round her, met her parents on the landing. The floorboards felt cold under her feet; she sneezed.

'Get out here now, the lot of you!' It was her uncle's voice, full of a Captain's authority and the power of the squire. 'You bloody lot get down here! I know it was you; it's so bloody obvious.' Lily could hear the door knob *rat-tat-tat.*

Father led the way down the stairs and to the back door.

'I know you are in there; come down, you coward! Now!'

Father opened the door; her uncle leant on the frame.

'So, you can face up?' His speech was slurred, his blonde hair dishevelled. His stubble chin was in shadow from the moonlight.

'Go home to bed, Uncle,' Lily pleaded.

'It was your doing.' He lurched and moved his finger to Mother's neck. 'You, Constance: you were trouble the day you moved in at the Manor and you've been trouble ever since. Nothing was done the way you wanted; arguing with father, arguing with Sampson, now arguing with me. And you, Lily, do you think Sampson was your father? The way your mother jumped

352

at marrying Sampson when Redver was in the war like that; she didn't wait for him long, did she? Who's to say, Lily, whether you were even Sampson's daughter?'

Mother moved, quick as a flash. She raised her arm and swung with full force. The palm of her hand smacked Uncle's face with a crack like thunder. Uncle Theodore staggered, sent to his knees. He stood up, quick; he grabbed mother by the wrists and pulled.

''Course, you should have had a real man, you should never have spurned me.' Father stepped forward. With one arm, he gently pulled Mother to him; with the other he pushed Uncle Theodore away.

'You should control that mare of yours; she's out of control.'

'You're a weak man, Theodore,' Father said. 'A very weak man. You can do whatever you want but you will never break what we have; it's more valuable than all the land, all the houses and all the money you have.'

'You're on borrowed time! I've lost it all, I've nothing else to lose.' He stumbled. 'And Lily, if you think you will ever finish that degree and own this farm, you're dreaming, because as long as I have breath in my body, no Kingson is ever going to be a landowner in this village.'

'Your trouble, Uncle, is you don't see what matters. The Great War may not have taken your sight but it has blinded you to what is important,' Lily said.

'Don't you lecture me!'

'You need a lecture! Someone in this village needs to stand up to you, or you will ride over all of us for the rest of our lives.' Lily said.

CHAPTER FIFTY-ONE

10th October 1943

Lily went to see Vicar Wrixon in his vestry. He'd asked her to go.

'Now, young lady, how is it all going?' He fiddled with his dog collar.

'It's going fine, but my Uncle Theodore – he is out of control.'

'Whatever do you mean?'

'He's been threatening again; he wants us out. He was behind the War Ag. When he didn't win that battle, it set him off; he is spiralling out of control. I fear to think what he will do next. He's been at the house in the middle of the night, calling us out.'

'It can't be easy for him, not after all he's been through: the war, losing his father, and now the fire.'

'But what can I do? He has all the power, he has all the control; he can make our lives a misery.'

'He's not the only one with power. You are stronger than you think, and you have some education, if not all that we wanted for you.'

'But he says that he's going to stop me from going back to university. He wants to put a stop to our way of life.'

'You will just have to find a way that you can outmanoeuvre him.'

'I don't know what I can do.'

'It will come to you, if you put your mind to it; if you have faith, you will be led.'

'It goes so deep, though, the hatred he has for our family. Deeper than I ever thought possible.'

'It's the way he is; he can't help himself.'

'What am I to do?'

'Keep the faith, keep going, keep believing, and trust you will overcome; you can do it, I'm sure.'

* * *

Lily wandered down Barrack Street. It was all very well for the vicar to keep believing but it was hard with everything that was going on around her. This damn war! Would she and Perry ever be able to settle down together? The cars in the street roared as engines raced to make the turn and head along St Andrew's road. She came around the corner and saw the wide façade of the Scientific Institute. The ground floor was still a reading room housing a collection of books, but the rest of the building had been commandeered. There was a medical detachment of American soldiers on the first floor, and the Red Cross were using the upper floors for collection and distribution. There was no library left in the Manor and she still loved books. She entered the tall stone building and went through the large doors into the reading room. In the corner was the billiard table, where two Americans were trying to play the game.

She cast her eye over the tall bookcases. The clean smell of disinfectant wafted into the room. She wandered aimlessly through the shelves that were much taller than her. It was good to be in peace, a time where she could reflect and get her thoughts together. There had to be a way, there had to be something; perhaps there was something in one of the great books, perhaps *The Canterbury Tales*, or even the bible. Perhaps that was the key: there must be a fable or story, something to help her turn things around, overcome her uncle's tyranny and put a stop to him trying to end their lives as they knew it. She gazed at book after book, taking each one from the shelves, scanning the pages, looking for something that would come alive from the page, something, anything that would come to her. When she found a book that might provide an answer she took it from the shelf and would read from it at the long table in the centre of the room. She made notes; it was like being back at St Hilda's. Time seemed to disappear, and that was what she didn't have on her side. There was no doubt that her uncle would be conspiring with his cronies, organising his lackeys, coming up with another plan that would finally get them from the land once and for all.

The light was fading outside and her stomach was calling for food. She'd forgotten to bring lunch; she hadn't even had a drink of water since she'd left home. Her arms were aching from lifting book after book from the shelves, then replacing them. This was pointless. Maybe she should just give up and resign herself to the fact that she wasn't as clever as the vicar thought, and that he was wrong to think she could do this.

The clock on the far wall was racing towards five o'clock and closing time. The busy librarian was clearing up and making sounds as if to pack up for the day. The Americans playing billiards had long gone. The natural light was fading fast through the large oval windows.

Crouching on her knees, she looked at another shelf, low down, in the row furthest from the window. She picked out yet another dust-covered book, one that looked like it hadn't been touched in years. She craned her neck and looked down at the spine. Its title didn't look exciting or inspirational and certainly wasn't a great work of literature. The author was unknown to her: George Arthur Johnston; and this was the second edition. The hard cover, a dark red with the lettering in black, held the title *The Agricultural Holdings Act 1906*. She'd looked at so many books, with no inspiration, no great insight; but maybe, just maybe, there was be a chance that there might be something in this dusty old book. There wasn't much time; the librarian would soon want to close the doors. Perhaps… The librarian was looking the other way; she was only a young girl, more interested in getting ready to go home. Lily didn't hesitate. Mother would scold her if she knew. She picked up her coat, hid the book underneath it and walked straight out, shouting 'thank you' on her way out through the large entrance doors.

* * *

Lily was out topping sugar beets with Father and Jeanie. Dusty was still forlorn, missing working with the sheep. Lily smiled as they worked; there was a glimmer of hope. After reading the book deep into the night, she thought there was a case that could be made. She had gone from farm to farm too, to the other tenants. The Fooks, the Crabbs, the Hansfords: all said it couldn't be done, but they were suffering. They had all suffered in one way or another at the hands of Theodore: having their rents raised, having the War Ag on their backs making their lives a misery. Uncle wasn't personal with them but it was still deeply unfair when war was raging, when the farmers were fighting their own battles to feed a nation that had, before the war broke out, imported a third of its food and forgotten about the farmers at home.

They loaded up the trailer with the beets, to be taken to the depot of the Ministry of Food, needed for sugar. Jeanie, with her chemistry background, was keen to point out that it took three beets to make one pound of sugar. Father drove the Standard Ford tractor with its large wide mudguards covering the big rear wheels, two smaller wheels on the front, and open to the elements. He seemed to be growing to like it as much as the horses. Lily hopped up onto the trailer and pulled Jeanie with her; Father slowly drove the tractor and trailer from the field and into the lane. There he was, her uncle, standing in his tweed, his hair looking tidier, his cane at his side. Father drew the tractor to a stop just inside the gateway. Lily dropped down.

'Glad I've caught you.' Her uncle looked more relaxed; he was clean-shaven, his hair neatly combed. 'I don't know what you're trying.' He took out the letter from his inside suit pocket. 'But you have no chance; I will wipe the floor with you.'

Lily had known he would come to them at some time. But it had all come from the book on the Act of 1906; she and mother had worked together on the letter and had sent it by registered post as they should, so that her uncle couldn't dispute it.

'You will know, Uncle, that if we can't agree on an impartial arbiter, then we will have a Justice of the Peace.'

'I don't know what your game is, young lady, but when it comes to the law I know whose side they will be on.'

'Do you?'

'I do; and money talks, if you know what I mean.'

'Well, I thought you didn't have any of that left.'

'Let's just say that the insurance has paid out just in time and I'm feeling so much better and clearer in the head; it's like a fire clearing away all the dead wood, and new growth can take place. I'm looking forward to our day in court; I have nothing to fear.'

'Stop with your posturing! Shall we agree, here and now, to have the Justice of the Peace?'

'Whatever, young lady; you have your day. Because it will mean nothing. You should know I've been talking to the Bridport Water Company; they couldn't believe how ideal the farmland around Home Farm would be for a reservoir.'

'You wouldn't dare! The ministries wouldn't allow it.'

'Well, the war won't last forever, and they would pay handsomely for the land.'

* * *

2nd November 1943

Lily walked up the steps of the town hall, the brick-built building with its cold draughts. The stone stairway was wide, and turned. She was arm-in-arm with Mother and Father. Another day in court, this time brought about by her. There had been no news from Perry, not even a telegram; and her small bump was growing. The odd kick into her bladder gave her the urge for a wee.

The courtroom was full, many of the village taking the day: the friends, the other tenants, the Fooks family so large it took up two rows, causing the town clerk to fret. Market day outside; everyone inside, squeezed in. There wasn't a chance that her uncle would agree on an impartial arbiter; they had settled on the Justice of the Peace. Lily walked through the imposing door and into the large room. She felt the cold air on her neck; it was icy and made her shiver. The large crowd were taking time from the war; a good local dispute was great entertainment if your livelihood didn't depend on it. The atmosphere was tense. It felt as though all the village was packed in.

Lily made her way to the front desks and Mother and Father sat down behind on the first seats. Her uncle did not care to give her a glance or a nod. But he looked well; he had his old confidence back and was in full flow, talking to his powerful cronies. There was Mr Milton, and Mr Rudyard, the magistrate. The hubbub of yapping, gossip and general discussion echoed around the high-ceilinged county court. The oak-panelled bench was where the magistrate would sit, high up, looking down on them.

The magistrate walked down the centre of the room to a hushed audience. She was tall, and walked as if her spine and shoulders were held straight by a thick silk thread, so upright was she. Her fair hair flowed curly to her shoulders, neat and coiffured; and she wore the black gown of the magistrate. It was Mayor Roberts, without her chain of office this morning. She made her way up to the bench from where she surveyed the room. The town clerk rushed in, whispering to the JP; last minute instructions.

'I'm to be the sole and only arbiter on this case; is that clear?'

'Yes, Madam,' Lily said, nodding, trying to keep the feeling of intimidation from overpowering her.

Uncle nodded.

'That's a yes, is it?' The JP looked down at her uncle. 'Cat got your tongue?'

'Yes, your honour.'

'It's not *your honour;* you address me as Madam. Is that clear?'

'Yes, Madam.'

'I see, Lily Andre-Kearns, you have brought this case to the county court under the Agricultural Holdings Act of 1906.'

'I have, Madam.'

'I see, I see.'

'And you, Mr Theodore Fox, you are the landlord of the Kingcombe Estate, Ashcombe: is that correct?'

'Yes.' He was quick to answer.

'I see, I see. So, Mrs Andre-Kearns, you bring this to me, and I thank you for the well-prepared documents; very clear and precise. You state that the landlord Mr Fox has on numerous occasions increased the rent which is in contravention of the Holdings Act. Is that correct?'

'It is.'

'I see, I see.' The Mayor shook her head as she read through the papers.

'And it says here that in January, Mr Fox brought you here to this courtroom and it was found that you had a lifetime tenancy agreement, but that he was entitled to the increase in rent.'

'Yes,' Lily said.

'I see also that the Ministry of Agriculture informed you that you had to drain and cultivate what had been pasture land and that you incurred the full cost of £2,000 to carry out these works.'

'We did, Madam.'

'Can I just say – ' her uncle said.

'No, you cannot; don't be so impertinent. You will speak only when I say you can. Is that not clear? Where were you brought up?'

Lily gasped, and tried to stand up straight. She had seen the Mayor in the town and had always been in awe of her power and forthright manner.

'I see, I see. I have been taking care to read this act and the acts of 1875 and 1883 and of course 1917. I've also looked at other cases; and this matter is very clear to me.' She cleared her throat, raising her voice even more. Lily swallowed hard. All she had worked for, all her family had struggled with: it was coming down to the words the JP would utter next. If they didn't get the verdict they wanted, it would have been her mistake again, making life worse rather than better.

She looked at her father and mother behind her, then to her uncle. He seemed so confident; they seemed so worried. If only her grandfather was still alive; if only he hadn't gone, life would have gone on much as it had before. They wouldn't have had to battle Theodore for ever and ever. Her throat seemed to tighten, and it was hard to breathe.

'This is so clear, and it's stated in law. I have no idea what my colleague magistrate Harold Rudyard was thinking in January. You see, the acts state quite clearly – as Mrs Andre-Kearns points out – that unless the holding has increased significantly in value then no rate rise can be given. To say that Mr Fox was wrong is incorrect; it wasn't just wrong, it was against the law. He was breaking the law; and second to that, the Act also clearly states that if the tenant improves the land, including putting in drainage, then the landlord will have to compensate the said tenant for this work.'

Lily felt a smile reaching from ear to ear. She looked at her parents. They were embracing, their faces relieved of stress and worry. Her uncle was blushing bright red.

'As the sole arbiter in this case, I'm to declare that the rent returns to the pre-war level, that Mr Fox repays the Kingson tenants the sum of £2,000 for the drainage works and £100 compensation for the time and effort carried out improving the land. Further rent rises levied at the same time to the rest of the tenants on the Kingcombe Estate are also to be reduced to the levels they were at before they were illegally increased.'

Lily's uncle's knees seemed to buckle. He leaned on his cane. Shouts and cheers broke out, only to fall to silence as the crowd cowered beneath the glare of Mayor Roberts.

'You, Mr Fox, have behaved deplorably. Not only have your actions been illegal, you have, it seems to me, at every step tried to thwart the Kingsons' efforts, and this in turn has harmed the country's war effort; you seem to have been thinking of profit for yourself at every turn. You are the worst kind of man, a man who has put himself first above the needs of his neighbour, and above the needs of the mother country in her moment of need. It is in my power as Justice of the Peace in the county court of Bridport to serve you with punishment for this illegal activity. To my mind, a fine which you could pay without hesitation or a moment's thought is far too lenient; therefore, I impose on you a six-month term of incarceration in the county jail at Dorchester.'

There were gasps in the audience, then utter silence. Lily looked at her uncle. The colour had drained from his cheeks; all his bluster, all his confidence had deserted him. It was as if he was standing naked. For all he had done to her and her family, she felt sad for him. She hadn't wished that on him; she had only wanted him to treat them fairly. She didn't want Montague to be without his father.

'Madam.'

'Yes, Mrs Andre-Kearns?'

'Please, if you would allow, could I approach?'

'Yes; come on, my girl.'

Lily walked to the oak bench and reached up to the imposing figure. She whispered in the JP's ear: 'Isn't that a little harsh? We only wanted a fair deal. He has a son he will be away from, and a wife; couldn't you reduce it to three months?'

'You're a fair child, I must say; you, my dear, are a credit to your family and your country. But my decision stands: he can do the six months. It will give him time to think and reconsider his actions.'

'But I don't think he will, I don't think he will change. It will just make him more bitter and more aggrieved against us.'

'I'm sorry, child; my decision stands. Now, let's get this finished. Town clerk, call in the officers now.'

The clerk bustled out to the landing, returning with two uniformed officers. They approached the front of the courtroom. They were tall and smart, their buttons shining.

'Take him down.'

Elizabeth screamed and both she and Montague were weeping.

The crowd celebrated, cheering loudly. Mother and Father came and hugged Lily close to them.

'I'm so proud of you, Lily; you were magnificent,' Mother said.

'You were that, young 'en,' Dad said.

CHAPTER FIFTY-TWO

6th November 1943

Hiding in the hayloft all day was a prison of a different kind. Thomas loved the fact that Nicole was close. But he had thought his war would have been over when he reached his sister; instead, it seemed more perilous. There were Germans coming and going all day long. Then there was the SS. When he peered through the gap between the window and wall, where the stone had weathered and fallen, he saw them in their black uniforms: square-jawed, tall, arrogant and loud. They would mill about in the yard, with their noses pointing to the sky. There seemed much more to lose; having made it all this way, to be caught now would be the end of his world.

The season was on the cusp, autumn moving to winter. The nights were cold, the sort that chilled to the bone. He and Romily missed Billy. Why had he been so brave and put his life down for them? Thomas didn't think he could have done the same. He didn't think he could even kill anyone, not even a German. Wasn't that against what God wanted? He and Romily chatted and dozed intermittently, talking about Billy, about home, about what was going to happen next. Much later, when evening had passed, when the hotel had become quiet and all the Germans had left, they made their way down to the hotel kitchen and met Nicole and Emma for a meal of hot mutton stew; steam came off their bowls. Thomas breathed in the meaty aroma. His bowl was full to the brim and there was fresh, crusty baguette that smelled and tasted of heaven. He tore off the bread and dunked it in the thick gravy; he savoured every bite and swore he would never leave a scrap of food ever again.

'We have to go tomorrow,' Nicole said in English, as she dished out a bowlful from the huge pot, then handed it to Romily.

'So soon?' Romily said. He took the bowl from Nicole. 'I was getting used to this.' Thomas saw him flash Nicole a smile, and she reciprocated.

Geordie walked into the kitchen and said: 'Yes, you need to get a move on; they won't be running the boats for ever.'

Thomas took a spoonful of stew, to feel the texture of meat, to have something to bite and to chew; it was as if heaven had landed in his mouth. He had forgotten the sheer pleasure of having such a thing. To think they could be back in England in as little as two weeks! They could be home for Christmas. It was unbelievable; he didn't dare believe it.

Geordie went over the plan, marked the safe houses to aim for, the friendly families, the network, on the trail home. They were to get a small fishing boat in Plouha which was over three hundred miles away on the Brittany coast. Once there, once on the boat, there was just the Channel to cross. He would be home with Mum, with Dad, Hamilton, Dusty and Ol' Parrot. The animals: Topsy, Turvy, Flotsam and Jetsam, the old cows, the chickens and the sheep. He would be home; he would see lambs playing in the spring sunshine, running and leaping over the Dorset hills. It sounded like heaven. He could work with Dad, find a lovely girl and settle down and never leave Ashcombe again. The hope bubbled up in him. He felt safe now. He smiled up at Nicole and she came and sat next to him. She held her spoon with one hand and put her other arm around his shoulder. They didn't talk. He was content. At last.

'I think we should celebrate our last night together.' Geordie got up and went to the cellar. When he returned he was carrying two bottles of brandy. 'I've been saving these for the end of the war. I think this might be the night for it.' He reached to the cupboards and took down the glasses.

As he poured out the measures, they all heard running footsteps on the cobbled yards. It was too late to run and hide. There was nowhere they could run. The door was flung open; but instead of Germans, in came Catherine and Louise, who despite their time incarcerated looked well.

'You have to go now. The Major has let us out but he says the SS have information on us all, that they are going to be here, soon. You have to leave; we all have to leave.'

'I'm not going anywhere,' Geordie said.

'Dad, if you don't, if we all don't, they will line us all up and shoot us,' Louise said.

'Well, maybe it's my time; I'm too old for running away.' He knocked back a brandy.

'We all have to go; we can't stay here. It's not going to be safe,' Louise said.

'I'm not leaving this all behind, not what I've built up all my life. I'd rather die here than run.' He poured out more brandy for himself.

Thomas sniffed the alcohol; it smelt warm and potent. He felt his heart sinking. He sipped at his drink and felt it run down the back of his throat; it seemed to light up a furnace in his stomach. He coughed.

'You all right, lad? It's good stuff, ain't it?' Geordie smiled. 'You sprogs, you're young enough; you go, you get home, and you tell your old dad that Geordie is still fighting Jerry twenty years on. I ain't too old yet.'

'Dad, no! You have to come. Please!' Emma said.

'You go; go to England, be with them,' Geordie said.

'I'm staying with you, Dad; I have to wait for Patrice,' Louise said.

'I'll stay; someone's got to stand up for Mother,' Catherine said. 'I can't have you two picking on her.'

'You're all daft! I don't think I can leave you,' Emma said.

''Course you can, dear,' Eliza said as she came in in her nightgown. 'You go. I want you to and that's my final word.'

Thomas looked at Emma, whose face was for once not full of fun and life, but set and serious and unhappy.

'Come on; I'll make you some sandwiches for the journey,' Eliza said.

'This one's for you,' Geordie said, handing Nicole the full bottle of brandy. 'Get it to your old man and make sure you have a drink on me!'

'We will; and I thank you all so much for looking after me all this time,' Nicole said as she went to Eliza and hugged her. 'You Tuckers are unbelievable.'

'You two better get back up in the loft, get a couple of hours' sleep, then be off,' Geordie said, looking at Thomas and Romily.

They said their long goodbyes; there wouldn't be time in the morning. Nicole and Emma walked across the cobbled stones. Thomas watched as leaves danced in the night breeze, pulled and twisted like puppets with invisible strings. He liked it when Emma was close, her faint sweet perfume and infectious spirit. What could he do to cheer her up? She looked bereft, knowing she was leaving her family to go with them. He couldn't think of anything to say that would make it better. He wanted to put his arm around her shoulder. They got to the stables and he followed Romily up the ladder. Nicole and Emma came up too and they all lay down in the hay.

'Nicole, thank you so much for everything. I don't say it enough, but I love you,' Thomas said.

'Oh, Thomas, I love you too,' Nicole said.

'Can you stay out here tonight with us?' Thomas said.

'Oh, Thomas,' Nicole said.

'I don't want to be away from you.'

'I'm only over the yard.'

'I know, but I want you closer.'

'You silly galley-bagger.'

Thomas looked at his sister, making sure to take in what she looked like with her pretty face and dark hair. Her eyes seemed wiser to him. They were all older, but he still felt like a boy.

'You will see me in a couple of hours.'

'I don't want you to go.' Thomas felt his tears welling up. All the time in the camps and on the run… He was finally with Nicole. It had been such an ordeal. He didn't want the hope ripped from his heart.

The sound of trucks filled the still night. Nicole and Emma jumped down to the stables. Thomas picked up one revolver from under the straw-stuffed pillow, and Romily did the same. Thomas looked at Romily and they shook their heads. They ran to the hotel kitchen.

'It's the SS; they're in the town, they're going house to house, taking people in the backs of the trucks; they will be here next,' Catherine stated.

'Here, take your packs; you're to go, now,' Geordie said. 'Everything is there; and don't forget that brandy.'

'Dad, I love you. Come with us,' Emma pleaded.

'I can't. You have to go now, to make all this worthwhile; you have to go, my little sprog.' Geordie hugged his youngest daughter. 'You have to for the family. Do you hear me, girl? You are to make it for this family.'

'Dad, I can't.'

'Yes, you can, girl; look at all you've done.'

'But Dad, I love you; I don't want to leave you.'

There came the sound of yelling, of German orders and of screaming. More sounds of vehicles. The sound of gunfire rang out.

'There is no time. We will stand together,' Eliza said.

Geordie pulled out the Sten gun from the back of the pots and pans cupboard, then ferreted around for more, before pulling out a further hidden treasure trove of weapons, grenades and more guns. He handed them out to Catherine, Louise, Edith and Eliza, who didn't hesitate to take them. Thomas felt his stomach urge.

'This is goodbye, I suppose…' Geordie said.

Thomas watched as Nicole embraced the Tuckers. Emma went to her mother and hugged her. He could see tears in their eyes. Thomas stepped out into the yard, the half-moon shining down. At last he was heading home, to be with his family.

'Go; don't wait for his goodbye speech,' Eliza said. She shooed them out of the back door. Emma was racing to hug each of her sisters in turn.

The Tucker family followed them out to the yard.

Thomas heard the unmistakable sound of jackboots, echoing off the underside of the arch.

The four of them ran with Nicole leading the way. Four leaving and running for freedom. As they made it to the garden, the SS arrived, their rifles to their shoulders. Geordie opened fire, along with his family. The SS hadn't expected a full onslaught of bullets.

Emma pulled at Thomas to turn around, to watch; but he pulled her away. Thomas looked over his shoulder. There was a huge fire fight; more soldiers flooded the yard.

'I can't leave them, not to face this!' Emma said. She pulled hard on his hand, slipped hers out of his and ran with her Sten gun swinging from her shoulder. Thomas looked on.

'No, Emma, no!' Thomas said. 'Nicole, wait!' His sister was ahead, running in the opposite direction. He was rooted to the spot with Romily.

He looked at Emma running towards her family. Nicole didn't realise.

Thomas looked at Emma and ran towards her. In the yard he could see the Tucker family, surrounded, with Geordie firing from the kitchen window.

Emma opened fire on the German troops; the sounds of gunfire filled the night sky. Thomas could smell the carbide in the air. The chill of the night was replaced by the heat inside him. He took out the pistol. They came to the wall between the yard and the garden. There must have been twenty or more troops. Then Nicole and Romily were beside them.

The Germans returned fire on them; more soldiers entered the kitchen. Thomas took aim, as best he could, the pistol useless at this range. Emma and Nicole were firing from the hip, their machine guns more effective.

'We can't help them,' Romily said.

'I have to!' Emma shouted above the gunfire.

'It's no good, Emma; there are too many of them,' Nicole said. 'Your family wanted you to escape.'

'I can't let them die!' Emma said.

Thomas watched on, helpless; they all were. Soldiers fired on them and they ducked behind the crumbling wall. Splinters of stone showered down.

Shouts, orders, movement. Thomas watched as half the troops gave cover and six in black uniforms swamped the kitchen. Gunfire went silent. What could he do? They should run, they should get away as Geordie and Eliza had said; they wanted them to escape, they wanted Emma to live. Six soldiers brought the Tuckers out, their hands up, Geordie with his head held high, Eliza, Catherine, Louise and Edith clinging to each other.

'Leave the girls, leave my girls!' Geordie shouted in French. 'It was all me; they are innocent! All of it was my doing!' He was punched, pushed and shoved, until they were all lined up in front of the stables.

Thomas and his group were pinned behind the wall.

The black uniformed soldiers took up position in a line opposite the Tuckers. There was no ceremony. Geordie was unbowed. Time stood still. The SS raised their guns, taking aim. Emma buried her face in Thomas's chest. He put his hands over her head. Time was broken by the sound of gunshots. Thomas watched as the family were executed. Nicole took out grenades and lobbed them into the yard of the hotel. There was the clink of metal on stone. More shouts. The explosions came and the fireball lit up the sky. Thomas took Emma's hand, tighter this time; they all ran for their lives.

CHAPTER FIFTY-THREE

10th November 1943

When they got to Plouha, they checked out the harbour; it was no bigger than West Bay, with a small fleet of fishing boats, one of which would give them voyage home. Thomas smelled the salty sea air, with wicker crab pots and the smell of mackerel. On the journey they had been staying in safe houses, travelling by night, walking and by cart, even once on a train, managing to avoid soldiers, troops and the SS. There seemed to be more troops than ever. Thomas was wearing his borrowed clothes and shoes, trousers too big, which he had to pull up at every opportunity, the belt not helping. They had documents. He'd even been picking up the language a little; he had the ear for it. It was Romily who struggled; when he did speak the words came out in a deep Dorset twang.

Soon it would be all over. Once they were on the boat, they would be only days from home. The excitement and nervousness built.

The safe house cellar smelled of damp and there was no natural light. Nicole had been gone for hours, making the contact.

'I miss them; how can I go on?' Emma said. She was close to Thomas and he could feel her chest heave.

'I know.'

'They're all gone, Thomas; all of them. All of my family, like that, in seconds.'

'I know. They died so you could live.'

Her chest heaved and she sobbed.

'I'm the only one, Thomas.'

'I understand. But you have us; we are your family now.'

Thomas put his arm around Emma's shoulder and she cried into him. They sat like this together for hours. In the pit of his stomach, Thomas began to worry about Nicole. Why was it taking so long? Had she been captured? He should have gone with her but she insisted he stayed with Emma and Romily. The old man and his wife upstairs in the house would take them up from the cellar later, if the coast was clear.

Thomas must have fallen asleep, because he woke with a start, with Emma sleeping by his side. He'd grown used to the light shuffling steps of the old couple; this was different, he was certain. There was the sound of banging doors, and the god almighty jackboots hammering around. This was going to be it: they were going to be found down in the cellar. The next time the light flooded in when the cellar door was opened they would be captured by the SS. They would then be carted off and stood up against a wall for the firing squad. There was no other way out. Romily looked over and nodded his head and put his finger to his lips. Thomas breathed in, trying to slow his breath, but it was racing. Emma came to, groggy. He mouthed at her to keep quiet. His heart was beating and the noise seemed to flood his eardrums. That alone would give them away. God, what if Nicole came back in now, when the SS were above, searching? Would she be able to talk her way out? Would they think her the daughter of the couple?

Thomas got up and walked to the stairs that led to the door. He stood at the bottom and tried to listen hard. This place reminded him of the outhouse at home where Dad made the wine. That seemed so safe and secure; now this place was a trap. Only one way out; no escape if they were found; it would all end here. He made out murmurings above, more heavy footsteps coming and going, but still they didn't open the trap door. He wanted to get out to get fresh air. This was what it must be like to be buried and in a grave. He preferred the hayloft; at least it smelt better. He wanted to make everything better for Emma, to say that it hadn't happened, that she would be all right; but he didn't know the words. God, how would he feel to have all his family taken like that? This was hell. Would she ever be able to smile or laugh again? If he could do anything to make her feel better he would try; just that he felt so hopeless. That's if they could ever make it home. Back in Dorset he would; he would make it better for her, make a better life, give her a new family.

The footsteps got closer above, walking from room to room. There was no light into the cellar. Thomas went back and settled down next to Emma. She looked at him with her tear-stained cheeks.

'My whole family, Thomas, all of them, gone,' she said.

He put his arm around her shoulder. He had no words that could soften her pain.

For another half an hour, he guessed, the boots wandered and stood, then wandered again. He couldn't settle. He thought he would burst. If the door opened and it was soldiers, would he fire his pistol? Would it be worth it? Should they go quietly? He felt his body shudder at the thought. He didn't want to die, not today, not for a long time. He wanted to be in love and to be home and die an old man in his bed. He was too young to go, before he had had a chance to live.

The boots came back louder overhead, coming for the trapdoor. He tried to catch his breath but it was racing from him. Where was Nicole? Had they got her? He waited in silence.

Then as quickly as it had arrived, the noise of boots subsided. Doors banged shut. They had left. He took a deep sigh of relief. They sat in silence for the next hour; then, when the cellar door finally opened, his heart leapt: it was Nicole.

She came down the stairs, shaking her head.

'It's no good. I've seen the fisherman; the route is closed. We're too late. It was shut yesterday. It's too dangerous; no other boats want the risk. The SS are everywhere.'

'What are we going to do?' Thomas said. 'The mountains?'

'We can't, can we?' Romily said.

'Dad would have wanted us to. We have to, to make their sacrifice worth it; we have to make it,' Emma said.

'But the length of France, to the mountains?' Romily said.

'It's possible. We know, don't we, Emma? We know the route; we get to Paris, a train to Saint-Girons. There is a way.'

'Well, I've had enough of cellars, attics, barns and haylofts to last me a lifetime,' Thomas said.

* * *

Thomas sat on the train. It wasn't full by any means. The people seemed normal; woman with children were in the majority. Though there were some men. He wondered if they had secrets, like his group did. Paris had been so busy and he had never seen so many people in one place; all the hustle and bustle, cars, horses, and of course soldiers. He had kept his mouth shut and his head down, walking quickly, holding Emma's hand. Romily did the same with Nicole. Now, Romily sat opposite, facing him. It was so good to be sitting on a comfortable seat. He watched the countryside roll by as the steam train pulled them onwards. There were rolling hills and long, flat plains. His heart was never far from his mouth. The stations where they stopped were full of soldiers, but it was the black uniforms of the SS that scared him most. They were only seconds from capture.

The train slowed, then pulled up with a jolt at a station. Soldiers got on and moved through their carriage. A mother with a baby walked on, holding a suitcase, the baby all swaddled up.

'Here, madam, have my seat,' Romily said, standing up and waving at his seat, as if he was at home. He spoke in English, Thomas thought; he bloody spoke in English, in his deep Dorset! This was it; they were done for.

Romily stood aside, smiling, not realising what a fatal error he had made. Thomas looked up the carriage and then behind. The woman sat down opposite, her face a picture of composure and motherhood. Thomas held his breath, praying and hoping. It

374

couldn't be. There was nothing: no soldiers rushing to grab them, no SS leaping on them and ordering them out. Romily still didn't realise what he had done as he looked down at the mother and baby. He even started to whistle.

Nicole and Emma started cooing over the baby and making a fuss, talking to the woman in French. Romily put his hand over his mouth, realising his mistake. He shook his head at Thomas. Thomas, relieved, laughed inside. What on earth? Would they ever make it out of this hell alive?

* * *

Thomas would have loved Saint-Girons if it wasn't for the Germans and the SS who seemed to be on every corner. The old medieval town, with stone buildings and sturdy bridge over the River Salat, was beautiful, the river full of the rush of mountain water from the Pyrenees.

Alfonso, the guide, had come to the safe house and the attic they now found themselves in. He was a sturdy little goat herder who lived most of the year in the mountains; he spoke French and Spanish and a language all of his own. He was tanned, short and wiry. His body seemed to be hewn from teak; he was hard and weathered-looking, and his face looked haggard. His eyes were narrow, his hair grey and wispy. His body was light, with no fat. His feet could almost be goat-like, his legs bandy and twisted like branches looking for light.

Alfonso gave them old coats that seemed too thin; he gave them shoes that were made from cord. He explained that this was the last chance before winter took hold; if they didn't make it, that would be it until spring. Once snow took hold high up, there would be no way through. He spoke and Nicole translated what she thought he was saying. They would follow the high route, as the lower routes had been closed down; there had been a huge betrayal and many of the leaders of the trail had been captured and tortured. This was one of the last passes open. The aim was to head for Mount Valier, then ultimately freedom in Montgarri, in

Spain.

'You stop, you die; you lag behind, you die.' Alfonso said, with a sneer. 'I've to look after the group. If you cause me trouble I will shoot you myself.' He spoke in French and Nicole translated.

Thomas looked at the others aghast and shrugged his shoulders. Alfonso handed them a piece of meat and two sugar lumps each.

'You are to obey me, every step. This is not an easy place, you understand.'

The four of them nodded their heads in agreement. Thomas didn't really know what he was letting himself in for.

CHAPTER FIFTY-FOUR

11th November 1943

Alfonso lead the way into the foothills of the Pyrenees. Thomas calculated that they were a group of about twenty. There were three RAF personnel, two US servicemen, a mixture of Jews, old men, young women, who carried suitcases and their bags; they made a ragtag bunch. Then there was the four of them. Nicole and Emma helped the Jewish woman who they had met on the train and who had come to their safe house after hers had been shut down. The temperature was cool and Thomas pulled the thin black coat around him. He wished he still had his army boots. They walked on wide cart tracks and the gradient was slight. There were loose rocks, and he could feel the small ones through the soles of his corded shoes. In his coat pocket he carried his meagre rations: some meat, bread and sugar lumps. There were seventy miles of walking to get to Montgarri, and the interlaced ridges of the Pyrenees and Mount Valier.

The silent night was filled with the shuffling feet of the slow human snake. Thomas walked; it seemed that this was what defined his war, the moving, the walking, the escaping. Alfonso kept them moving and at speed. The SS, the German patrols could be anywhere at any moment. Thomas couldn't believe the amount Alfonso was being paid: over £6,000 pounds for each person he got over the mountain. It was a huge amount. He was going to be a very rich man. The danger was immense. Only a week ago another group had been betrayed by a British serviceman, thinking that the Germans' terms were better; he had sold out his commander and the trail had been closed. This was why they were heading higher into the mountains than any previous attempt at escape.

Where the track was wide he fell in with Romily. They began to gain height and looking down to his left he could see over the trees.

'It won't be long now,' Romily said.

'Till we're home,' Thomas said. 'Romily, what can I do to make things better for Emma?'

'There's not much you can do. Be there for her. Listen when she wants to talk.' Romily sneezed and wiped his nose on his handkerchief.

'I feel like I should be more help.'

'You are. Do what you have been doing, that's all there is to it.'

'I don't know what to say.'

'Don't say anything; the words will come when you need them.'

'They're so brave, aren't they?'

'They are that.'

They kept on moving, walking in silence as they went. Gradually the track narrowed and entered the tree line. Many of the civilians began to meander, and grumbles went through that they would like a break. Nicole and Emma chivvied the lines. Thomas tried to do his bit, encouraging, motioning for them to continue. Alfonso wouldn't let them stop; he said stopping would get them killed. He waved at them to follow for all to keep up. To stay in their lines to keep the pace fast, to walk to freedom.

Thomas kept moving, beginning to feel the wind get up, the temperature dropping because they were higher. It was early morning; the light suggested that it was the time he would normally get up to milk the cows. The first snowflakes fell. They were soft on his coat; he could hardly feel them. Before long the wind was whipping up a blizzard full into their faces; the stinging made him half close his eyes. He felt his head become stifled, began to feel sick in his throat. An hour later, and he could only feel Romily in front; he couldn't see him, so heavy was the snow in his face. The temperature was well below freezing, the coat useless, his feet numb.

Alfonso pushed on into the deep of the morning. The snow on the ground became deeper and frozen hard. Thomas's shoes provided no grip or warmth. They came to the refuge; with relief they all piled in. With no room for them all to lie down, Romily and Thomas stood, as did all the servicemen. Thomas watched as Nicole and Emma lay down to sleep. After an hour both women got up and gave their spaces so Thomas and Romily could rest. They swapped back as dawn was rising.

There were the morning noises of people stretching, yawning awake. Thomas's coat was hanging from a rusty nail, straight and hard like an oak door. He walked outside in his shirt and jumper. The blizzard had cleared now in the morning daylight and the sun was inching its way up above one of the high passes. He could see the scale of the mountain in front of him. There was a series of interlocked ridges, each one higher than the last. He stared aghast, his jaw dropping. His breath escaped him like smoke from a fire.

He ambled over to Alfonso, who stood looking at the mountains ahead.

'*Nous nous tournons,*' Alfonso said. He motioned with his hands, pointing down the mountain the way they had come.

'*Non!* What? It is clear, sunny!' Thomas shook his head. His body felt drained of energy; every muscle in his body seemed to have a voice this morning and it was screaming at him to stop, to lie down and return to some kind of sleep.

'*Grande neige.* Great snows.'

'But it's sunny; the weather is good.'

'*Non, passage supérieur.*' Alfonso's face was stern; there was no reaction in his face. This was a man who was used to being obeyed.

'No, we have to go; we can't go back!' Thomas said.

'*Il n'y a pas de discussion.*' Alfonso shook his head, turned and entered the refuge to pass on his news.

Thomas looked out, forlorn. The panorama was awe-inspiring.

He was shivering and his teeth chattered. Now they would be shunted from safe house to safe house. They would be hunted all winter like wild animals. At least he would be with Nicole, with Romily and Emma. He should think himself lucky to be alive.

CHAPTER FIFTY-FIVE

25th February 1944

Nicole looked at Romily, his hair slicked back with water from the bowl which sat atop the dresser. The eaves of the attic meant that he had to bend double. She had fought the cell commander to be kept together; he had wanted to split them up at the last round but she hadn't come this far to be apart from her family. There had been more arrests, more captures. Their party was down to sixteen, two POWs being lost on the mountain when they had fallen behind on the way down; and two captured when a cellar was searched by the SS. Thomas and Romily slept on the mattress on the floor and she shared with Emma. Emma was beginning to become more like herself, although Nicole knew only too well how nightmares could take over the daytime too; they had haunted her for too long. She hoped Emma wouldn't suffer the same. Thomas was helping, telling her bad jokes and stories about home, about the animals, and the times haymaking, getting apples in the orchard or games of football. Whatever he told her she seemed to enjoy, her smile returning.

There were running steps approaching the attic door. They were light, more like raindrops; it would be the young girl of the family they were staying with. The door burst open and the dark-haired girl of about ten came hurtling in and jumped on the bed, carrying the aroma of fresh baking on her patchwork quilt of a dress.

'Mama says you can come down; *petit déjeuner*,' she said in French.

'Great; I'm starving. Lead the way!' Thomas said. He held his hand out for Emma, who took his hand, and the three of them skipped down the stairs. Nicole picked up the brush and began brushing out the tangles in her hair.

'Don't they make a good couple?' Romily said.

'They do; I'm happy for them both. Thomas seems to make Emma happy.'

'I can't imagine what I would be like, if I had seen what she did,' Romily said.

'Romily, what do you want if we get home?'

'To grow old with my sweetheart.'

'You're such a romantic!'

He grinned broadly at her as he moved to the end of the bed and stood looking at her.

'I think you're the only woman who could make a dress out of rags look good.'

'Romily Colman, you're such a charmer!' She turned her head over her shoulder and looked back at him. He stood tall. A winter of low activity and some hearty cooking had brought some colour back to his cheeks and now his frame seemed more like she used to remember. His arms still didn't seem to have the muscle or definition that she once remembered from when he was playing polo or lifting crates of bread. She put the brush down and returned to sit on the end of the bed; she picked her feet up off the floor and stretched them out. She touched the side of her cheek.

'And what about you, Nicole?' Romily said.

'Me?'

'Yes, you; what do you want?'

'To get home.' She moved her hand behind her neck and gathered her hair together in her palm, then pulled it all to the outside of her neck.

'If I've learnt anything it's not to think too far forward.' She ran her fingers down her neck. 'I don't dare imagine what's ahead, good or bad. I want to get Thomas and Emma home; I want to get home to see them all again. I want it so bad I feel like I will burst if I don't.'

Romily came down and sat next to her. He put his arm around her shoulder and the instant heat of his body was beside her. He turned and faced her, then moved his hand to her face. The touch of his light fingers was delicate and smooth. He traced his hand like a feather to her neck and pulled her in close.

He whispered in her ear: 'You've always been in my heart, Nicole.'

As Romily caressed her neck and shoulder, Nicole lost herself in the bliss of the moment. She moved her hands up to Romily's face and to the back of his neck; she pulled him in close. Then she put her lips on his; they kissed each other lightly, then more deeply. She took his hand and moved it to her breast. She could feel his heat and his desire. She moved her head back to the pillow, holding him all the while. He leaned down on her, kissing her. His hands were strong holding her waist; he leaned down, stronger. She held him tight, not wanting to ever let him go.

Romily pushed himself up on his elbows above her, paused, kissed her, then stopped.

'No, I can't, not before,' Romily said.

'What? Before what?' Nicole asked.

'Before we're married, of course.'

'It's wartime; we might not survive another day.'

'I'm sorry, I can't, I just can't. It's not the way I've been brought up.'

'Oh, Romily, no one will know! I want you.'

'*I* will know, Nicole, *I* will. I can't; it's that I just have to do it this way.'

He got up from the bed and knelt down at the side.

'Will you marry me, Nicole? I should rightly have asked your father first.' He looked up as she swivelled to face him. She had wanted him, to feel close to him, to have his love. And now he was proposing: what was she meant to say?

'Marry me, Nicole. I will make you the happiest woman alive.'

'I can't, Romily; I can't say yes. Neither of us knows how long we have.'

'Does it matter, the not knowing?'

'It does to me. I don't want to get your hopes up; I don't want to promise you and let you down.'

'Nicole, you will never be able to let me down.'

'If we make it over the mountain, Romily, if we both make it, I will.'

'That's a yes in my books; that's good enough for me.'

She saw the hope in his eyes and it opened her heart more than she could have imagined. They walked down to a breakfast of fresh croissants; it was as good as anything back in Albert and made her think of the time before the war. Romily and Thomas seemed in such good spirits; they said Jerry hadn't beaten them and the mountain wouldn't either. She was more realistic. It had been so hard the last time and they hadn't even reached the peak.

* * *

The track was similar but different, a new route out of Saint-Girons. Nicole walked with Emma and Thomas was with Romily, ahead. They were dressed as warmly as they could; she was wearing two layers, an old handmade dress, some old brown leather shoes which – with two pairs of socks – fitted. The spring day was still sharp and cold and not much different to the winter days. The message had got around that this was the day for the attempt. The group, numbering sixteen, walked the long track before narrowing to a single path which twisted and turned its way ever higher, through pine trees, then to an open plateau of grass that was in the first throes of growth. She was up near the front of the column and was first to hear the whistles: not man-made. Her eyes coasted over the rocks and grasses and looked down at a mound and gulley, overgrown with vegetation. There it was again: a loud, whistling call. Then she saw it out of the corner of her eye: the large fast-moving mammal. She pointed it out. There were four of them, a family all running for their burrows, like large rabbits. Alfonso, grumpy, told her they were marmots, shy and rarely seen.

She smiled and they walked on, higher, past the plateau of grassland to a more barren and rocky surface; the path followed the contours of the mountain. From time to time her shoes slipped on the loose scree. Rounding the bend she saw the task ahead of them. They had been walking continuously for hours with no breaks. If anyone lagged behind, Alfonso would race back on his branch-like legs and chastise and shout in his harsh gruff way. If people didn't move he would wave his pistol and shout louder. If that didn't alert roaming German patrols, then nothing would. He was curt, short and brusque in his manner and it riled her; there was no need to be rude. Magda suffered the most and Nicole took her baby to help lighten her load. Still, Magda would suffer, her light porcelain legs not used to the steep climbs. Servicemen who had been on the run, now wintered with little exercise, strained to take in oxygen as they slogged on, ever higher. Nicole dared to look up and saw the snowline was up ahead. What if they didn't survive? The enormity of it dawned on her. She'd seen it in the winter, the mountainous ridges, the sheer drops at every step and turn, the mad scrambling. Peak, then drop, then peak. It seemed never-ending.

Romily looked at her and smiled; she returned his smile with a wide grin and it warmed her inside. They tramped on, the human snake, barely talking, the shoes skidding on ice-covered stone. They walked on through sludge, then snow, then deeper snow that covered her shoes. Afternoon rolled into evening and they kept moving; she lost any sense of time. Her head became dizzy. She kept checking on Thomas and Emma who, like them all, were walking ever slower.

At last, and when her body was all but numb, they came to a refuge, a wooden hut; it was shelter. They got in and huddled together for warmth. The smell of Romily, his musky sweat, reassured her she wasn't on her own; she had her friends and she would like more than anything to be married to this good and upright man. It made her giggle, thinking of his principles; she felt more love for him.

The next day was much the same, trudging up and down rocky, scree-ridden paths, up through snow, down the other side, up another stretch of sketchy, washed-out path. Moaning, grunts and groans. They all looked out of place, ill-prepared in town clothes and normal shoes; they were dressed for Sunday worship, not mountaineering. The solid grey sky showed no shards of sun, so thick was the blanket. The sweat on Nicole's skin radiated the heat away. Her teeth gave up chattering, and she shivered to her core. Where the path widened, Romily walked alongside, putting his arm around her. They all took it in turns to carry Magda's baby. Nicole thought what a good father Romily would make. Alfonso was probably going to lead them all to their deaths, if he didn't shoot them first for being laggards. They pushed on further; she began to lose feeling and her thoughts were incoherent. The dizziness became worse. Why not stop a minute, to recover? There was no shelter, no refuge. Alfonso instructed them to dig a pit with their bare hands. They nestled. Fatigued. Sick. Too tired to sleep; only icy cold. No rations. Alfonso declared he would go and fetch more. Where was he going and who was he going to see? His shepherd friends? It made no sense. Minutes passed like hours. The cold. Romily beside her. Survive. Coughs, hollering coughs. Staying close. Alfonso returned with meagre handfuls of meat – goat or mutton – stale bread and more sugar lumps. Holding the meat, sucking on it till it thawed; then using more energy than she had, Nicole chewed on it.

They trudged upwards, the path narrowing, rising in height as they climbed towards another peak. So many times her foot had caught a stone. Nicole looked up, daunted by yet another rise, another twisting, icy, scree-covered path. Her concentration gone, she put her foot down on the edge of a smooth angular stone; her foot slipped, her ankle contorted and she went over with her full weight. She screamed in agony. Romily was first to her, then

Thomas and Emma; they gathered around and got her to her feet. She knew instantly the damage she had done by turning her ankle. She tried to put her weight down; there was searing pain right up through her body. Alfonso came back, telling the group to keep walking.

Nicole wanted to rip her shoe off as the pain throbbed and her right ankle swelled.

'*Enlevez pas votre chaussure*. Do not take off your shoe!' Alfonso shouted at her in French. '*Levez-vous; marchez!*'

She looked up at him, livid. Why didn't he shut up?

'Walk!' Alfonso said.

'I can't!'

'*Vous pouvez et vous devez*. We not wait.' He took out his pistol. 'If you don't, I shoot you.'

Romily put himself between Alfonso and Nicole.

'Leave us; we will catch you up, go on with your party,' Nicole said.

'Have it your way; *vous êtes bête*. You should stay with the group.' Alfonso glided past them and headed back up the line. The last of the group passed them by and kept moving up the mountain.

'Don't stay with me; leave me,' Nicole said. Thomas, Romily and Emma all looked at her.

'No way; don't even think it,' Thomas said.

Romily bent over her ankle, took a handful of ice and applied it on top of her shoe. It was comforting but did nothing for the pain. He tore the sleeve off his shirt.

'Romily, don't.'

He wrapped the makeshift bandage over the top of her shoe, covering it as much as he could.

'Come on, get up,' Romily said. He held her. She leaned her weight on him.

'You can't, Romily.'

'I can; and when I get tired, Thomas can take over.'

Thomas nodded and said: 'We ain't leaving you. You can lean on us for a change.'

'Don't; I don't want to slow you down.'

'Well, I haven't been walking much faster. Anyway, it gives me a chance to put me arm round you, don't it,' Romily said.

They staggered on, hobbling, one-sided. She chewed on her tongue when the pain got too much when her foot hit a rock she hadn't seen, or on a craggy part of the path. She thought she lost consciousness at one point, then recovered, and she saw that Thomas was holding her up. She looked up ahead and saw Romily, who kept looking back. Romily led them through the afternoon, then into the darkness. She had no idea how much longer she could keep going.

'Please, you leave me; I will follow on,' Nicole said.

'Not no way is that happening,' Romily said. He took her and indicated for Thomas to be on the other side. When had her little brother got so strong? He didn't hesitate; and between them they kept going, on up further and higher. No sign of the group. Up higher still; then Thomas called out and pointed at the small refuge from which a flicker of light escaped. It was still a way up ahead, but at least now she could see a target, something to aim for. They shuffled inch by agonising inch up the path as it further spiralled up to meet the shelter.

Inside there was already a fire blazing, with warm water. She drank from the canteen that was passed around and caught her breath, glad to sit in the corner with the weight taken off her ankle.

The heat from the fire brought some life back to the escape party. Alfonso came to the centre, his craggy features illuminated by the orange flame. There were deep bags under his eyes.

'This is as far as I take you,' he said in French.

'What?' Nicole said.

'Yes, this is as far as I take you.'

'But we don't know the paths, the way!' Nicole said.

'You follow this path, stick to it; it will take you to Spain. There are only another two days of walking.'

'We can't… You can't leave us! We will die without a guide!' Nicole said.

'*Non, non, non*, I have to return; more escapees,' Alfonso said.

'But you can't desert us!'

'This is not deserting; this is my job. You are on your own!' he shouted, then turned and walked out into the night.

'What? You can't do that to us!' Nicole looked at the others. A tremor of fear passed from the bottom of her spine right to the nape of her neck and she shivered, even though she was warm for the first time in days.

The night passed without sleep; the pain in her ankle did not subside. Romily packed it with ice. Her luck to be in the warm, with an ice-cold ankle. Morning came and she felt exhausted. She hobbled to help make weak tea with the few supplies that had been left in the hut. No one wanted the task of guiding the ragtag group through the remaining mountains. The servicemen were beyond fatigue; everyone was consumed with their own fights for survival.

Then Romily went to the front of the wood cabin, pushed his shoulders back and his chest forward.

'Come on; we can do this,' he said.

Nicole hobbled up, wincing as she went. She stood side by side with Romily, proud of the Dorset baker who was standing tall like she never believed he could. She chastised herself for not believing in him sooner.

Romily led them out into the freezing morning, colder than the day before. The blanket of thick dark grey cloud seemed to hover in front of her eyes, as if they were walking in it. How close to heaven she felt, which was funny because it was much more like hell. Every footstep took immense concentration, every breath seemed to be squeezed through a fine sieve. She had no energy; like the others, everything was a huge effort of willpower. People lagged behind. Romily didn't shout or holler, or be gruff. He put on his best smile, walked back, patted them on the back, let them take frequent breaks.

At lunch, they ate their small morsels of meat. She watched Romily stand and take the lead. Through his encouragement and praise, spirits in the group seemed to lift. But it was only temporary: when they came to the ice sheet, the hope vanished. There were two possible routes: either take the smooth-as-glass ice sheet in front of the frozen waterfall, or take the higher path that seemed equally as dangerous. There were arguments back and forward, shouts to take the higher path, counterarguments to carry on ahead, to risk the ice. There was little time left before nightfall and the loss of light would make any further walking nigh on impossible, maybe deadly.

Romily argued that they should keep on this path, risk the ice sheet, take their time, hold hands and look out for each other. Thomas and Emma both backed him up. There were louder voices. Nicole didn't want the group to splinter; for sure, they would be better together than apart. Romily swayed them back with his argument; drained and resigned, the group fell in. Nicole clung to Thomas as Romily led them to the ice sheet. To the right-hand side was the sheer drop, below which were the treetops. Up ahead was the bend in the path that clung precipitously to the mountain edge. The path seemed too narrow at the most awkward point. Romily led the way. He used a stone to chisel handholds on the ice wall. The path was narrow, covered in ice and snow; the drop below fell for hundreds of feet.

Nicole looked up and ahead, keeping her mind and body focussed on getting past the icy wall. Her heart began pounding in her ears. She forced herself to look ahead at Thomas's back, or to the left side, where there was only ice. She worried that if she didn't keep shuffling forward, she would never move, that she would be frozen in body and mind. The adrenaline coursed through her and there was a sense of panic building in her stomach. What if she fainted, slipped and fell? What if she pulled them all with her? It was no good thinking like this. She pulled herself together. Romily was already halfway across. Thomas followed, gripping the handholds, walking steadily and slowly. Emma was behind, with her arm soft on Nicole's shoulder. A shrill squawk from an eagle high above was the only sound; everyone was hushed.

Nicole stumbled. Lost her footing and began to slide. This was it; she would never get home, and never apologise, never see Hamilton's face. The world was so cruel. She felt herself being lost. She should have said yes to marrying Romily. They would both have been happy. She realised she loved everything about him: his tall, muscular frame, his cute shyness, his propriety, the way he did everything properly, the bravery he had shown in taking on the leadership. She was so proud of him.

Before she knew it, there was a strong hand around her wrist, then another on her waist, pulling her up as if she was a feather. It was Thomas. He pulled her to him and they struggled over to Romily.

'I do, Romily; I bloody well do.' She hugged him. He looked surprised; and then it dawned on him.

'Maybe I've changed my mind,' he said. A huge smile crossed his face. 'I ain't, though.' He grabbed her and kissed her full on the mouth.

'Do you two mind? We've a bloody mountain to climb yet!' Emma said, laughing. She nudged Thomas, who blushed.

They helped the party across the ice sheet, then continued on the path; they kept walking through the night, not bothering to stop. As dawn came the cloud cleared and the sun rose, casting the first rays of spring over the escapees. Nicole held Romily's hand and they looked over the panorama. Then she saw it: the settlement, the roofs of houses glinting in the light. It was the town of Montgarri.

'Come on, we can slide down on our bottoms!' Emma shrieked. She didn't wait for an answer; she was on her bottom sliding down the steep slope of snow, ice and scree. Nicole didn't wait. She led Romily and Thomas and they all joined Emma, sliding down the mountain, heading for the town, heading for Spain, heading for safety. Nicole let out a cry of pure joy as the wind rushed through her hair as they raced to the valley floor, with the imposing mountains behind them.

* * *

25th December 1945

They had made it the whole way across Spain, getting to Gibraltar and then taking a passage home. At last they were in Dorset.

Nicole stood looking at Home Farm. Romily held her arm tight. She was glad. Glad to be home, glad to be getting married to Romily, glad to be seeing her family. Deep down, she couldn't help but feel trepidation as to how she and Lily would be. She hoped they would be friends again. Each time she placed her foot on the clean white snow, it made a satisfying crackle. She looked back down the lane at her footsteps, mirrored by Romily's alongside. She breathed in the air; it was cool but the storm had passed. She was glad the journey was about to end. There was a light on in the kitchen. She neared the door. Eight years after leaving, her whole body seemed to be energised with excitement.

'Wait, Romily, wait. I want to listen; I want to remember this feeling.' She took in a deep breath. The anticipation was enormous in her stomach.

'Coalman's 'err, coalman's 'err, coalman's 'err,' Ol' Parrot sang out.

'That darn parrot – he's still going!' she said.

The door opened wide. Hamilton was on her before she could move, followed by Dusty.

'Let the girl in; let us see her!' Mother shouted.

Mother kissed and hugged her tight. She suddenly found herself beneath a deluge of hugs and kisses, like the warmest blanket.

'Come in, girl! I've the rhubarb wine for 'e; I've been saving it as

392

I know 'tis your favourite.' Her father hugged her. 'Hullo, Romily, come in, come in.' Father shook Romily's hand. 'Thanks for taking this one off me hands, boy.'

'You're welcome,' Romily said, beaming.

'You're so charming, Dad.' She laughed. She looked for Lily.

Lily came to her and gave her the biggest hug. She held her sister and squeezed her tight.

'I love you, Nicole. I'm so sorry; I should never have let a boy come between us,' Lily whispered in her ear.

'No, I'm sorry, I'm so sorry, Lily. It was all my fault.' The tears ran down her face in rivers.

She saw the tall stranger standing by Lily. 'Who's this, then?'

'He's my husband, of course: Perry.' Perry shook her hand and smiled. 'You can call him Percy, if you like.'

'Now darling, what have I said? You're the only one who can do that,' Perry said.

Nicole turned back to Lily. 'I was a silly young girl. I'm sorry. We were both so young. So much has happened,' Nicole said.

'You have nothing to apologise for, Nicole. I want you to know I love you,' Lily said.

She felt the tears come down her face. Lily pulled her to the cot in the corner and showed her baby Samuel. Lily picked Samuel up and handed him to Nicole, who held him in her arms, smelling his sweet warm fragrance.

'My, you've been busy, Lily!' Nicole said, smiling as she rocked the baby in her arms. Lily nodded.

'Where is Thomas? Where is he?' Mother said.

'I don't know; he was with us. Must be dilly-dallying,' Nicole said, looking up from Samuel. Romily stood by her with his arms around her shoulders.

'Oh, I've missed you so much,' Mother said. 'Come in, come in.'

It was so good to be in the heart of the house. There was the warmth and the smell of roast chicken in the oven. The yellow dresser was the same, though there was lino on the floor that was new. She could only look and smile at Hamilton, at Father, Mother and Dusty, Lily and her husband. She looked at Hamilton; he was so tall.

'Where is Thomas? Where is he?' Mother said to Father.

'He'll be here in his own time; don't 'e worry so.'

'Don't worry? I haven't seen him for years and you tell me not to worry?'

'He ain't far,' Father said.

'The bloody Christmas dinner will be ruined if he don't get here soon,' Mother said.

'Coalman's 'err, coalman's 'err, coalman's 'err.'

'Must be Christmas, 'cos that bird never speaks twice in a day,' Father said.

Hamilton was first up. He got to the door and opened it. Thomas was standing there, wearing a broad smile.

'Thought I'd stop and get 'e some holly, Mother.' He handed it to Mother, then they all piled on him, laughing and crying.

'Let me see him! Let me see!' Mother shouted.

'Cor, let me breathe, you lot!' Thomas said.

'What took you?' asked Father.

'Well, when we left Nicole and Rom, I found your bloody cows out, didn't I; had to stop to get 'em in.'

'Are you joking? And what do you mean *we*?' Father said.

'Come 'err,' Thomas said as he pulled Emma by the hand and brought her in to face the family.

'Bloody hell! Emma Tucker, you look a picture!'

Emma took out the brandy and said: 'Dad wanted you to have this; said it would make a change from that disgusting wine you brew.'

'I bet he bloody did, god rest his soul. You come in, dear; you're one of the family now, Mrs Kingson,' Father said.

'And you, of course, Romily, Perry; you're all part of the family now,' Mother said. 'Get around the table; that chicken is going to be done for. And I want to take a proper look at you all.'

Dusty sat to attention, her jaw gaping, her paw out.
'Yes, you too Dusty; you'll get some,' Mother said.
Dusty lay down, smiling, in front of the range.

Acknowledgements and Thanks

You have got to the end of my book. I hope that means you enjoyed it. Whether or not you did, I would like to thank you for giving me your valuable time and allowing me to try and entertain you. I am truly blessed to have such a fulfilling job, but I only have that job because of people like you: people kind enough to give my books a chance and spend their hard-earned money buying them. For that I am eternally grateful.

If you would like to find out more about my other books then please visit my websites for full details: https://www.christopher-legg.com and https://curious-writer.com. Also feel free to contact me on Facebook, Twitter or email (all details on the website) as I would love to hear from you.

I would like to thank my wonderful editor Penny Dunscombe who works tirelessly to improve all aspects of my writing and is so diligent and efficient, taking such care with my new creations. Thank you to Maggie Hamand without whose valuable guidance I would have wandered along dark and meandering paths away from the story.

Books that were particularly helpful to me on *In Time of Duty's* journey include:

Escaping Hitler by Monty Halls
Twenty-One by James Holland
Blackmore Vale Childhood by Hilary Townsend
Dadland by Keggie Carew

Sabotage and Subversion by Ian Dear
The Women who lived for Danger by Marcus Binney
Weird War Two by Peter Taylor

For the latest news, offers and freebies, sign up to the official Christopher B Legg Newsletter.

If you enjoyed this book and would like to help, then you could think about leaving a review on the Goodreads website or anywhere else that readers visit. Giving a positive review is a significant way of helping a book to sell, so if you leave me one, then you are directly helping me to continue on this journey as a full-time writer. Thank you in advance to anyone who does.

www.ingramcontent.com/pod-product-compliance
Lightning Source LLC
Chambersburg PA
CBHW072002190726
48293CB00001B/130